Rock's Redemption

An Insurgents MC Romance

CHIAH WILDER

Copyright © 2016 by Chiah Wilder
Print Edition

Editing by Hot Tree Editing
Cover design by Cheeky Covers
Proofreading by Darryl Banner

All rights reserved. This book or any portion thereof may not be reproduced or used in any manner whatsoever without the express written permission of the author except for the use of brief quotations in a book review. Please purchase only authorized additions, and do not participate in or encourage piracy of copyrighted materials.

Your support of the author's rights is appreciated.

Disclaimer: This is a work of fiction. Names, characters, businesses, places, events and incidents are either the products of the author's imagination or used in a fictitious manner. Any resemblance to actual persons, living or dead, or actual events is purely coincidental.

I love hearing from my readers. You can email me at chiahwilder@gmail.com.

Make sure you sign up for my newsletter so you can keep up with my new releases, special sales, free short stories, and other treats only available to newsletter readers. When you sign up, you will receive a FREE hot and steamy short story. Sign up at: http://eepurl.com/bACCL1.

Visit me on facebook at www.facebook.com/Chiah-Wilder-1625397261063989/

Description

Rock is the ripped, handsome Sergeant-At-Arms for the Insurgents MC. Being one of the club's officers, women clamor to share his bed. The biker's more than willing to oblige as long as it's a short-time hookup; *long-term relationship* is not part of his vocabulary.

He's only been in love once—a long time ago—and the end result was shattering. He learned his lesson: keep his heart encased in steel.

The tragic night that sent him to prison is over even though it still simmers inside him. But once he joined the Insurgents MC, he vowed to leave the past darkness and disappointments back in Louisiana. He's embraced his new life of brotherhood, booze, easy women, and Harleys. It suits him just fine. Some things are best left alone, especially a pretty brunette who destroyed his heart.

Easy sex has become his mantra.

Until his past crashes into his life….

Clotille Boucher is the wealthy, spoiled girl who'd stolen Rock's heart many years ago. From a young age, family loyalty was drilled into her, so when darkness engulfed her and Rock, fleeing seemed to be the only way out for her. Deciding to make a new life for herself, she didn't count on having to pay for the sins of her brother.

Just when her life doesn't seem like it could get worse, a face from her past gives her a glimmer of hope. Shamed that Rock has to see how far she's fallen, she pretends her life is exactly what she wants, but his penetrating stare tells her he's not buying her act.

Fearful that the secrets of the past will catch up with her and Rock, her inclination is to do what she does best—run away. Only problem is, Rock's not letting her slip away so easily this time.

Can two damaged people learn to trust one another again? Will Rock be able to reconcile the demons that have plagued him since that tragic night? Does Clotille offer him redemption or destruction?

As Rock and Clotille maneuver the treacherous waters of their past and present, someone is lurking behind the shadows to make sure the truth never comes out.

The Insurgents MC series are standalone romance novels. This is Rock and Clotille's love story. This book contains violence, sexual assault (not graphic), strong language, and steamy/graphic sexual scenes. It describes the life and actions of an outlaw motorcycle club. If any of these issues offend you, please do not read the book. HEA. No cliffhangers! The book is intended for readers over the age of 18.

Previous Titles in the Series:

Hawk's Property: Insurgents Motorcycle Club Book 1
Jax's Dilemma: Insurgents Motorcycle Club Book 2
Chas's Fervor: Insurgents Motorcycle Club Book 3
Axe's Fall: Insurgents Motorcycle Club Book 4
Banger's Ride: Insurgents Motorcycle Club Book 5
Jerry's Passion: Insurgents Motorcycle Club Book 6
Throttle's Seduction: Insurgents Motorcycle Club Book 7

Glossary of Cajun Words

A bientôt: See you soon

Arrêtez: Stop, stop it.

Attends: Wait

Ça va?: How are you? How are thing going?

Cher: sweetheart, dear. Term of endearment used for a male

Chérie: sweetheart, dear. Term of endearment used for a female

Chouchou: sweetie

Fini: Finished, done

Gris-gris (pronounced gree-gree): curse, hex

Je t'aime: I love you

Je t'aime aussi: I love you too

Maman: Mom

Mawmaw: grandmother

Merci: Thank you

Merde: shit

Mon beau trésor: my beautiful treasure

Mon Dieu: my God

Mon fils: my son

Mon petit chou: sweetheart, my sweetheart

Père: father

Petits: small, small ones, little ones

Petit bonbon: little sweetie, honey

Putain: slut, whore, hooker

Qu'est-ce qui se passe?: What happened?

Très bien: Very good, very well

Vite: Quick, fast

Vite alors: Then go on now, quickly

Voilà: Here you go, here it is

Prologue

Lafayette, Louisiana
1997

THE DARK-HAIRED BOY clutched the money in his hand as he walked through the wealthy part of the city. Earlier that evening, he'd gone to the butcher shop like his mother had told him to do, to buy some ham hocks for her to make for their supper. He hated going to Le Petit Cochon without his mother. When he'd been there, all the old ladies had run their rough hands through his hair and pinched his cheeks, laughing when he'd turned red. If he were with his mother, she would have told them to stop. They would've laughed and called her silly, but they would've backed away from him.

That evening his mother had sent him to the butcher alone because she'd taken on an extra job helping Mrs. Boucher with her dinner party. She worked as one of the housekeepers for the Boucher family and sometimes they'd ask if she could help serve when they had guests over. His mother always said yes because the need for money was so great. The eleven-year-old boy wished his mother didn't have to work so hard; she'd looked so tired when he'd gone over to get the money to pay the butcher.

The butcher, Mr. Despres, could be a mean sonofabitch. He'd told the boy—in a loud voice so everyone in the shop could hear—that he couldn't extend any more credit to his family. If the boy's mother wanted the ham hocks, she'd have to pay what she owed. All the people in the shop had stared at him, a few sniggering, and he'd wished the floor would've opened up and swallowed him up. Anything would've been better than the looks of amusement and pity the patrons had thrown at him. He'd walked backward out of the shop, nodding numbly. Once the sticky air hit his face, he took off running to Greenbriar Estates, where his mother was serving the elite on china plates that cost more than his family earned in one month.

"Roche," his mother said to him, surprise registering in her hazel eyes. "Has something happened to your father?"

A thread of anger slipped up his spine. She was always thinking about his father, even though he was drunk most of the time; beat her, him, and his brother regularly; and ran around with every *putain* on Louisiana Avenue and Johnston Street. Roche couldn't believe how his mother made excuses for his father all the time. She was such a loving and patient person, and if it hadn't been for her, Roche would have run away by now. He was scared to death to leave his mother with the monster who pretended to be his father.

The only respite the family had from his father's anger, his hard fists punching into walls and soft bodies, and his string of crippling verbal assaults was when he went to the bayou to the wooden shack on land that had been in his mother's family for more than seven generations. The monster would spend up to ten days fishing and hunting before he came back with some money in his pockets. Instead of paying the outstanding bills or buying his mother a much-needed new dress, he'd spend the weekend at the Three Kings Tavern, drinking it away and buying cheap perfume for his women.

And his mother always forgave him. It tore at Roche's heart to see her eyes puffy from crying all night, but in the morning she always had a large smile on her face as she doted on her children and husband. Roche wanted to scream and tell his father he didn't deserve a lady like his mom, but he knew his outburst would garner him a severe beating so he sat in silence, anger and hate churning in his stomach.

"Mr. Despres won't let me buy the ham hocks unless you pay the bill. He said it's been too long."

His mother's face softened and she ran her chapped finger over his cheek. "I'm sorry you had to go through that, *petit bonbon*. Here, take this money and tell him that's all I have. And he better wrap up those ham hocks. He knows I pay." She slipped her hand into a pocket of her worn dress, stuffing the bills in Roche's small hand.

"It smells good in here," the boy said, his stomach growling.

"The cook is wonderful." She watched him while she moved the hair out of his eyes. "Didn't you eat your lunch today?"

He nodded, cursing his stomach for making so much noise. How could he tell her the two bullies who picked on him stole his lunch? She had enough problems. Anyway, he didn't need his mother to fight his battles. He was learning how to fight from Guy, a teen neighbor, who lived behind their house. Soon he'd show the bullies they couldn't mess with him.

"*Voilà.*" His mother shoved a piece of French bread with a slice of roast beef nestled between in his hands, then a piece of chocolate wrapped in shiny green foil. He buried it in his pocket for later. She looked over her shoulder. "*Alors, vite!* I have to work. I should be home in a few hours."

Roche hugged his mom, took a big bite of his sandwich, and scampered outside.

The mansions loomed all around him as squares of light from their windows lit up the dark, quiet streets. Deciding to take a shortcut to the main street, he crossed the road and entered a park. Finishing his sandwich, he wiped his mouth with the back of his hand. He'd never tasted meat so tender—just like butter. He moved steadily, passing a large willow tree swaying in the late July breeze. As he went by a cluster of bushes he heard something crying. *Is an animal hurt?* He couldn't be sure.

He walked nearer to the bushes and the small sobs became louder. As he rummaged through them, the crying stopped. He froze, the only sound his own breathing. Ready to turn around and continue on his trek home, the crying started up again. He forged ahead, separating the bushes and sliding between them until he was in a small space surrounded by foliage. A girl of about ten years old sat on the ground, her hands wrapped around her knees that were bent close to her chest. Her big green eyes shimmered in the moonlight. Roche sucked in his breath; he'd never seen eyes like that before. They reminded him of a panther's—the ones he'd seen in books at school, anyway.

"Why're you crying?" he asked.

The girl wiped her nose. "It's nothing. I want to be alone." Her brimming gaze held his.

"There's always a reason for crying."

She looked down and then buried her head between her knees. He shrugged and turned from her, beginning to make his way through the bushes. Behind him, her soft voice called out, "Wait. Don't go. Not yet."

He swiveled around, his gaze catching hers. Her lips quivered as tears dropped from her eyes all over again. He hunched down. "You gonna tell me why you're crying?"

Without a word she pulled up her pants, exposing angry red streaks across her white skin.

He whistled. "Your pa do that?"

She shook her head, her light brown hair falling over her shoulders. "My *maman*."

"Your ma?" He whistled again. "Does your pa know she does this?"

Again her head shook. "He knows she beats my brothers, but this is the first time she's beaten me where he can see. That's why she made me wear long pants. She's mean when she drinks too much tea."

"You gonna tell your pa?"

Her eyes widened in fear. "No," she breathed. "My mother said she'd punish me severely if I ever tell him what she does to me." She bowed her head in shame.

He watched her for a few seconds before he sat down next to her. "I bet my pa is way meaner than your mom." He pulled up his shirt and, under the moonlight, showed her several angry lashes on his chest—some new, some healing, some scarred. He then pointed out the bruises on his arms and legs.

"Your father did all that to you?" she whispered.

"Yep." His dark eyes narrowed. "I can't wait to grow up so I can go away. My pa is always mad and he takes it out on me, my brother, and my sisters. I can handle it, but when he beats my ma, I get so mad that all I wanna do is slit his throat to make him stop. He's a bastard. Sounds like your ma's not too much better. How many brothers you got?"

"Two—one older and one younger. I wish I had a sister though. My older brother, Armand, is always telling me what to do. He's so bossy. My younger one, Stephan, isn't like us. He can't learn like we do, but I'm not supposed to tell anyone about him. I play with him a lot." She sniffled and wiped her nose again.

"What's your name?

"Clotille Boucher."

"Are you the Boucher girl who lives in the big house on West Bayou Parkway?"

"Yes. How do you know?"

"My ma cleans your house. I've never seen you before. I've seen your older brother a few times. He wasn't too nice."

"Armand's like that. So you're Mrs. Aubois's son?" He nodded. "You look like your mother." He smiled.

They sat in silence, each lost in their own thoughts until Roche remembered the ham hocks. If he didn't get them, his mother wouldn't be able to make dinner later and his father would be angry. He'd probably beat her.

Roche jumped up. "I gotta get going. I've got something to do." He shoved his hand in his pocket and felt the chocolate his mother had given him earlier. He pulled it out and handed it to her. "Here."

"For me? Thank you." Shyly she took the thin wafer from his hand, unwrapping the green foil slowly. She plopped the candy in her mouth and a large smile crossed her face.

All of a sudden he felt awkward as the pretty girl watched him, her green eyes dancing. "I gotta go," he mumbled, turning away.

"What's your name?" she asked after his retreating figure.

He glanced backward. "Roche."

"It means rock."

"I know." Their eyes locked and, in that moment, a friendship was born.

THEY SPENT THE rest of the summer sharing laughs, catching fireflies in jars, and digging for worms on the bank of the Vermillion River. He soothed her through the bruises her mother put on her in places her father couldn't see, and she sat quietly by him as he breathed heavily after a severe beating from his father. Together they found some solace, some lightness in the midst of their violent and hurtful world.

Their friendship was frowned upon by Mrs. Boucher and her older son, Armand. After all, Roche came from the poor section of Lafayette where dilapidated shotgun houses dotted the bleak landscape. His father fished and hunted for a living in the bayou while Mr. Boucher sat in his office in a suit and tie and made multi-million-dollar decisions pertaining to land development.

At first, Mrs. Boucher forbade Clotille from hanging around "the poor boy," but when she'd realized it kept her daughter out of the house for most of the day, she relented and poured herself another Long Island Iced Tea. Not having Clotille around kept Mrs. Boucher from beating her, and she welcomed the respite. She resented her daughter because she was "Daddy's little girl" and her father gave in to her all the time. He spoiled her, doted on her, and paid more attention to her than he did to his wife. And the fact that he carried on with his mistress—the *putain*—was more than Mrs. Boucher could bear. What was he thinking in setting up a woman nearly half his age in a luxury house in one of his developments in River Ranch? It was an embarrassment, something she couldn't do anything about except punish her daughter for her father's indiscretions and coldness. Each slap and sting of the belt on Clotille's tender flesh was meant for Mrs. Boucher's husband. He'd kill her for beating his precious daughter, and Mrs. Boucher derived an inordinate amount of pleasure from knowing that.

So she let the two children while away the summer, surprisingly calm when she learned that Roche would be attending the same school as Clotille due to an open enrollment policy the city had passed at the end of the previous school year. As long as she didn't have to *see* the boy, she was content to pretend that he didn't exist.

Four years later

"GASTON, I WILL never agree to sell the land. It's been in my family for generations and it's going to stay that way." Roche heard his mother's soft but firm voice coming from the kitchen as he scrambled to get ready for school. His father's loud voice bounced off the walls, and he knew if his mother didn't finish serving breakfast soon and get out of the house, she'd find his pa's fist on her face.

He wished his dad could understand that the land meant everything to his mother. She'd inherited a large amount of it in the bayou, where an old wooden shack with one room stood on the edge of the waters. When they'd married, she'd put her husband on the title on condition that he never ask her to sell the land. Now that oil and gas companies had approached his parents, his father's agreement was only a memory. He kept pressuring his wife to sell so they could finally have some money to get them out of poverty.

Roche scoffed at his dad's argument; he wanted the money to gamble at Cypress Bayou Casino in Charenton, buy booze, and purchase stinky perfume for the women he screwed. Roche admired his mother for not giving in to the pressures of his dad and the oil and gas companies who were decimating the bayous.

A loud *whack* startled Roche out of his musings, and he rushed to the kitchen to see his father backhand his mother across her face once more. She whimpered and raised her arms to defend herself. Before Gaston could hit her a third time, Roche grabbed his hand in midair. "Leave her alone," he growled.

Gaston spun around, eyes blazing, face contorted in rage. "You want a beating before school? I'll beat you so bad you won't be able to walk for a week."

"Don't touch her!" Roche's voice sounded stronger than he felt.

His mother rushed over to him. "Roche, go on to school. You'll be late. I can handle this. Your father and I were just having a disagreement, that's all."

His older brother, Henri, walked in before he could reply. "Roche, leave it alone. Pa's right anyway. We should sell the land so we can get out of this shithole house. It'd be nice to have some money."

"Shut the fuck up!" Roche glared at Henri.

"Roche, your language," his mother said, her face tight.

"When you get home, boy, you're getting a beating you won't forget too easily," his father growled. "Now both of you get out of here."

Roche glanced at his mother who nodded to him. "Go on," she said softly. "I'll be all right. You don't want to be late for school."

Henri walked out and Roche followed slowly, his eyes pleading with his mother's to let him stay so he could keep her safe. A knot twisted in his stomach when he shut the door behind him.

Images of what might be happening at home tortured his mind the whole way to school. Deep in thought, he jumped when someone lightly punched his arm. "What the hell?" He whirled around, laughing when he saw his buddy.

Andre laughed. "I can't believe you didn't hear me call out to you. What were you thinking about?"

A storm passed through his dark eyes and he looked down at the pavement. "Nothing really. Are you going with your pa this weekend to the swamp?"

"Yeah. You wanna come? My pa said it's okay."

Remembering the beating his dad was going to give him after school—his dad *never* forgot a promised punishment—he didn't know what kind of shape he'd be in. "Not sure. I'll let you know tomorrow."

"Okay. I hope you can. It's gonna be so much fun."

Roche nodded and looked away, and that's when he saw Clotille waving at a black limo that had just pulled away from the curb. She wore a pale blue sweater that molded over her soft breasts and made him feel funny inside. As a matter of fact, for the past year he'd been thinking too much about her breasts, wondering if they were soft and spongy or just soft, like one of the down pillows his mother made. Sometimes it took all his strength not to touch them or accidentally brush against them. And the softness of her hips drove him crazy in ways he wasn't used to before last year. He often used the image of her in her shorts and bikini top when he was doing something in the bathroom he knew he wasn't supposed to be doing, but he couldn't help it—it felt so good.

He waved at her and she waved back. Their classes were in different buildings since she was in the eighth grade and he was in ninth. After school they'd meet up, maybe get a soda if he could borrow some money from Andre. He couldn't wait for it to be three o'clock.

THEY MET ON the sidewalk near the tall chain-linked fence. She had two of her friends and he had three of his, but all he could see was how pretty she was. They decided to grab a pop at Soda Jerk's, agreeing to take the shortcut through the cemetery. Andre had come through for Roche and loaned him the money so he could buy Clotille her soda. He'd have to work extra hours the following week at the hardware store, mopping the floors and taking out the trash, to earn enough so he could pay Andre back, but Clotille was worth it.

As they cut through the cemetery, they crossed paths with Armand and two of his friends. Being sixteen, on the football team, and rich, Armand and his buddies held themselves above the poor kids who they felt disgraced the walls of their high school.

"Why're you hanging out with freshman white trash?" Armand asked his sister as he stared at Roche and his friends.

"Stop it, Armand. Leave us alone." Clotille turned to Roche and smiled. "Come on," she said softly.

Armand's friends blocked their way, then shoved Roche and his friends backward. The jocks laughed when Roche fell on his butt. Red stained his cheeks as he jumped up, brushing off the dust from his pants.

A surge of fire rushed up Roche's spine when he saw the way Peter, one of Armand's friends, ran his gaze up Clotille's body, stopping at her breasts. Peter smiled. "You need to stick with your own kind, Clotille. Hanging out with losers never does anyone any good." He reached out and grabbed her arm. She pulled back, unsuccessful in breaking free of his grip.

"Take your fucking hand off her!" Roche clenched his fists, the red stains of embarrassment replaced by streaks of anger.

Peter threw her backward, his nostrils flaring. "What did you say to me, you fucking scum?"

"You heard me." Roche breathed heavily.

Clotille brushed her fingers against his arm. "Let's go." She narrowed her eyes at Armand. "If you don't stop right now, I'm going to tell Dad."

Before he could answer, the cemetery groundskeeper rushed toward them shouting, his arms flailing, and they all scattered. Roche grabbed her hand and pulled her along as they ran, leading them behind a large cypress tree with Spanish moss that hid one of the large mausoleums. They both gulped for air as her brother and his friends looked for them. Grasping her shoulders, Roche pulled Clotille flush against him as he leaned against the large tree, obscured from sight. Clotille's back pressed against him, his jeans tightened as he held her closer to him, his arms snuggly around her waist.

"I think the dirtbag went this way," Armand shouted, pointing to the cemetery's exit. His friends grunted and followed him, taking them farther away from him and Clotille. As the boys' voices dissipated, Roche rubbed against her slightly to get some relief from the ache in his pants. It felt so good. As he moved against her lower back, she stiffened before turning around and tilting her head back, her green gaze locking with his dark one. A funny look crossed her face and her cheeks were a deep red.

He dipped his head down and kissed her. A jolt of desire shot through him and he brought her closer to him, his lips moving against her soft ones. Then she sighed and when her mouth opened slightly, he slipped his tongue inside. She tasted of cherry bubble gum and he pushed in deeper, losing himself in her warmth and softness. Then she jerked away.

"Why did you do that?" Clotille unwrapped his arms from her.

"You're so pretty. You didn't like it?" Roche's body was humming. He didn't want to stop kissing her.

Looking at the ground, she wiggled from one foot to the other, twirling a strand of hair around her finger. "It felt funny. I don't want you to do it anymore."

"It's natural to do it. Don't you like me?" He laced his fingers with hers.

She pulled away. "I do. I have to go." She whirled around.

"Let me walk you home." He pushed away from the tree trunk.

Panic laced her eyes. "No," she said too harshly. "I can go by myself." She ran from him but then stopped, waved, and yelled, "Bye!" Then she dashed between the graves. He watched her until she was nothing but a mere speck in the distance; then he sighed and walked in the opposite direction to his home.

In bed that night, his body racked with pain from the beating, he stared at the darkness, remembering how soft Clotille's lips were on his and how warm and wet her mouth was.

For several days after their kiss, she avoided him and when they finally got together, she made sure her other friends were with her. He noticed that she didn't want to be alone with him anymore, and a part of him wished the kiss never would've happened so they could go back to hanging out, just the two of them.

Something had changed between them after they'd shared their first kiss, and he felt like she was slipping away from him. When she entered high school the following year, she began hanging around girls who were considered the popular group in the school. All of a sudden she didn't have time for him. Their long walks along the Vermillion River ended, as well as their afterschool sodas at the local hangout. Soon she stopped saying hello to him in the school hallways, only offering a slight smile or nod.

He didn't understand why she'd pulled away from him; he only knew he missed her and thought about her too much. Fearing rejection, he kept his distance, and his heart broke the first time he saw her holding hands with Luc, a football player who was in his class. Roche had lost her, and he mourned the end of what they had shared for the past four years. If it bothered her, she certainly didn't show it, which made the cracks in his heart even deeper.

And so Roche went his own way, as Clotille did hers. Roche's family situation worsened, the only respite being when his father went to the bayou for several weeks to make some money from fishing and trapping. His mother still worked for Clotille's family, and his brother Henri had begun to take on the role of his father while he was gone. Henri tried to boss him around, but Roche wouldn't let him do it even if Henri was two years older and stronger. He mostly ignored Henri, but whenever he'd bully their sisters, Isa and Lille, or their mother, Roche would stand up for them and even fight his brother over his disrespect. His mother would pull them apart and tell Roche that his temper was going to get him in trouble one day.

She always acted like Henri's rudeness didn't bother her, but Roche would hear her crying softly at the kitchen table when she thought they were all asleep. It was during those times that he swore he'd give her a better life and take her away from all the disrespect and beatings his father inflicted on her. She was such a kind, selfless woman, and she deserved a better life than the one she had. Roche vowed to give it to her.

Henri had begun dating Lorraine, a local girl from the neighborhood. She was the same age as Henri, seventeen years old to Roche's fifteen. She'd dropped out of school to help take care of her seven siblings while her mother and father worked. Henri seemed crazy about her and always acted goofy around her.

One temperate afternoon in March, Roche came home from school to find Henri's blonde and busty girlfriend sitting on the couch filing her nails. When he entered the room, her face lit up as she beamed. "Hi, Roche. How are you?" Her blue eyes skimmed over him.

Roche shrugged. "Okay. Where's Henri?"

"At work. He got called in right after I got here." She pushed out her bottom lip in a faux pout. He nodded and moved toward the kitchen. "*Attends.*" She patted the empty spot next to her on the couch. "Come sit next to me for a minute."

"I got stuff to do." But he stood in place, staring at her.

She smiled, her lips glistening in an orange shade. "Just for a few moments?" She leaned back, thrusting her ample cleavage out.

Roche's gaze lingered on her chest as he licked his lips. Shoving his hands in his pockets, he ambled over and plopped down on the other side of the couch, his gaze still fixed on her breasts encased in her tight top.

Cupping them, she smiled. "You like these?" He gave a half shrug. "I think you do. You know, I've noticed the way you sneak looks at me when I'm over here." She clucked her tongue and scooted closer to him. "Do you want to touch them? I'll let you."

A surge of lust flooded him, and the tightness in his jeans made him uncomfortable. He glanced at Lorraine's face when she grabbed his hands and placed them over her breasts. "Squeeze them. They won't bite you." She laughed as he squished her lovely softness in his hands. "You're real cute, you know that? I bet you don't have any trouble getting girls."

He didn't answer. The truth was that girls did stare at him and want to date him, but he wasn't interested in any of it. The only one who owned his heart was Clotille, and she acted like he didn't exist. A streak of sadness ran through him as it always did when he thought of her.

"Harder," she breathed.

He squeezed them firmly, loving the way they felt in his hands. Lorraine threw her head back, her lips parted, and moaned. Without thinking, he leaned over and kissed her neck. She grabbed a fistful of his thick dark hair and jerked it. "I think you're the best-looking boy in the parish," she whispered.

He pulled away, heat engulfing him, before placing his hands on each side of her face. He kissed her hard, forcing the seam of her lips open and plunging his tongue inside her willing mouth.

"Let's go to your room," she said thickly against his mouth. Without hesitation he stood, helped her up, and led her to his room, closing the door behind them.

Half an hour later, he noticed the breeze picked up outside as he watched the budding leaves of the willow trees sway. He slipped on his boxers and jeans without looking at Lorraine. As he bent over to pick up his T-shirt, he heard the back door slam shut. He whipped his head toward her. "Get dressed. Now. *Vite!*" From the footsteps he knew Henri had come in.

Before Lorraine could slip on her clothes, Henri came into the room. His eyes darted between her and Roche, his face turning dark with rage as he rushed over to her, yelling, "*Putain!*" A loud *whack* bounced off the walls in the small room. Lorraine's hand rose to her face where she'd been hit.

As Henri readied to slap her again, Roche ran over and shoved him away. Suddenly the two brothers were tangled together, fists flying amidst all the swearing.

Roche looked at Lorraine who sat on the bed, a sheet covering her naked body, a red handprint decorating the right side of her face. "Get out of here," Roche said as Henri's fist landed on his jaw. She scooped up her clothes and ran out.

From that day on, a deeper wedge was drawn between the two brothers. Henri continued to see Lorraine, and the summer before his senior year of high school, Roche spent it sneaking over to her house and hovering over her, wishing it were Clotille he was thrusting into.

Most of his senior year was spent either in the principal's office or at home, under suspension. His main reason for going to school was to fight, smoke weed, and fool around with the fast girls. He'd bump into Clotille in the hallway or stairwell sometimes, and she'd fidget and clear her throat a lot if he said anything to her. He still thought she was the most beautiful girl he'd ever seen, but over the past few years his heart had hardened, bitterness replacing any tenderness he'd once felt for her.

During school assemblies or at the football games, he'd catch her sneaking glances at him, her eyes pained when he'd make out with one of the fun girls. He didn't have time for her anymore. He was a couple months away from graduating and getting the hell away from his father and Henri. No one or nothing was going to stop him.

On a cool April night, the senior class had a party down by the river. The teenagers huddled around a large fire pit, their faces appearing grotesque in the glow of the blaze. Roche walked toward the party, his arm wrapped around his newest girl, Sally. He greeted a few of his friends and they all took out cigarettes and lit them, the ends glowing in the dark. Sensing someone staring at him, he glanced over to the edge of the river and locked eyes with *her*. Clotille had her arm around Luc's waist, her long chestnut brown hair cascading down her back beautiful under the moonlight. Her gaze moved from him to Sally, who was wrapped around him like a snake on a branch. Clotille turned away, and Sally whispered in his ear, "Let's go somewhere and have some fun."

A couple hours later, Sally was flying high on coke and booze. Roche's buddy, Matt, came over to him. "Damn, Sally's wasted. You gonna take her home?"

"Why?" Roche knew Sally liked giving out freebies to the boys. He was pretty sure she'd screwed her way through most of the senior guys already.

Matt shrugged. "I'm going home, so I thought if you wanted to stay I could drop her off. I go right by her house."

Roche laughed, knowing full well what Matt wanted, and knowing Sally, she'd be more than willing to give it. "Sure, that works." He helped Sally into Matt's car, kissing her back when she covered his mouth with hers. "You sure you want to go home with Matt?" he whispered in her ear.

She nodded. "You don't mind, do you? You'll still call me, right?"

"Sure," he lied. He closed the door and watched as the red taillights disappeared into the darkness. He made his way back to the party, drank a couple more beers, and then decided to call it a night.

He'd borrowed his dad's beat-up old Chevy Impala, parking it down by the cluster of trees. He loved walking, especially at night. As he passed a large cypress tree, he heard crying—deep-in-the-chest sobbing—and he stopped, wondering if he should see if the woman needed any help. He decided to mind his own business and walked slowly away, but the sobs pulled him back. Roche walked toward the sounds, his eyes widening when he saw Clotille on her knees, sobbing into her hands.

At first, he almost walked away, but something about the way she cried reminded him of when he'd met her. His heart clenched. "*Qu'est-ce qui se passe, chérie?*" he asked.

She jerked her head up, wiping her damp cheeks. Recognition passed over her face, and he saw her features soften.

In two long strides, he knelt beside her, holding her hand. "You gonna tell me what's wrong? Where's Luc?" When Roche mentioned her boyfriend's name, she started crying again and sank into him, her cheeks wet against his shirt. "Did he do something to you?" A current of anger rode up his spine.

"No. Yes." She swallowed and her chin dipped down. "I went looking for him and caught him with Raine, the new girl in school. I can't believe he did that to me." She threw her arms around Roche's neck and cried.

He knew he should feel awful for her, but all he could think about was how wonderful she smelled and how good she felt in his arms. Her soft hair and the way her breasts crushed against him made all his senses jump to life and buzz. He'd never liked Luc and thought Clotille had only gone out with him to please her brother and mother since Luc was always in the papers after making touchdowns for the high school football team.

For a long time, he held her in his arms as she cried out all her anger and disappointment. She looked up at him and cleared her throat, startling him enough that he jumped a bit. He looked down at her and she smiled. "Do you think I'm pretty?" she asked in a hushed tone. *Fuck yeah. I think you're beautiful, chérie.* "You know you are."

"Then why have you stayed away from me? You've been going out with every girl in the school but me."

"Those other girls can't begin to compare to you," he said in a soft voice.

"Then why?"

He let out a long breath and crossed his arms. "I stayed away because that's what I thought you wanted. You began pulling away from me after we kissed that afternoon in the cemetery. Then when you came to high school, you treated me like I was dirt under your feet. I wasn't going to chase you. You decided our friendship was over. I went with it. Things don't ever last, *chérie*."

He watched as her face slackened and she looked at him with wet, dull eyes. "I thought you didn't want to be with me anymore. I thought you wanted a girl who was more fun. That time we kissed scared me because I was young and I felt weird in a funny, good way. I was confused and didn't know what was going on with me. When I got to high school, I kept waiting for you to come up to me and you never did. It hurt me a lot." Her voice hitched and her shoulders slumped. He watched her in silence, the hardness around his heart beginning to soften. "I've missed you, Roche," she whispered. "You're the only one I could be myself around."

"What about Luc? You seemed pretty close to him for the past three years."

She shook her head. "He was never *you*. I kept hoping he was, kept comparing you, but he was just a jock who loved all the attention, especially from the girls. Armand and my mom loved him." She pulled a blade of grass and put it between her teeth. "I never did."

"The way you were crying, you could've fooled me," he said, a steely edge to his voice.

"What he did tonight bruised my ego, hurt my pride. I know he's cheated on me before but I never caught him. And Raine is so smug and snotty. She's been after him ever since she came to our school." She lifted her chin. "She can have him as far as I'm concerned."

"The other girls meant nothing to me either. I was just having fun. It's always been you ever since I found you crying near your house. I've missed you too, *chérie*."

She leaned toward him and placed her hand on his arm. "You're the only one I've ever told about my mother and how she mistreats me. And you're the only one who knows about Stephan and how my parents hide him from everyone. I never found anyone else I've wanted to confide in, not even my girlfriends. It's always been you. You know that, *non*?" She ran her fingers up his torso, lightly scratching the material with her nails. He groaned and tugged her to him, covering her mouth with his. He relished the softness of her lips and her skin under his hands as he dug his fingers into her shoulders. She wrapped her arms tightly around his neck and they pressed together while they kissed under the moonlight.

"I want you," she said against his mouth.

His insides exploded as he pushed her gently down to the ground. Hovering over her, he said, "Are you sure, *chérie*? Because once I start I won't be able to stop. I've wanted you for so long."

"I've never wanted something as much as this. *Je t'aime*. I fell in love with you when you handed me the mint chocolate in the park. Remember?"

He nodded. "I've loved you for a long time too. Why did we waste these past three years?"

"I don't know, but we have the rest of our lives to make up for it." She drew him down and kissed him passionately, and he responded with every ounce of energy he had. He'd dreamt about this for years, and right then everything came together for him. All the grief, bitterness, and anger he'd been carrying around melted away with each kiss and stroke she gave him. Life was finally good to him, and he savored the enormity of it.

LATER THAT NIGHT he drove her home, tucking her under his arm as he maneuvered the car with one hand. Every few seconds, he'd brake and kiss her, the fifteen-minute drive to her house actually taking forty-five minutes.

He wanted to walk her to the door but they both agreed the risk of her mother or brother seeing them was too great. They'd deal with the logistics of her family the following day, but for that night, all that mattered was that she'd told him she loved him and he'd given her his heart.

On his way home, the realization that she'd saved herself for him hit him like a ton of bricks. He'd been shocked to learn she was a virgin. For these past several years, he'd been driving himself crazy thinking that she and Luc were doing it, but they weren't; Roche was her first, and the thought of that pleased him a lot. He couldn't wait to spend the following day with her. He'd told her he'd pick her up at eleven in the morning. Everything was all right. He loved her madly, and they'd found their way back into each other's hearts and arms.

He switched off the ignition and jumped over the small hedge that bordered the front lawn of his home. When he stepped on the front porch, he stiffened—the door was wide open. Cautiously, he entered the house. It was dark, not a single light on—not even the nightlight his mother always turned on in the living room. Knowing that Henri was at the shack in the bayou and his sisters were at their cousins' house in Abbeville for a slumber party, he wondered where his mother was. He was pretty sure his dad was out with one of his favorite street walkers.

"Maman?" he called out as he walked through the dining room to the kitchen. Low moans and whimpers came from it. When he entered the room, he stood still for a few seconds so his eyes could adjust to the darkness. The only light was the glow from the digital clock on the microwave. Scanning the room, he made out two forms on the floor. He switched on the overhead light and blinked several times. The horror of the scene in front of him remained the same: a huge pool of blood around his mother's torso and neck. As it flowed, it filled in the cracks between the linoleum tiles on the floor. Gaping knife wounds covered her arms, stomach, and neck. Her limbs were grotesquely flung outward. Her face was swollen and bruised, and her exposed teeth made her look as if she were growling. Several squadrons of flies and gnats buzzed around her head. There was so much blood, the strong copper scent hung thickly over the room.

"*Maman*!" he cried, rushing over to her and kneeling down, his jeans soaking up her blood in a matter of seconds. When his warm hands touched her cool body, he brought her hand to his lips and kissed it, murmuring, "No, *Maman*. No." His breath hitched and his chest felt as though it would crush his heart. All the feelings he could possibly feel were fighting together in his stomach, and he knew that the image of his mother's body would forever be burned into his memory.

From the corner of the room he heard a grunt. He whipped around and saw his father lying on the ground, an empty bottle of moonshine on the floor and a butcher knife smeared in blood next to it. Roche's ears pounded and his muscles tensed. A fire like molten lava bubbled inside him, rising steadily upward until it exploded, burning all his nerves, cells, and muscles.

"What the fuck have you done?" He rushed over to his father, who lifted his head and stared at him, his eyes hazy and unfocused. The smell of alcohol mixed in with the metallic odor of blood, and Roche had to swallow several times to keep from vomiting. "You killed her! It wasn't enough to beat her. You had to kill her, you worthless piece of *merde*."

As his father tried to lift himself off the floor, Roche grabbed him by the shirt and forced him up. He delivered the first blow against his dad's cheek, the cracking of bones like music to his ears.

Then he lost control.

RED AND BLUE lights created an eerie pattern on the front lawn as two paramedics rolled out a screaming and sobbing Roche, strapped down on a stretcher. Along the side and front of his house, he spotted the neighbors he grew up with, averting their gazes as the stretcher went past them. He saw his father's badly beaten body loaded into another ambulance, and his heart shattered when two men put his mother's body, encased in a body bag, in a black hearse. The door to his ambulance slammed shut and he was rushed to University Hospitals & Clinics. Still wired from the horror of it all, the emergency medical technician administered a sedative. In less than fifteen minutes, drowsiness set in and he closed his eyes, welcoming oblivion.

Five years later

AS THE METAL doors slammed behind him, Roche shuffled down the paved road without a backward glance. He had nothing to look at; five years of hell in one of Louisiana's most notorious prisons was more than enough. He'd received the maximum sentence for beating the shit out of his father that fateful night. He thought it was a gift because his goal had been to kill the bastard the way he'd killed his mother, only the police intervened. The neighbors had called them when they heard his father's cries and Roche's angry words, cursing him in Cajun. For the past five years, he'd tortured himself for not being home when his father had killed his mother. He'd been with Clotille while his mother had choked on her own blood. And it blew his mind as to why none of the neighbors had heard his mother's cries as she was hacked to death.

He squinted and spotted a car at the side of the road, a slender woman with dark curly hair waving at him as he neared. She ran up to him and hugged him tightly. "I'm so happy you're safe and coming home."

He nodded, pulling back a bit. His sister, Isa, looked beautiful and all grown up. She was the only one in his family who'd come to visit him. She'd also written to him regularly, and he loved her for it. His eyes lit up when he spotted her rounded belly. "When's the baby coming?"

he asked as he slid into the passenger seat.

"Not for another four months. You look good, considering what you've been through. You definitely got some muscle action going."

"I didn't have anything to do but work out. Had to make sure I could hold my own in there, you know?"

She nodded, a tear escaping. "It's all over now. You can start living again. This is all behind you."

He looked out the window as the countryside blurred by. It'd take a couple hours until he'd be back in Lafayette. His stomach twisted in a knot. So many memories, and he wasn't ready for any of them. He leaned his head back and closed his eyes.

"Charlie said that he can get you a job at the factory. He's the foreman, and they're looking for help."

"Not sure what I'm going to do."

"You should jump right in and get busy. Charlie said the work is good and the pay is decent. They always have overtime, so that's something, you know?"

"Does Clotille still live in Lafayette?" He immediately chastised himself for asking. He'd made a pact with himself that he wouldn't ask anything about her, yet he wasn't out even thirty minutes before he broke it.

"I think so," his sister said softly. "A few years back, I saw the announcement in the paper that she married Luc Gaulier. You remember him from high school, the star player?"

He nodded, his jaw jutting out.

"When you were in… prison"—Isa said it like it was a dirty word—"did you ever hear from her?"

"She wrote me a bunch of letters. The last one told me she was back with Luc."

"Did you ever answer her?"

"No."

"Why?"

He shrugged. "What for? She bailed on me. Most of her letters reeked with pity and an undercurrent of horror at what I'd done." He shook his head. "What did I have to say to her, anyway? I couldn't very well chat about 'my friends' on the inside. After she told me about Luc, I didn't see any point in her writing again. I had enough to deal with. I didn't need that shit, especially from her."

"Well, it doesn't matter anymore. That's all in the past. I can introduce you to a couple of my single friends. One of them remembers you from high school, and she always wanted to go out with you. You'll have a nice girl and family in no time."

"I doubt that." He was broken, but no one saw that except him. The pieces had shattered, leaving only bitterness and a dark rage. "Anyway, I'm not planning to stay."

"What do you mean?" Isa glanced at him her round eyes wide.

"I'm planning to head to Colorado. I got tight with a dude in prison who belongs to a club there. I'm thinking of checking it out to see if it's for me. His name's Bones. He was visiting some friends in New Orleans when he got into a bar fight and did some damage. Got six years for it. The way he talked about the club intrigued me."

"A club? What kind is it?"

"It's a group of guys who formed a brotherhood. They love the ride. I'll have to get a Harley, which may be hard since I don't have any money."

"You have money in trust from the sale of the land in St. Martin."

He sat up straight, his temples pulsing as the heat rose in him. "*Maman's* land was sold?"

"Yeah. I didn't want it to be, but I was outvoted. Henri and Lille wanted to sell it." She glanced at him, then darted her eyes back to the road. "Of course, Pa didn't have any say since he killed *Maman*," she said in a soft voice.

Their father was convicted of second-degree murder and was sitting in maximum security in the same prison Roche had done his time. *Fucking ironic.* The legal system didn't allow murderers to profit from their crimes, so the land went to the four of them. "How did they sell the land without my goddamned signature?"

"Henri said he sent it to you and you signed off. Your signature was on the paperwork." He pounded the dashboard. "He fucking forged my name!" He glowered and stared straight ahead.

"You've sure picked up some bad language."

"One of the perks of being in the joint," he deadpanned.

"I'm sorry that this came as a surprise. Anyway, *Maman's* gone, so what's the point in keeping it? I could never go there again."

He didn't answer, the darkness consuming him. He had to get out of Louisiana before he lost it and ended up back in prison. *Henri needs my fist in his face in the worst way. The fuckin' bastard!*

"So, you have money if you need it." She smiled weakly. "What's the name of this club that's taking you away from me so soon?"

"The Insurgents. And my name's not Roche anymore. It's Rock." He leaned back again and closed his eyes, working hard to push down his rage as the car sped along the freeway.

Chapter One

Pinewood Springs, Colorado
Seven years later

As Rock and Wheelie entered the Insurgents MC clubhouse, the hoots, whistles, and shouts were deafening. After four months of political bullshit, the two bikers had finally been released from jail. The Denver District Attorney's Office decided not to charge any Insurgents or Demon Riders in the fight that broke out at the Denver Motorcycle Expo that summer. Since there weren't any witnesses brave enough to testify, and none of the bikers were talking, both clubs walked away free and clear.

Each club knew they'd take justice into their own hands. One of the Demon Riders had been killed and two Insurgents had just spent four months in jail for a fight the Demon Riders instigated. Neither act would be forgotten by its respective club.

"Fuck, man. It's good to have you back," Throttle said as he gave Rock a bear hug. "I've missed your crazy ass around here."

Rock's dark eyes twinkled. "I heard you moved out and got bitten by the pussy-whipped bug. What the hell is this club coming to?" He lightly punched Throttle in the arm, then grabbed the shot that was waiting for him on the bar. Slinging it back, the fiery burn warmed his throat. *Damn, I missed this.* Before he could motion the prospect for another, his glass was filled.

He looked around, his cock stiffening when he saw the bevy of beauties in barely there outfits wiggling and shaking to the tunes of Guns N' Roses on the overhead speakers. Licking his lips, he picked out the women he'd be pounding into after a good game of pool.

"You gonna fuck all of 'em tonight?" Bones chuckled deeply.

Rock swung around and the two old friends tapped their fists together. "Damn straight. Shit, all I could think about was riding my Harley, pussy, and booze. Glad this shit's over. What've you been up to?"

"Just hangin'. We got some new chicks tonight. That's always fun. You up for some group fun or you want the bitches all to yourself?"

A wide grin broke out over Rock's face. "I love sharing. Damn, let's get three women and have a fuckin' good time."

"You know Throttle's out of commission now. He went and hooked up with Kimber."

"I heard that. Damn, I never would've figured he'd stop wanting easy pussy. You gonna go the same way?"

"Hell no. One time married to the bitch from hell was it for me. I don't need that shit. The only time a chick doesn't get on my nerves is when she's got her legs spread real wide." Bones picked up his beer and guzzled it.

"That's the truth. Anything more than fucking is asking for trouble." Rock threw back his third shot and ambled to the pool table. Hawk had just racked up the balls and was chalking his cue. Rock went over to him and clasped his shoulder. "Your woman did good by me. I don't forget what people do for me—good or bad. You got a Class-A woman."

Hawk nodded and smiled, then handed Rock a joint and lit it as well as his own. The smoke from the weed wove around them, each of them lost in thought. Then Throttle came over with three large cans of beer, handing one to Hawk and one to Rock. The three of them popped open their beers, clinked their cans together, and drank deeply from them. Warmth filled Rock as he drank, smoked, and played pool with his brothers. He'd never felt so close and unified with a group of people as he did with the Insurgents. The brotherhood was his family, and it was a damn better one than what he'd left behind in Lafayette, Louisiana.

After he was finished with his second game, he picked up the five hundred dollars he'd won, laughed at Rags's scowl, and snaked his way through the crowd as men clapped, gripped, and clasped his arm when he passed by. Spotting a pretty blonde with dark roots swaying to the music, he curled his arm around her waist and pulled her close to him, moving her back and forth while he sung the lyrics in her ear. She giggled and roped her arms around his corded neck, pulling him closer to her.

Soon he had his tongue halfway down her throat as she squirmed, rubbing her full chest against his so he could feel her stiff nipples. His large hands cupped the exposed underside of her butt, and he dug his fingers into her fleshy skin. He was so damn stiff. Not having pussy for four months drove him wild with desire for the stacked blonde, whose pouty pink lips would look good around his cock.

As he kissed her deeply, a soft voice next to him said, "Lela, did you see my phone?" Rock broke away from the blonde, who looked annoyed at the interruption, and stared at another blonde woman with blue eyes and one of the biggest racks he'd ever seen in person. For a split second he wondered if they were fake since they stood up so perfectly and her waist was so small. Deciding that, fake or not, he wanted his face buried in them, he smiled. "What seems to be the problem?"

Lela seemed angry that he'd shifted his attention from her to the new blonde. He saw the sparks of jealousy flash in her eyes and he laughed to himself. It always amused him how many women fought and clawed each other to have his attention when they didn't even know him. Sure, he'd been kissing and touching the ripe cutie, but he hadn't even known her name until her friend had said it. If he played his cards right, he'd be having double the fun with the two of them.

"I'm busy right now, Stacy. I don't know where your phone is." She turned away from her friend and jerked Rock's head down toward her lips. "Now, where were we?"

Stacy gave an exaggerated sigh and turned to leave when Rock grabbed her arm and pulled her back. "Where're you going so fast? Don't you wanna have some fun too?"

At first the two women looked confused. Then when Rock put his arm around both of them, each hand cupping one of their ass cheeks, they laughed as understanding spread across their faces. He kissed each one, drawing them closer to him. "You up for some fun together?"

They seemed nervous, but Rock thought it was more an act so he wouldn't think they were total sluts. Soon they were rubbing their tits against him and kissing him and each other. His dick was so hard that if he didn't release it soon, he was sure it'd break.

Bones came up to him then, his arm snaked around a tall, thin blonde. "Hey, bro. You look like you got your hands full."

"No shit." Rock raked his eyes lustfully over the blonde in Bones's arm. *Fucking these three hotties is gonna be awesome.* He turned to the two women wrapped in his arms. "This is Bones and we're real tight. We're so fuckin' tight that we do pretty much *everything* together. You get my drift?" His gaze locked with each of them, and he heard Bones's chick chuckle deep in her throat. *I can't wait to see how far down her throat my cock can go.*

Stacy nodded as she ran her hand through Rock's dark hair. "Oh yeah, and I'm loving where this is gonna take me." She blew against his ear and licked his earlobe. "You're so fuckin' handsome, and a club officer too. This is gonna be a night to remember."

Lela pulled him away from her friend's face and slipped her hand underneath his T-shirt, her nails lightly scratching his rippled chest. "I'd love for you and your friend to show us a good time. Just remember that I was the first one you saw and you came up to *me*." She ran the tip of her tongue along his jawline and up to his lips, brushing them. "Is your friend an officer like you?"

He shook his head, his body on fire from months of abstinence. "What're we waiting for? I got a room on the third floor." He practically dragged the two women behind him as he hurried out of the room and up the stairs. Bones's heavy footsteps sounded behind him.

When they reached his room, he told the women to strip and get on the bed. In less than a minute he'd kicked off his boots and stripped naked. Before he dove between the three women, Rock looked at Bones and grinned. "This is gonna be fun." He threw a condom packet at him after he'd ripped his open and rolled it on. Then he was on the bed, kissing, touching, squeezing, and playing with the chicks. Bones crawled over to him and the women, and soon Rock was buried deep into Lela's pussy while Bones owned her mouth. Stacy was under Lela sucking her tits while the thin blonde—he never got her name—lapped Stacy's mound as Rock shoved his finger in and out of her heated sex. *It doesn't get any fuckin' better than this.* Rock decided his blonde orgy made going without for all those months so worth it.

A couple hours later, they all lay tangled around each other, sated, a light sheen of sweat glistening on their bodies. Rock slid up and leaned against the headboard, chuckling when he heard Bones's snores. The three women clung to the two men like magnets. Rock leaned over, careful not to wake anyone, and lit a joint, inhaling deeply. Enjoying the deep sense of satisfaction humming through his body, he poured a shot of Jack and lifted it to his lips. As he threw it back, his phone bounced off the nightstand, sounding like a swarm of angry bees. He reached over and grabbed it, his sister's name flashing on the screen.

"Hey, Isa. *Ça va?*"

"I'm doing fine. What about you? You must be out of jail since you answered your phone."

"Yeah. Just got out this morning."

"That's good." He heard her suck in a breath. "What did they charge you with?"

"Nothing. They didn't have shit on any of us. Fuckin' badges," he grumbled.

Relief coated her voice. "I'm so happy it worked out. I was worried." Silence for a beat, but then it was broken with the loud bickering of his niece and nephew in the background. "*Arrêtez!* I'm talking to your Uncle Roche. Go in the other room." She laughed softly. "They drive me crazy sometimes. I don't remember us fighting this much when we were five and seven, or really at any age."

"You and I have always gotten along. Lille only gave a shit about herself, and Henri was another thing entirely. He fought with all of us, even *Maman*."

Another pause ensued. "So are you celebrating being back on the outside?"

He glanced at the three naked women and a wicked smile crossed his lips. "Yeah, you could say that."

"That's good. Very good." Another pause, that time longer than the last.

She wants to say something to me, but she's so fuckin' nervous. "Spill it. Why the fuck did you *really* call me?"

"I'm insulted. I always call to say hi and see how you are."

"Yeah, but you don't always act so fuckin' nervous that I can feel your sweat from way over here. Just level with me."

She breathed deeply and he imagined she was frowning, her brows creasing together like they always did when she was nervous, perplexed, or frustrated. "Okay. Promise you won't freak out on me and hang up."

Rock's stomach knotted. "I'm not promising shit. Just tell me."

"Pa's sick. He's been in the hospital, and they think it's cancer. They're doing a bunch of tests, and I thought—"

"What in fuck's name made you think I'd give a shit about *him*? He fuckin' murdered our mother, in case you forgot."

"I knew you'd be mad."

"Damn straight. I'm fuckin' pissed." His loud voice bounced off the walls and the thin blonde stirred, her eyes fluttering open. Her gaze locked with his and she blew him a kiss before closing her eyes again, her hand running up and down his thigh. "I don't wanna talk about it. I don't give a shit if he dies. The way I see it, it's fuckin' karma," he said in a low voice.

"Do you have someone with you? You're almost whispering."

"Yeah, so I gotta go."

"Please don't shut me out. I know Pa did something unspeakable and horrendous, but he was crazy drunk. That's why he got second-degree murder and will be eligible for parole in about ten years."

"And I'll make sure I make the trip back to the pen to tell the goddamned parole board to never let his murdering ass out. I'll never forget or forgive what he did to *Maman*."

"I understand, but everyone deserves a little bit of compassion, don't they?"

Rock's eyes narrowed, the warmth glowing in him from an amazing session of fucking replaced with icy cold hardness. "No. Some people deserve to die without an ounce of sympathy. He's fuckin' one of them. I really gotta go."

"You know *Maman* would've wanted you to forgive him," she murmured, barely audible.

He jutted out his jaw, his fists clenched. "Yeah, well, I'm not *Maman*. She was kind and forgiving and look where it got her—murdered on a cold floor in a shithole by a cruel, drunk sonofabitch. I'll take bitterness and hate any time."

"Okay. I'm sorry I brought it up. I thought that after all this time you'd have softened a bit."

"You were wrong. I'll never soften about what he did. To me, he's dead. I never want to hear about him again unless he's up for parole."

"When are you going to come out and see us? It's been too long. You'd barely recognize Aline and Michael. We talk about you all the time, and they love the gifts you send them. It's time to come home for a visit. I miss you."

Her cheerfulness didn't fool him. *Poor Isa. She's taken the role Maman had—the kind, loving peacemaker.* "I'll think about it. How are Lille and that piece of shit Henri?"

She laughed. "Lille is still trying to snag a rich man. She just divorced Robert and is already sniffing around Mr. Amelix."

"That old fart? Fuck, can he even get it up?"

She laughed louder. "Roche, you're so bad."

"I hope she gets what she wants. The trouble is when she gets it, she always wants something else."

"That's Lille for you. Henri has been working on a bunch of big deals. He says he's going to make a fortune. I don't know… I don't see him very often."

"He got a woman?"

"He's been going out with Suzette Terriot. You remember her from high school? She was the one who had the beautiful clothes, always flaunting her wealth in everyone's face."

"All I remember are the sweaters she wore 'cause she had a big rack. As I remember, she didn't have the prettiest face, but her rack made up for it. At least that's what the guys thought."

She chuckled. "Her rack is even bigger thanks to Dr. Anderson."

They both laughed. *Damn. When we're talking like this, I really miss Isa. I should go see her and the kids.* "Is Clotille still in Lafayette?" *Whoa! Where the fuck did that come from? I haven't asked about her since I left. Being locked up made me fuckin' soft in the head.*

"I don't know. She sort of disappeared. The whole family did when her father died in the condo he'd bought for his mistress. Can you imagine their embarrassment? Mrs. Boucher didn't go out of her house. Well, not until they took it from her. The family went broke because Mr. Boucher had a horrible gambling problem and threw away millions on the horses and at the craps tables."

"Really? I didn't know that. Fuck, that must've been hard for Clotille."

"She divorced Luc, and she and her family went into hiding. They must be doing better now because I read in the society column that Mrs. Boucher just bought a house over in Ranch River. She seems to be back on the circuit."

"Mean bitches like her never fall down. They may falter, but they get right back up on their hoofed feet."

"Not a fan of hers?"

"Nah."

"Hey, handsome, I need some attention." Stacy's hand curled around his dick and it started waking up.

"I gotta go. We'll talk soon." He hung up the phone and moved his hand on top of the blonde's head, guiding her mouth to his cock. "Suck it," he ordered.

She opened her mouth and slipped his length inside, licking and sucking while she cupped his balls. He leaned his head back, eyes closed, groaning as the image of a brown-haired woman with shimmering green eyes invaded his mind. As Stacy sucked him, he imagined she was Clotille. In a matter of minutes he blew his wad, wishing for the first time in a long time that the blonde was his old love swallowing his come and licking his dick clean.

The other two women stirred, and then Bones sat up. Rock looked at his clock, which read eleven thirty. Deciding another round with the blondes was what he needed to shake the green-eyed memory from his mind, he pulled Lela up to him, covering her tit with his mouth. Bones was now fully awake and the two other women began pleasuring him.

The night was just beginning.

Chapter Two

THIRTY PEOPLE IN a room meant for twenty made for an uncomfortable club meeting. Each time the brothers attended church, especially during the hot months, the discussion would come up about taking down walls to make the room bigger. When the members were uncomfortable they tended to argue more, shove each other around, and break out in fistfights. That afternoon was no exception.

As Rock came between Wheelie and Rags, Wheelie's fist, aimed for Rags, slammed into the side of Rock's face. "Fuck!" He grabbed the brother's hand and bent it backward.

"Sonofabitch! Stop, Rock. You're gonna fuckin' break my wrists!"

"That's what I wanna do, asshole."

Soon several brothers were taking sides: some were in Wheelie's court, others in Rags's. All of the membership was in Rock's since he was just trying to break up the fight. Being the Sergeant-At-Arms, it was Rock's duty to make sure order was kept among the brothers most of the time, especially during church and at family gatherings.

A thunderous bang stopped everyone in their tracks, and they turned to the front to see where the noise had come from. A red-faced Banger stood tall, a splintered chair in his hands. A heavy hush filled the room, and Rock smiled at his president's style.

"Each one of you fuckers sit down. This is church. You do whatever shit you wanna do before or after but *never* during." He scowled, his piercing blue eyes flashing.

"What the fuck started the shit anyway?" Rock asked under his breath to Throttle.

"Wheelie called Rags's vintage Harley a rusted can."

"He said *that*? No wonder Rags wanted to bust him up. I'd kill anyone who said shit about my bike."

"Wheelie knew it'd piss Rags off. He's pissed at Rags 'cause he's lost the last four pool games to him and he's out five grand."

"Still was a low blow to talk shit about a guy's Harley."

Rock realized the room was dead silent and he glanced up and locked gazes with Banger.

"Is it okay if I continue, or am I breakin' into yours and Throttle's private time?" The brothers in the room all sniggered. Rock and Throttle squirmed in their chairs. "Just let me know 'cause I wouldn't wanna be disturbing you motherfuckers." Banger's steely glare bored into Rock.

Clearing his throat, Rock said, "Just trying to figure out what happened so I can make sure it doesn't spill into the great room when we're done here. Just doing my job."

Banger's clenching jaw was visible. "Your job right now is to keep your damn mouth shut and show respect to your president. Is there something you don't understand about that?"

Rock shook his head slowly, then leaned back in his chair. He motioned with his hand as if to tell Banger to continue with the meeting. He knew he was being a prick but, president or not, he didn't like *anyone* patronizing him. For a few seconds he and Banger glared at one another, each of their chins held high in defiance, neither of them ready to acquiesce.

Finally Banger broke away and folded his arms against his chest. "Liam's asked us to do him a favor."

Liam was an Irish arms dealer and smuggler who the Insurgents MC had worked with on and off for years. Before marijuana was legalized, they depended on illegal deals to fund their club, and in the murky world of arms smuggling, finding trustworthy people was about as rare as a midsummer snowstorm. Liam had proven to be a fair, salt-of-the-earth type of guy who had the guts to work with the Insurgents and the brains to not fuck them over. Since weed had been legalized, the club had shifted directions and began making money the legal way. They rarely got involved in arms smuggling anymore; however, their respect and relationship with Liam continued.

"What's the favor?" Jax asked.

"He wants us to do a bodyguard gig."

Groans and cussing circled around the room, and Rock stared at the redness creeping up Banger's neck. Before it hit his cheeks, Hawk stood up and motioned the crowd to shut up. He cleared his throat. "I know we don't do this type of work—"

"Yeah, we're not losers like the fuckin' Deadly Demons," Bones interrupted. Fellow members laughed and pounded their fists on the table in agreement.

Hawk threw him a dirty look. "As I was saying, we don't do this type of work, but we owe Liam for the job Shack fucked up last year in Nebraska. Besides, Liam never asks favors from us."

"Who're we protecting?" Rock propped his elbows on the wood table.

"Frederick Blair. He's a billionaire who's having a dinner party at his estate in Aspen and he wants some muscle. The total worth in the room makes him and his guests targets."

"What the hell does Liam have to do with him?" Jerry asked.

"He buys big, expensive, and illegal toys for the ultra-wealthy. Men like Frederick Blair have too much money and time on their hands. That's what makes them dangerous as hell. But what they buy and what they do with it isn't our business. We're there to babysit a bunch of rich fucks. That's pretty much it."

"I know I'm gonna be on this fuckin' babysitting duty," Rock said aloud.

"Me too." Jax shook his head. "The muscle of the club always does this type of work. Shit."

"Yeah. Shit."

"So, Rock, Bones, Wheelie, Throttle, Jax, Rags, Chas, Bear, and Axe will be the ones to cover this detail. The party is this Saturday night. You have to be there at six o'clock in the evening. The security at the estate will brief you on where things are and the lay of the land. The money earned from this job will go in the club fund after the brothers who work it get their pay. Rock is in charge. Any questions?"

"Is this gonna be something the club's gonna start doing regularly?" Bruiser asked. "I remember doing this shit before some of the brothers were even born." He chuckled. "We used to do the nightclubs and concert halls. You remember that, Banger?"

Banger smiled and nodded. "You're taking us back pretty far, dude." Bruiser grinned, and Rock noticed a warmth pass between the two older brothers. "Anyway, we're just doing this to help Liam and make some money too. We'll see how it goes, and if the rich fuck needs us again, we'll do it. It's easy money." Banger looked around the room. "Any more questions?"

The members shook their heads and their president picked up the gavel, hit it on the table, and announced that church was adjourned.

By the time the guys shuffled to the great room, the sun had begun to set and a golden pink glow bathed the room. The scent of hickory chips tantalized Rock's nostrils as wisps of smoke filtered in from the opened back door. Two large grills were smoking as they waited for Bruiser, Bear, and Hawk to cook up steak and chicken. A large pot of baked beans simmered on a hot plate, and mountains of potato and macaroni salad were placed on the long buffet table by Wendy and Rosie. The club girls had made up the sides, and the tinge of pink in their cheeks told the brothers they were excited to start the party.

Rock, beer in hand, walked out back. The smell of grilling always brought him back to his childhood. His mother would use the grill they'd had in the backyard to smoke ribs and andouille sausages. She'd also boil crawfish in big pots on their outdoor propane cooker. Since he'd moved to Colorado, he hadn't had a crawfish boil, and he suddenly missed it. *Damn. Why the fuck is my mind back in Lafayette? What the fuck's going on?* For the past seven years, Rock rarely thought about his life back in Louisiana; there was no need for it. But talking to Isa the previous night stirred something inside him. Something he had buried deep where it couldn't hurt him.

"You hungry?" Hawk laughed as he lined up the steaks on the grill.

"Huh? Oh, yeah. I'm fuckin' starving." Rock watched as the juices from the steak sputtered and sparked in the flames. "You need some help?"

"Nope. I have a handle on it."

Soon the members and the women—both club girls and hoodrats—congregated near the food as Puck and Blade hurriedly set up a makeshift bar adjacent to the buffet table. Rock grabbed a spot at one of the aluminum picnic tables and scanned the crowd, soon spotting a pretty brunette whose hair ended right above her butt. As if she sensed him staring, she turned around and smiled at him, her eyes moving over his six-foot-one body.

Rock was a sight to behold with his dark wavy hair curling right above his collar, inky black eyes, strong jaw, and a perfect Roman nose. His tanned skin was taut above hard, defined muscles that moved and flexed in a mesmerizing way, making the tats adorning his flesh come alive. Several earrings dangled from each ear, and a thick silver-chained necklace gleamed against his corded neck. When women spotted him, they vied for his attention, but he'd walk past them, a smirk dancing on his full, sensuous lips. He knew women wanted him, and when they spotted the Sergeant-At-Arms patch on his cut or jacket, they promised him wild sex any way he wanted it. Sometimes he took them up on their offer, but most times he'd just smile and say, "Another time," in a low, throaty voice that stroked the women's senses like velvet. He rarely went with citizens, preferring the no-strings-attached sex the club women and hoodrats offered.

Kristy, one of the club girls, slipped in the space next to him, her nails running up and down his forearm. "You want me to get you a drink?"

Rock noticed the look of disappointment on the pretty brunette's face as Kristy fused herself to his side. He slid over a bit and put a sliver of space between them. "I'll get my own. Bones was looking for you."

"I want you. Don't you want me?"

His gaze lingered on her breasts as they practically popped out of a crop top a size too small for her. He'd licked, sucked, and fucked those tits more times than he could count. Kristy was a club girl who'd be available the following day, week, month, and, most probably, year. That night he wanted something new, not a club girl he could fuck any time. "I've already decided on someone, babe. Be a good girl and go find Bones." He dipped his head down and kissed her gently on the cheek. "Tomorrow, okay?"

She squeezed his inner thigh, her fingers close to his dick. "We got a date for tomorrow. Where's Bones?"

He lightly brushed her hand away and then jerked his head toward the back door. "He's in the great room playing darts."

Kristy stood up and he smacked her jiggling ass as she walked away from him. She threw him a big smile and headed toward the back door. He watched her until she disappeared, then turned back to find the cute brunette he wanted to bang. She was next to the buffet table, plate in hand, spooning some macaroni salad on it. He saw Rags giving her the eye and Rock scrambled over to her before Rags could reach her.

"You don't want any steak?" he asked her.

She smiled broadly when she turned around and saw him. She shook her head. "I'm vegetarian."

"How the fuck does that work? You never eat steak or ribs? How the hell can you live without them?"

She laughed and moved close to him so her orchid-scented body brushed against his. The softness of her touch, her scent, and her cute upturned nose made his dick jerk. He figured he'd be fucking her senseless right after they finished eating. With his arm around her shoulders, he carried her plate back to the table and pulled her close to him.

The night was turning out like most of his nights at the club: strong booze, delicious food, and hard fucking. He lived a hedonistic life of drinks, parties, and sex, and he couldn't imagine what more a man could want.

The brunette leaned into him and placed her soft hand on his face, turning him to her. She kissed him passionately and moaned when his fingers kneaded her tits.

Another night in paradise.

Fuck yeah!

★ ★ ★

ON SATURDAY EVENING the bodyguard brigade made the one-hour trip to Aspen to the lavish estate of Frederick Blair. Hidden behind thirty-foot stone walls, the Blair mansion had twelve bedrooms, sixteen bathrooms, twenty wood-burning fireplaces, and two kitchens. It also had a fully finished basement that was off-limits to the staff who lived and worked at the estate.

Rock whistled under his breath. "Fuck. The place looks like a hotel. You could fit a small town in there."

"Why the hell would anyone want to live in something so big?" Axe asked. "Shit, if your woman is pissed at you, it could take a week to find her."

The brothers laughed as they waited for the iron gate to open and let them in. In a few minutes they were roaring up the driveway, parking their iron machines to the left of the house in a small parking lot, as they had been instructed to do. They met with a large-framed man who sported a reddish-brown, bushy moustache. He tilted his head at them. "The name's Kevin, and I'm head of security for Mr. Blair. Tonight your duties are making sure the outside is secure. Mr. Blair has five thousand acres, but you'll be responsible to make sure no one gets near the house. Three of you will be stationed in the house and the others will be outside. Do you have any questions?"

Since Rock was the Sergeant-At-Arms, he was in charge of every security gig the club did. He shook his head. "It seems pretty basic. How long do you figure this shindig's gonna last?" Rock didn't want to waste an entire Saturday night babysitting a bunch of rich people.

"I don't know. Mr. Blair will let you know when it's over. Sometimes his parties can go all night, and other times just a few hours." Kevin turned and pointed to Rock, Wheelie, and Bear, motioning them to follow him. "You three will do inside duty. The rest will be out here. I'll be in and out all night, so let me know if you have any questions or need anything."

The three brothers followed him to the house, entering and then staring up at a wood staircase that spiraled around an enormous wrought-iron chandelier that Rock surmised to be about three stories high. Their leather boots tapped loudly on the pristine white marble floor as the men followed Kevin into a spacious room that had large cushy couches, several armchairs, an enormous fireplace, and, in the back, a large wooden table with twelve chairs around it.

"This is where the party will be. Mr. Blair wants two of you present in the room and one in the front hallway. At no time does he want you to engage in conversation with him or his guests. You are not to talk with each other. Your job is to be alert for anything amiss, nothing more."

Rock clenched his jaw. The prick was starting to piss him off. He looked over at Wheelie and Bear and saw their tight faces, and clenched fists. He chuckled inwardly. Insurgents didn't like anyone telling them what the hell they could or couldn't do. This Mr. Blair could take his rules and shove them up his ass.

Kevin bowed his head slightly. "I'll leave you, then." In a few seconds he was gone, disappearing down one of the many hallways.

"This is gonna fuckin' suck," Rock said to Bear and Wheelie, who nodded in agreement. "I can't believe Banger got us into this shit."

Before the other two bikers could answer, a tall, lean man in his early forties entered the room. He had blond hair and pale blue eyes surrounded by fine lines. He wore perfectly pressed khaki trousers and a lime-green sports shirt with yellow pinstripes. He smiled when he stopped before them, his too-white teeth looking ridiculous against his overly tanned face. "You must be the backup Liam promised me."

You fucking know we are, asshole. For reasons Rock couldn't articulate, he didn't like their employer. There was something about him that was cruel and evil just below the surface of his too-tanned skin. Rock could sense it, smell it, and its scent was rotten to the core.

The three bikers stood stone-faced before him, and Blair chuckled nervously while he jammed his hands in and out of his pockets repeatedly. "I'm sure Kevin explained everything to you. Right?"

Rock jerked his chin up.

Blair licked his lips, then pressed them together. "Okay. Well then, I don't need to tell you that anything that goes on inside the house is private. I don't want the names of my guests or what we do or talk about ever leaked out. Understood?"

Rock crossed his arms and stood stiff with his legs spread apart. His tattoos rippled as his muscles tensed. "We're not fuckin' snitches," he growled.

Blair's eyes widened. "No, I didn't mean that you were."

"Then you don't have to tell us that shit," Bear gritted.

Rock glanced at Bear's darkening face. *He hates this asshole too.* He stood frozen to his spot, his eyes boring into Blair. An awkward silence fell over them and they stood rigid as soldiers as their employer ran his hand through his short hair.

"Well then," Mr. Blair's voice sliced through the tension, "take your positions. The guests will be arriving shortly." He turned around quickly and disappeared from the room.

"What a fuckin' prick," Rock said. Wheelie and Bear voiced their agreement.

Wheelie would man the hallway, and Bear and Rock would stay in the living and dining room. They stood around for about thirty minutes before the doorbell rang and Blair appeared out of nowhere to answer it. "John, Sebastian, Alex, it's so good to see you. Peter and Roger, you both as well. How've you been?"

"Very good, Frederick," several voices chimed.

Rock turned to look toward the hallway, watching Wheelie's eyebrows rise and then lower immediately. Five men from their late thirties to early fifties came in with five attractive women behind them who wore raincoats. When they entered the living room, the men turned to their women and gave them a hard stare. They each took off their coats, handing them to one of the staff. Rock sucked in his breath and heard Bear do the same: the women were naked except for black collars. Long leashes were attached to the metal D-rings on the collars. *What the fuck?* Frederick gestured to the men to sit and they sank down on the couches and armchairs while the women knelt—butts against their calves, hands on their thighs palms up—next to their partner.

"What the fuck is this?" Bear said in a low voice.

"A dinner party." Rock grinned. "Getting some ideas, are you?"

"I can't see the club girls kneeling next to us without a cock in their mouths. No way."

"Yeah, they're not the submissive type. This must be a play party."

"All of a sudden this gig doesn't seem so bad." Bear turned his gaze back to the living room.

The waitstaff filled drinks, passed hors d'oeuvres, and acted like it was an everyday occurrence to have a dinner party with naked women kneeling in front of their men, collared and silent. It blew Rock away; he surmised they must be part of the lifestyle. The caterer came out of the kitchen, bent down, and said something in Frederick's ear. He smiled, stood up, and announced that dinner was ready. The male guests rose to their feet and followed him into the dining room, tugging their crawling women behind them.

Rock couldn't help but gaze at the women, catching the eye of one who quickly looked down, her face reddening in embarrassment. He felt bad and made himself stare at the paintings on the wall, but out of the corner of his eye, he caught her looking at him and wiggling her butt on the rug. The man with her yanked her leash hard, jerking her forward. She yelped and he said in a cold voice, "Be still, slutty vixen, or I'll punish you." She immediately shifted her gaze downward.

"And where is your beautiful fucktoy, Frederick?" one of the men asked as he brought a glass of white wine to his mouth.

"She's coming. If I didn't know you, I'd swear you're trying to steal her away from me, John." Frederick laughed, but Rock picked up a hard edge in his laughter.

"She is beautiful," a portly man said as he patted his woman on the head. "Have you changed your mind about lending her out?"

Frederick's eyes narrowed. "No, Sebastian. I haven't."

As if on cue, a woman with brown hair streaked in golden highlights entered the room. She wore a tight-fitting red dress that hugged all her curves, three-inch-heeled shoes that made her rounded ass higher, and a black collar with metal studs. She walked with elegance over to Frederick. Her long hair hung over the side of her face, and all Rock could see was her ripe body busting out of her dress. When the scent of amber and vanilla ribboned around him, his dick twitched and he cursed under his breath.

"Come here, pet." Frederick stretched his hand out and smiled when she placed hers into it. He yanked her down to his face, kissed her, and then placed his arm on her shoulders. "Kneel," he ordered. She immediately dropped to her knees, her head bowed.

Rock watched the lust shine in the eyes of the men seated at the table, and he wished he could see the woman in red's face.

"It doesn't seem fair that we lend our whores to you but you keep yours all to yourself." Sebastian licked his lips as he boldly stared at the woman kneeling next to Frederick.

"You and your slaves signed a contract allowing for lending out. My pet and I did not. However, I may feel generous tonight and let you touch her."

Rock saw the woman in red jerk at his words. For a split second, Rock wanted to know how she'd ended up kneeling on the floor next to the rich sonofabitch. But he reminded himself it wasn't his business. The power play between the men and women was something they all wanted.

As the men gorged on steak, asparagus, and potatoes, the women knelt patiently by their partners. Every once in a while, the men would cut a piece from their steak, pick it up, and put it in their women's mouths, letting their fingers linger so the women could lick them. As the women were fed, they seemed to become more aroused—except for the clothed one. She opened her mouth and took the morsels of food Frederick fed her, but she didn't seem to enjoy his fingers lingering in her mouth.

From where he stood, Rock could feel her resentment for the man who controlled her, and for a quick moment he wondered if she were willingly his submissive or was being forced into his world. Bear grunted and Rock turned to him. "This is fucked, man," he said under his breath. Rock shrugged, his gaze pulled back to the woman Frederick was feeding.

For some reason, Rock was drawn to her. The pull was strong, but he knew it was insane; he didn't know anything about her, and she was Frederick's wife or partner. Plus, she hadn't even noticed him. Some of the women sneaked peeks at him, but the clothed woman stayed perfectly still, her hair half in her face. The only thing exposed to him was her full, shining red lips that wrapped around the piece of steak each time it was given to her. *I'd love those lips around my cock. What the fuck am I saying? Why the hell did Banger take this shitty job?* Something about the woman touched him; he wanted to find out her name, where she was from, and if she were with Frederick of her own accord.

Before he could explore the odd feelings swirling around inside him, Frederick said something in her ear. His tone was sharp, a bit jagged, but Rock couldn't make out the words.

She jumped up while saying, "Yes, Sir."

He looked at his dinner guests and grinned wolfishly as he pushed back his chair. "Come here, my sweet fucktoy," he said sternly. She stood up and then dropped to her knees between his, spreading them out, her head down. Frederick grasped the hem of her dress and yanked it up, revealing no panties and a smooth, shaved pussy. He fisted her hair and pulled her up by it, a small cry escaping from her lips. He placed his hands on her waist and spun her around so she faced the men at the table. "Bend over."

Rock heard her say in a low voice, "Please, Frederick, don't do this." Her voice was as soft as a kiss and washed over Rock. His insides clenched and a single bolt of anger burned up his spine.

As if Bear sensed it, he muttered, "Easy, man. This isn't our business. It's part of a game they have going between them."

"I don't fuckin' think she's playing." A primitive instinct to protect her flooded all his senses.

Frederick glared at the two bikers, his stare piercing. Rock fought every urge he had to beat the shit out of him, toss the red-dressed woman over his shoulder, and take her back to his cave. The host turned back around and slapped her ass hard. She gasped as he continued slapping her, the men laughing and egging Frederick on to hit her harder. From where he was standing, Rock could see her lips quivering, a flushed sliver of neck showing through her hair.

"He's fuckin' humiliating her on purpose," Rock growled.

"I know, but it's their scene, man." Bear crossed his arms.

Both bikers were uncomfortable with the way the woman was being treated. Even though they fucked hard and rough, they fooled around with women who wanted it, and they wouldn't embarrass a woman in public unless she enjoyed it. *But maybe she does enjoy this. I know people get off on this type of play. Damn, why do I give a shit what's going on here? Fuck you, Banger!*

Frederick stood up, pulled down the woman's dress, and then wrapped his hand in her hair, pulling her toward him. When her face was close to his, he kissed her and she curled her arm around his neck, leaning into him. Rock watched as the woman passionately kissed the man who'd just humiliated her. The host stood up, grabbed her leash, and tugged her behind him. In a loud voice, he said, "Gentlemen, let's go to the playroom for some fun."

The men followed their host, their subs obediently crawling behind them. Rock and Bear followed them to the basement door. Frederick turned to them. "You aren't allowed downstairs. Stand guard in the room until we are finished," he said in a dismissive tone before closing the door, the lock clicking loudly.

A few hours later, the dinner guests returned except for the woman in the red dress. Rock wondered if the prick had hurt her too bad and she was collapsed on the floor in the basement. Frederick walked his friends to the door and they exchanged "Thank yous" and "Good-byes." He closed the door and stared at Rock, Wheelie, and Bear. "I wasn't pleased that you talked during the dinner party when you were told not to. That won't fly the next time. You can go."

Rock, trying to control his temper, said, "We don't give a fuck if you were pleased or not. And your attitude doesn't 'fly' with us. You didn't like it? Tough shit."

"Let's get outta here," Wheelie said, clasping Rock's shoulder.

"Come on, man. This shit ain't worth it." Bear stood next to Rock. Frederick glared at all three of them.

"Fuck it." Rock stormed out, welcoming the cool night air. He had to clear his head, rid his mind of the woman who knelt so silently and obediently.

"Why's he so pissed?" Chas asked as Rock jumped on his Harley, his face dark and brooding.

"Some intense shit went down inside this fucker's house. Damn. Did you see any of it, Wheelie?"

"Yeah. It was cool 'cause they all were into it. Why the hell is Rock so pissed? It's not like it's all that different from the initiation of a club whore. Everyone is down for it, including the chick."

"Will someone tell me what the fuck you're talking about? We were outside all night. What was going down in there?" Bones asked, while Axe, Chas, Rags, and Throttle nodded in agreement.

"I'll tell you when we get back to the club. I'm fuckin' dying for a beer." Bear swung his leg over his bike.

"Your old lady gonna let you stay out late tonight?" joked Throttle.

"Yeah. What about yours?"

"Nope. She's got something romantic planned."

The brothers laughed and made kissy noises as they switched on their ignitions and roared into the night.

When they got back to the clubhouse, a party was in full swing. The brothers who had old ladies left after one beer while the single ones stayed and mingled with the partygoers. Rock was on his fourth shot of Jack when the pretty brunette from the previous night came up to him. He smiled when he saw her, the memory of his cock buried in her ass still fresh in his mind.

"Hi, sexy. I was hoping you'd show up. Where've you been?" she said as she pressed close, her hard nipples crushing against him.

"I was doing something." He threw back his shot, then motioned for another. "You couldn't find another brother?"

"No one here compares to you." She squeezed his bicep, then bent down and traced his tattoo with her tongue. "Wanna have some fun?"

Rock wished he was feeling it the way he had the previous night. "Sorry, babe, not tonight. I'm so fuckin' tired. Another time."

Her eyes widened. "Didn't I please you last night?"

"Yeah, and I did the same to you. It was great. It's not you. I'm just fuckin' tired, that's all." That wasn't all. The woman at the mansion had disturbed him. He couldn't get her out of his mind.

The brunette stayed next to him until Bones came over. "You having a good time with this one?" His whiskey breath fanned over Rock's face.

"She's cool. We had some fun last night. Passing on it tonight."

The brunette smiled widely at Bones, and Rock knew she'd found a replacement. He blew out a relieved breath as she walked away from him, her arm around Bones's waist and his draped over her shoulder.

Rock stared at the party unfolding before him, but his mind was on the woman at Frederick's party. *I want to see her again. Fuck, what am I talking about? I don't know why she's still in my head.* But she was. Maybe it was the way her full lips took the pieces of food in her mouth, or the way her delicate hands gripped the table when her partner humiliated her. He didn't know; he couldn't make sense of it. All he knew was that she stirred something deep inside him. It was like she was a magnet drawing him to her. *She didn't even know I was in the damn room. This is fucked.*

Shaking his head, he left the party and stumbled up to his room. When he closed the door, he took out a bottle of brandy, put on a CD of Lee Benoit's music, and sat in his easy chair by the window, looking out into the darkness as the music filled the quietness around him. The spirited melody played by the fiddles eased the muddled feelings he had rustling inside him. He closed his eyes and let the rich, dynamic sounds of the button accordion take him back, and for the first time since he'd left Lafayette so many years before, he felt homesick. Right then he'd kill for a proper jambalaya, a lively two-step on the dance floor at Clementine's Bar, and Clotille wrapped around his body. *Why the hell did she pop into my mind? I haven't thought about her in a long time.* And when he *had* thought about her, disappointment and bitterness filled him. But at that moment the bad feelings weren't there, and he was eighteen again and loving his sweetheart. And it *had* been good for that one single moment when they'd come together, their hearts flashing and throbbing as one. But that had been before he'd found his mother cold and bloody on the kitchen floor.

Fuck! No!

He poured more brandy into his glass and cranked the music louder.

That night, he wasn't letting the demons in.

Chapter Three

I CAN'T BELIEVE Roche was here last night. What's the chance of that after all these years? Clotille paced back and forth in the small room off her bedroom. She remembered she'd heard he'd left Lafayette right after he was released from prison. Someone had told her he'd joined up with a motorcycle gang, but she'd never expected to see him again. Being back in the same state as Roche made her feel better in a strange way. She'd missed him terribly over the years, and in her mind, she'd played the fantasy of running into him many times over years. It had finally come true, but it wasn't at all the way she'd imagined it.

Red stained her cheeks and her stomach clenched when she recalled the humiliation of the previous night. The minute she'd spotted Roche, she'd made a concerted effort to keep her face hidden as much as she could. She'd have died if he'd recognized her, knowing what she'd become. But he didn't seem to know her even though he'd watched her. She'd sensed it, and when he was whispering to the other biker, she'd stolen glances at him.

She rubbed her sore arms and wrists and tried to sit on the loveseat next to the window overlooking the garden. She gasped in pain and breathed heavily as she settled onto the cushion. *Frederick went too far last night.* Earlier that morning, after he had left to play golf, she'd run to the bathroom to look at her behind in the full-length mirror. Angry red stripes, welts, and the beginning of bruising on her ass showed off his handiwork. She knew he loved seeing how beautiful her butt looked, and sometimes he'd have her bend over on her knees for a long time as he sat on a chair, legs crossed, admiring it.

She sighed, happy that she had a slice of aloneness. The only room that she had any privacy in was the small room off the bedroom they shared; the rest of the house had cameras in every room and hallway. When she'd first come to Frederick's house, she'd insisted upon having one room that was all hers or all bets were off. He'd agreed and it had become her refuge. Clotille especially welcomed her cocoon after a very intense session, like the one she'd just endured.

Her thoughts drifted back to Roche. She still couldn't believe that he'd been less than ten feet away from her. A shiver shimmied up her spine. *From what I could see, he's still handsome. He's built himself up, and he looks so damn good.* When she'd first recognized him, her heart had skipped a beat and her insides clenched, but then she'd become consumed with him not recognizing her. It'd been his soot-black eyes that had given him away. They still flashed with fierceness and pride. They were the same ones that had once dragged her into their depths and made her fall in love with him. And she knew if she wasn't careful, his dark orbs would pull her back in again.

She glanced at the clock and a knot formed in the pit of her stomach. Frederick would be home soon and he'd expect her to be in her full submissive pose, waiting for him at the door. She couldn't slip up or he'd punish her, and she didn't think she could take another one of his whippings so soon. Absently, she rubbed her bruised wrists where he'd tied the rope too tightly. The longer she'd stayed with him, the less she wanted to be part of his lifestyle. For the first few years, she'd actually enjoyed the pain mixed with the pleasure, but in the past year, his obsession with her had increased as well as his punishments. Just the week before, she'd used her safe word when he used the crop on her aroused sex, but he hadn't stopped. He'd beaten her badly until she'd almost passed out from the pain. Later that night, he'd apologized to her and held her close, gently stroking her cheek. He'd told her that he was so consumed with passion for her he'd lost his head. He'd sworn it would never happen again—her safe word would be honored.

She'd forgiven him, but her trust in him had disappeared. Clotille no longer wanted the life he provided for her, and since she'd seen Roche, she wanted to break away from Frederick more than ever. But she knew she couldn't; she was obligated to him. Besides, he'd never let her go; she was too entrenched in his life, and his love and passion for her went far beyond the regular Dominant and submissive relationship they'd shared in the beginning. She shivered imagining what he'd do if she ever tried to leave him.

The loud buzz of her timer startled her. She looked at the clock again, panic weaving through her. *I should've been in the shower twenty minutes ago!* She leapt up and scurried to the bathroom. When she'd finished, she slapped on her makeup in the way Frederick liked, fastened her black collar, and rushed down the stairs. When she was home alone with Frederick, he forbade her to wear clothes, but if guests were over, she'd wear what he picked out for her. He loved tight, revealing clothes that made her blush when she wore them. The more men ogled her in the outfits, the prouder he was of her. It made her happy that he was pleased and proud of her. When he was disappointed, shame would spread through her, making her feel so sorry for displeasing him. After all, he *did* take care of her, and he'd helped her so much in her life.

Damn! He's going to be here in less than a minute. I can't let him see my face red from rushing. He'll know I was dawdling too much. Frederick was compulsively prompt and she knew if he told her he'd be home at five o'clock, he'd be home right at five—not a second before or after. She dropped to her knees on the marble floor and faced the front door. She sat upright on her heels and clasped her hands behind her back, her knees spread as wide apart as they would go. She'd stay in this position until he told her to move.

As the grandfather clock in the grand foyer struck five, she heard Frederick put the key in the lock and turn it. He walked in and his gaze locked with hers, a smile twitching at the corners of his mouth. *He's pleased with me.* Her nerves relaxed a bit.

He bent down and patted her head. "I love seeing my sweet pet waiting for me at the door when I come home. Now go and get me my drink."

She jumped up and rushed to the bar. His chuckling told her he was enjoying the way her beaten ass jiggled as she ran. She made him a scotch and soda, then scurried to the family room where he sat on a chair, his leg crossed over his thigh. She handed him his drink and dropped to her knees next to his feet.

He smiled. "How was your day, pet?"

She smiled back but didn't answer. She'd learned early on that speaking without his permission resulted in being punished.

Frederick gently stroked her cheek with the back of his finger. "You have my permission to speak, pet."

"I had a nice day, Sir."

"Is there anything you want to talk to me about?"

Apprehension rose in her and the tension of the moment made her insides scream. *Why is he asking me that? Did I do or say something that I wasn't supposed to? Did he find out I know Roche. Oh God, no. He couldn't have found that out.*

She felt his hand pull her hair hard.

"Answer me."

"No, Sir. I don't have anything to talk to you about." She didn't dare breathe.

He ran his fingers through her hair. "You're such a good little pet."

She smiled demurely, her body relaxing. "Do you want me to fix your dinner, Sir?"

He shook his head. "Not yet. I want to look at you for a while." And so they stayed for a long time, his intense gaze taking in her naked body with an admiring look in his eyes. Then he reached out and his fingertips brushed across her soft skin, sending shivers up her spine. Her nipples hardened, and his mouth curled into a smile. "You like that, pet? You're so beautiful, and you're all mine. Your body is mine to do with as I please. And you like that, don't you?"

She nodded.

He pinched her nipples gently and she suppressed a moan. Frederick didn't like her making a lot of sounds when he played with her. Then he pulled and twisted her reddened buds until she squirmed. Yanking them harder, he dragged her closer to him and kissed her deeply. When she began to respond, he fell back in his chair. "You can make my dinner now."

"Thank you, Sir," she said before she stood and went to the kitchen.

As she grilled his steak, she looked out the window at the Rocky Mountains, noticing a tinge of gold beginning on some of the trees. The air had the feel of autumn to it, even though summer wouldn't officially be over for at least another month. She wondered what it would feel like to be on the back of Roche's motorcycle, her arms clutching his waist as they rode high up the mountain passes. *I wonder what he's doing right now. Stop, Clotille! These kinds of thoughts will bring heartache, not only to you but to him and a lot of other people. You must forget you ever saw him.* But how could she? He'd been her first love. *We were so young.* Where had all the time gone?

"Clotille!" Frederick's harsh voice broke through her recollections.

She scurried to the family room, her large breasts swaying. "Sir?"

"I need another drink. You should've brought it. You know this. I shouldn't have to ask you." A displeased frown spread across his forehead. "What were you doing to make you so disobedient?"

I was remembering who I was before my nightmare started. I was remembering how much I loved Roche and thinking about how I have to see him again. "I was making sure your steak and baked potato wouldn't burn." *I'm lying to him. Can he tell? Oh God, I hope not. This is the first time I've lied to him since we've been together.*

Frederick's eyes pierced right through her. She stood her ground, her gaze never wavering from his. Finally he smiled at her. "I'll forgive this one indiscretion, my pet, but don't try my patience any more tonight."

"Yes, Sir. You are kind." She scampered away to fix him his drink. She knew he loved her. He reminded her all the time of how much she meant to him, and how important she was to him. He'd told her everything he did was because he loved her. He controlled almost everything in her life: what she did and didn't wear, what she ate, how many times she exercised, what time she went to bed, when she could go out with her friends—the list went on and on. She really didn't mind the control; it helped rein in all her distractions and gave her meaningless life some purpose. Before Frederick had come into her life, she had made a mess of it, but he'd taken control and organized it for her.

That night, he let her sit at the table and eat with him. Usually he liked her at the table with him, but sometimes if he was in a foul mood, or didn't care to see her, she'd eat alone in the kitchen while he took his meal in the dining room.

He brought his glass of red wine to his lips and sipped it. "What did you think of our bodyguards last night?"

Her insides froze. "I didn't really notice them." *Another lie. I'm getting good at this.*

"They were outlaw bikers, and they kill without batting an eye. They live in their own world and have their own rules. They are violent brutes." She cringed but then remembered how soft Roche's lips had been on hers when they were young and in love. "They scare most people, even the bad guys." He laughed and slathered sour cream on his baked potato. "Is your salad tasty, pet?"

She nodded as she chewed slowly.

"I'm going to have them again when I have the Peak Five meeting at the house. With all the money that's going to be there, I can't take any chances."

Please let Roche come again. Wait, what am I saying? I can't risk Frederick finding out that I know him. And I don't want him to see me like this. A flush of shame filled her when she replayed how Frederick had humiliated her in front of the other guests, and Roche. *I can't let him see how far I've fallen.*

"You're not with me tonight. I don't like that. I demand one hundred percent of your attention. What's been on your mind this evening?"

"I was just thinking about home. I don't do it very often, but whenever fall is in the air, I get a hankering for Cajun-style jambalaya and crawfish. Maybe I'll make some jambalaya next week. Would you like me to?"

He watched her intently. "If you like."

"Excellent." She smiled sweetly, her insides playing a game of handball against her stomach.

"Excellent, what?" he asked firmly.

"Excellent, Sir."

After she cleaned all the dishes, she joined him in the family room. She began to kneel when he patted the space next to him on the couch. "Sit next to me, pet."

She sank down on the couch and soon he began to touch her, softly at first but then harder, making her wince as pain mixed with pleasure. "You please me very much, little one," he murmured. "Turn over and go on your knees. Remember, spread wide. I want to see your ass and pussy." She turned over and propped herself on her knees, her back arched. "Fucking beautiful," he rasped.

She heard him unzip his pants, and she moaned when he touched her sore ass, making him dig his nails into her tender flesh. "You want me to ass-fuck you?"

"Yes, Sir." The truth was she didn't want him anywhere near her ass right then, but she wanted to please him and have it over with, so she'd lied to him again. If she told him the truth, he would question her for hours until she admitted that since she'd seen Roche, the old Clotille had awakened and she wanted her life back.

Frederick spread lubricant over her crack, making sure she was good and wet. Without warning, he plunged into her hard and fast. As he jackhammered her, she buried her cries in the couch's cushion.

She also guarded the image in her mind of Roche's ripped body covering her as he made love to her.

Chapter Four

One month later

"WHERE DO YOU want us to put the couch?" Rock asked Throttle as he and Bones walked into the family room, each of them holding one end of it.

"Kimber wants it in front of the fireplace," he said as he cleared boxes out of the way.

They put the couch down and Rock wiped his brow. "You got any beer?"

Throttle nodded, went into the kitchen, and came back with a six-pack. "Let's take a break."

Bones and Rock sank onto the couch and popped open their cans. Rock looked around at the spacious family room, stone fireplace, and cathedral ceilings. "You got a real nice place here. Beats your room at the clubhouse."

"Yeah. I never thought I'd like living away from you guys, but I have to admit this is way better."

"Having your woman with you helps a lot," Bones said as he brought his can to his lips.

"You good with just one woman?" Rock asked.

Throttle spread his hands out on his jean-clad thighs. "Totally. It's so fuckin' awesome to have a deep connection with a woman. I never really had that with Mariah, and I'd given up on finding it. Then Kimber crashed into my life. We still bicker like hell, but we have a great time making up." He wiggled his eyebrows.

"I'm good with club pussy. Being tied down to one woman isn't my style. I like it easy. That's why I never go out with citizens. The club women and the hoodrats know the score. Hell, they don't want to be tied down either, and it suits me just fine." Rock popped open another beer.

"I'm with Rock on this one. I had a wife years ago who turned out to be nothing but a tramp." A darkness crossed Bones's face. "Bad things happened. I'm not ever gonna let another bitch do that to me again."

"Yeah. My ex did a number on me too, but when someone right comes in your life, all the past shit doesn't matter anymore. It just hits you head-on like a fuckin' train at top speed." Throttle grinned and shook his head. "I still can't believe how great this all is."

"My ex did me wrong when I was laid up in the pen. Fuckin' cunt." Bones crushed his can with his hand. "Your woman did the same shit to you, right?" Bones looked at Rock.

Clotille didn't stand by me. She fuckin' up and married Luc, leaving me with nothing but the memory of her soft body and tight pussy. Venom burned through his veins as he nodded.

"See? You can't trust 'em. When life's good they're there, but when it goes to shit, they split with the first cock that comes their way. Fuck." Bones lit up a joint.

"So we gonna get back to work?" Rock stood up. He didn't want to bring the memories from his past back. For the past month, he'd done a good job in keeping them away.

The other two bikers jumped up and the men headed out to the rented truck to bring in some more boxes and furniture.

A couple hours later, Rock and Bones tilted their heads at Throttle as they made their way to their Harleys.

"You wanna go to the Charred House and grab some steaks and cold beer?" Rock asked Bones once they reached the bikes.

"In Aspen?"

"Yep."

"Sure. Let's head back to the clubhouse so we can clean up before we go."

Rock nodded, swinging his leg over his bike. In a matter of seconds his iron machine roared to life. He and Bones pulled away from the curb and headed back to the club.

When Rock and Bones got back to the clubhouse, Wheelie and Rags wanted to join them on the ride and dinner. The bikers never passed up an opportunity to ride, and a good steak and beer were a bonus, so an hour later the four bikers twisted and turned around the back mountain roads leading to Aspen.

They pulled in front of Charred House and stretched their legs. Rock took off his gloves and placed his sunglasses in his saddlebags. "Damn, I'm starved," he said as he shook out a kink in his leg.

The four men walked into the restaurant, Rock blinking as his eyes adjusted to the low light. The steakhouse boasted the finest steaks in the western Rocky Mountain region, and the aroma curling up from the grills was intoxicating. The hostess sat the men at a table near a picture window showcasing the peaks of Maroon Bells.

After placing their order for porterhouse steaks and mashed potatoes, the brothers kicked back, drank their beer, and shared riding stories. For the amount of screwing the motorcycle club did, most people would think that the main topic among the brothers was fucking, but it wasn't. The conversations that made them excited were always about Harleys: riding them, customizing them, and buying them. The ride was what they lived for—and, many times, died for. It was just that simple.

As Rock leaned back in his chair, he scanned the restaurant, trying to spot their pretty waitress so he could order another drink. That's when he saw *her*. Actually, he saw Frederick first, but the woman with the lush hair cascading a little past her shoulders sat across from her partner, her back to Rock. But he knew it was her; he could sense her, feel her, and almost hear her soft voice. His groin pulled and he caught his breath. He had to see her and catch a whiff of her vanilla-scented body.

Frederick's mouth kept moving and every few minutes, he'd throw his head back and laugh. Rock saw him place his hand over hers, and a sudden urge to see her consumed the biker.

He pushed his chair back. "I'll be right back. If the waitress comes over, order me another Coors." He walked toward Frederick and the woman who'd been invading his thoughts since he'd first seen her a month before.

When he approached the table, Frederick acted like he didn't know who he was, which pissed Rock off to no end. If it had not been for the woman who intrigued him, he never would've acknowledged the rich asshole.

"Mr. Blair, correct?"

Frederick's lips curled down in disgust as he nodded. The woman shifted to the side and bowed her head, her hair falling in front of her face. *Fuck! What the hell is up with her? Why does she keep hiding her goddamned face?* As hard as he tried, he couldn't get a glimpse of her. He squished his brows together and gave Frederick a perplexed look.

Frederick pressed his thin lips together. "My pet is very shy. What can I do for you?"

Rock's body tensed and his expression grew tight. It took all he had to stop himself from smashing his fist into the arrogant sonofabitch's face. "Nothing. I was just passing by."

"And you can continue passing by." Frederick turned from him, acting as though he weren't there.

The woman moved slightly in her chair, and Rock was rewarded with the seductive fragrance of amber, creamy vanilla, and sandalwood. As the delicate thread of her perfume wound around him, it reminded him of the glowing embers of a campfire under an inky deep blue sky studded with brilliant stars. *Now that makes putting up with this shithead worth it. I wish I could see your face, darling.*

He turned around and went back to his table. When he scooted his chair in, he caught a quick glimpse of the woman as she turned to look at him. It was so fast that he thought he may have imagined it, but then he spotted Frederick's face, dark with disapproval as he clutched her hand… tightly. Rock noticed she squirmed in her chair. When her partner released her hand, her shoulders slumped a bit.

All through dinner, Rock watched her, half listening to what his buddies were saying. A few times, Frederick leaned in and whispered something in her ear. Rock heard her laugh and it resonated deep inside him like a lost echo in a cave.

The waitress set down another beer for him. "Compliments of the redhead." She pointed to a table a little past Frederick's; three women in their late twenties waved, the redhead winking at him.

Rock held up his beer and jerked his chin, his eyes roving back to Frederick and the woman he was with. It was at that moment that he saw her stand up and head toward the restrooms. He waited a few seconds and then rose from the table, ambling past Frederick's table, through the bar, and over to the bathrooms. He leaned against the wall as he waited for her to come out. A couple minutes later, she exited the bathroom and he pushed in front of her, "accidentally" running into her.

She glanced at him for a second, then quickly bowed her head. "Sorry," she mumbled as she tried to get around him. He blocked her way. "Can you please let me pass?"

"I want to talk to you," he said.

"I can't. Please don't talk to me." Panic laced her voice.

"You intrigue me, sweet lady." He heard her suck in her breath. "Ever since I saw you, I've had the feeling you're in something you want to get out of."

"That's not true. I'm sorry if I made that impression on you." She brushed against him, her head still bowed.

He grabbed her hand, her moan as they touched skin-to-skin making his insides burn.

"I'm not asking for an apology from you."

"What are you asking for?" she whispered.

"To see your face. Why do you keep hiding it?" He felt her hand stiffen before she pulled it away.

"I have to go. Please." She squeezed his hand then slipped it away from it.

"I worry about you." He brushed his finger against hers; he needed to touch her again.

"You don't need to worry about me. I'm fine. Forget about me. I've stayed much too long. Fredrick will be displeased. Please."

"Do you ever think about me?"

She looked up at him through the tendrils that fell over her face like a veil, then turned away from him. "Oh yes... so much," she whispered. "I have to go. Please."

"That's all I wanted to know." He moved aside and she walked away from him, her enticing scent lingering behind her. He inhaled and it coursed through him, stirring something deep inside: a tenderness he'd buried a long time ago. He stepped out of the corridor and watched her go to her table, her curvy hips moving provocatively in her tight black dress. As she pulled out her chair, he noticed the way Frederick frowned, his mouth a jagged line. The minute she sat down, he grabbed her wrist and yanked her to him, then said something in her ear. Her back stiffened, and he saw Fredrick pull her hand under the table, the maroon tablecloth covering what he was doing.

Something doesn't seem right. Damn, why do you give a shit? So she said she thinks of you. Big fuckin' deal. She's the jerk's woman. Move on. Forget about her.

But he couldn't forget her. She'd already pulled him in. There was something about her that seemed familiar yet unfamiliar to him all at the same time. This odd, fragile woman summoned memories that had been hidden under the weight of many years and experiences. This woman, whose name he didn't know and face he hadn't seen, threatened to detonate those memories that he had worked so hard to forget.

"Your friends told me you'd be here." A flirty voice grounded him.

He turned to his side and saw the redhead who'd bought him the drink. Shaking his head as if to rid himself of the spell the strange woman had cast on him, he laughed. "I was going to come over and thank you properly. You live in Aspen?"

She nodded and moved in close to him, pretending there wasn't enough room for them to talk. He knew she wanted him to feel her big tits against his chest and smell her overpowering musk perfume. *If only she smelled like my mysterious lady. Fuck, you're acting lame. This one's a hot one. Dump the fucked-up woman who gets off on men like Fredrick and go with the sure thing.* "You're pretty cute." He smiled down at her and she giggled. "Why don't you and your friends join our table? How many friends you got with you?"

"Two. Is that a problem?"

"Not for me." He laughed and led her to his table, his arm tight around her shoulders. He strutted past Frederick's table, catching his partner's gaze on him for a brief second before she looked away. The woman who was tucked under his arm motioned to her friends to come to the bikers' table. The two women scrambled out of their booth and joined the four men.

"What's your name, darling?" Rock asked as he motioned the waitress over.

"Zoe." She giggled and snuggled closer to him.

The waitress brought another round of drinks and the women and men talked, mostly flirting with each other. The bikers knew they were in for a good time by the way the women "oohed" and "ahhed" over their biceps, tats, and patches. Zoe looked especially pleased that the Sergeant-At-Arms had taken an interest in her. And even though Rock laughed, drank, and rubbed his hand on Zoe's thigh, his gaze kept going over to the table a few rows from his. A few times the strange woman would tilt her head as if trying to hear his conversation with Zoe, and he sensed she wasn't too happy about the redhead and her friends joining his table. And for reasons he couldn't articulate, he was happy she didn't like seeing him with the sexy redhead.

When Frederick paid the bill and stood up, helping his companion to her feet, Rock's heart dropped. He liked being in the same room as her. An emptiness gnawed at him when the couple left.

"These sexy ladies have invited us to their house for some fun. You down for that?" Bones nudged Rock's shoulder.

"What? Uh… yeah. Why not?" *And why the fuck not? I'm not gonna sit around thinking about* her.

The bikers paid the bill and walked out with the women into the cool night air. Rags turned to the group. "Sorry, but I can't stay. Throttle and I have an early morning landscaping job. I gotta get back."

"Me too," Rock said. *Did I just say that? What the fuck?* The redhead bit her lip, a frown crossing her brow. "Sorry, darling. It's an hour drive back, and I promised my buddy I'd open his bike shop for him in the morning."

"You can come over for just a half hour or so. I promise I'll make you glad you did."

As his eyes roamed over her small frame, landing on her blue eyes, he wasn't feeling it. He could get pussy anytime at the club and at parties; he didn't like taking up with a citizen. Although, she lived far enough away that it probably wouldn't be a problem.

Sensing his hesitation, she drew closer to him, grabbing his hand and placing it on her tit. "You like that?" she breathed against his ear.

"I like it, but I still gotta go. Give me your number and I'll call you next time I'm up here." He knew he wouldn't, but it always made the citizens feel better when he asked for their numbers. *Club whores are so much easier.*

She smiled weakly and wrote her number on a piece of paper she took out of her purse. "You're sure you can't stay?" she asked as she handed it to him.

"Yeah, but I'll call you." He swung his leg over his bike and winked at Wheelie and Bones. "Have a good time."

The men grinned wickedly, and Wheelie tugged Zoe to him. "Let's have some fun," he said.

Rock and Rags pulled away from the curb and made their way to the highway. When they stopped at a light, Rags turned to Rock and said, "We're getting old, dude."

"Or bored with easy pussy."

"Probably both."

As they merged onto the highway, Rock turned and looked over his shoulder at the twinkling lights of the ski resort, knowing he'd be spending a lot more time in Aspen.

He had to.

The urge was too great.

Chapter Five

Lola placed a white legal-sized envelope in front of Rock as she handed out the mail to the brothers in the great room. Rock took a bite out of his breakfast burrito as he watched cars speed around a racetrack on the big-screen TV on the back wall. He glanced at the envelope and moved it to the side of his plate.

"How's the burrito?" Wheelie asked as he plopped down on the chair beside Rock.

"Damn good. Rosie and Kristy can cook. Where the fuck have you been?" He wiped his mouth.

"Aspen."

"You and Bones have been there since Monday? Fuck, those chicks must've been damned horny."

"More than horny, man. It was fucking awesome."

"You tell him about our sex fest?" Bones chuckled and put his plate down on the table. "You and Rags missed a damn good time. Those women were open to anything. I mean *fucking anything*." He bit into his roast beef sandwich, then washed it down with a bottle of beer. "And the redhead who was into you was fuckin' wild. She told me to tell you she'd be waiting for your call."

"Maybe you should call her since you all know each other a whole lot better." Rock winked.

"Maybe. If she lived closer I'd consider it."

"Bones and I were surprised you and Rags bailed. What the fuck was up with the 'I have to get up early' bullshit you guys were feeding those chicks? Did you have something waiting for you when you got back?"

Rock shrugged. "I just wasn't feeling it. No big deal. Anyway, four guys are a crowd for fucking. I prefer two. You had the right ratio."

"Don't think you're fooling me. I know you got a chick on your mind, maybe even on your cock."

Rock smiled and took a gulp of his orange juice. He pushed his plate away and picked up the envelope. His name and address were handwritten in blue ink, and the writing looked like it'd been made by an unsteady hand. He opened it up and a small flannel bag fell out, indigo with twine securing the top of it. A flush of adrenaline tingled through his body. He unfolded a piece of paper that was in the envelope that read "Beware. You have a *gris-gris* on you." Rock reread the two sentences several times, then picked up the bag and held it in his hand.

"What the hell is that?" Wheelie said.

He quirked his lips. "It's a mojo bag."

"What the fuck is that?"

"It's to protect the wearer from evil. It basically wards off curses and hexes. I haven't seen one of these in a long time." He picked up the envelope and noticed the postmark was Lafayette, LA.

"What's in it?" Bones said. "I remember when I was doing time in Angola that a lot of the inmates had bags like that one. They were in all kinds of colors. Don't you remember?"

Rock slowly nodded. "The bayous are full of superstitions. Mojo bags have different herbs, roots, bones, and minerals in them depending on what they're used for. This one probably has white sage, devil's shoestring root, and maybe Dead Sea salts. Sometimes tobacco soaked in whiskey is placed inside for extra protection. This is fuckin' strange."

"You got a hex on you? Which chick did you piss off?" Wheelie laughed.

"Who's putting a hex on who?" Jax asked as he sat down on one of the chairs.

Bones pointed to Rock. "Someone's put a curse on him and he's trying to find out who did it." The guys laughed.

Rock read the note again. "It says someone has given me a *gris-gris*."

"What the hell are you talkin' about?" Jax motioned for Puck to bring him a drink.

"*Gris-gris* means curse in Cajun. I wonder who's messin' with me." Rock scrubbed his hand against his face.

"You scared, big guy?" Jax tipped his chair back. "We'll protect you."

"Shut the fuck up. I don't believe in this shit. My mom and aunts were into it. Both of my sisters believe it too. Fuck, more than half of the bayou believes in some sort of curses or spells. I'm just wondering who sent it to me, and why now? I haven't been back home in over five years."

"Well, if you're down on smokes, you can always smoke your bag." Wheelie howled and Bones and Jax followed suit.

Rock laughed. "You've got a point there." He glanced at the clock. "Come on. Church is gonna start in a minute." The men all rose to their feet as Rock announced to all the brothers in the great room that they had to go to the meeting. He slipped the bag in his pocket and followed his friends to the meeting room.

Antsy, he leaned against the concrete wall, his massive arms crossed against his chest. *Who the fuck sent me the mojo? Is Isa trying to get me to come visit? She seemed real anxious about it when we last talked.* Deep in his gut, he knew it wasn't Isa. But who, and why? *Fuckin' weird.* His attention focused on Banger when he heard him say, "Frederick Blair."

"This time the gig is during the day. I'm gonna send the same crew unless there's an objection." Banger took a gulp of his beer.

"No objection. But this time we want to be inside. Rock, Wheelie, and Bones can be outside." The crew who'd been at the house sniggered.

"Who stands where at the house is shit you can all figure out. Anyway, Rock's in charge of all that. What I got from Liam is that it's a meeting of a group of billionaires who belong to some elite group—Peak Five. It'll take place in a couple days." Banger glanced down at a large calendar he had on the table. "Yeah, Saturday at two o'clock. It's gonna be…"

Rock's heart pounded; he'd get another chance to see *her*. Since their last encounter, all he'd gotten was a quick glimpse of her green eyes before she looked downward. Her hiding her face from him made him think about her all the time. She was mysterious and had a sexy body that had been the fodder for some of his fantasies for the past couple days. *I've built up all this shit in my head. I gotta see what she really looks like. Then I'll be good.* He hadn't thought he'd get the chance to see her so soon. This time around, he wasn't playing her bullshit game.

"How much we making for this babysitting? Seems like we got better things to do," Axe said.

"About a hundred fifty thousand a gig." Banger held up his hands to stop the grumbling that was circulating around the room. "I know that's a good week at our dispensaries. But remember, we're doing this as a favor for Liam."

"So is this some permanent shit we're doing?" Throttle said.

"No. I told Liam we'd help out a few times, but then we're done. It seems like this rich dude had a big problem with the last several security people he used. Things leaked out about his lifestyle and business dealings. Liam suggested a biker club for security. And here we are. I was thinking to pass it to the Iron Dogs MC."

"The Iron Dogs are cool. We've always gotten along with them," Chas said. "I'm pretty good friends with their Road Captain. They're always looking for some easy cash."

Banger nodded. "Now on to a problem that Hawk and I think could be huge. I'll let him explain."

Hawk stood up. "The word is that the Demon Riders are forming a bond with the Gypsy Fiends to buy some fuckin' hardcore weapons from them."

"The Gypsy Fiends? What the fuck are the Demon Riders doing with them? Iowa is a long ways from Louisiana." Rock shoved away from the wall.

"That's what a lot of the MCs wanna know. Rock, you're from their territory. Did you ever come across them?"

"I met a few when I was in the pen, but I didn't know much about them except that they were bikers who scared the hell outta people. I'd see them around Lafayette when I was young, heard they ran some of the casinos in the nearby parishes. I know they have charters in Mississippi, Arkansas, and Alabama, but them venturing into Iowa is fuckin' crazy."

"They're not aiming to set up any chapters, just selling high-powered shit to the Demon Riders. I didn't think they had that kind of money to buy the shit to sell."

Rock shook his head slowly. "They don't. I know they're in a turf war with the Hellbenders in Georgia. Gypsy Fiends are claiming the territory and so are the Hellbenders. Is Liam supplying the arms for them? That's gotta be expensive. Where the fuck are they getting the money? Last I heard their casinos weren't doing all that great."

"Liam's not involved in the deal. We're positive the Demon Riders have their hands in this. The word is also out that the Gypsy Fiends are buying some hardcore shit directly from an international dealer."

Rock and Bones exchanged looks before Bones cleared his throat. "There's no way they're acting alone. Some company or person is backing them financially. Remember when I was out there visiting my buddy who was in the Devil's Legions in New Orleans?"

"How could we forget? Your drunken brawl got you six years in the pen and put you outta commission for the Insurgents," Banger said.

"Yeah, but I met Rock, so it wasn't a total loss." The brothers hooted and Banger smiled. "Anyway, they were telling me that the Gypsy Fiends had started putting their fuckin' noses in places they never even knew existed, like oil stuff and banking shit."

Hawk narrowed his eyes. "They most probably have a group of investors who need them to do the dirty work. MCs are an asset to crooked people. They know we don't snitch or leave evidence. But if the Demon Riders get a partnership going with the Gypsy fucks that puts our club and affiliates in jeopardy. As we know, Dustin and Shack have been aiming to take us down since we threw them outta the Insurgents, and with one of our brothers killing one of theirs at the expo, you know the Demon Riders are chomping at the bit to get back at us."

"We gotta find a way to make sure the fucks don't buy the weapons from the Gypsy Fiends, then see who's backing the Gypsy assholes in buying the expensive as hell weapons," Jax said.

"Exactly. We got Liam working on it through his network, and that's why we gotta do this fuckin' babysitting job." Banger tipped back on his chair. "We're on high alert until we find out something. Once we do, we'll strike first if need be."

"It's been a while since we've gone to war, but if that's what they want we'll fuckin' give it to them. We'll show them not to mess with Insurgents." Hawk banged his fist down on the table, bringing the brothers to their feet, their arms held high in the air with their fists clenched as they chanted, "Insurgents forever, forever Insurgents."

After going over the financials for the club, the meeting was adjourned and the somber group headed to the great room. The thought of going to war weighed heavy on them. For the past several years they'd enjoyed a truce with the Deadly Demons, and the violence of the turf wars hid in the dusty corners of their minds. At that moment, the threat from the Demon Riders was real, especially since they were gearing up to buy some pretty intense weapons. To the brothers, it signaled that the rival club was preparing for an attack on them. No MC would take that lightly, especially an outlaw one.

Rock slammed back his double shot, tilting his chin at Hawk when he approached. "This is some crazy shit, huh?"

Hawk nodded. "Yeah, and the worst fucking timing. Cara's not gonna understand this at all. We got our wedding coming up. How do I tell her and her parents that their society friends are gonna have to be cool with the brothers surrounding the country club during the reception?"

"I wouldn't put it past the fuckers to strike at your wedding," Rock said.

"Me neither. Fuck. What a mess." Hawk threw back his shot. "I think it's time for Puck, Blade, and Johnnie to wear the full patch. We got three more prospects who're coming in, and we could use a few more full patches to deal with the shit we got going all around us."

"I agree. They've earned their patches. At the next church we should put it to a vote." Rock popped a couple pretzels in his mouth.

"How do you like the guard job? The truth." Hawk grinned.

Rock shrugged. "It's okay."

"You're fucking outside on Saturday and I'm in the house," Rags said as he scooped up a handful of pretzels.

Rock stiffened and his eyes turned to slits. "I'll decide what's going down for Saturday."

Hawk and Rags exchanged puzzled glances, and then Rags laughed. "Just joking, man. I know you're in charge."

"Yeah." *There's no way I'm leaving without talking to her. If I have to beat the shit outta the pansy-ass rich guy to get to her, I'll do it.*

"I gotta go." Hawk placed his empty shot glass on the table.

"I'll walk out with you. I gotta make a phone call and it's too damn loud in here." Rock followed the vice president outside. Threads of blackberry-colored clouds striped the sky as twilight approached. He waited until Hawk drove away, and then he pulled out his phone and called his sister. After he'd exchanged pleasantries with her, he asked, "Did you send me a mojo bag?"

"A mojo bag? No. Why would I do that? Do you need one? I can get one made for you from Madame Vincennes."

"No, I don't need one, but someone sent me one. You don't know anything about that?"

Her gasp filled his ear. "What color is it?"

"I don't know. It looks like blue but it has some purple in it too."

A louder gasp. "Have you pissed someone off in a big way?"

He chuckled. "I'm always pissing people off."

"Roche, this is serious. You have a mojo to ward off curses or evil."

"I know what it means. I was just wondering if you sent it."

"Why would I do that?"

"To mess with me so I'd come home for a visit."

"You don't joke around with mojos or *gris-gris*."

"So who do you think would do it? Lille? I don't know that many people anymore back home. It came from Lafayette."

"Lille would never do that. Anyway, she's been in the Hamptons with her new boyfriend, the old, rich guy. That *is* strange. Any note with it?"

"Yeah, some shit about someone putting a *gris-gris* on me. It's no big deal. I was just asking because I found it strange, that's all."

"I'll see if I can find something out. I'll pay a visit to Madame Vincennes and have her do your cards. I'll let you know what she says."

"Isn't she like a hundred years old? When we were kids she looked about eighty."

Isa laughed softly. "She's not as old as she looks. She's had a hard life. When her husband was killed in the coal mines in Tennessee she had to raise all her young children by herself. *Maman* used to go to her for amulets, mojos, and card reading. You knew that, right?"

"A lot of good it did her," he muttered under his breath. "Her whole family was fuckin' superstitious."

"It's not superstition," Isa whispered.

"Well, I don't fuckin' believe it. I got shit to do. Take care of yourself."

"I'll let you know what Madame says."

He snorted. "Yeah, you do that."

Rock slipped his phone in his pocket, lit up a joint, and watched the sun begin its descent. He wondered if *she* was watching it too.

Chapter Six

On Saturday at one thirty in the afternoon, nine Harleys roared past the iron gates and up the driveway. The idling engines had an uneven, syncopated cadence that crashed through the quiet in the exclusive neighborhood. When they switched off their ignitions, the quiet returned except for the clink of swinging chains from jeans and the clomping of steel-toed boots on the pavement.

When they arrived at the front of the house, Rock said, "This is a meeting of a bunch of rich guys, so we gotta be on extra alert. I'll do both inside and out, alternating with Jax. Chas and Rags can be inside and the rest of you will be outside. Make sure all the exits are covered. If there's a problem, use the remotes." The men nodded their acquiescence and then spread out to man their posts.

Rock rang the buzzer, his stomach tightening. He fucking hated the way his body was doing weird shit over a woman. A tall man dressed in a black suit opened the door and ushered in the three men. Chas and Rags whistled under their breaths as they stood in the enormous marbled foyer. "My whole fuckin' house could fit in here," Chas said under his breath. The butler's forehead creased in annoyance.

"You want us to wait for Blair here?" Rock asked.

"Yes. *Mister* Blair will be down shortly." The thin man slipped away.

"Guess we're not fuckin' good enough to go to the living room or whatever the hell it's called." Rags's head went back. "How many feet do you think that fuckin' chandelier is?"

"Who the fuck cares?" grumbled Rock.

"Thirty feet, and obviously your colleague cares," a cool, detached voice said.

Without turning around, Rock knew it was Frederick. He was getting sick and tired of the asshole popping up out of nowhere. He turned slowly to him. "I think each of us should cover an exit."

A smile twitched on Frederick's thin lips. "You'd need double the men you have for that."

"I got men outside. We'll cover what they don't inside." Rock wanted to slam the dude against a wall when he saw the look of disdain in his eyes as he ran them over the biker.

"My colleagues will be here soon. I will need your services until they leave." His tone was dismissive.

"Let's go and check this out." Rock walked away from him without a glance.

After the men checked out the entire first floor, Rock placed Chas at the back of the house where triple French doors opened onto a veranda overlooking a well-manicured lawn. Rags took the north side, and Rock stayed in the front by the foyer. From that viewpoint, he could watch the other rooms. The woman of the house was glaringly absent.

At two o'clock five gentlemen appeared dressed in khaki pants with sports shirts. They carried briefcases and greeted Frederick as he walked into the foyer from one of the rooms. The host escorted the men to the dining room where they sat down and began their power meeting.

Rock expected the woman to show up and serve the drinks, but the butler seemed to be the one in charge of doing it. *I wonder if she's at home. Maybe he had her go shopping while he and his buddies decide how to fuck up the economy and start wars.*

After thirty minutes, Rock contacted Jax on the remote and told him to come to the house so they could switch positions. He wanted to do a perimeter check to make sure everything was cool. The amount of wealth in the room was staggering, and he could understand why Blair wanted security during their meeting. The risk of a home invasion, kidnapping, or worse was too high.

It took a long time to walk the grounds, but he wanted to make sure they were secured. When he came around the backside of the mansion he stopped. He sensed her at the fringes of his awareness, felt her pull—like magnet to steel. He took a deep breath and looked up, and there she was on the second floor, leaning against a small window, her gaze locked with his. For a long moment they were tied together through silence and anticipation. Then she turned away and was gone. Rock licked his lips and took a couple gulps of air while he tried to clear his head, then quickened his pace to finish up his round.

When he entered the house again, he headed for the massive circular stairway leading up to her. As he climbed up, Frederick's voice echoed in the foyer. "Stop! You're not allowed up there."

"I'm just doing my job in making sure everything is secured."

"It's not necessary to go upstairs. Just check the main floor and the grounds. The second and third stories are private."

Reluctantly Rock turned around and headed down, each step heavier in the knowledge that he was going farther away from her. *It fuckin' kills me to know she's up there and I'm down here. Is it killing her too? She was definitely staring at me, but maybe she'd have stared at Wheelie, or Chas, or any of the guys. I'm worse than a pussy. I'm a fuckin' pussy sissy.*

"You want me to go back outside?" Jax asked as Rock hit the bottom of the stairs.

"Hold on for a few. I'm gonna check out all the doors and windows. We shoulda had more guys for this job." Rock marched around the house, making sure everything was locked and not tampered with. *This house is so fuckin' big it's taken me almost an hour to check everything out. Give me my room at the club anytime.* As he came back to the foyer, he saw Frederick and the woman walking down the stairs, his hand holding hers. Rock held his breath, but the moment she saw him she bowed her head again, her hair covering her face. *No way, darlin'. One way or another, I'm gonna see you before I leave.*

As they passed Rock and Jax, Frederick said to the woman, "Fix us lunch and bring the drinks, pet." He escorted her into the dining room, the men standing as she came to the table. Rock doubted that the group was in the lifestyle, and Frederick acted differently with her this time than he had the last time the bikers had been there.

She took their drink orders and then served the drinks, telling them she'd be out in a little bit to serve lunch. In less than twenty minutes she placed a bright seafood salad on the table, a plate of croissants, small bowls of lemon and lime wedges, and a platter of watermelon, cantaloupe, and berries. She refilled the glasses with white wine.

"Leave the bottle here, pet. I'll pour the wine. Why don't you start cleaning the kitchen?"

"Yes, S—I mean, Frederick." She rushed out of the room.

Rock came close to Jax. "I'm gonna check around again," he said in a hushed voice. He went the other way, knowing from his earlier security check that he could enter the kitchen from the other side of the house.

As he approached the kitchen his heart pounded against his ribs. *Calm the fuck down. What's up with you, pussy?* He stood in the doorway, admiring the way she looked in her knit dress as she bent over to put dishes in the washer, her lovely hair free-flowing.

"Need some help?" His voice came out louder than he wanted.

She whipped her head up, her back to him, stiff and straight. "No. You have to go." She glanced sideways out the door leading to the dining room.

"He's eating. He won't bother us. I wanna talk to you."

"Why can't you leave me alone?" she whispered, her voice hitching.

"I don't know."

An uneasy silence fell over them.

"How've you been?" Rock asked gently.

"Fine," she muttered. "I can't talk to you."

"Why not? Because *he* tells you not to? You're a grown woman. You can decide for yourself."

"I can't." Her voice was so low he could barely hear her. The few words they had spoken between them had always been in hushed tones, as though she were speaking from the shadows that lurked around her.

"Okay, but before I go I want to see your face," he blurted.

She gasped. "No."

Without arguing, he was beside her in a couple long strides, spinning her to face him. She didn't resist; it was like she'd been waiting for this moment since their breaths had first shared the same air. He lightly moved her hair from her face and placed his finger under her chin, tilting her head back so he could see her. He scanned her face and his gaze fell on her big shimmering green eyes. Beautiful eyes that reminded him of—*Clotille!*

"Fuck. It's you, Clotille, isn't it?"

She nodded then smiled.

"No wonder you were hiding your face. I'd never forget your eyes. What the fuck are you doing in Aspen with this asshole?"

She touched the base of her neck. "Please don't tell Frederick we know each other. He's very jealous." She wrung her hands as she glanced out the door again. "Do you live in Aspen?"

"Pinewood Springs. I've been here since I got outta prison."

"I heard you left Lafayette. I didn't know where you'd had gone."

"I'm with the Insurgents MC. We're doing this piddly ass job as a favor to a longtime friend." His gaze roamed over her body. *She's still so beautiful even though she's lost a lot of weight.* He didn't remember the dark circles under her eyes. "How can you be a part of this jerk's lifestyle?"

She shrugged. "It's nice not being in control. I like being submissive and he loves being dominant, so it works for us." She laughed nervously before looking out the door for the umpteenth time.

"That wasn't who you were when I knew you."

"That was a long time ago. I don't think either of us knew who we were, Roche."

"I'm not Roche anymore. I'm Rock."

She smiled faintly. "And I'm no longer Clotille. I'm Pet." They stared at each other for a few seconds, and then she cleared her throat. "Are you married?"

"No."

"Girlfriend?"

"Nah."

"I can't believe a handsome, rugged man like you isn't taken."

"Don't wanna be."

"Don't you get lonely?"

"I said I wasn't taken, not that I'm living like a monk. I got plenty of women. No worries there."

She skimmed her eyes over his body. "I bet you do. You grew up to be quite a good-looking man."

"*Merci.*"

She smiled, a touch of red kissing her cheeks. "I can't believe you're here. It's so good to see you again," she said in a low voice.

"Let's go for lunch and catch up," he said, his gaze lingering on her full lips.

"I don't think I like you asking my pet out." Frederick's voice was sharp and steely.

Clotille's hand flew to her mouth and she trembled.

"I don't give a damn what you like," Rock gritted, his six-foot-one frame looming over the other man.

Frederick ignored him and stared hard at Clotille. "Why were you talking to him without my permission?"

"I'm sorry," she mumbled.

"You're sorry, what?"

"I'm sorry, Sir."

"You disobeyed me, didn't you?"

"Yes, I disobeyed you, Sir."

Before he could continue, Rock cut in. "Don't blame her. I'm the one who came in bugging her. She told me to leave and not talk to her. I kept pushing it."

"And she kept talking to you. My point exactly," Frederick said matter-of-factly. He glared at Rock. "If you think for one minute that I'm going to let you paw and soil my pet, you're dumber than you look."

"You better fuckin' watch your mouth 'cause I won't think twice 'bout beating the shit outta you. I don't give a fuck if you own the goddamned world. You show respect or your prick friends will be scraping you off your white marble floors."

Frederick looked at Clotille. "Get upstairs. Now!"

"She's not going anywhere. We're not done talking." He saw Clotille blanch, her lips quivering.

"I don't want any of you bikers in the house. Just stay outside."

"Fuck you. Come with me," Rock said to her.

She looked at Frederick. He smiled. "Pet, you have permission to speak."

"I can't. I'm with Frederick."

Frederick looked at him smugly and Rock clenched his fists, willing himself to keep his temper in check. *If she wants this fucked-up life, she can have it. I'm sick of this shit. How the hell is Clotille even here? Who gives a fuck? First thing when I get back, I'm telling Banger to assign another brother to this bullshit job.*

She went behind Frederick, her hand on his shoulder. He laughed. "I think my pet has spoken. Just because you're younger and ride a motorcycle you think all the women want you. I can give my pet more than you ever could."

Rock looked one last time at the woman he'd loved since he was eleven years old. Even though her hand was firm on the asshole's shoulder, a solitary tear spilled from her eye, leaving a wet trace down her face. As he watched it, he could feel her heart breaking.

Rock marched out of the room and went up to Jax and Chas. "He wants us outside only." The three guys left the house, and Rock went over to his bike and got on. His cams screamed to life and he ignored the baffled faces of his brothers as he sped away from Clotille.

Chapter Seven

The wind slashed at Rock's face and body as he rode furiously back to Pinewood Springs. The last person he ever thought he'd see again was Clotille, and she turned out to be the woman who had been pricking at his mind for the past five weeks. *She's living as a slave for some rich man's amusement. What the fuck, Clotille?* He didn't buy it for one minute that she wanted to be part of that asshole's lifestyle. Hell, he *knew* her, plus he saw it in her eyes and heard it in her voice that she was lying. She was with Frederick Blair for a reason.

Rock rounded the corner along the pass so low to the ground his shin was inches from the asphalt. As he pulled up, he remembered Isa telling him that Clotille's father had gambled away all their money and they'd lost everything, but now her mother was living in a big house in a ritzy neighborhood. A wry smile cracked his face; he'd just figured out where the money came from to allow her mother to live in luxury.

He couldn't believe Clotille had ended up in such a situation. *Shit! If she needs money, I can help her out.* He yelled and the wind swallowed up his cuss words. Rock had money from the sale of his mother's land, and he hadn't wanted to touch a penny of it. He hadn't even wanted to sell the land in the first place. He thought of it as blood money, so he'd placed it in an investment account which had been growing steadily for years. The club also gave a generous stipend to all the members thanks to their dispensaries and various businesses in Pinewood Springs.

He hung a sharp right down the small dirt road leading to the clubhouse. Pulling up, he jumped off his bike and walked inside, the familiar scents of beer and weed welcoming him home. Before he reached the bar, Bruiser said, "Banger wants to see you in his office."

Rock stiffened. Had Frederick contacted Liam already? *The whiny pussy.* Rock rapped on the office door and entered when Banger's voice boomed out. A scowling president greeted him as he walked into the room then sank into a chair in front of the desk.

"Why the fuck did you leave your post? And what the fuck were you thinking by hitting on a client's wife? Shit, don't you have enough pussy in the club and town?"

Rock's eyes widened for a second when he heard "wife," but then his complacent expression returned. "It turns out I know her from back in the day. We're both Cajuns from the same parish."

"So what the fuck does that have to do with you hitting on her and leaving your post?"

Rock stared defiantly at Banger's piercing gaze. "I wasn't hitting on her. And I don't like the sonofabitch who owns the house. We don't get along, so I thought it was best that I leave before I beat the shit outta him."

For several seconds Banger and Rock engaged in a stare down, neither one giving an inch until the president slowly shook his head. "Fuck, man. You may have blown the whole thing with Liam. You know how it is—it's all about the money. There's no way Liam is giving this fucker up for us, and we need him to get info on the Demon Riders. You shouldn't have lost your head."

"Yeah, well, I did. I don't like the way he's treating her. She's like a goddamned slave." Rock crossed his arms and jutted his jaw out.

"Yeah, I know all about the dinner party from the last time you were up there. Some of the guys told me about it. It sounds to me that's what they're into. It might not be for everyone but it seems like they fucking like it. It's not for you to decide what's right or wrong for her. You need to back the fuck off. This isn't just about you and some pussy; it's about the Insurgents. The club has a job and its reputation, and I can't have one of the brothers fucking things up because he has the hots for someone else's wife."

Rock just glared.

"I'll call Liam and smooth this out. The guy doesn't want you near his place so—"

"That suits me just fine 'cause I have no fuckin' intention of going back there." Rock stood up. "We done here?" He wanted to take a hot shower, drink some brandy, and maybe fuck Lola and Rosie. The last thing he wanted to do was think about Clotille and how beautiful she looked. He wanted to leave that far behind.

"We're done." Banger looked at his computer screen, his action dismissing Rock. He left and climbed the stairs to his room, the shock of seeing his old flame still reverberating through him.

After his shower, he poured himself a brandy and sipped it slowly. Clotille's eyes had always captivated him, but at that moment they haunted him. He sighed. *She saved her family by selling herself to the guy. Are they really married or is Frederick using "wife" lightly?* He wouldn't put it past Frederick to be saying that on purpose to piss him off. *Why the hell do I care? We haven't had anything since we were teenagers.* Then he remembered how she'd gone back and married Luc a few months after Rock was incarcerated. That had hurt more than anything. He'd acted like it didn't, especially to Isa, but inside he'd been shattered. He'd needed her—his mother had been killed by his father, for fuck's sake—but she'd left him when the going got tough. *She fuckin' bailed on me.*

He downed the rest of his brandy and headed downstairs, not wanting to be alone. Being with people kept his mind quiet. And that night he definitely had to keep the memories and all the demons they conjured up at bay; otherwise, he'd do something he'd regret, like riding back to Aspen and taking Clotille with him after he stomped the rich fucker to death.

Wendy and Rosie were seated at one of the tables leafing through *People* and *Cosmopolitan*. He grabbed a beer at the bar and plopped down on a chair at their table, his eyes riveted on Seth Rollins as he attempted to throw Brock Lesnar on the ground. Several brothers were gathered around the television cheering and cussing at it as the top-notch WWE wrestlers entertained the crowd.

"You doing okay, honey?" Wendy asked Rock. "You look tense."

"I've been better." He took a long pull of beer. *I can't believe Clotille's in Aspen. She must've recognized me the first night we were doing that shitty gig. That's why she kept hiding her face. She fuckin' knew it was me and didn't say shit about it at the restaurant. She just keeps fuckin' with me. Been doing it since we were kids.*

"Want a massage?" Wendy pushed her chair back and knelt in front of him, gently pushing his legs apart. She settled between his legs and began giving him a hand and arm massage.

"Scoot your chair forward, sweetie," Rosie whispered in his ear. He moved forward a bit and Rosie slid behind him and began massaging his shoulders. "Damn, you are tense. Your muscles are like cement." She kissed his shoulders gently as her strong fingers dug into his skin. It felt so damn good the way Rosie worked out his kinks and Wendy moved her adept hands up and down his arms. Watching her tits bounce in her very low-cut top was a bonus. While they worked their magic on him, his thoughts flitted back to Clotille. He was getting real pissed at how she kept creeping back into his mind. For some unknown reason, he felt responsible for her, at least in her current situation. It wasn't that he wanted her back in his life; he just wanted to help her get hers straightened out. After all, they had known each other since they were kids, and if he turned his back on her now he knew the guilt would nag him the rest of his life. *If she really doesn't want to leave, then I'll stay the fuck out of her life forever. I want her to look me in the eyes and tell me to go away without that motherfucker around. If she does, then that's it.* Fini.

"You want us to give you a full-body massage?" Wendy cupped his crotch and squeezed suggestively.

"I'm good. There's some stuff I have to do. I'll catch you later. Thanks, ladies." He bent over and kissed Wendy quickly on the lips, then craned his neck and nipped Rosie's cheek. The two women returned to their chairs and resumed thumbing through their magazines. He went up to his room and grabbed a small bag, throwing in his toiletries and a couple of T-shirts and changes of underwear. He'd have to stake out the house for a few days to get the feel of Frederick and the staff's routine. He wanted to make sure he had time to talk with Clotille and take her out of there if that was what she decided.

He sat on the chair and looked out at the dirt road that led up to the thirty-foot chain-linked fence which surrounded the clubhouse. It ended on the edge of the two-lane highway that was a black ribbon wrapping around the mountains. When dust clouds obscured his view, he knew the babysitting brigade was back from their gig. Rising up, he left his room to meet them as they came into the club.

Rock stood against the bar as the men entered. Throttle threw him a wide grin and headed in his direction, followed by Bones and Wheelie. "What the fuck happened today?" Throttle asked as he picked up the shot of Jack the prospect placed on the bar.

"I was ready to beat the shit outta that motherfucking asshole. That's all."

Bones and Wheelie joined Throttle in guffawing. "I'd have loved to have seen that," Bones said between gasps for air. "That dude has such a big stick up his ass."

"I'm surprised you're back so early." Rock put his beer bottle to his lips.

"I think you pissed the dude off big time. Not too long after you left, the other guys took off." Wheelie settled on the barstool.

Rock's stomach churned when he thought of how Frederick would make Clotille pay for talking with him. He'd been careless and selfish in his haste to see the woman who'd held his interest since the dinner party. He hadn't considered what would happen to her if the fuckwad caught her talking with him. And now that *she* was Clotille, the thought of any harm coming to her made his anger burn.

"The arrogant fucker made sure to tell us that you're not allowed on his property anymore. Hell, we decided we're gonna tell Banger the next time the asshole needs us, he's gonna have to find someone to replace us. We're done with this shit." Throttle motioned Puck for another shot. The rest of the guys came over, mouthing their agreement with Throttle.

Rock nodded and touched fists with several of the brothers. *There's no way in hell that fucker's gonna keep me away until I hear Clotille tell me face-to-face without* him *around*. After a couple games of pool, Rock went to Banger's office and knocked on the door, opening it when he heard his president's voice.

Banger was slipping on his jacket and shoving his phone in its pocket when Rock walked in. "Can I talk to you for a minute?" he asked.

Banger glanced at the clock on the wall. "If it won't take too long. I was supposed to be home like fifteen minutes ago. What's on your mind?"

"I just need a few days off. I got some shit to sort out."

The president stared at him. "Yeah, you've seemed tense and off-kilter for a few weeks. Taking a few days off seems like a smart move. I'll have Jax take over while you're gone."

Rock nodded and left the room. If Banger knew the real reason why he was taking some time off, he'd be livid. Since Banger didn't know, there was no risk in Rock going against his president's orders. He climbed the stairs, wanting to get some shut-eye before he slipped out of the clubhouse into the early morning darkness and made his way to Clotille.

Chapter Eight

CLOTILLE LAY ON her side, knees bent and close to her body, finger gripping the steel bars of the cage Frederick had placed her in after he'd lectured her on what she'd done wrong by talking to the biker. He'd started her discipline by pulling her hair with a series of "what did you do wrong" question-and-response routines with an occasional swat on her behind with her hairbrush. Normally, that would have sufficed for her punishment for being a bad girl, but he'd been so angry and disappointed in her, he'd told her he'd have to do something more so she would never do it again.

When he dragged her by her hair to the cage he kept in one of the locked rooms on the main floor, her heart had dropped. The steel cage was too small and she had to crumple herself into a ball in order to fit, unable to stretch out her limbs or turn around.

As he watched her get inside, he'd said, "I know you hate the cage the most, and that's why I'm using it as your punishment. You've angered me more today than you ever have during our time together. You humiliated me by talking to that dirty biker. I know you're attracted to him. I could see it in your eyes. Since you humiliated me, you will lie in your cage until I decide you should come out. Do you understand why I am doing this to you?"

"Yes, Sir," she said in a low voice, the embarrassment in lying naked in a cage with him watching her, so pathetic and immovable, hitting her in her core. He locked the steel door, then sat on a straight-backed chair and gazed at her for what seemed like an eternity. Every once in a while he'd chuckle at her shame and pain. He was deriving an enormous amount of pleasure from her punishment, but then she was there to pleasure him. Her body was his to do with as he wanted. He owned her.

She heard him stand up from his chair and walk out of the room. Soon she smelled the delicious aroma of grilled meat, and she knew he'd bring his food into the room and eat it while he watched her. Of course, she'd have no food until the following day.

As she lay on the cool steel floor of her cage, her mind filled with images of Rock and her stomach clenched. *Seeing him up close, talking with him, sharing that very short moment with him makes this damn cage worth it.* She was proud of how well she'd lied to Frederick when he'd questioned her repeatedly about her attraction to the biker. She never once revealed that they knew each other, and he believed her. He even admitted the biker was more at fault than she was, but he punished her hard anyway. Clotille suspected it was because the younger, buffed Rock made Frederick feel insecure and jealous. So she was punished for Rock being a stud. The irony hit her and she almost laughed aloud, but she held it in for fear that he'd think she was enjoying her punishment. Some subs enjoyed the punishment aspect as much or more than the pleasure element of their relationship with their Dom, and they would manipulate their Master by purposefully misbehaving so they could be punished. Clotille was definitely not one of those.

Since Rock had come back into her life, she'd begun questioning the whole lifestyle that had provided her some comfort in a chaotic world. *Is Rock in my life? He's close to me physically, but I'm not* in *his life. I doubt I'll ever see him again. I told him to go away.* He'd had no idea how she wanted to wrap herself around his hard body, his strong arms holding her close and making her feel safe and protected. But there would be consequences if she did that, and she wasn't prepared to face them. She couldn't.

"Are you hungry?" Frederick's voice broke in on her internal thoughts. She'd forgotten he was there, and she hadn't even smelled his dinner… until now.

"Yes, Sir."

"Then you shouldn't have been such a bad pet." There was a long pause and she closed her eyes, trying to bring Rock's face back into her mind. "Because I love you so much, I will allow you to eat, but you'll have to do it from the bowl."

Redness crept up her neck and spread out over her cheeks and forehead. A loud bang on her cage made her eyes fly open, and she found herself staring into Frederick's face as he crouched low on his haunches beside her. He was fucking mocking her. There was no way in hell she was going to eat her dinner from a damn bowl while he watched. She'd rather deal with the hunger pangs than submit to that.

"So what does my disobedient pet have to say?"

"Thank you for your kindness, Sir." A smirk covered his lips. "But I'd rather not eat." The smirk turned into a thin line of displeasure.

"You think you're holding on to your dignity?"

"No, Sir. I'm just not hungry." Her gaze locked with his, a defiant sheen in it.

He stood up and kicked her cage. "Remember you belong to me, not to yourself or anyone else. Only me." He stormed out of the room and a rush of joy filled her. For one brief instant, Clotille Boucher had resurfaced, pushing pet away. She smiled and closed her eyes again.

When he finally let her out of the cage three hours later, her joints were so sore that she could barely walk on her wobbly legs. He told her he didn't want her in his bed that night, so she slept on the pallet he'd laid down on the floor at the foot of their bed. She was elated to sleep alone, and derived some pleasure out of knowing his final punishment had backfired. She washed up and stretched out on her pallet, tugging the blanket under her chin.

As she drifted off to sleep, Frederick's gentle voice broke through her sleepiness. "I do love you, pet. Very much."

Her pulse pounded in her ears, and she pretended to be asleep. After many minutes, she heard Frederick's even breathing, and her body relaxed and allowed sleep to take her.

★ ★ ★

FOR THE PAST two days, Rock had been watching the house waiting for a weakness in Frederick's stringent routine. So far, the man rarely went out and when he did, Clotille was with him. The way she moved, the way her clothes hugged her curves, and the way she'd toss her long hair over her shoulder was a natural aphrodisiac, causing Rock's jeans to tighten.

While Rock had done the security gig at the house, he'd noticed all the cameras, but also a weak link in approaching the house from the forest of trees on the fifty acres of land. He'd intended to mention it to Frederick Blair, but then he discovered Clotille and he made a mental note that he may need to use the breach in security to his advantage.

As he stared through his long-distance binoculars, he spotted Frederick leaving the house, briefcase in hand. The driver pulled up the black limousine and he went into the backseat. The sleek limo pulled away and drove out the iron gates. *Fuck yeah! Game's on.*

He approached the house by coming through the forest. Once he was close enough, he took out a small device not much bigger than a cigarette pack. He knew the cameras were wireless, having seen them enough during his two stints at the mansion. He figured they were only set up so Frederick could watch them later and see what Clotille did during the day. Pushing the buttons on his frequency emitter, he jammed the reception, thus making the cameras inoperable. There was no way Frederick would have his security people in tune with them—they were for his pleasure only.

He tried the French doors off the veranda, and to his surprise, they were unlocked. Rock pushed them open and found himself in the family room. For several minutes he stood frozen, his ears pricked for anything that may signal danger. Nothing. He moved cautiously through the main floor, checking all the rooms. There was no sign of Clotille.

As he crossed the foyer, the circular staircase beckoned him, and he remembered the last time he'd been to the house he'd spotted Clotille staring out at him from a window on the second floor. He slowly ascended the stairs.

The second floor had a shitload of rooms, but she had been standing in one on the right side of the house so he went in that direction, opening doors and scanning each room for any signs of her.

He turned the knob to the door in the middle of the large hallway and it swung open. Adrenaline pumped in his blood as he perused what was definitely the master bedroom. He noticed a pallet at the foot of the bed, sheets and a blanket neatly folded on top of it.

He entered and went through the room, trying to figure out where she could be. *Maybe the sonofabitch locked her in his goddamned playroom in the basement.* He opened a couple doors only to reveal large walk-in closets bigger than his room at the clubhouse. To the right of the closets, there was another door. He slowly opened it and his eyes washed over Clotille as she sat stiffly on a chair, her gaze overly bright, her face ashen. She wore her hair up in a high ponytail and the tendons stood out on her neck, a small pulse visible.

"*Chérie*, you don't need to be afraid," he said in a soothing voice as he approached her.

"W-what are you doing here?" she stammered, her face strained.

"I need to talk with you."

Looking downward, she shook her head. "No. The cameras. He'll see you. This is bad, Roche, very bad."

"Don't worry about that. I fixed it. It'll just show as a malfunction. How much time do we have before he comes back?"

"He said he'd be back at five o'clock. He's always prompt."

Rock glanced at the digital clock on a side table near the chair. "Good, we have several hours." He reached out and stroked her cheek gently, her skin so soft. "Are you his wife?"

Her head jerked up. "No."

"I didn't think so. Are you with him because you love him, or is it for the money? I know he's helping your mother."

Crimson painted her cheeks. "I knew you did. At first I thought I could love him the way I loved… well, the way a woman should love a man. I tried, but I couldn't. He's been good at taking care of some things I messed up over the years. My mother adores him."

"She would."

She shrugged. "He makes a lot of things possible in my life for me and my… family."

"If it's money you need, I can help you. You don't have to be with a man who humiliates you like he did at the dinner party."

She covered her face with her hands and sank down on the chair. "I hate that you saw that. You don't understand. It's part of the lifestyle, and it was pleasing to Frederick."

"I understand that but I know this isn't your lifestyle, even though you've tried to make it that way."

She stared at him, her eyes flashing. "How do you know what I like? You and I haven't seen each other since we were fools in high school who thought the world was ours. You don't know a damn thing about me."

He grinned. "I thought you were submissive."

"Fuck you!" She leaned back, placing her hand over her mouth as her body shook. Then a peel of laughter escaped from her lips.

He joined in, laughing loudly. "It felt good, *non*? *Chérie*, you're about as submissive as the women at the club. This life isn't for you. I've come to take you away."

Tears were rolling down her cheeks as she gulped huge breaths of air. After she calmed down, she took a tissue and blew her nose. "If I were the only one involved in all this, I'd go with you in a heartbeat, but it's not so simple."

"You want to stay with him?"

"It's not a matter of *want*. Things are complicated."

"I'm not going to beg you to come. I'm helping you out as a friend and because we have a history together, but if you tell me you don't want to go with me, I'll wish you a good life and walk out of it. It's your choice."

In a monotone voice, she said, "I'll stay with Frederick. *Merci*, Roche… for everything."

Rock exhaled slowly, a bitter smile whispering on his lips as he shook his head. "Okay, Clotille. Have a good life." He whirled around and marched out of the room, a heaviness descending on him. All he wanted to do was jump on his Harley and ride it fast and hard all the way back to Pinewood Springs. *You tried to help but she wants this bullshit. Your hands are now clean of it.*

He went down the stairs and walked toward the French doors. Just before he stepped outside, her voice echoed through the house. "Roche! *Attends!* Are you still here?" Panic played on the edges of her words. Warmth radiated throughout his body as he silently walked back to the staircase. She stood at the top of the stairs gripping the bannister, her knuckles white. Her watery gaze scanned his face as she rocked in place.

Stone-faced, he crossed his arms. "Hurry it up."

A slow grin spread as the color slowly came back to her face. She spun around and scurried to her bedroom.

"I got my bike, so don't bring a bunch of shit," he yelled after her.

He figured they'd be back at the clubhouse in a couple hours. *I wonder what the fuck Banger's gonna say about this.*

He knew his president wouldn't be happy.

And at that instant, he didn't give a damn.

★ ★ ★

Frederick opened the door at exactly five o'clock, his gaze turning dark when he didn't see her kneeling on the floor, waiting for him. Anger sizzled inside him and he took long strides into the family room, expecting to see her sitting on the couch. She'd lost track of time before when she'd become too immersed in a book. The family room was empty and an eerie silence blanketed the house.

He ran upstairs calling her name, but there was no answer. When he saw that her small room was empty, he knew she'd left him. Disbelief mixed with raw anger and sadness befell him. He sat on the edge of the bed trying to make sense of what had happened. Frederick pinpointed the restlessness he'd sensed in her beginning when he'd had the outlaw group watch his house. *There's something not lining up. I caught her talking to that muscle head in the kitchen, the same one who stopped by our table at the restaurant. Has she left me for* him? The idea seemed inconceivable. He could give her the world. Maybe he'd been too hard on her after the incident with the biker in the kitchen. He'd been so angry it'd taken him over an hour to cool down before he'd punished her for her disobedience.

He picked up the phone and dialed her number, but it went straight to voice mail. *Maybe she's been hurt. Kidnapped.* He rushed downstairs to his office and turned on the monitors, rewinding the tapes to see what had happened. He leaned forward and stared at the screen, the rage creeping through his body threatening to explode. The snowy screen confirmed what he'd known since he'd realized she wasn't there: she'd run off.

We had an agreement. If the cunt wants to break it off, there will be hell to pay.

Frederick had never been the forgiving type, and he had no intention of changing that.

His pet would regret humiliating him like this.

He was bringing her back. And then she would pay for what she did to him: slowly, painfully, until she was hoarse from begging for mercy. His eyes narrowed and his jaw clenched.

He'd take her out of her misery.

He'd choke her until her body crumpled down on the floor in a lifeless heap.

Chapter Nine

Clotille's hair whipped around her face as the Harley sped past evergreens and pine trees. Each curve made her stomach lurch and she buried her face in Rock's back, not daring to look down at the steep drop-offs on the narrow, twisting road where guardrails didn't exist. Every once in a while she'd sneak a quick glance at Rock, whose eyes were fixed straight ahead as he maneuvered the scariest road she'd ever been on. The wind tangled his hair and she longed to run her fingers through it, but she didn't dare release her death grip on him. She closed her eyes again and made herself concentrate on Rock's hard stomach muscles under her hands and his scent of leather, cloves, and earth that filled her nostrils. She'd always thought he was incredibly handsome, but he had matured into a panty-melting hunk. She squirmed a bit on the leather seat as she remembered how powerful his thrusts inside her had been that night they made love in the park when they were teens. How little she'd known about pleasing a man back then.

After forty minutes of terror around the mountain pass, they finally hit a long stretch of road. She breathed a sigh of relief that they'd made it in one piece. Expecting him to take her into town, she was surprised when he turned down a narrow dirt road. They bumped around for several minutes before stopping at a concrete and steel security booth. The man sitting inside waved at Rock, opening the gates so they could ride in.

When she got off the bike, her legs felt like jelly and she collapsed into his arms. He laughed. "Was this your first time on a motorcycle?"

She nodded, loving the way his strong arms felt around her. "It was thrilling, but I never want to drive on that road again."

He smiled, his fingers gently pushing her hair away from her face. "I took a back road for extra security. The road is definitely not for novices. It's even shut down in the winter. You think you can walk now?"

The strength had come back in her legs, but she wanted to stay in his arms. She felt safe in them, and being cocooned by him made it feel like none of the crap she had going on in her life existed, like it'd all been a bad dream.

"So can you?"

His deep voice melted her and she nodded. The minute he let go, she missed his closeness. He took out her small bag of essentials and cocked his head toward a large three-story brick building.

"Where are we?" she asked as she followed him.

"My clubhouse."

"I thought I'd stay in a hotel. I have some money." The truth was she had quite a bit of money since she'd been extremely frugal in spending the monthly stipend Frederick had given her for the past four years. Most of what he'd given her she'd stashed away. Knowing she had money of her own had given her a sense of freedom in her regimented life.

"Too risky. The security at the club is top-notch. There's no way anyone can come in here unless they break through with a fuckin' tank."

She had no doubt in her mind that Frederick would purchase a tank and crash through in order to take her back. She shivered and walked through the door he held open for her.

When they entered, she spotted a few men sitting at the bar and a couple more shooting pool. Hard rock music played in the background. The men's eyes took her in and all at once she felt self-conscious, scared, and insecure about her decision to leave the world she'd known for the last few years. The world where all decisions had been made for her. There had been comfort in that.

An older man grinned at her while he greeted Rock. "Dude. You're back." His gaze slowly ran up her body and she flinched. "Now I know why you went away. Fuck, dude, you got taste." The other men at the bar chuckled, each of them assessing her boldly. Instinctively, she circled her hands around his arm, pressing closer to him.

He laughed at the guys and dismissed them with a wave of his hand. He looked down at her. "Come on. I'm on the third floor." He pulled away from her and clomped up the stairs.

She walked into a room she presumed was his. Posters of barely clad women in various poses on Harleys dotted his walls, along with Cajun folk art paintings. The room was well lit since it was a corner one, sunlight bathing the room in a hot, white light.

"Is this where you live?" She stood by the door, her arms crossed around her.

"Yeah. You can stay here until you figure out what the fuck you're gonna do."

"Have you always lived here?"

"Yeah. Everything I need is close by. I like it."

"It's a big room. Do all the men live up here?"

"The third floor is reserved only for officers. We got a few free rooms up here for visiting officers. The guys who live here have rooms in the basement. The club girls live in the attic."

"Club girls?"

He grinned. "The women who like the protection of the club. We give them room and board and a monthly allowance."

"And what do they do for you?"

"Keep the place clean, cook, and keep us satisfied." He winked.

With a pinched expression, she tugged at the hem of her top. "I can see why you live here."

He raised his eyebrows and chuckled. "It definitely has its perks." He walked over to a short dresser. "I'll clear out a drawer so you can put your stuff in there. I'll crash in one of the empty rooms in the basement."

Panic zigzagged through her. "I don't want to be alone. I'd prefer it if you stayed with me, or else every noise will have me thinking Frederick is busting in." She laughed nervously.

Rock paused and stared at her for a long moment, then blew out a long breath. "Okay. You can take the bed and I'll sleep on the floor."

She shook her head. "No. I can't kick you out of your bed. I'll sleep on the floor." Memories of her pallet at the foot of Frederick's bed and the cage she sometimes slept in flitted through her mind. "I'm good with that."

An incredulous look passed over his face. "There's no fuckin' way I'm gonna let you sleep on the floor while I'm in the bed. You take the bed. *Fini.*"

Warmth spread over her like honey. "*Merci*, Roche."

"For what?"

"For helping me out… for everything." She smiled and took a few steps toward him.

"Of course. We're from the same parish. We were friends a long time ago."

Her heart sank a bit and her stomach tightened. *Is that all he remembers of our times together? Just friends? Was our lovemaking something between friends? I recall it differently.*

"And I'm Rock, not Roche, okay?"

She nodded and stared straight out the window. "And I'm Clotille." From the corner of her eye she noticed him glance at her, a smile on his face. She wanted to go over to him and hug him hard, bury her head in his chest and breathe in the scent that tantalized her during their ride to Pinewood Springs, but she only stood there, watching him.

"You can settle in and rest. I'm gonna go downstairs and have a couple drinks with my brothers. If you want something to eat, just text me and I'll come up and get you. Don't wander around here alone. You're not wearing my patch, so the guys will think you're open for business. You know what I'm saying?"

Her eyes widened. "You mean they'll think I want to have sex with them because I'm *here*?"

He nodded. "That's the way it is. They'll think you're a hoodrat, who's looking for some fun. The only women who hang at the club are the club women and the hoodrats, and fucking is the main reason they're here. You need to stay close to me. The old ladies wear their man's patch, so they can come and go as they please, but if you don't have a patch you're telling the brothers you wanna spread your pretty legs."

"That's insane!"

He shrugged. "That's the way our world rolls." He opened the door and looked back. "Text me and I'll come right up." Then he was gone.

Emptiness spread through Clotille as she stood alone, looking at the closed door. She sighed and moved over to her small bag on the bed, taking out her toiletries and going into the bathroom. She turned the water on, loving the way the steam encased her. She needed a hot shower to ease her aching muscles from the hellish ride into Pinewood Springs, knowing she'd feel a lot better after. *I wonder if Roche—I mean Rock—is interested in me anymore. He looks at me like he is, but then he acts like a distant friend. Maybe it's for the best to leave the past behind. There are things that he'll never forgive me for. We haven't seen each other in twelve years. We really don't know each other at all. He's very different from when we were in high school. His outlaw world frightens me. It kills without flinching. How did everything get so messed up?*

She shook her head as if to dislodge the shadows of the past and then stepped into the shower.

★ ★ ★

WHEN ROCK ENTERED the great room, several brothers grinned at him and gave him the thumbs-up approval of Clotille. Rock smiled smugly as he swaggered over to the bar and grabbed the shot of Jack that Blade had waiting for him.

"Who's the woman in your room? She's fuckin' gorgeous," Hoss said.

"How come you been hiding her from us, bro?" Chicory punched Rock in the arm.

"She's just a friend from back home. She's visiting for a little bit."

He threw the whiskey back, the amber liquid warming his throat.

"Then you don't mind if I get to know her?" Chicory propped his elbows on the bar and held Rock's gaze.

"Don't even fuckin' go near her," he gritted before he threw back another shot. Chicory sniggered. "Yeah, I wasn't buying the 'just my friend' bullshit."

"Whatever. You guys staying for a while? Maybe we can get Bones and play a few rounds of pool. I'm feeling lucky tonight." Rock took out three joints and gave each of the brothers one before he lit his and took a deep drag.

"With that cutie, I bet you're feeling all kinds of lucky." Chicory nudged Hoss, who nodded in agreement.

"Yeah, we're not talking about her anymore. So you wanna play pool or not?"

"I'd like to, but my mom is sick so I gotta go and see her in a little while," Chicory said. "I gotta do duty at Dream House tonight. I hope Crystal's working. She can dance real good." Hoss smiled broadly.

"Yeah, like you're lookin' at her dancing." Rock laughed and took another hit from his joint.

"I appreciate the art of dance." Hoss brought his beer bottle to his mouth.

"More like an appreciation of tits and ass. And Crystal's got a fine-looking rack," Chicory said. "Who's your favorite dancer at Dream House, Rock?"

Rock bent his head back and blew his smoke toward the ceiling. "Fuck, I haven't been there in a while. I used to work there a lot, but now Banger wants me at the club more. Janelle is pretty hot, and Sasha has an ass that a man could sink his teeth into." The three men chuckled and compared notes on the different strippers who worked at Dream House.

Rock turned around when he felt someone clasp his shoulder. Bones stared at him stone-faced. Rock smiled and offered his brother a joint, but Bones just shook his head.

"What the fuck's up with you? I don't ever remembering you turning down a smoke, dude." Rock put the joint back in his pocket.

"Are you drunk, high, or just plain fucking crazy bringing that rich prick's wife to the club? What the fuck, bro?"

"I didn't tell you, but I know her from my hometown. Isn't that a fuckin' small world?"

"Shit's gonna hit the fan when Banger finds out."

Rock shrugged. "Shit's always hitting the fan around here for some damn reason or another. I'll deal with it."

"You fucking her?"

"Nah. We're just friends."

"That's the best kinda fucking. You know each other, no love involved, just admiration for each other." Bones glanced at his cell phone. "Damn, I promised my brother I'd help him fix his truck. I gotta go. Looking forward to the fireworks at our next church." He drained his glass and placed it on the counter. "Later." Bones rushed out the door.

After a couple hours, Rock checked his phone to see if Clotille had texted him, but there were no messages or calls. He wanted to make sure she was all right, so he took the stairs two at a time until he came to his room. He opened the door and saw her lying on his bed, wrapped in one of his many quilts—Isa was fucking obsessed with them—fast asleep. He padded over to her and took in her beauty: flawless skin, hair as golden as honey in the sun, lips full and parted slightly, and long burnt-umber lashes. *She's so fuckin' beautiful.* As he gazed at Clotille, he felt magnetically drawn to her, and he brushed her pinkish cheeks with the back of his hand. *Fuck, they're so damn soft.* He sucked in his breath, the desire to kiss her, thread his fingers through her tresses, and trace her body with his tongue overwhelming. He longed to see her creamy breasts and suck their nipples to hardness. His desire grew and his pulse quickened as he looked on, his jeans tightening as the need for her burned from his head to his stiff dick.

For such a long time he'd thought about her, replaying their last night together over and over in his mind, like a movie projector set on autopilot. Mixed with loving thoughts of her were strains of bitterness, anger, and... hate. When he'd needed her the most, she'd dumped him for the rich high school star quarterback, whose father had paid his way to Harvard. Rock had been the troubled bad boy, who started fights, smoked cigarettes, and skipped school. He'd been from the other side of the tracks—white trash. Then he'd beaten his dad nearly to death and had ended up in the slammer. How could he ever blame her for bailing? Even so, it'd hurt when she'd given up on him so quickly. And looking at her at that moment, the hurt he'd buried deep inside began to resurface. He wanted her desperately, but he didn't want to be dragged into her web again. He had vowed that he'd never let that happen. *My sweet Clotille. You're a ball buster, that's for sure.*

"I like you looking at me. It reminds me of when we were young," she said as her eyes fluttered open.

His head jerked. "Uh... I was making sure you were okay. I still can't believe you're here after all these years." He ran his hand through his hair. "You gonna tell me what the fuck's going on with you?"

She pushed herself up and leaned against the headboard, then wrapped her arms around her knees that were pulled close to her chest. Her gaze locked with his. "Not now," she said softly. "Tonight, I want to pretend that everything is wonderful and nothing bad ever happens to anyone."

He watched her as her face flushed and she buried her head between her knees. It took everything he had not to reach out and stroke her hair, then press her close to him and soothe away the bad memories she had locked in her mind.

She lifted her head, a warm smile lighting her face. "Do you have food around this place? I'm starving."

"Yeah. We got some food downstairs. You like barbecue?"

"Yes. I'm so hungry I could eat anything."

"You lost a lot of weight since I last saw you. You didn't need to."

She pressed her lips together and looked away. "Frederick liked me very thin. He controlled what I ate and how much."

He walked over to the other side of the bed and sat on the edge of it. "Why did you let him control you like that?"

She pulled her hair into a ponytail and stretched out her legs. "I don't want you to think Frederick's a monster. He isn't. He's just used to being in control. It's his personality. He came into my life when there was nothing but chaos, and I yearned for someone to take over and tell me what to do. It really can make things simple when you let go… at least it did for me."

"Were you happy with him?"

Her brows knitted together as she paused before answering. "I wouldn't say I was happy, but I was safe and knew things in my life were taken care of. It's kind of hard to explain. Frederick cherished me and I pleased him. It was a give and take." Her stomach growled and she blushed, her hand flying to her belly.

He laughed. "Let's go down and get you some food. You definitely need some fattening up." He stood up and wanted to give her his hand to help her up, but he knew if he did, he'd never let go. He stood aside as she passed through the door.

She followed him into the kitchen and stood behind him as he rummaged through the refrigerator, her creamy vanilla scent coiling around his dick as want ribboned through him. "Here's the pork. I can nuke it. Coleslaw. And some kickass potato salad. Pickles, tomatoes, and cheddar cheese slices. Perfect." He brought his armload of goodies to the kitchen island.

"Is there any lettuce? I can make great salads." Her eyes sparkled like a dew-misted meadow in summer. As long as he lived, her gaze would always pull him in.

"We got lettuce. Look in the vegetable bin." A familiar easiness settled between them as he assembled the pulled pork sandwiches and she made a salad for them. He liked the feeling of being with her, acting like they were two people who didn't have the history they did between them. He could get used to this with her. *Fuck no. Remember how she ripped out your heart. So you're having a domestic moment with the girl you* crushed on all through high school. So the fuck what? You're acting like a goddamned pussy.

"These carrots are so sweet. Here, taste them." She placed her finger on his lips and put the chunk of carrot in his mouth, her finger lingering inside. He closed his mouth and sucked it, a jolt of lust zapping his cock like lightning. "Good, huh?" She slid her finger out. "Did you guys get these at a farmer's market? I'm positive they didn't come from the grocery store."

I want to fuck you so bad, chérie. *I don't give a shit about the damn carrots. You're the only thing I want to taste.* "I don't know where they came from."

She smiled at him and ran her hand lightly down his arm. "Us being together like this is nice, isn't it? It makes me remember how good life can be."

His gaze followed her hand, wishing like hell it would go lower to palm his throbbing dick. *Damn, she's killing me.* He lifted one shoulder. "I guess."

Her laugh surrounded him and slid down his body, landing on his pulsing shaft.

"You done with the salad?" She nodded. "Let's eat in the great room." He carried out the food and she followed him, the salad bowl secure in her hands. He set everything down on the table and plopped on the chair. She joined him and ordered a glass of wine when Blade came over to give Rock a beer.

She ate two sandwiches, and he loved looking at her as she took dainty bites. He used to love watching her eat because she did it so delicately. He'd forgotten about that until right then. He had to admit being with her was comfortable as hell. It soothed an ache in him he'd had since he'd left home, but he didn't trust her. He couldn't let himself be lured in by good memories.

Be careful with this one. Don't let her burn you again. Keep your distance. She's keeping shit from you. Something's not right. I can sense it.

As he placed a forkful of salad in his mouth, he smelled Wendy's fresh scent before she stood behind him and draped her arms around his neck. Leaning down close to him, she breathed in his ear, "You wanna have some fun later on?"

He craned his neck to see her and noticed Clotille giving the club girl a hard look. A deep, satisfying feeling filled him when he realized she was jealous of Wendy. Rock grasped the club girl's hands and said softly in her ear, "Not tonight. Another time."

Wendy's eyes darted from Clotille back to Rock's hands on hers. She pressed closer to him, her low-cut top displaying her breasts. "Who's she?"

"A friend from back home. We got shit to catch up on."

A slow smile spread over her face. "Oh. I got ya. When you're done catching up, let me know." She kissed his cheek and then ambled away, her hips swaying seductively in her short dress.

Rock turned his attention back to his food, mindful of Clotille's change in demeanor.

"She certainly isn't shy, is she?" she muttered under her breath.

"She's a club girl so they act differently, you know? No worries. I'm here with you."

She shoved back in her chair and laughed dryly. "Don't mind me. You're a free agent." He nodded. "I know that. I can catch up with her another time." He smiled inwardly as she sneaked peeks at Wendy, sitting on Wheelie's lap a couple tables away from them.

As they finished their meal in silence, a series of beeps emitted from her phone, and she kept ignoring them.

"I think someone's trying to get a hold of you." Rock pointed to her phone as it danced on the table.

"You think?" Clotille leaned back and crossed her arms.

She's still fuckin' pissed about Wendy. Damn, that's a surprise. "You gonna pick up?"

"No. It's Frederick. He's been texting and calling me nonstop since I turned my phone back on after Miss Hospitality moved on to another one of your club friends."

"That's what she's here for. You don't need to worry about her. You could spin circles around her." He winked and threw her one of the crooked smiles that made women flush with desire. Redness crept up her neck. *The fuckin' smile does it every damn time.* "Don't you want to see what he wants?"

She shook her head. "I know he's anxious that I may be hurt or in trouble." She drummed her fingers on the table.

"Then why don't you answer it and tell him you're okay?" Rock wanted to throw the beeping phone across the room and place his hands over her nervous fingers.

"I'm not ready to talk to him."

"Text him."

"He'll drive me crazy with questions."

"Don't answer 'em. Tell him you're fine. That's it. It's not so hard."

She smiled at him. "I'm glad to be here with you right now. It just feels good, you know?"

It feels fuckin' awesome, but I can't be drawn back into her fucked-up world. "Sure. You wanna go back up to my room?"

"Do you have any Cajun music?"

He nodded and couldn't help grinning when he saw her eyes light up as she clapped her hands together. "Let's go up. I'll bring some brandy."

In his room, he poured brandy for both of them and kicked off his boots. "Get comfortable." He sank down in the easy chair by the window.

"I didn't really bring that much," she said as she took off her heels. "I'll have to head into town tomorrow and buy a few things."

He went over to his dresser and pulled out a T-shirt. "Put this on."

She unfolded it and a menacing grim reaper grinned ghoulishly at her. "That'll give me nightmares."

"It's an Avenged Sevenfold shirt. I saw them in Denver last year. It was a kickass concert. You want another one? I got a ton, but most of them have skulls, images of blood, or guns on 'em."

"I'll stick with this one." She went into the bathroom to change as he went over to his CD collection, pulling one out and placing it in the player. When she came out, his gaze traveled over her, taking in every bit of her. She shifted from one foot to the next. "It's too big and too short, but it's comfy."

The T-shirt fell over her ample breasts and came down mid-thigh on her, and she looked delicious wrapped in black with just enough to cover her to make his imagination go into overdrive. "It looks fine. Here." He handed her a glass of brandy and turned on the CD.

She sat on the bed cross-legged, her hair spilling over her shoulders as she took a sip. "Mmm... good." Then she leaned back against the headboard and closed her eyes as the melodic strains of fiddles and accordion filled the room. When the first lyrics of the song sang out, her eyes flew open. "Huval Family. My favorite Cajun band. You remembered." Her grin lit up her whole face.

He wanted to scoop her up, cover her in slow passionate kisses, and savor every fucking inch of her body before he made love to her. "I remembered. How could I forget? Each time I saw you at the Lafayette Crawfish Festival, you'd always be hanging around the stage when they played. You were nothing but a groupie."

She giggled. "I was." She faced him, her green gaze shimmering. "It's been such a long time since I've heard Cajun or Zydeco music. *Merci.*"

He lifted his glass and tipped it to her. "You're welcome." He watched how she fell into the music, her body swaying with the beats, each movement pulling him in more. He stood up and walked over to her, his hand extended. "Let's dance, *chérie.*"

Uncertainty shadowed her face, but then she placed her hand in his and he drew her to him. Soon they were twirling around his room to the rhythm and quick fiddle action. Turning too sharply, they tripped and landed on the bed, laughing and breathless. Rock hovered over her, and when her pink tongue touched her top lip he took hungry possession of her mouth, devouring it with deep sweeping strokes of his tongue. He wanted to consume her whole.

As he kissed her, he breathed in each of her tiny moans and whimpers. She hooked her arm around his neck, bringing him even closer to her. When he pulled away to nuzzle her neck, a soft moan escaped from her throat and he felt his cock swell in his jeans. He tugged down the too-large T-shirt, revealing her shoulder, and peppered kisses over it while he breathed in deeply, filling his lungs with her, intoxicated on the scent.

"Clotille, *ma chérie*," he whispered as her hot skin trembled beneath his hands. She whimpered and arched her back, pressing closer to him, her hard nipples pushing against the fabric of the T-shirt. "Fuck," he gritted as he pulled back to look at her. Her lips were red and swollen from kissing and lust misted her eyes. His gaze journeyed over her curves, his hands following its path. When he slid his hand under her shirt, she gently moved it away. Their gazes locked on each other, their breaths ragged. "Why're you stopping me? I know you want this as much as I do."

"I don't know what I want," she said softly.

"The fuck you don't." He straightened up. "You've always known exactly what you wanted, and you made sure you got it."

"Not really. You thought that about me because my father was rich and it seemed like everything was wonderful for me…. It wasn't." She brushed her hand against his. "Roche, please don't be angry. I just think it's too soon. I do want you, but I've been in a fucked up situation for the past four years. I can't just switch things on and off that easily. Can't we give it some time and get to know each other again? If we jump in too fast, it would just confuse everything"

"For the last fuckin' time, my name is Rock. And nothing would be confused. It'd just be two old friends fucking." He stood up and turned off the music.

"Is that what we were? Friends."

"Yeah, babe. Nothing more." He sat at the edge of the bed and pulled his boots on.

"Where're you going?"

"Downstairs where everybody knows the score." He opened the door and walked out, anger pricking at his body. *Now she can wonder if I'm gonna fuck Wendy. Just like I wondered if she was fucking Luc when my ass was in the pen and I didn't hear from her. Fuck this shit!*

By the time he came back to his room, she was already asleep, her soft breaths filling his ears. He stripped down to his boxers before lying down on the makeshift bed on the floor. He hadn't fucked Wendy or any other woman downstairs. How could he? He had Clotille on his mind. *I gotta stop this shit before anything happens. I got plenty of pussy to get lost in. I don't fuckin' need her.* But the tent he was pitching in his boxers said otherwise, and he cursed under his breath.

He knew sleep would elude him that night, but somehow it didn't matter. All that mattered was she was with him for the moment, and he knew that was all he could really count on from her.

Chapter Ten

Clotille's eyes snapped open. Streaks of sunlight filtered through the blinds. *Oh God! I've overslept. Frederick is going to be so angry with me.* She rubbed her eyes and looked around the room, realization of where she was dawning on her. There was no Frederick anymore, and she could do whatever the hell she wanted. All of a sudden, she felt ultra-awake, adrenaline rejuvenating her. *I'm in Roche's room.* Smiling, she inched her way over to the edge of the bed and looked down, expecting to see him. He wasn't there. She glanced around and noticed his pillow, sheet, and blankets were stacked neatly on one of the chairs by the window.

She wasn't sure he'd even been there the previous night. He'd been so angry and she couldn't blame him. She'd wanted to make love to him, but she couldn't. She knew if she spent the night with him, she'd never be able to leave him. She'd given up so much since he'd gone away to prison. And he kept telling her they were friends. *I definitely don't want Roche as a fuck buddy.* It seemed like he wanted to have fun *and* keep her at bay at the same time. She needed time to think and figure out how she was going to right all the wrongs that littered her past.

Pangs of jealousy stabbed her as she thought of Wendy pleasuring him. She could hardly expect him to stay celibate just because she was staying in his room. He was such a gorgeous man, so of course women wanted to be with him. She had no right to be mad at them; she was only the visiting *friend*, after all. But the way he'd kissed her had taken her breath away. *I'm going to have to be careful that I don't lose control. I want him so bad,* but she couldn't risk both their hearts again.

She held her head between her hands. She'd had too much to drink, but it had been a good night: listening to music, sipping brandy, and reminiscing about crawfish boils, sneaking out at night, and so many other things. It'd felt good to talk to him about home, and she'd made sure to steer their conversation away from anything negative. Then he'd asked her to dance and she loved being in his arms. It'd been perfect until the kiss and her rejection of him. If only he knew how badly she wanted and needed him. He'd been in her mind and between her legs ever since the first night she'd recognized him in Frederick's house. *Frederick. What the fuck am I going to do about him? I know he'll be spiteful. I have to get back to Lafayette and smooth everything over. I have to make sure my—*

A thunderous rumble shook the glass panes, and she scrambled out of bed and ran over to the window. Several motorcycles roared into the parking lot. The men all wore black leather and the sun bounced off the chrome, creating beacons of white light. When the men turned off their engines, stillness crept back in. She watched as the men dismounted and walked into the building. She tried to see if she could spot Rock, but he was not among the group of bikers.

Walking back to the bed, she saw her phone sitting on the nightstand. With trepidation, she turned it on, a series of beeps assaulting her ears.

She had numerous calls and texts from Frederick, one or the other coming through every fifteen minutes practically the whole night. Guilt washed over her as her chest tightened. She knew Frederick was probably beside himself with worry, and he didn't deserve to be treated like that. After all, he'd helped her so much; an explanation from her was merited. It wasn't his fault that she couldn't fulfill the agreement, that Rock had reentered her life. Fate had decided it, and who was she to argue with such a power?

She picked up her phone and began to text him when it rang. It was Frederick. Exhaling a long breath, she picked up.

"Where the fuck are you? Do you know how worried I've been about you? I called the police, the hospitals. Fuck, pet, how could you let me worry like this? Why didn't you answer my calls or texts?" He sounded so worried and upset that she cursed herself for being so selfish.

"I'm sorry, Frederick. I needed some time by myself. I'm exhausted and I need to think."

"Where are you?" A hard edge had crept into his voice.

"I'm safe. You don't have to worry."

A long pause ensued and his anger radiated through the phone, curling around her neck and squeezing it. "You need to come home. Now."

"I can't just yet," she whispered.

"You've made your point, pet. You're throwing a tantrum, and I find it childish and distasteful. If I've been too hard on you, you should've told me. You know you can talk to me."

"I used to be able to, but over the last year you've become too possessive and it scares me."

"We can talk about it. Everything I do is because I love you. You know that, right?"

"Sometime it's too much."

"How can love ever be too much?"

"When it suffocates and swallows up who I am. I miss who I used to be." Her voice hitched.

"You miss the confused, broke, sniveling coward who couldn't even figure out how to make a go of her life? Think about what you're saying, pet."

"I have to go, Frederick. I'll talk to you later."

"Are you with the biker?"

"What? No. Of course not."

"You better not be or else I'll have to do something you'll regret for the rest of your life. You knew what my conditions were and you agreed to them. Now you're breaking them, and innocent people will be a part of the fallout. You'll have their blood on your hands. Don't be foolish, pet. You and others have so much to lose if you leave me."

His words chilled her bones and she shivered as his subtle but powerful threats weaved around her, choking all the breath from her.

He snorted. "I think you understand, pet." The phone clicked off and she stood there staring at it for a long time. She knew what he was capable of, and there was no doubt in her mind that he would make good on his threat. She couldn't let it happen; she had to do something about it. One thing was certain—going back to Frederick wasn't an option. She'd have to figure out how to stay one step ahead of him.

She rubbed her pounding temples with her fingertips. *I'm going to have to ask Rock to help me without him knowing why. How the hell am I going to do that?* Clotille knew Rock didn't trust her because she'd abandoned him when he needed her the most, but she'd had no choice at that time. What he hadn't known, hadn't wanted to hear, was that she'd let him in her heart, and that had never faltered. Even when she'd married Luc and knew she'd shattered Rock's heart, she'd loved him. Life was hard and she'd had to play with the cards it had dealt her, knowing Rock would never have understood that. *How could he? He came from a different background from me. I was expected to behave and live in a certain way. The only person who could've supported and saved me was locked up in prison, hate and rage clouding everything in his life. I didn't know what I was doing, and I fucked up big time. That is my private hell, just like his is the image of his murdered mother burned into his brain forever.*

She'd need a lifetime to correct a decade of mistakes and secrets but she'd have to try, even if she died doing so.

★ ★ ★

BANGER STOOD SILENT in front of the brothers, muscles and veins straining against his skin, his lips pulled back and baring his teeth. His icy blue gaze bored into Rock, whose shoulders slumped as he braced himself for the rage his president was ready to unleash on him.

"What in the goddamned fuckin' hell made you think it was a good idea to bring the rich fuck's wife to the Insurgents' clubhouse?" His face was mottled, and he clenched and unclenched his hands.

"She's not his wife," Rock said.

Bones whistled softly under his breath. "Wrong fuckin' answer, bro."

Banger picked up a wooden stool and slammed it on the table, the splintering wood sounding like cracking bones. "I don't give a shit if she is or isn't. Why the fuck is she in our clubhouse?"

Rock didn't flinch. "I'll take care of it. This is my personal affair and it doesn't involve the club."

"Every goddamned thing each of you does involves the club. How can you have been part of this brotherhood for as long as you have and not fuckin' know this? You got shit for brains? The fuckin' minute she stepped her ass in here, it involved the brotherhood. Fuck!"

"I get that, but this is my problem that I have to take care of."

"You fuckin' put the Insurgents in a bad position. This isn't some bitch you saw at a damn nightclub and wanted to fuck. This is a client's wife, a big-ass client for one of our loyal outsiders. Liam doesn't deserve the shit you just dropped on him. This is bullshit!"

All eyes were on Rock, and several brothers had their heads down out of respect for the verbal beat down their president was giving to a fellow brother.

Rock lifted his chin in defiance. "I said I'd take care of it. The rich fuck doesn't know she's here, and she'll be gone before he finds out. Liam doesn't know either. She was in a bad way and needed my help. We go back a long time."

"What are you planning to do about it?"

"I'm not sure yet."

"Well you fuckin' better get sure real fast 'cause her ass is out at the end of the weekend. And the only reason it isn't tomorrow is 'cause we got the celebration for patching Puck, Johnnie, and Blade in on Saturday. We got enough shit going on with the Skull Crushers, Demon Riders, and now the goddamned Gypsy Fiends. I can't fuckin' afford to take on an asshole who's got enough money to buy an army and raze this place to the ground just to get his bitch back. Fuck! I never expected this shit from you, Rock."

"I said I'd handle it."

"You fuckin' better."

"If you need my help, bro, let me know," Bones said.

"Same goes here." Wheelie stood up, followed by Jax, Chas, Chicory, Bear, Bruiser, Axe, Throttle, and—except for four of the older members—everyone else in the room.

Rock straightened his shoulders and looked at his brothers, a gleam in his eye. The magnitude of support the brothers just gave him reinforced the love he had for the brotherhood. He'd never experienced such love and loyalty in his life, not even with his mother. Her undying loyalty had always been with his pa, and he could never figure out how she could've stood by such a selfish, cruel-hearted sonofabitch. But that was over. She was gone. His pa was locked away. Rock was in the Insurgents. And Clotille was up in his room.

A wolfish smile crossed his face.

"We're already so deep in shit over this that I don't give a damn who helps you. Just get it fixed." Banger cleared his throat. "Now, on to other business. We're meeting with Baylee to draw up plans for our new strip mall...."

An hour later, Rock went into the great room, laughing and talking with his buddies. When he spotted Clotille sitting at one of the tables, a cup of coffee in her hand, his heart soared. She was wearing another one of his T-shirts and it turned him way the hell on. She had on a pair of yoga pants, and he couldn't wait to check out her ass in them when they went upstairs. *Damn, she gets my blood boiling.* As he approached she looked up from the magazine she was reading and smiled at him.

"Where have you been?" she said as he took the chair next to her.

"Church." He laughed at her quizzical look. "A meeting. We call it church."

"Why?"

He shrugged. "Just do."

"Okay. What was your meeting about?"

"I can't talk about what we discuss during church. It's club business."

She nodded. "I talked to Frederick this morning."

He stiffened. "What did he have to say?"

"The expected: he loves me, he wants me to come home, he'll destroy me if I leave him." She laughed as she pulled at her hair.

Rock scowled. "What does he mean by 'destroy you?' Does he got something on you?"

She licked her lips and averted her gaze. "He's helping a lot with my family, so I guess he means that he'll pull the financial plug."

"Is he supporting your brothers too?"

She nodded. "Mostly Armand."

"Isn't he ashamed to have a sugar daddy?" He chortled.

Her face was taut. "Armand isn't going to be happy about me leaving Frederick," she said in a low voice.

"Fuck him. He's always been a pain in the ass. 'Bout time he learned how to work."

"Yeah." She put her fingers to her mouth and chewed her cuticles. "I'm not sure what my plans are. Frederick has given me twenty-four hours to decide, and he's always prompt."

"My prez gave me a timeline too, only mine's longer. We'll figure it out." He stood up. "I'm going to get a beer. Want something?" She shook her head and he walked toward the bar.

Lola was leaning against the bar laughing with the new prospect when Rock came up. "Hey, prospect. Gimme a Coors on tap. Now." The young man's smile wiped off his face as he rushed to serve a patched member. Rock chuckled.

"You're such a mean SOB sometimes," Lola chided as she ran her fingernail up his arm.

Rock drew his arm closer to his body. "You gotta show the new ones they're in for hell so they appreciate the patch even more. What the fuck is this dude's name, anyway?"

"Buzz. He's pretty cute."

"Yeah, well he's off-limits 'til he's patched."

"I know. I was just commenting. Oh, I forgot to give you a letter that came for you in the mail yesterday." She pulled a white envelope from the pocket of her jean shorts, placing it in his hand. "Here you go, handsome."

He looked at it, noticing the address was handwritten again and the postmark was Lafayette. He ripped it open and a single sheet of paper fell out. Written on it was one sentence: "Your father did not kill your mother." The sentence was also handwritten, but it wasn't in the same script as the one that had contained the mojo bag.

"What the fuck is going on?" he muttered under his breath as he reread the note again and again. *Like I fuckin' believe this.* He shoved the envelope and note into his jeans pocket and headed back to the table.

For the next half hour, Clotille tried to make small talk with him but his mind was on the strange note and what it said. Was it true? How could that be? His dad had the goddamned bloody knife by him and his damn fingerprints were all over it. At the trial, he'd insisted he hadn't hurt his beautiful wife, Marie. He'd testified that he'd had some moonshine at the casino and it'd hit him real hard so that by the time he'd come home, he'd been drunker than he'd been in a long time. He hadn't been able to remember much of anything about that night except a lot of banging around, yelling, and a woman screaming. The jury hadn't bought his story, and he was convicted and placed in maximum security. Rock hadn't bought it at all either. He still didn't.

He reread the note again. *Is this fuckin' possible? I know Pa killed Maman. Why would someone kill her? She was the sweetest woman I've ever known. No fucking way. So who the hell is messin' with me?*

Rock turned the note over in his hands again before he folded it in half and placed it back in the envelope. For as long as he could remember, he'd hated his old man and he thought the bastard got exactly what he deserved.

But now the note had arrived and for the first time since his father's conviction, a scintilla of doubt poked at the dark recesses of his mind.

Chapter Eleven

"How the fuck didn't you know that Rock lived so close to Aspen?" the man growled. "That's sloppy work, and you know I don't like it. I'm giving you too much money to be fuckin' something like this up."

"What's the big deal if he's there?" a deep voice answered. "He's joined a damn motorcycle club, so he's out of the picture."

"He fuckin' saw Clotille." The dark-haired man leaned against the desk in his tastefully furnished office. He had a bitter tang in his mouth—dealing with trash always had that effect on him.

"How the hell did that happen?" The shorter man sat down on one of the plush chairs lining the wall.

"Frederick hired some outlaw biker club to do security for one of his fucked-up dinner parties. Rock was one of the guys. What the hell are the chances of that?" He laughed wryly.

"Why the fuck would he hire a biker gang? He's supposed to be smart."

"Fuck if I know. Damnit! He's livid. Clotille's run away."

The shorter man rose to his feet, sweat tickling down his face. "And she's with him? Fuck!"

The man adjusted the lapel on his Armani suit. "Don't panic. He doesn't know if she's with him, but you and I do. We know her and we fucking know Rock." He tapped his fingers against his desk.

"Does Frederick know Clotille knows Rock?"

"No, and I don't plan to tell him, so don't shoot off your fucking mouth. Got it?"

The shorter fellow wore casual pants and a striped polo shirt. He wiped his sweaty palms on his pants. "As long as the old man lives we risk going down for the murder, especially since there's still a living witness."

"The old lady kept her mouth shut, and as long as we keep paying her, we're good. The problem is if Clotille doesn't go back to Frederick. Then he'll cut me off which means you're off the payroll. We can't risk losing the money. When I get a hold of Clotille, she better get her ass back or else I'll take away the one thing she loves the most. She had an agreement and she's fucking blown it."

"And if we can't pay the old woman, then her memory will miraculously come back. You watch and see."

The taller guy walked behind his desk and sat down on his buttery Italian leather chair. "I'm not going to wait to see if that happens. I'll have to take care of everything because you're a dumbass and Clotille's a fuckup. I should've had Rock killed when he was in prison."

"Let's just deal with one thing at a time. The most important thing right now is getting Clotille to go back to Frederick. If that link's gone, the whole fucking chain breaks."

"And there's no way I'm going to let that happen. If she doesn't cooperate, I'll make her watch everyone she's ever loved be destroyed, and then I'll kill the spoiled little bitch with my own hands. She's not going to fuck this up for me." His eyes narrowed as he opened the mini fridge near his desk, took out a sparkling Pellegrino, and poured it in a tall glass.

Clotille knew the score and she'd agreed to play.

He hated when things changed mid-game.

He was a competitive bastard, and he played to win.

At all costs.

Chapter Twelve

CLOTILLE WATCHED OUT the window as a large van pulled into the club's parking lot and stopped at the front door. A burly man jumped out of the driver's seat and walked around to the back of the vehicle, then slid the door open. Several women came out carrying makeup cases. More than the majority had on tight jeans and tops that showcased their ample cleavage. They scurried into the club as the van pulled away and parked in the back of the lot.

A steady stream of chrome and metal made its way into the Insurgents' lot, the riders clad in black leather and denim. A few women teetered on four-inch heels waiting by the guard station until the prospect cleared them for entry. There was an air of anticipation among the women and men, and Clotille felt a rush of excitement skate over her just from watching the people below.

"You can have the bathroom. I'm done." Rock's scent of cloves and leather wafted around the room. She loved the way he smelled. When he'd leave the room she'd rush over and pick up his pillow or folded sheet, inhale deeply, and let herself get lost in his scent.

She turned around and her breath caught as she took in six-foot-one inches of raw power and manliness. He was shirtless, rummaging through the second drawer in his dresser, and she took the opportunity to admire his hard muscles beneath taut, tanned skin and the enticing tats on his arms, back, and chest that danced with each breath he took. He stood up and caught her ogling. She spun away, blushing.

He chuckled. "You don't need to turn away. I like it when you check me out. It's hot."

Under half-lidded eyes, she gazed up at him and locked onto his rock-hard torso, his to-die-for sculpted six-pack, and the dusting of dark hair trailing from his belly button and disappearing beneath the low-riding waistband of his tight jeans. All of a sudden the room grew smaller and hotter, and her body hummed with desire. She licked her lips and gave him a crooked smile. "I definitely like what I see."

He winked at her and slipped his T-shirt over his head. "We're going to have to do something about that, *chérie*, but for now, I gotta get downstairs. When you're done getting ready, text me and I'll come up. Tonight there'll be a lot of guys from the other chapters in the state, as well as Wyoming, Utah, and Nebraska."

"I noticed some of them riding in. I also saw a van of women being dropped off and some more women standing by the gates. This party feels different from the one the other night."

"It is." He slid his belt through the loops on his jeans. "Three prospects are going to get their colors, their full patch. It's a fuckin' big deal. The women who got out of the van are some of the strippers from our club. They'll entertain the brothers in one of the rooms. We have a stage and pole set up. The other women are hoodrats, who come to the parties to let loose. You know: drugs, fucking, and booze. They all gotta get cleared through security to make sure we don't have any rival club people or badges slipping through."

"Do you think the black dress I bought in town the other day will be okay? Some of the women had on sexier outfits."

"Who do you want to look sexy for? If it's me, I already think you are. If it's for another brother, don't even fuckin' think about it." He attached several strands of chains onto his belt loop.

A warm shiver skimmed across her skin, and she melted at the intensity with which he watched her. "I was just saying that because I thought I may stand out like a sore thumb."

"Are you kidding? You're all kinds of crazy in that dress. And just 'cause someone's looking at you doesn't mean you have to play Miss Social and talk to them. In my world doing that will get you a fucking, not an invitation to a charity ball."

She shook her head. "So basically I'm not to look at or talk to anyone but you?"

"Pretty much. I gotta get down there to make sure everything's good. Remember to text me when you're ready." He walked out, closing the door behind him. The jiggle of the knob made her smile; he was always making sure she was safe.

She walked back to the window, her eyes widening when she saw the throngs of bikes parked in the lot and the women gathered at the gate. A fluttery, empty feeling played in her stomach, and she gripped her arms to try and quiet her nerves. She pulled away from the window and headed to the bathroom to take a shower.

By the time she entered the great room, Rock's arm hooked with hers, the place was teeming with people. The haze from the smoke was so dense that she had to tilt her head in several positions to make out any faces. Punctuating beats from a Metallica song pounded in her ears as Rock led her to the bar. Without warning, he grasped her waist and hoisted her up, placing her on a barstool.

"You want wine?" he yelled in her ear.

She nodded as she looked around the room. Three men wearing clean new vests stood on tables drinking one shot after another. She surmised they were the ones who received the patch Rock and the others seemed so fond of. Clotille turned to look at the bartender and noticed that he placed drinks on the bar before anyone asked for them, like he knew what the brothers wanted.

"How does he know what they want to drink?" she shouted in Rock's ear.

"That's one of the duties of being a prospect. He's gotta know what the members in his club drink and have it ready the minute he sees them come in. The prospects start learning that shit when they're just hangarounds. Once someone sponsors them and they become prospects, the crap they have to know and do goes way up."

"Seems like a lot to do for just a couple of guys for a big club like yours."

Rock shrugged. "We all had to do that shit, so we're not asking them to do anything more than what we did."

A burst of shouts and whistling drew her attention away from Rock and to the center of the room. There was a line of women, and the three newly patched members went to each one, kissing them, touching their breasts, and squeezing their behinds. Clotille leaned in to Rock. "What the hell are they doing?"

He yelled out to the guys and then laughed. "They're picking which club girl they want to fuck. They've been talking with them, flirting with them, and watching them fuck different brothers for the past two years, but they couldn't touch 'em or do anything with 'em. Since they have their full patches, they can have fun with the club girls. I bet Puck's going to fuck Rosie. He's been pitching a damn tent for her since she came on board a year ago."

Clotille watched in fascination as each man yanked a woman to him while the others cheered and clapped with each choice. The women picked seemed thrilled, and they clapped their hands and kissed the men who chose them.

This is a strange world, but is it any stranger than the one I lived in with Frederick?

After the men left with their chosen women, the crowd thinned a bit as people filed out into the backyard. Rock wrapped his arm around her waist and guided her off the stool. "Let's get something to eat." He grabbed her hand and led her out the back door.

After securing a plate of ribs—it seemed like barbecue was all they ever ate—salad, green beans, and cornbread, she and Rock sat at one of the many tables strewn around the area and dug into their food. Eating whatever she liked felt like a guilty pleasure for her. For the past several years, her meals consisted of salad, steamed vegetables, and cottage cheese. Frederick dictated what she ate, and since he wanted her to be stick thin—a hard thing to be for an hourglass-figured woman—she rarely ate the tantalizing meals he required that she prepare for him.

A lump formed in her throat as she thought about what she'd put up with in her relationship with him. When she had agreed to become involved with him, she never would have imagined his lifestyle would have controlled her whole life. She'd erroneously believed his desires would be satiated with some kink in the bedroom, but she was wrong. By the time she'd realized what she'd gotten into, it was too late to change her mind. Things had already been put in place, and upsetting the balance would've been detrimental to—

"You want some more food?" Rock's voice cut through her thoughts.

"No, thanks. It's good but I couldn't eat another bite." She began to rise to throw the paper plates out when his hand on her thigh anchored her to the bench.

"I'll do that." He took her plate and slid off the bench, pitching their trash in the nearest bin. When he came back, he put his arm around her. "Let's go inside." He gave her his hand and she took it, following him into the club.

As she walked past several groups of people, she noticed many of them were in various stages of having sex: women on their knees giving blowjobs, men sucking women's tits, threesomes, and full-on fucking. *It's like a play party without the whips, restraints, and equipment.*

When she entered the great room, Rock pulled her close to him and said, "Let's dance." He grabbed her hands and flung her around while people stepped back and watched the couple. After several fast tunes, a ballad crooned over the speakers and Rock pressed her tightly to him, his arms looped around her waist. The touch of his hands burned into her skin and her heart raced. She circled her arms around his neck and placed her head against his chest, listening to his heartbeat as they swayed to the music, his scent engulfing her. Together they moved to the music as one, their bodies fused and heated as a sweet sensation formed between her legs. She was lost in his touch and while they danced, it felt as though they were the only two people in the room. Everyone but Rock ceased to exist for her and she held him tightly, never wanting to let him go.

As his hands journeyed down her back, landing on her butt, quivers ran up and down her spine. Rock's hard dick pressed against her, causing her heart to beat erratically. For so long she'd fantasized about being back in his arms.

"You're so sweet, *ma chérie*. Do you feel what you're doing to me?"

She tilted her head back and her gaze locked with his lust-filled one. She traced his jawline with her finger. "And do you know what you're doing to me?"

"I got a pretty good idea. I bet if I touched your panties they'd be sopping." He leaned down and kissed her neck, his warm breath tickling it. "Fuck, *chérie*, you're making me think dirty thoughts." His words shimmied down her neck and landed smack dab on her aching sex.

Bending down, he peppered kisses along her neck before taking her earlobe into his mouth and licking it while moving his teeth against its softness. "It's so good to have you in my arms. You're killing me."

Clotille buried her face against his throat; he placed a finger under her chin and gently lifted her head up. His gaze caught and held hers, and she gasped at its smoldering intensity. He dipped down and his mouth hungrily covered hers, his hand at the small of her back holding her flush to him. His tongue forged through her seam and tangled with hers as his breathing deepened. Desire raced through her, but then he pulled away—too quickly for her liking—leaving her mouth burning.

All around them people danced to the fast beats of Warrant, and they both realized at the same time that the slow song had ended a while ago. They laughed, his hand squeezing her behind, her head resting on his shoulder, the sexual tension still crackling between them.

"Let's go back to my room." He guided her toward the stairs and she readily climbed them to the third floor, lust spiraling though her.

Rock unlocked the door and she slipped in, turning to look at him. The sight of him took her breath away. He filled the doorway, his broad shoulders nearly touching each side of the frame while his bulging biceps gleamed with sweat. A cocky smile danced on his lips and she knew she was staring, but she couldn't drag her eyes away from him. He exuded such virility and savageness, and her body threatened to lose control. She wanted to lick every inch of him and then claw him with her nails, leaving her mark in order to brand him as hers only.

He stepped in, shut the door, and approached her, his gaze feral and sexy as sin. Heat flared through her like a flash fire. Then he was next to her, his mouth crushing hers and his hands scorching her skin as they slid under the hem of her dress, skimming her hips and thighs. Her body tingling from the contact, she drew his tongue farther into her mouth and sucked on it, his low growl hitting her right between the legs. Brushing her breasts against his sculpted chest, his hands cupped them as he teased her nipples to hard points between his fingers. She squirmed under his touch and he pulled away slightly.

"I want to suck your tits, *chérie*," he rasped as he slid her dress higher up her body.

When his hand slipped inside her lacey bra and touched her skin-to-skin, she threw her head back and moaned, gripping his shoulders so hard that her nails dug in. In one smooth movement, he'd pulled her dress over her head and tossed it on the floor. He trailed his tongue from her bottom lip, down her throat—where he paused to kiss the pulsing hollow at the base—past the creamy swells of her breasts, and finally rested on her impossibly hard nipples. With a growl, he drew her hardened nipple into his mouth and sucked on it. When she whimpered, he chuckled softly.

"You like that, sweetie? You're making me hard as fuck," he growled.

Instead of answering, she arched her back, thrusting her tits deeper into his mouth. His hands hadn't stopped exploring her, making her body tingle and hum as sexual tension flowed through her veins. Then his finger glided under her panties and encased itself between her swollen folds. His touch was like the spark of a match, igniting all her nerve endings. She moaned loudly and his mouth was back on hers, swallowing all her cries of pleasure. The deep emotions from their past expanded between them and they clung to each other in a passionate dance of want, need, and remembrance.

"I love that you're so fuckin' wet for me. *Chérie*, I need your hot, sweet pussy wrapped around my cock," he said huskily as he inched her backward toward the bed. When the backs of her knees hit the bed, she sat down, pulling him with her. He lay on top of her, their lips fused together as his palms skidded down her velvet skin before slipping under her ass, squeezing her luscious globes.

Drawing back slightly, she breathed in his ear, "I can't believe I'm here with you."

The molten steel of his eyes burned into hers. "I'm the fantasy that you've had in your mind." Then he kissed her again. Hard. Deep. Wet. He pulled back and their gazes held each other's, their lips raw with desire.

She shoved his shirt up and he tugged it over his head, kicking his boots off and shrugging out of his jeans and boxers as lust filled her eyes. He knelt next to her reclined body, his heated gaze roving over her nakedness. "You're so fuckin' beautiful. I want to taste and feel every inch of your body."

His chest hovered inches from her and she arched her back even more, trying desperately to press her tits against him, the desire to feel him against her skin overpowering. He chuckled and dipped his head down, brushing kisses across her cheeks and chin. He kissed and nipped her skin as his hands moved down her body. His mouth and tongue blazed a trail to her lacey panties and he grasped the waistband with his teeth, pulling them down as his hand lightly scratched her taut skin.

"Oh, Roche," she murmured. Desire coursed through her, lacing around her nipples and sending jolts of pleasure to her throbbing sex. She'd never felt this alive, this desired, this cherished since she'd lost her virginity to him when they were teens. The feel of his mouth on her skin, his fingers on her quivering thighs, brought tears to her eyes. *Careful. Don't go over the edge.* But at that moment, all she wanted was to feel him inside her, move in rhythm with him, and soar to euphoric bliss with his name on her tongue.

She looked over at him when he sucked in his breath, his shining black orbs focused on her glistening, shaved pussy. "Damn. I gotta taste you." He spread her bent legs wide and nestled between them as she watched him intently. Slowly he licked her inner thighs, moving closer to her mound but never quite touching it. Each time his lips came close to her clit, she thought for sure that would be the time he'd touch her and release the throbbing ache, but he kept narrowly missing it.

"I need you to touch me. Please." He chuckled against her inner thigh and goose bumps pebbled her skin from the warmth of his breath. "Please, Roche."

"You begging me?" He chuckled again.

"I am. Please touch me." She grabbed the back of his hair and tried to guide his mouth to where she urgently needed it to go, but he resisted her attempts.

"I'm getting there, *chérie*."

She moaned and attempted to close her legs so she could rub them together and have some relief, but his hands anchored them exactly where he wanted them to be. The sweet pain pounded and she tried to touch herself, but he moved her hand away. The tension and desire he built inside her was over the top, and her craving for him inside her was fierce.

"I bet you taste delicious." He looked up at her and grinned.

"Why don't you find out?" She held her breath in anticipation of his wicked tongue on her sensitive and madly aroused sex.

"You'd like that, wouldn't you?"

He scooted down a bit and lapped her in one long sweep from her puckered hole to the top of her hood. *Holy shit!* Her stomach did several backflips and her nerves sizzled and zapped as he continued to lavish deep strokes over her most private part. She moaned and gripped the sheet, balling it in her hands. He looked up and caught her gaze, his lips and chin glistening with her juices.

"You taste fuckin' sweet, just like I knew you would." He slid his hands under her soft ass cheeks, clenched them, and pulled her closer to his eager mouth. Dipping his tongue back between her engorged folds, he swirled the tip of it in her juices while he sank a finger deep inside her. "Too fuckin' good, *cherie*."

She wanted to reply but her throat was too dry and her building tension rendered her speechless. All she could give him were guttural moans as she watched him lick and fingerfuck her to orgasm. She was on the brink of exploding when his hand went behind her knees and lifted her legs over his shoulder. Her eyes widened when she saw his thick, long dick positioned at her heated opening. "Oh" was all she could croak out.

He smiled as he leaned down and kissed her on the lips, his tongue plunging inside and tangling with hers so she tasted the musky sweetness of her arousal. He backed away and opened the drawer of his nightstand, withdrawing a condom. Rolling the sheath over his pulsing shaft, he winked at her. "I wanna feel your pussy clamped around my cock, squeezing the fuck out of it." He held his dick in his hand and then, with one hard thrust, he buried himself in her.

Holy fuck! Her walls molded around his hardness, coaxing him in deeper as her arousal sent her senses reeling. He pulled out slowly and then pushed back in as his finger flicked her hard nub. Bending over, he kissed her again.

"You want it gentle or rough?" His words vibrated against her lips.

"Rough. I want to *really* feel you."

A wolfish grin crossed his face. "*Très bien, chérie*. I'll give it *all* to you." He withdrew and then began hammering her pussy hard and fast, pulling all the way out with each thrust before slamming back in. As he pounded her, his balls slapping against her ass drove her wild, and she thrashed and moaned each time he buried his dick inside her. With each plunge, her body moved up until her head hit the headboard. Leaning over, he placed a pillow behind her head and then continued his relentless, wild pounding of her dripping pussy. When his finger massaged the side of her beaded nub, the sparks that had been teasing her nervous system combusted; she flailed her head, wailed loudly, and shivered uncontrollably. Her release trembled through her, shaking her core with an intensity she'd never experienced before. A feral growl came from Rock as he stiffened and came, his pulses throbbing against her warm walls. Placing her legs on the mattress, he wrapped his arm around her waist and placed his damp forehead between her heaving breasts. Sweat misted over his body, and she raked her fingers through his hair before gently kissing his shoulder. He breathed deeply and rolled over, then tugged her close to him.

"That was fuckin' amazing. Damn, woman, you know how to please a man."

She smiled and lifted her head to plant a kiss on his chin. "You're amazing."

"It felt real good to be back inside you, *chèrie*. Real good." He kissed the top of her head as his fingers lightly tickled her upper arm.

She wanted to tell him she felt the same way, that she wanted to stay with him forever, but she couldn't. How could she destroy his life a second time? She had to face the reality that all she and Rock could ever have were memories. At least she'd given him a good one that night.

He held her tighter and soon his even breathing told her he was sleeping. She closed her eyes, happy to be safe in his arms again, even though it would be short-lived.

Chapter Thirteen

THE AROMA OF coffee drifted up the stairs and seeped under the door crack, waking Clotille. Peeking through sleep-encrusted lids, the bright rays of morning stabbed through the open shutters. She shut her eyes again as she soaked in the warmth of Rock's arm around her belly. She inhaled his familiar scent, then burrowed her head deeper into the crook of his arm. *This is the first time in forever that I've woken up happy to start the day, and it's all because of Rock. He's wonderful. Maybe I can make this work.* She brushed her fingertips over his arms and traced his colorful tattoos with her fingernail. *I never liked tattoos, but I adore them on him.* Shifting her body, she raised her eyes up at Rock and smiled when she caught his simmering gaze, a grin teasing at the corners of his mouth.

With a quiver in her stomach, she kissed his chin tentatively. He yanked her up, his mouth covering hers as he cupped one of her bare ass cheeks. She moaned into his breaths and slowly lowered her hand toward his crotch; brushing past it, she kneaded the insides of his thighs for several minutes. Inching her fingers upward, she curled them around his dick—it was hot and hard. He groaned and sighed as he tangled his hand around her hair. Alternating between one and two hands, she changed her grip and stroked the top and underside of his shaft. Midway through her hand job, she languidly glided her fingers down toward his balls, softly fondling them. A moan deep from his throat fell on her ears as she cupped his soft sac in her hand and gently squeezed it.

"Fuck, *chérie*, you're killing me," he said between pants.

Glancing up, she made eye contact with him and held his gaze as she scooted her hands back around his stiffness. She moved them up and down in a steady rhythm, only slowing when she saw the pressure building in his face. As he went rigid, she eased her grip on him and he grunted loudly, his hot seed erupting over her hands.

"Fuck, yeah.... Shit, that's good." His pelvis thrust forward as his hotness trickled down her hands onto his thighs and sheets. He jerked her to him and kissed her deeply before circling her in his arms and pressing her close.

She lay there quietly, listening to his breathing return to normal. When he'd dozed off, she went to the bathroom and washed her hands, returning with a warm washcloth and cleaning him tenderly as he slept. Watching him, his face peaceful, his breaths escaping from his parted lips, she felt an overwhelming connection to him. It was like a deep magnetic field was drawing her to him, and instead of fighting it, she wanted to give in to it wholeheartedly. *Fuck my family. Who cares what they think or expect of me.* A renewed vigor vibrated through her until she thought of the one person she could never risk hurting or losing. *I know what Frederick, Armand, and Mom will do to sweet—*

"What are you thinking about, *chérie?*" he said as he pulled her down on top of him.

She kissed him tenderly. "That I'm happier than I've been in a long time, and it's because of you." A shadow passed over his face and her heart lurched for a nanosecond. "Should we get some breakfast? I'm starving. What about you?" She smiled warmly even though a chill had begun to settle over her.

Rock sat up, dragged his feet off the bed, slipped on his boxers, and stretched his arms over his head. "We need to talk."

How she hated those four words. Men were always saying those four evil words to her, and it always meant something bad. With Luc it had meant he had cheated on her, with Frederick it had meant she would be punished, and with Rock it would probably mean she was a one-night stand. *How could I be so stupid to think we had a chance?*

"What are your plans? You know you can't stay here."

With her head down, she said, "You're already tired of me?"

He stood up, went over to his jeans that were rumpled on the floor from the previous night's fucking, and took out a joint. "Want one?" She shook her head. He lit it up and took a long drag, the smoke encasing him like a fly in a spider's web. "Banger's told me you gotta go. You being here puts the club in an awkward position. It's not me telling you this but my prez. You have any idea what you're going to do?"

Bringing her fingertips to her temples, she massaged them lightly in a feeble attempt to thwart an encroaching headache. She pressed her lips together and shook her head again.

"You wanna stay in Pinewood Springs?" He leaned against his dresser, his eyes boring into her.

Her heartbeat picked up as hope fought with despair inside her. "Do you want me to?"

He shrugged. "You gotta do what's best for you. You and I are just friends."

"Do friends act like we did last night?" she said softly.

He blew out a long breath. "Last night was fuckin' awesome and this morning was pretty damn good." He grinned and she wanted to slap him hard across the face because she knew he was going to crush her hope. "But a lot of time has passed between us. We're different people than we were in high school, and we got different lives."

"What do you see in your future? Do you want a family?"

He laughed and stubbed out his joint. "The last thing I want is to be tied down. I love the freedom of easy livin', if you know what I mean." He winked at her.

"You never want to settle down and have kids?"

"Not for a fuckin' long time. I don't have time for a family. For one thing, I'm an Insurgent. I'm the Sergeant-At-Arms for the club. There's no way I'd want to risk an old lady or a kid getting hurt."

"I know you belong to the club, but you could leave it if we rekindle what we once had."

He looked at her as if she'd gone insane. For a short moment, she thought he was going to have a stroke his eyes were opened so wide.

"Leave the Insurgents? That'll never fuckin' happen. When I joined the MC, it was a life commitment. A person doesn't stay for a few years and leave. It's a brotherhood of support, love, loyalty, and respect. It's who I am."

"I didn't mean to upset you. I guess I don't understand what the club is and how it affects you. I'd like to understand it so I can know you better." She clutched the sheet in her hand. "I honestly don't know what I'm going to do. After last night, I thought maybe you and I could try and explore this connection we have between us. It's strong, like a magnet pulling me to you, and I suspect you to me. You feel it, don't you?" She glanced at him.

He nodded as he stubbed out his roach in an ashtray on the dresser. "Yeah, I fuckin' feel it, but I wonder if it's just 'cause we got a history. I'm going to level with you, *chérie*. I don't know if I can trust you."

Her hand flew to her chest as she leaned forward. "Can't trust me? Why would you say that?"

"Are you fuckin' kidding me? When I needed you the most you fuckin' bailed on me. I hadn't even had my trial yet and you were back dating Luc. Don't you remember that, or do you have selective memory?"

Don't condemn me for something I couldn't help. I want to tell you everything, but in doing so, I risk losing it all. "I know it looked like I didn't care, but you must believe me when I tell you that I *never* stopped loving you. Not for one minute did my heart belong to anyone but you." Her voice hitched, and she noticed his eyes had softened a bit.

"Well, that's in the past anyway. Now I gotta deal with a pissed-off prez and what I'm gonna do with you."

"I'm not your problem. You don't have to worry about me."

"I've cared and worried about you since I first saw you kneel beside that rich fucker. I'm not going to abandon you now. I can help you get a job and place here, but I think you've got to go farther away if you don't want the fuckwad to find you. Have you heard from him?"

"Only texts telling me he's desperate to have me back." Clotille leaned back against the pillow. "I have to go home for a bit to straighten some things out with Armand and my mom. My mother's been frantically trying to get ahold of me, but I told her I needed time to think. I don't want her to know I'm thinking of going back to Lafayette. Not now, anyway."

"We got some club business in Louisiana." He raised his hand, silencing her. "I can't tell you shit about it, so don't ask. I'll take you home. We can stay at Isa's house until you decide to tell your family you're back. I'll be helping the club out and making my prez happy all at the same time." He walked toward the bathroom and said over his shoulder, "And it'll let me spend some more time fucking you. A good decision all around." Then he closed the door.

The running water filled in the silence around her. *I'm going back home, and Rock's taking me.* Fear and excitement battled within her, and she tried to suffocate the fear so she could relish the awesomeness of spending more time with Rock. *Maybe everything will work out. I must get my cards read by Madame Vincennes when I get to Lafayette. It never hurts to know what's coming in life, and when we get there, I can explain everything to Rock. Even if it means losing him forever, he has to hear me out.* She stretched out her legs and snuggled up in the sheets that were still scented with Rock's arousal and cologne. She closed her eyes and drifted off to sleep.

★ ★ ★

LATER THAT AFTERNOON, Rock knocked on Hawk's office. The VP was usually at home on Sundays with his old lady, but since all the shit started up with the Demon Riders and Gypsy Fiends, he'd been pulling in more hours than usual with club business.

Rock walked in and sat in the chair in front of Hawk's desk. The vice president tilted his chin and stared at him. "Where's your woman?"

"She's in my room, and she's not my woman. We're just friends. We grew up in the same parish in Louisiana."

"You could've fooled me. The way you were dancing last night came off as being more than friendly." He grinned.

"We have a history, but that was a long time ago. I don't want any woman. Anyway, she's moving back home. I'm just going to help her, and that's why I came in. I'm going to take about ten days off to take Clotille to Lafayette and visit with my people. While I'm there I can covertly look into what the fuck's going on with the Gypsy Fiends and the Demon Riders."

Hawk shook his head. "I don't want you to do anything stupid 'cause you're gonna be out there all alone. Insurgents don't have any major reinforcements in that part of the country."

"The Devil's Legions have a chapter in Lafayette, and I can see if they can steer me in the right direction. Bones has a few close friends in the MC, so he can give them the heads-up I'm coming and to play ball with me."

"Okay, but take it real slow and smart. We don't need any brothers vying for martyrdom. We need you alive. Got it? If things look bad, get the fuck outta there. I'm still working on seeing who's backing these Gypsy fucks. Damn! We can't let Dustin and Shack get a hold of those weapons. If that happens it'll be war for sure."

Rock nodded, then both he and Hawk sat silently as they contemplated the gravity of the situation.

In the outlaw world, declaring war was the same as nations declaring it on each other. The war was fought until one side or the other won, regardless of the casualties. Nothing less would do, and there weren't any rules. What made these wars so dangerous and bloody was that the clubs had no fear of the consequences; jail, prison, or death meant nothing to them. The only thing that mattered was preserving the brotherhood and its colors. Outlaw one-percenters mostly kept the battle in the rival MC circle, and it rarely spilled out into the citizens' world. But families, girlfriends, and sometimes parents and siblings were pulled into the violence and bloodshed. Many times support clubs to the main rival club would become involved and the confrontation could last years.

It'd been many years since the Insurgents found themselves on the bloody battlefields against a rival club. During the Biker Wars, the Insurgents had viciously defended their Colorado territory against the Deadly Demons. After years of car bombings, shootings, clubbings, and stabbings, the war-weary president of the Deadly Demons had called Banger to negotiate a truce. Both sides had realized the bloody corpses of their slain brothers had been enough. At the end of it, Colorado remained Insurgents territory and New Mexico belonged to the Deadly Demons.

Now, the Demon Riders wanted to take on the Insurgents because two of their members craved vengeance. The Insurgents would defend their brotherhood to the death, but they would prefer to avert a bloody confrontation with an out-of-control club. The Colorado brotherhood also had more to lose than they did back during the Biker Wars. Many of the brothers had old ladies and children, and the club had thriving businesses making their income mostly legitimate—a first in their history.

"When are you planning on leaving?" Hawk asked, breaking the silence.

"Tomorrow. Banger wanted Clotille out by then."

"You want some of the brothers to go with you?" Concern creased the VP's face.

Rock smiled. "Nah, but thanks. I got some personal shit I gotta look into." The mojo bag and two notes he'd received flitted across his mind. "I may see my old man in the pen. He's not doing so good."

"I'm sorry for that."

"Don't be. He was a fuckin' bastard my whole life. He's in there for offing my ma."

"I heard. Fuck, that must be hard, dude. You're a better man than I am for going to see him when he's sick. I don't think I could do it."

"Well, I told my sister I didn't give a shit if he died a slow death, but something may have come up. I don't know. I gotta look into it. That's the only reason I'm going to see him. I wanna make sure the right man's been paying for the crime. Fuck, I don't know. It's gotten complicated all of a sudden." Rock stood and shoved his hands in his pockets. "I'll let you know if something comes up with the Gypsy Fiends."

Hawk nodded. "Remember you're not fuckin' invincible. Later." He held his fist in the air and Rock returned the gesture, then walked out.

After drinking a few shots of Jack and shooting the shit with some of his buddies, he headed upstairs to tell Clotille about the plans. When he arrived at his door he heard her talking. He slowly opened the door and looked in, spotting her as she sat on the bed, her back facing him. Her soft voice said, "You have to take him away. I know Frederick will hurt him. I'd die if anything happened to him."

A pause, then, "I'll definitely pay you double what I normally do. I'll wire it. I'd like to leave tomorrow. I don't know if I'll be able to talk to you, but text me when he's safe." She grabbed the back of her neck. "I can't fuck this one thing up. Rock's taking me back so I'll have limited time to talk to you. Texting is best."

Another pause. She sighed. "I'll wire the money now. Please make sure he's safe. And I understand what you're saying, but I can't tell Rock just yet. The reason doesn't matter. I thought I could, but I just can't. I need a little more time with him."

Rock felt a knot form in the bottom of his stomach. *What the hell is she talking about? What can't she tell me? And who is* he? *Is it Luc?* His eyes narrowed. *Fuck! Something isn't right here.* He ground his teeth as tightness crept into his expression. He thought they'd worked past all this, yet there she was still hiding things and trying to trick him. *That's why she wanted to fuck me last night. She probably has another man in Louisiana and needs me to help her escape from Frederick. She's a vixen I can't trust.* Heaviness spread through him as images of the previous night and the morning assuaged him. *Damn, she's good. She almost had me convinced it was all real, that she wanted to try and make a go of it. Fuck her.*

He banged the door open and smirked when she jumped from the bed and whirled around. With eyes wide, she laughed nervously. "You startled me."

He glanced at the phone in her hand. "Don't you think you should finish your conversation?"

She stiffened, then placed the phone to her ear and whispered, "I have to go. Text me." She placed her phone on the mattress. "Did you play a round of pool?"

He shook his head. "Who were you talking to?"

For a split second panic crossed her face, but then she smiled. "A friend of mine from back home. I'm so excited to be going home that I called her up to share the news."

"Who's the *he* you were talking about?"

She hesitated for a moment, then quirked her lips. "I was talking about my brother."

"Armand?"

"No. Stephan."

Rock stared at her but she didn't flinch. Stephan was her younger brother and an embarrassment to the Boucher family since he was born developmentally disabled. For years they acted as though they only had two children, except for Clotille. She'd always talk about her brother and share funny stories about him to Rock when they were growing up. He remembered the day she'd called him out of the blue when she was a sophomore in high school and he was a junior. They'd drifted apart at that juncture in their young lives, and, on that day, she'd been very upset. She'd asked if they could meet in the alcove in the park, their secret hiding place from the cruel adults in their lives when they'd been kids.

He'd met her and had been blown away at how pretty she'd looked in her short skirt and knit top, her hair shining in the sunlight. Then he'd noticed her eyes were red and puffy, her face swollen. It had been on that day that he'd fallen in love with her. She'd flung herself into his arms and cried for what seemed like hours. Her parents had taken Stephan away and put him in a place for "children like that." She'd cursed her parents, especially her mother, who had been the instigator of ridding the household of Stephan, and lamented the emptiness in her heart since he'd gone away. She'd told Rock he was the only person who knew about her younger brother. Then, when the sun had begun to descend, she'd told him she had to go. As she ran from him, she'd stopped, turned around, and simply said, "I love you. I always will." Then she was gone.

"Rock? What's wrong?" Her voice heralded him back to the present.

"Nothing. I'd forgotten about Stephan. How's he doing?"

"He's happy. He's still at the same place so that's good. I had to sell all my jewelry to keep him there after my dad died and we had no money."

"Fuck. Is your mom paying for him now?" Her jaw hardened and she shook her head. "Then Armand? Isa tells me he's doing pretty good for himself." Again she shook her head. "Then how's he staying at that fancy place?"

She lowered her head. "Frederick. But then I suppose he'll stop that if I don't go back to him. So much that is good in my family is tied to him."

"Don't let all that sway you. You made the decision to leave him. You can't give up your life for your family. We'll figure it out." He crossed the room and pulled her into his arms. She shuddered beneath his touch. Hugging her, he stroked her hair. "We're leaving tomorrow. Pack real light 'cause we're going by bike."

"No heart attack-inducing mountain passes, right?"

He threw his head back and laughed. "No. I promise." Then he kissed her deeply, the urge to keep her safe and happy overpowering the feeling that she still wasn't telling him the whole truth. *I should take her to Lafayette and walk away. But how the fuck can I? I've been addicted to her since I was a boy. And like an addict, my sweet craving is going to fuckin' kill me.*

"Rock? I have to send some money for… Stephan by wire. I'm sending it to my friend to pay the facility. Can you take me to the grocery store so I can send a MoneyGram?"

"Why don't you send it directly to the place?"

"I don't want Frederick tracing it back here."

"Won't he be able to trace it to your friend? You're still leaving a paper trail."

"Are you going to take me or not?" Irritation had crept into her voice.

"Yeah, sure. We can pick up some stuff for the trip. We'll leave at nine in the morning."

"Then we better get to the store so I can get everything arranged."

He scanned her face. Although it didn't reveal anything, he knew without a doubt she was bullshitting him big time.

He grabbed the keys to his Harley. "Come on. Let's go."

She walked out and he followed her down the hall.

I wonder how this is going to play out.

I wonder if I'll ever be able to get her out of my blood.

I wonder if I want to.

Chapter Fourteen

THE SMALL WOODEN house crouched in the shadows under the sprawling boughs of a large cypress tree. Inside the abode, there were four rooms and an enclosed back porch where Madame Germaine Vincennes kept various concoctions for spells and potions. Customers usually came over in the evenings, under cover of the darkened sky, to pick up a healing salve, a love potion, or a mojo bag to bring them whatever relief they desired.

For over forty years Madame had offered her services to help others. She believed God had given her the gift of healing and warding off evil spirits, as she'd had an uncanny sixth sense ever since she'd been a young child. She charged only what it cost her to make the candles, powders, mojo bags, and spells. It never occurred to her to make money from her gift; it was enough that she could help an unsettled person find comfort and meaning in his life.

The small house was where she'd raised her children, laid out her husband when he was killed in a mining accident, and gave tea leaf readings for the distraught. She was a great-great-grandmother and lived alone, fiercely proud of her independence.

On a side table, among the numerous pictures of her children, stood a framed black-and-white wedding photograph. The bride sat in a chair with a bouquet of roses resting in her lap, and the groom stood behind her looking so handsome in a black suit. Upon waking each day, Madame Vincennes took the portrait in her hands and held it to her heart as she wished her husband a good day. After a half hour of prayers and recollections, she'd place the wedding photograph back in its place, knowing that one day she and her husband would be reunited.

The perimeter of the largest room was chock-full of mason jars stuffed with various herbs, stones, animal bones, and powders. Small vials of oils filled several curio cabinets. The scene was repeated on the back porch.

That evening, the old fortune teller rose from the chair, her knees cracking, when her doorbell rang. The wooden cane in her hand clacked on the wooden floor as she went to answer it. Peering out the curtained window on her door, her face tightened. *What does he want?* She paused, debating on whether she should let him in. A gust of wind rattled her windows at that moment and her cat skedaddled across the floor, disappearing under a worn couch.

"Germaine, I know you're in there. I have to talk to you. It won't take long."

Pushing down the apprehension that clawed at her psyche, she turned the lock and opened the door. He walked in and smiled at her. His suit was perfectly pressed, and there wasn't a hair out of place. "How are you?"

"I'm doing okay. Why are you here? You already gave me my money for the month."

"You're all business, aren't you? I came over to talk to you about something. Come on, let's have a seat." The tall man threw her a toothy smile, and she didn't trust him at all. Evil surrounded him.

He sat down when she did, then spread his hands on his thighs. "We have a slight problem here."

Madame Vincennes tucked a loose strand of silver hair into the bun on top of her head. She stared hard at him, her sharp blue eyes clear and young. Her orbs held the echoes of her youth, unlike the rest of her. The lines in her face were deep and saggy, like the skin no longer had a connection to the skull underneath it, and age spots gave her skin a coffee-stained look. She gave him a twisted smile. "What's the problem?"

"You've not been entirely silent about that night, have you?" His stare was piercing.

"I have. You made it very clear what would happen to my children and grandchildren if I told anyone."

"And receiving two thousand dollars a month hasn't been too shabby." He crossed his leg and smoothed down his pants."

"*Mon Dieu*, just tell me why you're here."

"Why did you send Rock the mojo bag?" His face was taut, his eyes narrowed into slits. A damp chill gripped her like a hand from the grave. "You didn't think I'd find out about it, did you? And the note telling him that his father didn't kill his mother was stupid." He pressed his lips together and they looked like a slash across his face. "Actually, it was… suicide."

This is the night I'm going to leave the Earth. Mon Dieu, if I'd known, I wouldn't have chastised Delphine this morning. I would've told my family I love them. Her eyes misted as she stated to her would-be killer, "I've been having what happened on my conscience and in my soul for too long. I couldn't let a son go to his grave thinking his *père* murdered his *maman*. I need to have peace."

"I understand." He rose from the chair and moved behind her. "And now that you cleared your conscience, I'll clear mine. I can't have any loose ends. You understand." Then he placed his cold hands around her skinny neck and squeezed.

Her hands flew up to her neck as she tried to pry his away, but she knew she was no match to his strength so she let them fall to her lap. She noticed the soil beneath her fingernails from constantly digging in her garden for her mojo bags and healing spells, and she was ashamed that her children would see it on her corpse. She would've cleaned them had she known.

As he choked the life out of her, her gaze drifted to the wedding portrait, a surge of joy filling her as she realized she'd see her François again. Then the pictures of her children and their families danced in front of her, and a heavy sadness weighed on her. She'd hoped to be around for a few years longer.

Dark spots shrouded her gaze.

The clawing panic of not being able to breathe began to dissipate until it was all gone.

Chapter Fifteen

They parked in front of a nice two-story brick house in a neighborhood where everyone had well-maintained lawns and shrubbery. Before he turned off the ignition, Isa and two children ran down the concrete walkway toward him. He grinned and his eyes sparkled when he saw his niece and nephew.

"Rock, you're really here," Isa said as she threw her arms around him and kissed him on the cheeks. "I kept telling Charlie I wouldn't believe it until I saw you in the flesh. Let me look at you." She pulled back and gave him a quick assessment, then threw her arms around him again.

"Mom, let us in," a young boy said as he tried to squeeze between Isa and the Harley.

"Hang on." Rock chuckled. "I gotta get off the bike." He swung his leg over the leather seat, then wrapped his arms around Isa and her children in a big bear hug. From the corner of his eye he saw Clotille standing off to the side, watching the family reunion. She'd done a great job traveling the long distance from Colorado to Louisiana on the back of his bike, and, to his surprise, he'd fucking loved her warm arms clinging around his waist. The way her tits pressed against his back was a major bonus. He normally liked riding solo but every once in a while, if a chick was an especially good lay, he'd reward her by taking her for a spin on his Harley. In his experience, chicks were suckers for that kind of thing. But having Clotille hold on to him was something entirely different. It was like they fit together, their bodies molding as one.

Don't start these pussy-assed observations. It would have felt good if any chick's tits were against you for that long. Remember, she's lying to you and keeping too many damned secrets. Not fuckin' interested in figuring it all out.

"Is that Clotille?" Isa whispered in his ear.

"Yeah." He turned to her. "Clotille, get over here and say hi to Isa. These two hoodlums are her kids." He picked up a giggling child in each arm. "Maybe we need to go shopping to get you some presents."

His niece's and nephew's eyes lit up. "Did you bring us anything from Colorado? Are the mountains really as big as they are in movies?"

"Michael! That's not polite." Isa's brows knitted.

"It's perfectly okay to figure out what kind of loot you're going to get. Yeah, I got you something, and yeah, the mountains are big as hell." He laughed and set the two kids down next to Clotille, who had sidled up beside him. "Isa, you remember Clotille."

Isa nodded as her eyes scanned the other woman. "Yes. It's been a long time. How've you been?"

Clotille smiled. "I've been okay. It has been a long time. Look at you—a house, family, husband. It must be nice."

Watching her children rifle through the saddlebags on the Harley, she shoved her hair out of her face. "It can be, and sometimes not so much, but I don't know what I'd do without these two *petits*." She ruffled Michael's and Aline's hair. "*Vite alors!* Let your Uncle Rock come into the house."

Rock pulled out a multi-colored stone with an acrylic dome over it and a tarantula sitting on it, immortalized forever. He handed it to Michael. "You can find these creeping around in southern Colorado. The rocks are found in the Rocky Mountains where I live. See all those gold streaks?"

Michael's eyes opened wide as he took the gift in his small hands and tapped on the dome. "Cool. Uncle Rock gave me a spider. Look, Mom. Is that real gold?"

Rock nodded. "Real gold flecks." He handed Aline a doll with long blonde hair in ringlets dressed in prairie clothes with several other outfits.

Aline's hazel eyes sparkled. "Thank you, Uncle Rock." She shyly took the doll he handed her and hugged it tightly.

"Let's go in the house. Charlie's still at work, but he wants to take us all to dinner when he gets home."

Clotille's eyes darted to Rock. "Yeah, well, we're kinda bushed. It's a damn long ride, you know?" he told Isa.

"I didn't even think about that. I'll call Charlie and tell him we'll go out tomorrow. We can have pizza tonight."

"Pizza! Yay!" The two kids jumped in the air and then dashed up the walk to the house.

Rock laughed and slipped his arm around Isa, pulling her to him. "I've missed you. Your kids are pretty fuckin' cute. It's good to be back."

She looped her arm around his waist and they went inside as Clotille followed behind.

When Isa and Rock were alone at last—Clotille had lain down for a nap and the children were playing—he sat at the kitchen table, guzzling a bottle of beer. "You mind if I smoke in here?"

"I don't want you smoking pot around the kids." She brought over a pitcher of lemonade and placed it on the table.

"The kids aren't around."

"I know, but the smell and all." She poured the lemonade in her glass. "Charlie wouldn't like it."

He slipped the joint back in his pocket. "That's cool. I can smoke later in the open."

A worried frown crossed her forehead. "Be careful. It's not legal here. I mean, if you really want to, we could go out on the patio."

He stood up. "Let's go." He ambled out back and lit up his joint, the mellow effect taking hold as he smoked. "Clotille doesn't want her family to know she's back in town. She really doesn't want anyone to know right now, so don't tell anyone, okay?"

"Okay, but why?"

He shrugged. "I don't know. She's got some shit going on with Armand and her mom. She wants to lay low for a while before she tells anyone."

Isa smoothed her hair off her face. "I never would've recognized her. But then I didn't really know her. She never came to the house when we were growing up. You always went to her. I just remember seeing her when I started high school and she was a senior. We never even talked. Are you two back together?"

He shook his head. "Nah. I'm just helping her out, that's all. She got herself in a bad situation in Colorado, so I'm just trying to make things smooth for her. She feels awkward being here 'cause she feels like she's imposing since you two didn't really know each other."

"Tell her I love having her here. And it would be great if you two got back together, especially since it seems like you both have been miserable without each other all these years."

He sniggered. "I don't remember being all that miserable."

"I'm talking about a real relationship, not sex. You know there's a difference. Henri is close to marrying. He and Suzette have been going out for over a year. Her family owns Petries, the department stores."

"I'm sure Henri loves her money."

She tapped his arm. "Oh, you. He's very much in love with her." She lowered her voice. "And her money." She covered her mouth with her hand and laughed.

"I'm done smoking. Let's go inside. It's too damn humid. I forgot how awful it can be."

After they settled on the kitchen chairs, she poured them both some lemonade. He took a deep breath and finally asked, "How's Pa doing?"

Her fingers touched her parted lips as she looked at him with wide eyes. "Not so good. He's in the prison infirmary. He was getting better, but he fell ill again. I'm real worried he's not going to make it." He jutted his chin out, his jaw clenched. "I was planning to see him. Do you want to go with me?"

"I'm not sure."

She licked her lips. "Think about it and let me know."

He shoved his chair back. "I'm going to check on Clotille."

"Are you going to share a room with her?"

"Not sure 'bout that either. *A bientôt.*" He walked out of the room and went downstairs to the guest room Isa had given to Clotille, knocking softly on the door.

"Come in."

He went into the room, making sure to lock the door after he closed it. "How're you feeling? It must've been a brutal ride for you."

She smiled. "It was pretty intense. I didn't think my butt would ever have feeling in it again. I guess twenty hours on the back of a bike will do that, huh?"

He chuckled. "Yeah. Imagine if we'd ridden straight through." He went over to the bed, bent down, and kissed her deeply. "That's for being such a good sport."

She grasped his arms and yanked him down before she sat up, the sheet falling off her. He held his breath when he saw her rounded tits and pink nipples, he reached out and pinched one of her nipples. "You got beautiful tits, *chérie.*" Dipping his head low, he pulled one of the buds into his mouth, licking and sucking it until it hardened. He fucking loved feeling a nipple harden under his touch. He moved his mouth to her other one. Her gasp made his desire heighten, and when she squeezed his inner thigh a low moan came from his throat.

She palmed his thighs, hips, and belly, then unbuttoned his jeans and slipped her warm hand inside. Breathing heavily he waited for her to touch his cock, but her hand stayed right above it, her fingers lightly pinching his skin. *Fuck! I'm going to blow my wad if she keeps up this teasing shit.* But the truth was he loved it. The women he screwed usually went for his cock right away and it was nice, but the anticipation he was feeling with her at that moment was more than hot.

With her other hand, she lifted his head and kissed him gently on the lips. "And that's for being such a kind soul and helping me out."

The desire in her eyes sent him over the edge and he crashed his mouth against hers, sucking her bottom lip with such intensity that he was sure it would be bruised. He wanted to fucking devour her whole. "What the fuck are you doing to me, *chérie?*" In response, she wrapped her fingers around his throbbing cock and squeezed. "Fuck," he groaned, then bit the side of her neck hard. Her whimper was his undoing. He gripped the sheet and tore it away from her, then ripped off her panties before he stripped. He searched through his jeans pockets. "Fuck," he said under his breath.

"What's wrong?"

"I don't have a goddamned condom in my pocket. Fuck. It's in my bag upstairs."

"I'm on the pill and I'm clean. What about you? The club girls have been around."

"I always use a condom."

"Not always… remember our first time together?" She smiled and took his hand, pulling him back to her.

"Yeah. That was the only time I did it raw." He ran his hands all over her body and feasted his eyes on her exquisite nakedness. With her arousal, the tips of her tits had become stiff peaks that taunted him. He pinched and pulled each one, each moan from her driving him wilder with desire than the last. As she arched her back he devoured her flesh with his teeth, lips, and tongue, her pebbling skin making him harder than he'd ever been. He wanted all of her: her body, heart, and soul. And at that moment, as he consumed her, he knew nothing less than that would do.

She was his fucking weakness.

And she knew it.

A couple hours later, they lay tangled in the sheets, completely sated with his arms around her, her hair covering his chest like a blanket. *I'm so fucked with her. Now that I've tasted her I can't walk away. Shit, how the hell can I be so wrapped up in her when I don't even fuckin' trust her? How does she pussy-whip me like that, and why the fuck do I let her do it?*

It was because her hair smelled like wildflowers in the spring, her skin was like silk, her lips were soft, and her pussy tasted like salty honey. He fucking craved this woman, and he was madder than hell that he did. Each time her scent filled his nostrils, her hand touched him, and her whimpers fell on his ear, his damn dick would twitch. He didn't want her. He'd written her off years back, decided she was a bitch of the worst kind, yet there he was getting hard again as she lay across his chest. *Damn!*

Maybe she'd bewitched him. He wouldn't put it past her to have ordered some kind of mojo bag from Madame Vincennes to entice him. What other explanation could there be? He'd never felt this way with all the women he'd screwed over the years, and there had been too many to count. She was the only one who grabbed him. But then, it'd started when he was eleven.

Fuck. I wonder if Madame has something to exorcize a sexy vixen who smells like heaven out of my life.

★ ★ ★

THE FOLLOWING MORNING, Rock woke up and reached over but Clotille's spot was empty beside him. Sitting up, he yawned and looked to the bathroom, but the door was open and the room was dark. Figuring she'd already gone upstairs for her morning coffee—she couldn't function without it—he rose to his feet and went to take his shower.

When he entered the kitchen he expected to see her sitting at the table with a coffee mug in her hand, so he was surprised to find his sister alone. She smiled at him. "Did you have a good sleep?" The twinkle in her eye made him grin.

"Yeah. Have you seen Clotille?"

"No. I thought she was still sleeping."

"No." He sent her a quick text and poured himself a cup of coffee. "I wonder where the fuck she could be. She's not answering my texts."

"She doesn't have a car, so maybe she went out for a walk."

"She went in a yellow car," Michael came in, his hand clutching the tarantula paperweight.

"Yellow car? Did it have words on the doors?"

"Yep. Mom, do we have any of the cereal with the colored marshmallows?"

Where the fuck did she go, and why did she take a cab? She could've asked me to take her. She's fuckin' playing her secrets game.

"Do you want some cereal, Uncle Rock?"

He ruffled the boy's hair and smiled. "Nah, I'm good. You're a growing kid so you need all that sugar." He shrugged when Isa glared at him and then stepped out onto the patio, plugging in Clotille's phone number. No answer. Concern swept through his body as he stared at the blank screen. *Where the fuck are you?*

He hadn't even realized he'd stayed out so long until he heard Isa and Clotille speaking in the kitchen. He jumped to his feet and rushed in, his nostrils flaring. "Where the fuck have you been?" he demanded.

She placed her hands on her hips and cocked her head to the side. "Good morning to you. Since you're monitoring my whereabouts, I met up with a friend. I didn't want to wake you up to take me. What's the big deal?"

"The big deal is I didn't know if you'd been hurt or fuckin' kidnapped."

Isa slipped between them. "I'm going to give you guys some privacy."

After she left, Clotille glared at Rock. "How dare you speak to me that way, especially in front of your sister. Am I your prisoner?"

"No, but you fuckin' should've left me a note, or answered your goddamned phone. And for the record, I don't believe your shit at all. You didn't want anyone to know you were here and all of a sudden you're meeting a friend. You better start leveling with me or you're on your own, *sweetheart*." His chest was heaving.

"I didn't think you'd get this mad, and I didn't get your call. My reception wasn't good."

"You fucking someone?"

"What? No! Why would you ask me such a ridiculous thing?"

"'Cause you're keeping shit from me and I don't know why."

She walked over to him and ran her hands up his arms. "I went to see Stephan. He was so happy to see me. It's been a long time… The last time I was here, I was only able to spend a couple of hours with him." She bowed her head down. "I miss him so much. I wanted to be alone with him. I hope you understand. Please, let's not fight." She leaned in to him and brushed a kiss over his jaw.

He stood rigid, but his anger and tension were melting under her touch, her scent, her nearness. *Fuck!* He wrapped his arm around her waist and drew her closer. "Don't fuckin' do this shit to me again. You need to tell me where you're going so I know in case something happens. You know Frederick's pissed at you. I wouldn't put it past him to figure out you're here and come after you."

"You've been in an outlaw club too long," she breathed in his ear, gently biting his earlobe.

"And you've got a real mouth on you, especially for being a damn submissive."

"You've liberated me."

"So you're blaming it on me?" He sounded stern, but the merriment in his eyes gave away that he was teasing her. "Give me your lips." And she did. He cupped her ass cheeks and slammed her against him so they were pressed together as one. Then he kissed her and she kissed him back, and they stood in Isa's sunlit kitchen kissing as though it would be the last time they'd taste and feel each other.

"Uncle Rock," a small voice said. He reluctantly pulled away from Clotille and looked at Michael. "Do you wanna go swimming with me, Aline, and Mom tomorrow? She told me to ask you."

He bent down on his haunches and looked the boy in the eyes. "You can count me in." He lowered his voice and asked, "Can Clotille come along?"

Michael looked her over and then nodded. "Sure, but you have to go down the slide with us. It's really fun, and Dad does it all the time."

"I wouldn't want to miss the slide. I'm a killer dunker, so I'm just warning you."

Michael chortled. "It's gonna be fun. I'm going to the day camp now. The bus picks me up. It's so fun. We play, swim, and eat our lunches."

"That does sound like fun. Does Aline go too?"

"She's too little for my camp, but she goes to one for little girls."

"Michael, the bus is here," Isa called out from the living room.

The boy whirled around and dashed out of the room. "See you later, Uncle Rock."

"He's such a darling little boy. You're so good with him," Clotille said as she sat down.

Rock shrugged. "I still can't believe Isa was the first one to have kids, and she's the youngest."

"Are you talking about me?" Isa walked into the kitchen, a wide smile on her lips. "Everything good now?"

Clotille nodded and Rock tilted his head. *For now. Damn, chérie… I wish I could trust you.* "Have you been to the bayou since *Maman's* land was sold?"

Isa pulled out one of the kitchen chairs and sat down. "Charlie and I went out there a couple years ago. It was so disgusting it made me cry. The oil companies are destroying the natural landscape. It's horrible. A big sign has replaced the shack on *Maman's* land. It's everywhere—Elite Power Inc. I'll never forget the name. The oil and gas companies are destroying the bayou."

"That's Frederick's company," Clotille said softly.

Rock jerked around. "That fucker is raping my mother's land?"

"Who's Frederick?" Isa asked.

Clotille and Rock exchanged glances. "Someone I knew in Aspen," she said.

"Well he must be pretty wealthy because his signs are everywhere in that part of the bayou."

"Did you know he bought my mother's land?" Rock said.

"I wasn't sure. I knew he was doing explorations in the bayou in the Lafayette area. That's how we met when I was still living here. I didn't know exactly where your mother's land was."

"The company is all over the bayou. They own most of St. Martin." Isa brought her leg up under her buttocks.

"I knew he was heavily involved in the St. Martin project, so I guess if I'd thought of it, I'd have realized it was where your mother once had land."

Is this what she's been hiding from me, that she knew that rich fuck had decimated our family's land? "Did you ever go to see what he was doing?"

She shook her head. "I wasn't deeply involved in his business."

Silence fell on the trio until Rock broke through the barrier. "When are you going to visit Pa?"

"Day after tomorrow. You want to join me?" Isa ran her finger around the rim of her glass.

"Yeah."

She smiled at him while nodding. He hoped he'd made the right decision. He hadn't seen his dad since the night he'd almost killed him. *Life has a funny way of twisting everything up when you think you got it all figured out.* He let out a long breath and went out on the patio to smoke a joint.

★ ★ ★

CHARLIE HAD INSISTED on taking everyone out for dinner, so Rock asked if they could go outside the parish since Clotille didn't want her family to know she was back in town. Charlie hauled everyone in his Chevy Suburban and made the drive to Baton Rouge, an hour away. They went to a Cajun restaurant, and both Rock and Clotille raved about the food. It was the first time in years that Rock had had authentic Cajun dishes, and he relished every bite.

On the way back, Michael and Aline fell asleep, and Rock nestled Clotille into the crook of his arm while he listened to the music of his favorite Cajun bands playing over the SUV's speakers. He smiled when Charlie leaned over and kissed Isa, that simple gesture warming him. *Isa deserves to be happy and with a great guy who'll treat her right. She—fuck, we—put up with such bullshit growing up. Charlie's good for her.*

Less than an hour later, Charlie pulled into the garage and he and Rock carried in two very sleepy children. When they'd tucked them in their beds, Charlie told Rock he was going to turn in. Rock grasped his shoulder and squeezed it, an understanding of friendship and gratitude passing between them before Rock padded down the stairs.

"This is for you," Isa said as she handed him a white envelope. "It was stuck between the iron grid on the screen door. I always check to make sure everything is locked and I saw it. It has your name on it. That's strange, don't you think?"

Rock took the envelope from her and saw that the handwriting was the same as the one on the note he'd received stating that his dad was innocent of killing his mother. "Yeah. Probably someone who knows I'm back."

"Didn't you say that you received some strange letters in the mail just recently?"

"Yeah." He tore open the envelope and found a folded piece of paper inside. He unfolded it and it read "Come to Madame Vincennes' home tomorrow night at nine o'clock. Wait under the cypress tree. It's very important. Come alone." He folded it back and slipped it in the envelope.

"Well? What does it say?" Isa said.

"Just welcoming me home. It's someone playing with me."

"Maybe one of the many girls you used to date in high school." Clotille laughed. "Isa's been telling me how several of them have been asking about you in the past year. Seems like many of them have recently gotten divorced." She poked him in the side.

He'd never told Clotille about the mojo bag or the strange notes he'd received. He didn't see how it would concern her, and he didn't want her to get involved in whatever was sucking him in. "Probably. I'm beat. I'm going to get some shut-eye." He turned around and walked down the stairs, the sound of Clotille's soft footsteps echoing shortly behind him.

They lay entwined in each other's arms, and the soft noises she made while she slept comforted him. A sliver of moonlight spilled into the room and the windows clattered in the strong wind. Sleep eluded him as his mind whirred with images and thoughts like a spinning top. Rock hoped he'd find some answers when he met whoever sent him the note the following night. He hated when he couldn't fit all the pieces of the puzzle. He'd thought for so long that his father had killed his mother, and now the puzzle was jacked up. Finding out Frederick owned the oil and gas company on the land once owned by his family was a shock to him. He hoped Clotille was telling the truth about not knowing anything about the fuckwad being on his mother's land. None of it made any sense to him: the strange mojo bag, the notes, and now an appointment.

He listened to the pounding of his heart as it drowned out the moaning wind.

Chapter Sixteen

Hawk leaned against the meeting room's wall as he watched the brothers file in. He and Banger had decided to call an emergency church once Hawk had found out some pertinent information from Liam. He'd been working extended hours to figure out where the Demon Riders were getting their money to purchase the arms from the Gypsy Fiends, and who was funding the Gypsy Fiends' arms deal. He couldn't let the fucking Demon Riders get their damn hands on such high-powered weapons. Just thinking of the bloodshed the Insurgents would be subjected to enraged him. The brothers would gladly die for the brotherhood, and he was no different, but when he thought of any harm coming to Cara, his heart squeezed. She was his everything, and he couldn't even begin to entertain the idea that he could lose her.

He knew the other brothers with women and children felt the same, so it was imperative that the weapons didn't fall into the hands of rival clubs, like the Demon Riders who were led by the fuckers Dustin and Shack.

"Hawk and I called this emergency church 'cause we found out some shit about the gun sale that's due to go down soon. The one with the motherfuckin' Demon Riders. I'll let Hawk take it from here." Banger sat down and gave his attention to the VP.

"After a lot of digging and hacking into programs and layers of security, I found out the Demon Riders have taken on a few more illegal activities. I wasn't surprised by that since Dustin and Shack made money the same way when they were giving Banger and the mother club the finger and doing whatever the fuck they wanted in Nebraska."

The brothers grumbled among themselves, cursing the renegade

Insurgents who'd sullied their club and disrespected its colors. Chas pounded his hand on the table. "I know I say this every time those fuckers come up at one of our churches, but we shoulda killed 'em when we had them." The members yelled out their agreement.

"I agree with Chas. I'm goddamned pissed at myself for letting over twenty years of friendship cloud my judgment. I should've ordered the execution of those two sonsofbitches. I fucked up and now the brotherhood is paying for it." Banger scratched his chin.

"What's done is done. We've all fucked up, so now's not the time to rehash old shit. We gotta deal with the fuckin' mess we have in front of us." Hawk took a gulp of beer. "As I was saying, the money to buy the arms is coming from the Demon fucks' newest endeavors. They're into prostitution—and they're using minors again—counterfeiting, forgery, and it's looking like they're dipping into trafficking women."

"Fuckin' pussies," Chicory yelled out.

"I say we should ride to Iowa and burn their fuckin' clubhouse down with them in it." Throttle shoved back in his chair, his tattoos shimming across his tense arms.

Hawk watched as the brothers screamed out what they wanted to do to the rival club. He had half a mind to take a posse and ride up to Iowa to kick some Demon Riders' ass, but he just leaned back and let the anger dispel. After many minutes, the brothers quieted down, resumed their seats, and looked at the vice president.

"Their businesses are something we gotta discuss at another time since we have to break the money flow, or else we'll be putting fires out like this for too fuckin' long. Liam found out where the Gypsy Fiends are getting their funding. It's from Frederick Blair." Hawk held his hands up as if to quell another outburst. "Frederick Blair is the money behind this deal. He's getting the weapons from a Russian dealer. And Liam's goddamned pissed that Blair didn't use him to make the deal."

"And Liam kissed his ass by asking us to be the fucker's babysitter. I knew the guy was a piece of shit the first time I met him. Thought he was too good for us, and he's as dirty as mud." Bones shook his head and crossed his arms.

Banger stood up. "Agreed. And the asshole's fired us from any future guard gigs. Like we give a shit." All the brothers laughed. "But I'm worried about Rock down in Lafayette by himself. The Gypsy Fiends are there, and I got a feeling Frederick fuckface isn't too far away."

"How the hell did a rich dude like him get mixed up with the Gypsy assholes?" Bear said.

Hawk cleared his throat. "According to what I uncovered, Blair owes the Fiends for helping him with a problem he had in Louisiana several years ago. Seems like he cheated some stockholders. Only a couple were brave enough to agree to testify against him, and they ended up disappearing. The whole incident had the markings of an outlaw club. The Gypsy Fiends also run the casinos that Blair owns in Louisiana."

Banger wiped his forehead with a tissue. "The more shit I'm hearing about this bastard, the less of a good feeling I'm getting with Rock being all alone in the thick of this. It seems like the rich fuck is in tight with the Gypsy Fiends. And he's still livid about that chick Rock's taken up with. Liam said he wants her back real bad, and he's not too happy about Rock plucking her out from under his fuckin' nose."

"She wants a man instead of a wimpy fucker," Wheelie said. "Can we help it if women love biker cock?" The men hooted and whistled as Banger and Hawk laughed.

After the noise died down, Hawk said, "I think we should get some brothers together and go to Lafayette, see if we can offer the Gypsy fucks a better deal with a much bigger price tag. Rock can help us out since he's already down there. Let's take a vote on it."

The vote was unanimous, and by the time church was over it was decided that Hawk, Puck, Throttle, Blade, Axe, Bones, Wheelie, Chicory, Tigger, Bear, Hoss, Blade, Ruben, and Chas would leave early the following morning to make the long journey to Lafayette.

As they drank beer and shots in the great room, Hawk looked around and a swell of pride spread over him. *This is what the brotherhood is to each of us. Love, support, loyalty, and respect, and we'll fuckin' come together to crush anyone who threatens that.*

He finished his beer and left the club, anxious to spend the night making love to his woman.

Chapter Seventeen

Rock tucked his 9mm Glock into his side waistband, his knife went down his boot, and he placed a large padlock with a bandana tied to it in his back pocket. The padlock was like a blackjack and could do some serious damage to someone; it was a favorite weapon of his and many of his Insurgent brothers.

He went into the bedroom. Propped up on several pillows, Clotille watched him, her face illuminated by the flickering screen of the television.

"Where're you going?"

He walked over to her and kissed her firmly on the mouth while his hands cupped her tits and kneaded them. "Club business." He pulled away, not wanting to arrive too late. He'd decided to get there early and hang out to see if he could spot anyone. He wasn't sure if it was an ambush or a person who wanted to help him, so he'd be prepared.

"What time will you be home?"

"I don't know."

"Is your business dangerous?" Worry creased her brow as she sat straighter.

"*Chérie*, life is dangerous. I'll be okay. Don't worry. When I get back, I'll fuck you real good." He moved forward and kissed her again, but when he tried to move away that time, she looped her arms around his neck and pulled him close to her while her tongue pushed against his teeth, coaxing his mouth to let her in. He parted his lips and her tongue invaded his mouth as she grabbed a fistful of his hair and yanked. "Fuck. You're making it hard for me to go," he said against her lips. Her tongue kept pushing in deeper, and his thumbs rubbed her taut nipples. His jeans had grown uncomfortably tight in the crotch, and he knew if he stayed any longer he'd end up fucking her until morning.

He gently loosened her arms around his neck. "I'll be back," he whispered in her ear.

"Be careful," she said, concern punctuating her words. "I really care about you."

He nodded and headed out of the room. Isa was sitting with Charlie watching television when he walked through the family room. "I've got something I have to do. Can I borrow your SUV?" The last thing Rock wanted to do was announce to the neighborhood that he'd arrived with his cams screaming. Charlie and Isa looked at him with wide eyes. "Don't ask any questions 'cause I can't answer them."

"The keys are in the basket on the side table," Isa mumbled.

"I'll be back later." Before the couple could reply, he'd slipped out the door into the inky night.

Rock had been to Madame Vincennes's house many times when he was a young boy with his mother. She had come to the fortune-teller to find out how she could calm the restlessness in her husband's heart. She'd leave the house with a bag of potions for all sorts of desires: curing the need for alcohol, keeping him home, making him love only her, and keeping the family safe. Rock couldn't remember a time when his mother didn't have a candle burning and some mixture of herbs she'd bought from Madame.

Hidden in the bushes, he looked at the old wooden house and wondered if Madame had seen how his mother was going to die in her tea leaves. He waited, his senses all on high alert, but except for the nocturnal sounds of nature, nothing was amiss. He looked at the time—twenty minutes past nine o'clock. *Maybe this is someone playing a joke on me.* Deciding to give it ten more minutes, he kept his vigil. Then he saw a figure dart from behind the house and approach the cypress tree. The figure's head moved right and left as though searching for him. He slowly walked out of the brush and came around the house from behind.

"You looking for me?" Rock said in a deep voice.

The figure yelped and then came closer, and he realized it was a woman dressed in black leggings and a long black tunic. Her black hair was pulled up in a high ponytail. She looked to be a little older than him. "Do I know you?" he asked.

"Let's go inside," she said in a low voice, her head constantly turning as she looked all around her. He followed her inside. Instead of turning on the lights, she lit a kerosene lamp, the flame dancing as it created long shadows over the wood floorboards. The flickering light illuminated their features, and the woman motioned for Rock to take a seat.

He sat down. "You going to tell me who the hell you are and what the fuck's going on? Why did you wanna meet me?"

She spread her hands out on the table. "I'm Madame Vincennes's great-granddaughter. My name's Tessa." Her blue eyes bored into his. "You're sitting on the chair my great-*mawmaw* was murdered in."

"What the fuck?" Rock jumped up.

"*Mawmaw* was killed a few days ago." Her voice hitched. "She was strangled. The killer used his bare hands."

Madame Vincennes is dead—killed? This is some crazy shit. How the hell does this involve me? "I'm sorry 'bout that, but I still don't know why the hell you wanted to meet with me. Did Madame send me the mojo bag?"

Tessa nodded.

"And you sent me the second note, the one saying my dad didn't kill my *maman*."

She nodded again. "*Mawmaw* asked me to send it because her handwriting was too shaky." She looked at the windows, then lowered her voice. "She saw who killed your ma, and it wasn't your pa. She swore it was two men, but she only really saw one. She got a good look at him, and he saw her. She ran as fast as she could hoping he didn't recognize her, but everyone in the parish knew *her*."

Is this for fuckin' real? Pa is innocent? "Why was she in our neighborhood that night?"

"She had to perform a healing for your neighbors a few doors down.

Their daughter was very ill with the fever. After she finished, she began to walk home and came to your house. She felt an evil presence surrounding it. At least that's how she told it to me. Anyway, she went up to it and was going to make sure your parents were okay. She always liked your ma. When she got up to the porch, she heard loud voices, moaning, and a gut-wrenching cry. She ran in and that's when she saw a tall man with a knife stabbing your ma. Your pa was on the floor, crying and jabbering. The man looked at her, and she told me he had the devil in him. He was pure evil. When she told me that, it gave me the chills. I'm getting them again just telling you."

"Why didn't she call the police? Why did she let my *maman* be gutted like a pig?"

"Don't blame *her*. Your ma was already gone when she got there. Her eyes were flat. The next day the tall man found my *mawmaw*, and he threatened to kill her children and their children. He told her she must never talk. And she didn't for years, but it always ate at her."

Rock sat there in silence, trying to make sense of the information he'd just been given. If his dad hadn't killed his mother, who did? Who was this tall man Madame had seen that night? He'd have to find him and tear him apart with his bare hands. "Did your grandma get paid to keep her mouth shut?"

She nodded then added hastily, "It wasn't like you think. She had to help the family. We were born poor, and she did her best to help all of us out as best she could. She had a bad dream a couple months ago and you were in it. She saw an evil force trying to swallow you up whole, and your ma was there trying to protect you but she wasn't strong enough. Anyway, it scared the daylights outta *Mawmaw* and she felt that it was your ma telling her to give you some protection and to tell you the truth about your pa. It killed her that you hated your pa for something he didn't do." She pursed her lips. "And now she got killed for telling you."

Rock's gaze locked with hers. "How'd the killer find out she told?"

Tessa shook her head. "I don't know. It's like evil always knows when something is comin' to destroy it. I met with you tonight to tell you the truth. That's what she would have wanted me to do. I'm also telling you to be careful. The evilness that destroyed your ma wants you."

Silence fell between them, the spitting of the wick in the kerosene lamp the only sound in the small house. After a long while, Rock stood up. "Thanks for telling me. I'm sorry Madame had to die, but I promise you I'll find the fuckin' sonofabitch who killed her and my ma. Where do you live?"

"Not so far from here."

"I'll walk you home."

"Thanks for the offer but I drove. I parked a few blocks away."

"I'll walk you to your car, then. I want to make sure you weren't followed."

She extinguished the kerosene lamp and darkness engulfed the house. They walked quietly to her car and he watched her drive away until he couldn't see her anymore. Then he went back to his sister's car and headed home.

★ ★ ★

ROCK SLIPPED THROUGH the back door and went downstairs. He didn't want Isa asking him a lot of questions, and he had to be sure the information Tessa had given him was true before he told his siblings. His gut told him it was. *Why would anyone want to kill an old lady who didn't have anything but concoctions of herbs, bones, and oils?* He quietly went into the bedroom and stripped down to his boxers. Watching Clotille's body as it moved up and down with her steady breathing, he pulled back the covers and slid in next to her. She stirred slightly and he flung his arm over her waist, pressing close to her. Vanilla mixed with sandalwood wisped around him and he kissed the top of her head. She craned her neck and smiled, her eyes sleep-filled.

"I'm glad you're back. How'd it go?" she asked in a soft voice.

"Fuckin' intense." He squeezed her gently.

"I tried to wait up for you but I fell asleep."

"That's okay, *chérie*. I'm fuckin' tired."

She pushed back into him, not leaving any space between their bodies. "I love being in your arms."

"And I love holding you, *chérie*."

He held her until she fell back asleep. For a long time, Rock stared at the surrounding darkness as he attempted to make sense of what the hell was going on. A couple months ago, life had been so much simpler. Now it was all kinds of complicated.

Simpler is way the fuck better.

Then sleep overtook him, and the tumble of thoughts was put to rest until morning.

Chapter Eighteen

THE GLOOM OF the day reflected the mood of the four siblings as they sat in the waiting room of the Louisiana State Penitentiary. Isa twisted her purse strap over and over around her fingers, Lille fooled around with her phone, Henri kept glancing at the large wall clock, and Rock stared stone-faced at the concrete walls. Being at the prison brought back rough memories; he never thought he'd see the inside of this hellhole again. Their father's impending death brought them together as they waited to see him at the medical department on site.

After a twenty-minute wait, a corrections officer told them to follow him. Inside the treatment center, they passed by rooms housing ill inmates, who were chained to a bed, overseen by bored prison guards idling away their time with TV and card games.

The officer stopped in front of a room on the east side of the building. Normally it would've received a lot of sunshine, but that day the sun was blocked by gray, dense clouds that carpeted the sky. "He's in here. You only got thirty minutes with him."

Rock held back and let his siblings go in front of him. Since he'd entered the medical facility, a cold clamminess had settled into his bones. For so long he'd hated his father for killing his mother, and he didn't know how to change that.

"Pa, can you hear me? We've come to see you. It's me, Lille, Henri, and Roche," Isa said. Rock entered the room and saw her bending over their dad, who was hooked up to beeping monitors with tubes of fluid flowing into his veins.

"Roche?" his father said in a hoarse, low voice. Isa stroked their dad's cheek and looked at Rock.

He walked over to the side of the bed. His father had aged so much since he'd last seen him: gray hair, deep wrinkles, hollow cheeks. Due to his illness, lesions dotted his face and his eyelids were swollen. *Fuck, he's lost so damn much weight.* Rock's stomach dropped. "Hey, Pa." His dad's bony hand reached out for his and he grasped it, surprised at how cold it was.

Lille and Henri came close to the bed, each of them rubbing their hands over their father's arms or legs. Isa sniffled and turned to the nightstand to retrieve a tissue. Henri sighed and shook his head while Lille brushed a tear from her eye.

Pa isn't gonna make it. This fucking sucks. Being in an outlaw club, Rock had seen his share of death, but looking at his dad dying and chained to the bed, broke his heart. For so long he'd hated this man, but now, knowing the truth, he felt sorry for him. The truth didn't negate that his dad was a mean sonofabitch to him, his siblings, and his beloved mother, but he didn't deserve to be punished for a crime he didn't commit while the killers roamed free.

Rock turned to his siblings. "Say your peace with Pa and then get the fuck out. I wanna be alone with him for a few minutes."

"To upset him?" Henri said. "I don't think so."

"Henri's right," Isa chimed in. "He's too sick, and I don't want you unleashing on him. This isn't the time nor the place, Roche."

He glared at them. "It's Rock," he gritted. "And I'm not going to upset him. I wouldn't have fuckin' come if I was going to do that. I wanna be alone with him. Fuckin' deal with it and get the hell out." He stood back, his arms crossed over his chest.

Henri shook his head again, then went over and whispered something Rock couldn't hear in their pa's ear. Isa and Lille followed suit, and then they filed out of the room.

Rock waited a few minutes before he approached the bed again. His father's dull eyes peeked out from red, puffy lids, following Rock's movements. He bent down low, his hand covering his dad's, and said in a hushed voice, "I just learned you didn't kill *Maman*. I hated you for years thinking you took her life, took her away from me, but I know better now." His father raised his eyebrows and a trickle of wetness leaked from his eyes. "I wanted you to know that. I wasted time hating you, and you wasted years doing time for something you never did. I'm fuckin' sorry about that, Pa. Fuckin' sorry." His father squeezed his hand weakly. "I'm gonna tell the others, but not until I find out who killed *Maman* and set you up. I promise you one thing: When I find them, I'm going to fuckin' kill 'em."

"*Merci, mon fils. Merci.*" His father breathed heavily as though talking had taken all his strength.

"You better wrap it up. Your time's almost over," the corrections officer said.

Rock stroked his father's cheek, then went out into the hallway and said to his siblings, "I'm done. If you want to say something more to him, go on." They shuffled back into the room.

Almost an hour later, as they drove back to Lafayette in silence, Isa received the call that their father had died. She burst into tears, Henri sucked in his breath, Lille moaned, and Rock narrowed his eyes and stared straight ahead, his stomach in hard knots.

I'm going to make good on my promise to you, Pa. I'm gonna fuckin' destroy the bastards.

★ ★ ★

"I ORDERED AN autopsy to be done," Isa said the following morning.

"Why?"

"Because I want to see why Pa died. I saw him two weeks before and he looked great. He wasn't that old, and I want to see what took him down."

A few days later, Isa leaned against the kitchen counter. "Pa was poisoned."

Rock set his beer down. "What the fuck?"

"The autopsy report came in. It said he was filled with arsenic. Someone in the prison poisoned him. The prison officials are treating it as a crime and have turned it over to the police. Who would want to murder him?"

"When you're inside, every day is a fuckin' battlefield. I saw inmates get killed because another guy didn't like the way they walked on a particular day. Crazy shit happens." *The killers wanted to make sure another loose end was tied up. Motherfuckers! They paid someone on the inside to kill the old man.*

"What a sad end to a tragic chain of events. At least now we can have the funeral. This is so awful. I hope they find out who did this and punish him."

Rock nodded. *Don't worry, Isa. I'll find out, and I'll fuckin' make sure they're punished.*

★ ★ ★

ROCK'S PHONE VIBRATED against his thigh and he grinned when he saw Bones's name. "Hey, dude, what's up?"

"Not much except a group of us is here. We're staying at the Devil's Legions' clubhouse. Fuck, it was a long ride."

"What the hell? What're you doing in Lafayette?"

"We got a lot of shit to tell you. Get your ass over to the clubhouse 'cause Hawk's called an emergency church. We'll see you in fifteen minutes. One more thing. I'm sorry about your old man, bro. That fuckin' blows. I know you hated him and all, but fuck, it still sucks."

Rock hesitated, then said, "Yeah, it fuckin' sucks ass. See you soon."

He quickly pulled his jeans on and smacked Clotille's bare ass as she watched him dress, her elbow propped on the mattress and her head in her hand. "What's up?"

"Some Insurgents came into town, and Hawk's calling an emergency church." He yanked on his boots and strode over to her, kissing her shoulder. "I'm just glad they didn't call while we were fucking." He winked at her.

"When will you be back?"

"I don't know. I'll call you. Why don't you go swimming with Isa and the kids?"

She shrugged. "Don't worry about me. I'll find something to do. I just worry about you, that's all."

He walked back over to her, fisted her hair, and pulled her head back, kissing her deeply. "That's sweet, *cherie*. Gotta go," he said against her lips. He picked up his keys and left the room.

It seemed surreal to be in church with only a handful of brothers in a clubhouse that wasn't the Insurgents'. After expressing the brotherhood's condolences for the death of his father, Hawk and the others caught Rock up to speed about the dealings of the Gypsy Riders and Frederick Blair. When he heard the asshole's name, his blood boiled. He then told the brothers about learning his father hadn't killed his mother, the murder of his father, and the fuckface's company owning a lot of the land in the bayou, most notably his mother's.

"I got this gnawing feeling in my gut that the rich fuck's the one who killed my mother. I bet the other guy was a Gypsy Fiend." He pounded on the table.

"Could be. I admit something's not right here. The first thing we gotta do is meet with the Gypsy Fiends' prez. Dogface, the president of the Devil's Legions, said he could arrange it." Hawk tipped his chair back. "The important thing is we gotta stop the sale of the arms to the Demon Riders. The rich fuck isn't going to give the Fiends a percentage of the profits in the sale of the weapons. We've since learned that they are buying the weapons through providing services to him like security at the casinos, extortion, roughing up some enemies, and a bunch of other shit. I'm pretty sure the Gypsy asses would like to have a lot of cash, and we can make this deal worth their time. We gotta play it cool, like this is strictly about business and not anything personal with the Demon Riders."

For the next two hours, the Insurgents talked about the execution of their plan and what they'd do if it backfired. After church was done they went into the main room of the Devil's Legions' clubhouse and met up with Dogface and some of the other members. The Devil's Legions didn't have as many members as the Insurgents, but they had a good relationship with the Gypsy Fiends, which the Insurgents were counting on to change the direction of the arms deal with their rival club.

Rock and Bones meandered to the pool tables to play a game with two Devil's Legions brothers. In that moment of camaraderie, Rock forgot about all the family drama and lost himself in the brotherhood.

★ ★ ★

CLOTILLE SAT ON the big cushy chair in the screened-in back porch, the ceiling fans cooling her off. She was engrossed in a romance novel when her phone rang. Her heart leapt; she'd been waiting to hear from Rock for the past few hours, and she'd been so worried. She grabbed her phone and said breathlessly, "Rock, I've been waiting for your call."

"It's a pity I'm not the Neanderthal," Frederick's crisp voice said. "I don't think I ever heard such excitement in your voice for me."

"What do you want, Frederick?"

"You."

She exhaled loudly. "It's over. I don't get why you don't understand that."

"Because I never lose."

"This isn't a game."

"You're wrong about that, pet. This is very much a game, and I've just raised the stakes."

"What does that mean?" she said, her heart thumping.

"You'll find out soon enough. Of course, the game can stop if you just come home like a nice pet."

"I know you can find another woman, a better one who is totally into your lifestyle. Believe me, you'll be happier with someone who wants what you have to give her."

"I want you."

"But you can't have me anymore."

"Ah, and that's where you're wrong, pet. Game on."

The phone went dead and ice flowed in her veins. Frederick could be a very cruel man, and she knew that he didn't like to be the one who didn't call the shots. He'd never leave her alone, even if he had another woman, which she suspected he did. He couldn't go without the control and a compliant submissive.

Maybe I should go back to him so he won't exact vengeance on the people I love. I know he'll kill Rock, but how could I ever be with any other man now that I've experienced him? I love him so much.

She decided she'd call her mother and let her know what was going on; plus, she wanted to see Stephan again before she left. When she'd gone to see him the day before, she'd switched the payments for his care to her and taken Frederick out of it before he did it first. She could anticipate what he was going to do because over the past few years she'd studied him meticulously. Her only hope was to anticipate staying one step ahead of him until he couldn't do anything to her. Then she'd disappear.

Chapter Nineteen

CLOTILLE LOOKED AROUND the Devil's Legions' clubhouse, noting that the main room was a lot smaller than the Inurgents'. The clubhouse was a house located on the fringes of the city. The yard was a patchwork of green and brown squares, and a big sign reading "Devil's Legions MC Private Club, Bikers Only" hung on a chain link fence. Several German shepherds roamed the backyard, barking incessantly as the women and other bikers entered the club.

The main room was in the basement, and its concrete floor was left bare. The walls were painted black, a large, cloth banner of a skull and crossbones hung against the back wall, and the club's logo—devil with fire—hung over the small bar that had a few wooden barstools around it. A pool table, big screen television, and two tattered couches completed the room. There were a lot of bikers, and under the low lights Clotille would've thought she was at an Insurgents' party. The women were the same: heavy makeup, long hair, overly glossed lips, partially exposed butt cheeks, and big breasts bursting out of too-tight tops. Several of the women were fused against the men, but the majority strolled around the room waiting for the urge to strike one of the bikers. As with all MC parties, there was a disproportionate amount of men than women.

When Rock called her and told her he'd pick her up for a club party, she was happy she'd bought the short black skirt when they'd gone shopping in Baton Rouge. She paired it with a cute black lace crop top, a pair of short boots with a three-inch heel, and a ton of silver bangles on each arm. Large silver hoops and smoky eyes completed her look.

She'd stayed in her room waiting for Rock to text her, not daring to venture upstairs and endure the stares of Isa and Charlie. She normally dressed a bit more conservatively, but since she was going to a club party she'd pulled out all the stops. Sometimes not giving a damn was liberating.

Rock came into the room, startling her. "Oh. I thought you were going to text me."

"I gotta use the bathroom, *chérie*." When he came out, she was putting her lipstick in her purse. His low whistle made her spin around. "Fuck, you look tempting and damn gorgeous. Get over here."

The smoldering flame she saw in his eyes sent an electric tremor through her. Smiling, she shook her head. "That's for later."

"Woman, I said get your ass over here." She slowly walked toward him but he reached out, grabbed her hands, and jerked her roughly to him. "You're taking too fuckin' long." His demanding lips caressed hers, sending her stomach into a wild swirl. His hand slid underneath her skirt, his fingers kneading her skin as they inched up toward her ass. When they touched her bared cheeks, he grunted. "You're wearing a fuckin' thong. You're so damn sexy."

She let him run his hand over her firm globes while she pressed against him, feeling the bulge in his jeans tighten. Placing her hands on his chest, she pulled back a bit. "We need to get going."

"I need you bad, *chérie*."

She laughed and twisted out of his arms. "You're so impatient. Anticipating something is sometimes more enjoyable than getting it."

"Never been good with patience, and anticipation is fuckin' overrated. Get your ass back over here."

She snatched her purse off the dresser and opened the door, stepping out. Glancing over her shoulder, she chuckled. "Not going to happen. Let's go." She was sprinting up the stairs when he came up behind her, his arms locking around her waist. She cried out playfully, "Let go of me."

Rock nuzzled her neck and whispered, "I'm never letting you go, *chérie*." His hands scorched her exposed midriff as he showered her neck with kisses.

"Are you two going out?" Isa's voice rang out from the kitchen.

Pulling away from Rock, Clotille straightened her hair. "Yes. Some friends he knows are throwing a party." She suppressed her laughter as Rock swatted her butt until they reached the top of the stairs.

"We may crash at the clubhouse. We'll see you." He held the door open for Clotille and soon they were riding toward the Devil's Legions' party.

Unlike the Insurgents' parties, this one didn't have any food except for pretzels, peanuts, popcorn, and chips—hardly the best choice for dinner, but it would have to do. Many men checked her out boldly, and she buried herself deeper and deeper into Rock's chest. Even though she should have been used to it after years of male attention, she wasn't. She hated men ogling her now as much as she had back when she'd been in middle and high school.

"What's up, *chérie*?"

"Nothing much. Is there somewhere we can sit? My feet are aching."

"Sure. You should've told me sooner." Taking her hand, he pushed through the crowd and went to a couch that had several people on it. Squeezing in at the end, Rock sat down and tugged her on his lap. "Better?"

Next to them a man was getting a blow job from a naked blonde woman who was fingering herself as she worked the biker's dick. "I'm not sure if it's *better*, but it's more comfortable."

He laughed and placed his hand on the back of her neck, bringing her face close to his. "You're so fuckin' adorable, *mon petit chou*." He kissed her, then nibbled her earlobe.

"*Mon beau trésor*." Burying her face in his neck, she pressed a kiss there. His low groan vibrated against her, and she felt his hardness under her thighs.

Bones and Puck came over, their arms around a stacked, inebriated brunette each. "Hey, dude, this fuckin' party rocks. It's great to have new pussy." Bones laughed and kissed the woman with him deeply while he cupped one of her tits. "Puck's enjoying the shit outta being a full patched member, aren't you?" The newest member of the Insurgents bobbed his head in agreement while Rock and Bones laughed. "You and your woman wanna do some sharing?"

Clotille looked quickly at Rock, her stomach tightening. When he shook his head, she relaxed and sank deeper into him.

"Do you wanna watch?" Bones said.

Rock put his lips to her ear. "You wanna watch them fuck? It can be hot."

She stiffened. "Do you want to?"

"It's up to you, but there's no way we're fucking in front of them. I'm not letting anyone see your body but me. It's definitely your call. I'm already hot for you without watching another couple get it on."

She brushed her lips across his ear. "I feel the same about you. I'm not interested."

Rock placed his hand on her thigh and squeezed. "Nah, we're good, Bones. You and Puck go have some fun."

As the night wore on, the bikers and the women became drunker, more drugged out, and hornier, and Clotille felt like she was at a porn festival. Everyone around her was going at it, and the only ones left in the room who were still sitting or standing upright were her and Rock, Hawk, Chas, and Axe. The four brothers were drinking shots and talking Harleys and "best of" lists for biker songs, movies, rallies, and a slew of other categories. After a while, Hawk stood up from the couch and announced he was turning in. He stepped over different couples having sex and headed downstairs.

"You getting tired, *chérie*?" Rock stroked her cheek and she nodded. She slipped off his lap and he held her hand as they maneuvered down the stairs, Chas and Axe following them.

The Devil's Legions had roomed all the brothers together who wanted to fuck, and the ones who didn't were paired up separately. Since the club wasn't that big, rooms for guests and those crashing overnight were limited. Rock and Clotille lucked out; there was one empty room left since a couple of bikers from their New Orleans chapter left that night.

Before Rock closed the door, he had Clotille in his arms, kissing and biting her. The slow flame of desire that had been burning through her ever since he'd come home to pick her up for the party exploded with the fiery kisses he was stippling along her charged body.

"Fuck, I've been wanting you all night. I'm ready to burst." His hoarse voice pebbled her skin and skimmed over her, from her stiffening nipples down to her damp sex. "You turn me way the fuck on all the time. I can't get enough of you. Damn, woman. What kind of mojo shit did you do to me?" He kicked the door closed and slammed her against it, grabbing her arms and pinning them over her head.

Clotille was wild with passion and her legs weakened by his demanding touch. The slip of his hand under her top made her hold her breath as his fingers stroked their way to her bra. He reached inside it and pulled out one of her breasts, his thumb and index finger pinching the aching bud to hardness. He pulled on it and she yelped, which seemed to please him. Shoving her top over her large tits, he took the other out of her bra and pushed them together, licking, biting, and pinching them. She writhed under his wicked touches and leaned eagerly into him, craving more. Each time he bit one of her red tips was like a hot poker straight to her wet pussy. "Oh, Rock. You're driving me crazy. I love the way you touch me."

"I love your tits, *chérie*. I could play with 'em all day." One of his hands went under her skirt and his finger slipped under the fabric of her small thong. "You're sopping. I love that you're so wet for me. I can't wait to taste your juices." His smooth-as-whiskey voice melted over her and she moaned.

She fisted his T-shirt in her hands, shoving it up until he pulled away from her briefly and yanked it over his head. She dropped her arms and grasped his shoulders as she tilted her head down and traced his chest tattoo with her tongue. His lust-filled gaze caught hers as she licked his tats while her fingertip moved back and forth over his nipples, flicking them occasionally.

"Fuck, Clotille," he growled. He pushed her hands away and

dropped to his knees, bunching up her skirt and tucking it in her waistband. Licking his lips, he swiped his tongue on each side of her inner thighs before he pulled the skirt down around her ankles, helping her step out of it.

She bucked from the intensity of the contact and the heat of his tongue lapping at her juices. "So good," she murmured, grabbing a handful of his hair and tugging at it.

"You taste fuckin' amazing, *cherie*." The vibration of his lips against her pussy as he spoke made her tingle all over from both immense pleasure and sweet pain. The sounds he made as he moved his tongue all around her wetness drove her beyond insane.

She pulled so hard at his hair that he stopped and said, "Fuck, *cherie*. Not so damn hard." He chuckled and resumed his steady licking, over and over until his tongue delved into her slick slit. At that moment, white heat burst inside of her, spreading sizzling embers to all her nerves. She screamed out her climax, her legs losing all muscle control.

He stood up and scooped her in his arms, bringing her over to the bed. As she whimpered he kissed her damp face, slowly peeling off the rest of her clothes so she lay naked and trembling on the sheets. He stripped off his clothes and lay beside her, tucking her into his side as he stroked her hair.

When the rush of euphoria calmed to a pleasurable hum, she looked up and met his eyes as they watched her. She smiled and strained up to kiss him tenderly. His hand slid down her back and rested on her ass cheek, his fingers digging in. Her kiss intensified and she pushed her tongue into his mouth. He tangled his around hers and the harder they probed each other's mouths, the hotter they got until his cock was poking into her and her stiff nipples jutted into him. She squeezed her body closer to his, rabid for the feel of his skin against hers.

"Come on top of me," he said, lying down on the bed. Once she'd knelt and straddled him, facing away from him, he guided her down until she was lying on his chest, her head resting on his shoulder. Rock put his hand under her chin, tipped her head back, and kissed her deeply. His hands covered her tits, kneading them while she moaned into his mouth. "Play with yourself," he whispered against her lips.

Clotille lowered her hand and buried her finger into her pussy, wet with arousal. She slowly stroked her clit while she gyrated against him. As she fingered herself, Rock pinched and squeezed her tits while he bit and licked her neck and shoulders. Tingling pleasure skipped over her body as the tension in her sex rose.

He gently moved her hand away and replaced it with his as he entered her from below. His thick cock filled her, and she loved the way her warm walls molded around his hardness. As he thrust up and down, his cock stimulated her G-spot, and the way he was rubbing her clit stoked a desire that was hotter than fire.

"You like that, *chérie*?" he asked as he kept thrusting in and out of her, his finger still stroking her clit, his hand squeezing her tit, and his mouth biting her neck between his pants. She was on fucking sensory overload, and just when she thought she wasn't going to be able to take it anymore, he slid his hands under her back. "Sit up and ride my cock hard."

She sat up, her back facing him, and began grinding on him as he pushed against her. Then she bounced harder up and down on his magnificent dick; it felt so good inside her. He was breathing heavily when he grabbed her ass and massaged it, his fingers sinking into her flesh. "I love your ass, *chérie*. You want me to play with it?"

Holy fuck! "I love that."

"You do? Fuck yeah." He spanked her ass lightly, then increased the pressure until her cheeks were red and she was moaning in pleasure as she alternated between grinding and bouncing up and down. "Lean forward and fuck me good."

She leaned forward and rocked in and out while she lightly cupped and played with his balls. The wave was building in her and her insides tensed in anticipation of the flood of pleasure ready to combust. When he pushed his finger inside her puckered hole, she couldn't hold it back any longer, exploding in thousands of sizzling pieces as the walls of her pussy clamped around him. "Roche!" Her voice was raw and unrecognizable to her.

Rock's feral growl came next as he gripped her ass and ground against her, spilling his warm seed inside her. "Clotille. Fuck!" Behind her, he lay breathing heavily.

She bent down, her head between his legs as her body slowly returned to normal. He stroked her damp back and guided her off him as he eased out of her. Drawing her close to him, he placed her head against his heart, the thrumming of it comforting her. He kissed her head. "You're incredible, *chérie*." His words warmed her and she snuggled closer to him. He grabbed the sheet that lay tangled next to him and flung it over them, then whispered, "I'm happy you're back in my life."

"Me too, Rock. I waited so long for us to be like this. There's so much I want to tell you. That I *have* to tell you."

"Shh… we got time for that. For tonight, let's enjoy what we just experienced. It was the best fuckin' I've ever had."

"And it was the most intense I'd ever come before."

"We're good together. I always knew that. Life just kept fuckin' up what we had. This time we won't let that happen."

"I never want us to be apart," she whispered. "There are things we have to talk about. I've wanted to explain about Luc and—"

His deep breathing told her he was asleep; she'd have to talk to him another time. With his arm snug around her, it was like the years that had separated them disappeared into nothingness. Feeling safe and happy, she closed her eyes and fell asleep.

Chapter Twenty

Armand reclined in his leather chair and observed the well-kept garden in front of the Cathedral of St. John the Evangelist in downtown Lafayette. Completed in 1916, the cathedral's red and white brickwork was built in the Romanesque Revival style. It was a slice of history amid the modern buildings surrounding it. He glanced at his watch when the bells from the octagonal steeple tolled. He silently counted along with each strike as the person on the other end of the phone continued his tirade about "their agreement."

He'd chosen his office just for the unobstructed view of the cathedral, and he'd usually swivel his chair to face it when he was on the phone. At that moment, he wasn't interested in what Frederick was saying; he just wanted him off the phone. If Clotille didn't want to stay with him anymore, it was her choice. He sighed; his sister had been a pain in the ass ever since he could remember. Over the years, he'd tried to guide her, but she was willful and spoiled thanks to their father, and there was nothing he could do about it. When she'd taken up with the family's housekeeper's son, he'd been appalled just as his mother had been, and he'd pushed Luc at her so she'd forget the white trash who had entered her life. But she hadn't wanted Luc, and now she was throwing in the towel with Frederick—a man who could give her everything. In Armand's opinion, Clotille had never been the same since she and Roche became friends. He shook his head, then focused his attention back to the phone.

"I don't know what you want me to do about it. I agree that Clotille has broken her agreement, but I don't even know where she is."

"Your business wouldn't even be where it is if it weren't for me.

Remember, your debt still hasn't been paid. I don't think you want to go back to where you were before I stepped in to save your ass, do you? You love money, and you squander it—that's your weakness."

Armand rubbed the bridge of his nose with his thumb and index finger. "Again, I don't know where she is. She hasn't called me or my mother."

"She's in your fucking backyard." Frederick's anger over the phone was palpable and Armand cursed Clotille for messing up *again*. *She's such a disgrace to the family, just like Dad was.* "Did you hear me? She's in your goddamned city."

"Clotille's in Lafayette? That can't be true. She would've contacted me, or at least our mother. You're mistaken."

"I don't make mistakes. She's there with that lowlife biker. Rock's his name. She left *me* for a *biker*. It's so ludicrous."

"Rock? Oh yeah, Roche. They knew each other many years ago. I just can't believe she hasn't called our mother."

"I can't believe any of this. That goddamned piece of trash has made her forget who she is. I'm not surprised at all by what she does anymore."

"Have you heard from her?" Armand said.

"We spoke a couple days ago."

"Did she tell you she was in Lafayette? Is that how you found out? She was probably trying to throw you off." Armand glanced at his watch; he'd been on the phone with Frederick for over an hour listening to him lament about losing Clotille. *He fucking thinks she's the only woman around. He has so much money he could get any woman he desires. Clotille isn't that great to carry on like he is. Mom's going to be beyond pissed when she finds out Clotille's been in Lafayette with Roche and hasn't even bothered to call.*

"She didn't say where she was. I know a few guys in the Gypsy Fiends, a local motorcycle club. They told me. Seems like another club—the Insurgents—are trying to muscle in on a deal I have going. Anyway, they said Clotille came with the biker and they've been in

Lafayette for over a week."

"I can't believe it. I'll try and call her and see what's going on. I have to end our conversation. I'm meeting my girlfriend for drinks." Jolene had arranged a small party to meet for happy hour at a new chic bar downtown, and she would be dour for most of the evening if he were late.

"You better make this right, Armand, or there'll be hell to pay, not just for Clotille but for you as well. I do *not* intend to just walk away. Clotille is mine until I tell her she isn't. Do you understand me?"

"Yes, I do."

"Good, then you know what needs to happen."

"I'm surprised you haven't come to Lafayette."

"I was there a few days ago on some… business. At that time, I didn't know she was there."

"I didn't know you were in town. You should've called me and we could've met up."

"It was a very short trip. There was something I had to do."

"Gotcha. I hate to do this, but I do have to go. Jolene doesn't like it when I keep her waiting."

Fredrick's dry laugh sounded through the phone. "You need to be better in controlling your woman unless your scene is having the woman control you."

"My scene right now is getting off the phone so I can clear up my desk and meet Jolene. We'll talk soon. I'll try and call Clotille and see if I can't convince her to go back to you."

"She'll come back to me," Frederick said in a low, hard voice. "Either dead or alive, I will have my pet. Remember that." The phone went dead.

Armand shook his head, cleared off his desk, and scampered out of the office.

Chapter Twenty-One

Rock walked back into the kitchen and grabbed a paper towel to dry his hands. "This time the water ran clear, so I put some salt in with it to make sure the crawfish are totally cleaned." Rock had watched his mother prepare crawfish boils since the time he could walk, and while he was in the back rinsing and filling the tub with water several times to clean the crawfish, he felt as though his mother were watching him.

"We're almost done with cutting up the vegetables. We'll have to boil the craw in batches." Isa rushed around the kitchen while Clotille cut up the potatoes and halved the corn on the cob.

Rock liked watching Clotille make Cajun food; her eyes always lit up. A few nights before, she'd been humming while she'd blended the spices for the killer jambalaya she'd prepared. Watching her sway her hips to the tune had made him damn horny, and if Isa and her kids hadn't been in the next room, he'd have had Clotille bent over the counter, licking some sweet paprika and cayenne pepper off her firm globes as he slammed into her pussy.

Fuck, just thinking about it makes me hard.

"I hope your friends will like the food," Isa said as she placed the cut-up potatoes, celery, corn, mushrooms, onions, and garlic in a big bowl.

"They're easy—they like anything that has beer as an accompaniment." Rock popped the top of his beer can. "And I bought a shitload of it."

"Clotille made a hot and spicy blend of seasoning for the first pot, and I made a milder one for the other pot. Not everyone likes it hot." Isa wiped her hands on the dish towel.

"Fuck, will you calm down already? It'll be fine. Hot and spicy is just the way I like it," he said in a gravelly voice, winking at Clotille when she looked up and met his gaze. He groaned inwardly when the tip of her pink tongue touched her top lip. What he wouldn't do to be able to suck it into his mouth and play with it.

"I've just never entertained a bunch of bikers before." Isa laughed nervously. "Charlie's so damn excited to see all the motorcycles. He's been dying to get one but I won't let him. I have enough to worry about without him having an accident."

"He must be bummed. Hell, if you wanna ride, you gotta do it. It's in your blood. You should let him have one." Rock drifted his gaze back to Clotille and watched how her tits bounced up and down as she chopped the parsley vigorously. *I wish she were bouncing like that on my cock. I'm pitchin' a damn tent. Fuck, I didn't know it was so hot to watch a woman cook.*

"I got Charlie to let it rest, but since you've been here with your badass bike he's started up again about it. Now he'll be impossible after seeing all the bikes tonight."

"Yeah, and Hawk—he's our vice president—has a wicked Harley. He customized it all himself. It fuckin' rocks."

"I didn't think I'd like riding on one, but I have to say that I love it. At first I was scared shitless, but now I enjoy the ride." Clotille pushed a fallen strand of hair off her forehead with her forearm.

Rock chuckled. "The first road I took you on was hairpin turns all the way. It wasn't a good introduction to riding." *I love the way you put your arms around me, your fingers slipping down on my dick whenever I hit a bump. Definitely enhances the ride with you clinging onto me.*

Charlie walked in and stole a stalk of celery from the vegetable bowl. "I heard my name. What things are you telling them about me?" He came behind Isa, wrapped his arms around her small waist, and pulled her back to him. Nuzzling her neck, he said, "Are you saying good or bad things about me, *chouchou*?"

Isa giggled and pretended to be embarrassed, but Rock knew she was loving every peck Charlie was bestowing upon her. "She's telling us you want a Harley, dude."

A big grin broke over his face. "I've been thinking about getting a motorcycle." He kissed her neck again when her brow furrowed. "Not sure about a Harley."

"What the fuck? A Harley's the only bike to get. Man, if you get a fuckin' rice burner, I'm going to have to act like I don't know you." Rock laughed when concern crossed Charlie's face. "Dude, I'm just shittin' you. But Harleys are the best machines. When my brothers come over later, you can check them out. Some of them are beyond wicked. They're the best on the market."

"If you ever need to supplement your income, you could get a job at the Harley-Davidson showroom," Clotille said, a smirk on her lips.

"You little vixen, I outta spank your ass for that." He threw her a lascivious grin, and her eyes darted to Isa and Charlie. He glanced over and saw their discomfort as they fidgeted in place, pretending to be busy wiping imaginary crumbs off the counters. He guffawed and then rose from the table. "I'll put the pots on the propane burners." He swaggered out the door.

A few hours later, the crawfish boil was in full swing as the Insurgent brothers stuffed their faces with the star of the event, along with boiled potatoes, spicy sausages, boiled corn on the cob, mushrooms, and crusty toasted French bread slathered in butter. The multi-colored paper lanterns Rock had hung up earlier under the eaves of the patio's roof swung in the night breeze, casting a warm glow on the lawn. Cajun music interspersed with Zydeco and hard rock as everyone enjoyed the chance to eat good food, share stories and memories, and guzzle a bunch of beer.

"I can't fuckin' believe I'm eating mudbugs," Axe said as he popped another piece of crawfish in his mouth.

"We're eating bugs? What the fuck do you serve in the south?" Chas laughed and Rock joined him when Isa's face fell.

"Biggest damn bugs I've ever seen. But they're tasty as hell," Wheelie joined in. "Throw me another can of beer so I can wash them down."

"Actually, they're not *really* bugs." Isa stood with her arms wrapped around her. "They're freshwater crustaceans."

The men stared at her, then burst out laughing. "Well, that fuckin' cleared everything up," Bear said.

"They're like small lobsters." Isa, red-faced, looked at Rock, who was smiling at her. "Roche. Help me out here."

"They're freshwater lobsters, so you fuckers are eating high-class grub." He looked at Dogface and the other officers of the Devil's Legions MC. "Am I right?"

"Fuck yeah. These fuckers are the best." Dogface slurped the meat out of the shell, the buttery juices running down his chin. The other Devil's Legions bikers grunted their approval.

"Ma'am," Catfish, the VP of the Devil's Legions, said to Isa, "this is one of the best fucking crawfish boils I've ever tasted." The rest of his brothers voiced their agreement.

A big grin spread over Isa's face. "Well, thank you. I didn't do it all alone. Clotille helped me. You can taste how delicious her spicy blend is."

Dogface winked at the women. "You both did a kickass job. We appreciate being invited over."

The Insurgents agreed that the crawfish, mudbugs, freshwater lobster, or whatever the hell they were called, were lip-smacking good. And they ate a ton of food. Rock hadn't seen his brothers eat that much since the charity poker run they'd done six months before. It gave him a warm feeling to see his brothers gathered at his sister's house sharing in his heritage. It made everything come full circle: being with Isa, his niece and nephew, Clotille, and his brothers.

The talk turned to a biker's favorite topic, motorcycles. An excited loudness hovered over the backyard as anything related to Harleys and riding was discussed. Rock noticed Charlie had pulled his lawn chair closer to the group, his eyes shining. *Poor bastard's got the bug. Isa's going to kill him.* But he knew Charlie would get a bike. He had to. When the need to ride grabbed ahold of a person, there was no letting go.

As the men talked, Rock watched Clotille go into the kitchen, and he jumped up and followed her. When he walked in, she was rolling her hips and swinging her arms to one of the songs playing outside as she kicked one of the cupboard doors shut. He caught her in his arms and whirled her around as he danced with her in the kitchen and family room. She felt so light in his arms, and she smelled of vanilla, cayenne pepper, and sweet paprika. He pressed her closer as they two-stepped around the room.

Clotille laughed breathlessly and he put his hand behind her head, holding it while he covered his mouth over hers, kissing her deep and hard. Then they were all lips, teeth, tongue, and hands as they groped each other fiercely like it was their last time together.

"You've been driving me wild since you started cooking, *chérie*," he breathed against her shoulder as he licked, sucked, and bit it. "Every fuckin' time I see you, or even *think* about you, I get so hard. What're you doing to me, woman?" He sucked on her lower lip and she moaned, melding her body into his until there was no space between them.

She caressed his face and locked her gaze with his. Her green eyes shimmered with desire, love, and fire, pulling him in deeply. It was as though he were inside her, feeling everything she was, and they were one. It was damn mind-blowing, and it was something he'd never felt with any other woman. She did things to him with her eyes that most women couldn't do with their entire body.

With an intensity burning through him like an inferno, he filled her mouth with his tongue, pushing in as deep as he could. It was as though he wanted her to swallow him whole. She whimpered and he swallowed it, their breaths passing through each other. "*Je t'aime, ma chérie,*" he murmured against her lips. "I really love you." And he did. He always had. It'd been pushed down and buried by bitterness, cynicism, and hatred, but it'd still been there, just waiting to be revitalized.

"I love you too. I never stopped loving you. Ever." She peppered kisses across his face, murmuring, "*Je t'aime, cher,*" over and over. "I want to tell you something special even if it makes you mad."

"Ssh... *chérie*. We've got time to talk. Tonight is for love only." He cupped her ass and squeezed it, his hardness rubbing against her as he grunted and pushed his fingers into her flesh.

"Is this the entertainment?" Henri's voice boomed from behind them.

Rock looked over Clotille's shoulder. "Only if you watch." He then kissed his red-faced woman. "Don't let him bother you, *chouchou*," he whispered. "He's always been an asshole."

"Aren't you going to introduce me to your lady, or is it just a one-night thing?"

Rock growled deeply from his throat and the veins in his throat pulsed. "Shut the fuck up! Why the fuck are you still standing there? You aren't getting enough action from your woman?" He heard a woman's gasp and looked more closely at his brother. Behind him stood a blonde woman with a long face that was heavily made up. Her false eyelashes made her look like Lamb Chop, and if he didn't know better, he'd have mistaken her pink, silicone lips for a toilet plunger.

"Henri, Suzette, I didn't think you were going to make it. Lille went back to the Hamptons with her new guy. Come on back, there's still plenty of food." Isa rushed over to them.

"I'm guessing you got a bunch of bikers out there. I saw all the motorcycles lined up and some creepy-looking guy watching them." He bent over and kissed Isa on both cheeks. "Whatever possessed you to have *that* type of people over to your home?" He curled his lip while shaking his head. "I suspect Rock's had a bad influence on you."

"Don't be talkin' shit about my bro," Bones's voice bounced off the walls. Henri stepped back and the terrified look on his face made Rock feel it was almost worth having Henri and his plastic surgery pinup show up.

"Bones, this is my older brother, Henri. He never caught on to the whole respect thing." Rock walked into the kitchen, his arms snug around Clotille.

"That's no fuckin' good." Bones glared at Henri who seemed to shrink a little more, especially when the back screen slammed and Puck walked in.

Puck was tall, muscled, and tatted over every inch of skin except for his face, and with a face that rarely smiled, he was an intimidating figure. "Hawk wants a bottled water," he said. Rock laughed, opened the refrigerator, and tossed him the bottle. Puck caught it in one hand. "Everything good in here?"

"Yeah, just catching up on shit with my big brother." Rock turned to Henri. "Wanna meet my brothers?"

"No. Suzette and I are leaving."

"Are you Suzette Terriot? I remember you from high school."

"Hi, Roche." She smiled widely and it frightened the hell out of him. "I heard you moved to Colorado."

"Yeah. I didn't recognize you." *Fuck, Isa was right. She made her big tits even bigger. Something's all kind of crazy with this chick.*

"Is that Clotille Boucher next to you?"

Clotille straightened her shoulders. "Yes, I'm Clotille. I'm sorry, but I don't remember you."

"I didn't think you would. I was in Armand's class. How's he doing?"

Rock noticed a glint of anger in his brother's eyes when his date asked about Armand. "Did you used to go out with him?" Rock knew asking the question was childish, but he took delight in the visible flush in Henri's face.

Suzette nodded and giggled. "The last year in high school, and then on and off for a bit."

"When did you get in town, Clotille?" Henri said, and Rock smirked at him to show he knew Henri was diverting the conversation away from Suzette's interest in her ex-boyfriend.

"Not too long ago," Clotille answered.

"She's leaving real soon. Just a passing-through trip, right?" He darted his eyes to her and she nodded.

"So you two are dating now?" Henri smiled thinly.

"Just hanging out." Rock motioned to Bones to throw him a beer. "And the question and answer session is fuckin' over now. Come on, *chérie*, let's go back outside." Rock latched his fingers around hers and they walked out back with Bones right behind them. He laughed when he overheard Henri tell Isa he didn't want to stay. Rock didn't want him to stay either; they were like oil and water, and always had been. It'd be better if Henri came by after Rock went back to Pinewood Springs.

Later that night, after everyone had left and all the dishes and pots had been cleaned and put away, Rock sat on the chaise lounge on the patio, Clotille between his long legs, leaning back against him. A soft breeze ruffled her hair, and Rock smoothed it down with his hand before returning his arm to her waist. The Spanish moss moved gently in the warm breeze, and the lights from the paper lanterns softened the darkness. Behind them the house was dark—everyone had gone to bed. They sat for a long while holding each other and listening to the constant chirping of the crickets.

"Do you want to go to the bayou tomorrow?" she asked.

"Nah. It'll just piss me off if I see what's happening to it," he said as he nuzzled her neck.

"You're probably right," she replied, then inhaled sharply as his hand slid down her top, grasping one of her nipples and tweaking it with his thumb and finger.

"It sucks Suzette saw you tonight. I'm pretty sure she's going to use it as an excuse to call Armand." He tugged her nipple, loving the way it had a direct circuit to her pussy. She arched her back, bringing her tits closer to him while her legs moved back and forth.

"Armand's dating someone. I doubt he'd even take her phone call," she said in a raspy voice.

"Never know." His other hand glided down slowly, and he chuckled softly when she gasped. "Did you have a good time tonight?"

"Yes," she croaked as his hand dipped beneath the waistband of her panties.

"That's good. You and Isa made some kickass food. We should go to a Cajun club to dance. We can go to Baton Rouge. Would you like that?"

She squirmed under his skilled touch, each movement rubbing against his cock which had grown rock-hard.

"Uh-huh."

"It'll be fun. I love dancing with you." He licked her jawline, then tilted his head lower to gently bite the place where her neck curved into her shoulder.

"Oh, God," she groaned.

Then his hand was on her hot and sopping pussy and he slid his finger between her folds, covering it with her juices. He withdrew and placed the digit in his mouth, licking and sucking. She craned her head and he caught her heated gaze. "Fuckin' tasty, *chouchou*. Try it." He slipped it into her mouth and she licked it, driving him fuckin' wild. She pushed herself up and tugged off her panties, then undid the button of his jeans and zipped them down. His cock, harder than marble, jutted straight out and she placed her mouth over the crown, gliding her hot tongue across it. He let her play with his hardness until his balls tightened. Then he pulled her off and pushed up her skirt, moving her to straddle him while he entered her. He pulled her top over her head, unhooked her bra, and grabbed her tits with both hands as though they were food for a starving man.

She placed her feet on the ground, grabbed the arms of the chair, and began to ride him as he played with her tits. Leaning down, she kissed him deeply before moving back up, grinding and bouncing on him. He loved watching her tits jiggle and sway as she moved. *She's fuckin' gorgeous, and I can't get enough of her. I'm fuckin' addicted to my beautiful Clotille.* He gently eased her back a bit to give him better access to her pink pussy. He gazed at it, her clit swollen and peeking from its hood, begging for attention. Rock placed his finger next to her bud and stroked steadily as he felt her warm walls clutch his cock like a vise.

They rode each other under the moonlight and stars, their breathing heavy, their bodies coated in a thin sheen of dampness. As she stifled her cries against his shoulder, her teeth bearing down hard, guttural grunts rose from his throat. They came together, holding, biting, and loving one another.

And it was good.

It was fucking perfect.

Chapter Twenty-Two

The Insurgents arrived at the diner on the far west side of the city. The smiling crawfish with the chef's hat blinked on and off in neon blue, while the name of the diner, Crawdads, lit up the parking lot in neon yellow. Crawdads had catered to the bikers in the area for the past forty years, and it was generally considered a neutral zone for rival clubs. Dogface had told the Insurgents that would be the best place to meet with the Gypsy Fiends' president.

When they entered the eatery, Rock noticed several men in leather and denim seated at a big table in the back. Most of them sported bushy beards and long stringy hair. The president patch on the cut of the guy at the head of the table directed the Insurgents toward them. When they approached, Rock noted the name, Copperhead, stitched on the president's cut. The dude had long blond hair and a lengthy beard in a slightly darker shade. Icy blue eyes stared out of a face that had a patchwork of scars, cuts, and moles. He sat expressionless as they stood in front of the table.

"I'm Hawk, the VP of the Insurgents, and these are my brothers. You're Copperhead?"

The president nodded while his brothers stared at the Colorado club. Copperhead motioned Hawk to sit down, and he grabbed a chair, the other Insurgents following suit.

"I'm not gonna fuck around. You know why we're here. You got the weapons we want and we got the cash you need." Hawk and Copperhead stared at each other, neither of them giving the other any slack.

Rock sat at the end of the table so he could watch what everyone was doing. He was on high alert since a seemingly calm interaction could turn bloody and deadly in a matter of seconds. In the outlaw world, anger and hate were always bubbling right beneath the surface.

"The shit we got is for someone else. We can get you some more. It'll take some fucking time, but we can get 'em." Copperhead scratched his beard.

"I don't give a fuck who it's for. We got the cash. I'm not waitin' for shit. If you don't want the money, then we're wasting our goddamned time."

Hawk tilted his chin at his brothers and pushed his chair back. He and the rest started to get up when Cooperhead said, "Where the hell you going? Sit the fuck down. I didn't say I wasn't interested in doing business."

Hawk paused for several seconds, then eased back into the chair. His brothers followed his lead, all of them stone-faced. Rock was laughing on the inside. *We've got these greedy fuckers. Kiss our asses, Demon Riders.*

In the end, the Gypsy Fiends agreed to take the cash deal and to "fuck the rich dude." Rock and his brothers knew exactly who the "rich dude" was, and he took an enormous amount of pleasure in screwing the Demon Riders *and* Frederick.

To seal the deal, both clubs ordered a feast of crawfish, shrimp, red beans and rice, gumbo, and a slew of other local favorites. As the men ate, they talked about the one thing that bound all the outlaws together—Harleys. And not once did Rock have to smash someone in the face. The meeting had been a huge success.

★ ★ ★

CLOTILLE HAD JUST finished putting away the leftovers from dinner when her phone jingled. She grimaced when she saw Armand's name flash on her screen. Clutching it tightly, she went out to the screened-in porch, sat on a cushy chair, and answered it.

"Why didn't you tell us you were in Lafayette?"

She sighed. "I wanted some time to myself. I was planning on calling sooner or later." *Damn you, Suzette! Rock was right… she called Armand.*

"Sooner or later? What the hell's that supposed to mean?" his voice rose slightly.

"I was going to call. How've you been?"

"Busy as hell trying to keep Mom happy and in the lifestyle she's become accustomed to. It takes a lot of hard work and money to do that, you know?"

Here it comes. "I'm sure it does." She kneaded her forehead with her fingers.

"And if Frederick stops helping out, we're fucking toast. You do get that, don't you?"

And here it is. The real *reason Armand called me. He wants me to go back to Aspen. Frederick is working overtime trying to get me back.* "I get that things may become tough, but I'm planning to help out. I don't want you to do it alone… I never have."

He clucked his tongue. "Why did you leave him? I thought you were happy with him."

"Content, in the beginning, yes. Happy? Never. I became restless and realized I was missing out on so much. I missed seeing the ones I loved."

"Frederick would've brought you to visit. He said you never asked."

"It doesn't matter. Anyway, he was becoming too possessive. I didn't think it would be safe for me to stay with him anymore. I felt like I didn't really have a choice when I made the agreement with him, but now I do. I wanted out."

There was a long pause. "Well, I suppose you have to do what you think is best. It's your life."

"I can't believe you just said that. Wow, you've changed for the better since you've been going out with Jolene." She tucked her feet under her butt. "How's Mom?"

"The same. She's busy with all the committees she's on for a bunch of charities. It'd be nice if you called her."

"I'll call her in the morning. She's probably pissed off big time at me." She laughed dryly. "It wouldn't be anything new. I always rubbed her the wrong way."

"She'll be glad to hear from you. Where are you staying?"

"With friends. You don't know them." *There's no way you don't know about Rock, but I'm not going to bring it up.*

"That's good. I gotta go. Remember to call Mom."

"I will."

She put the phone down on the side table and leaned her head on her hand. She couldn't believe Armand didn't read her the riot act. She said a small prayer of thanksgiving for Jolene being in his life. *Sometimes it takes a woman to soften a man's rough edges.* She smiled. *Like Rock. All tough and badass, but such a sweetheart when we're together. I love him so much. It kills me that I'm going to have to break his heart. He's never going to forgive me. He told me that he wanted an easy, unfettered life. He'll never get that with me. Damn, I don't want him to feel obligated to me, but I love him so much, and I want to try and make a future with him. Every time I try to talk to him, he shuts me down. I have to choke back my fear and make him listen to me regardless of the consequences. I can't lose him again.*

She stared out into the night, wiping the tears that trickled down her cheeks. *I never should've let Rock go.* She sighed and wrapped her arms closer around as she let the lull of the crickets and the winds numb all thoughts.

★ ★ ★

By the time Rock came home, Clotille was fast asleep. He quietly put his gun, knives, and padlock in a metal box and locked it, then went into the bathroom to take a shower. The humidity made him sticky all the time; he missed the dry, mountain air in Pinewood Springs.

When he'd finished he walked to the bed and tossed his towel across a chair, then slipped between the sheets, the warmth of Clotille's body radiating to him. When he moved close to her and slinked his arm around her waist, she pushed back, her ass hitting his hard dick. She made a few sweet noises in her sleep, then returned to her steady breathing. His shaft was on fire. No woman had made him hard as often as she did. All he had to do was see her, smell her, or hear her and his damn dick would wake up. He dipped his head and kissed her silky hair, the scent of lemon and cucumber filling his nostrils.

I'm so fuckin' hooked on her. I've never loved any other woman but her. I can't believe we fuckin' wasted all those years, but now that I have her, I'm never letting her go. She's a part of me. She makes my life whole. She was the one who filled all the dark places in his heart. She'd become his comfort from the storm of life. And he loved her for it.

His trust had begun to come back since she'd told him she loved him. And he knew she did by the way she watched him when she didn't think he noticed, or the way she'd wrap her arms around his neck and stipple kisses all over his face even if Isa and Charlie were in the room. Whatever it was that still haunted her, he could ride through it. He could weather anything now that his *chérie* was back in his life.

And he was never letting her go again.

Chapter Twenty-Three

Rock sat at the kitchen table dunking a praline in his cup of coffee while he watched Clotille exercise to a DVD in the family room. *I love those yoga pants. Fuck. Best invention after the thong.*

"I'm thinking of going over to Madame Vincennes to get a reading. It's been ages since I had one done." Isa poured a cup of coffee and sat on the chair opposite of Rock.

He raised his eyebrows. "You didn't hear?"

"Hear what?"

"She died a few weeks ago." He snatched another praline from the plate in front of him.

"Oh... that's too bad. I'm real sorry to hear that. She was a nice woman. I knew she was old, but I guess I never thought she'd die. Silly, huh?" Isa stirred a lump of sugar in her coffee.

"It wasn't old age that got her. She had some help. She was murdered." He wiped his hands on a napkin.

"Murdered? Oh my God." Isa's hand covered her mouth. "Why would anyone kill Madame? She was so poor, I can't imagine anyone thinking she had any money. How did you find this out?"

"I heard it. I'm surprised you didn't know."

"I'm not friendly with anyone from the old neighborhood, and Aline and Michael keep me pretty busy. I hardly ever watch the news. Where did you hear it from?"

Rock glanced over at Clotille and figured she had another forty-five minutes left of her exercise routine. He leaned across the table. "I have something to tell you that's going to fuckin' blow your mind."

Forty-five minutes later, Clotille came into the kitchen and ran her fingers through Rock's hair as she passed him on her way to the fridge. She took out a bottled water and guzzled it down. Rock stared at her tight body that looked fantastic now that she'd put on some weight. Sweat glistened over her bare arms and neck, and those damn yoga pants had him adjusting his jeans. *Damn, she's so sexy after she works out. I can't stop looking at her.*

"I'm going to take a shower." She broke off a piece of the praline on Rock's plate and popped it in her mouth. "What're you two talking about? You look so serious."

"Family shit," Rock said after yanking her to him.

She wriggled out of his grip. "I'm covered in sweat. I'll be back." She laughed when he smacked her behind as she walked away. He loved seeing her tight ass shake in her yoga pants.

When she was out of earshot, Isa—a dazed look on her face—wrung her hands over and over. "Have you told Lille and Henri about Pa? I can't believe he spent twelve years locked up for something he didn't do. Poor Pa." Tears glistened in her eyes.

"You're the first one I told. I wanna find out some more shit before I tell Henri and Lille."

"Do you believe Tessa?" Isa stared wide-eyed.

He nodded. "There's no reason for her to lie to me. And Madame sent me the mojo bag. Why the hell would she have reached out to me after all this time? And… someone murdered her. I checked it out with the public records."

"Do the police have any leads on who may have done it?"

He shook his head. "Not that I can see. Poor old woman. If she would've just come clean that night, she'd still be alive. Fear is a terrible thing to have. It makes people do all sorts of crazy shit they'd never do."

"Do you have any idea who would've killed *Maman*? She didn't have an enemy in the world."

"I have an idea. Working on how to put it all together. When I do, then I'll tell Lille and Henri. Just keep it to yourself, okay? I wanted to tell you 'cause I know you went to see Pa a lot, and you were the only one out of all of us who couldn't believe he killed *Maman*."

She shook her head. "I still can't believe all this. Thanks for telling me. It makes the whole tragedy less horrific to know Pa was innocent." Rock placed his hand over hers and squeezed it.

They stood like that until Clotille came in. "A good shower feels wonderful after a workout. It's so quiet around since your kids went back to school. It was adorable the way Michael danced around the house after you came home with his school supplies. I don't think I was ever *that* excited about school."

Isa laughed and wiped the corner of her eyes. She slid her hand from under Rock's and stood up. "I have a ton of errands to do." She glanced at the wall clock. "Damn, look at the time. I have to run." She rushed out of the kitchen. Rock watched her until she was gone.

"Everything okay?" Clotille asked, grasping his hand.

"Yeah. We gotta think 'bout heading back. The club business is going to be finished in a couple days. I gotta go back home." He skimmed her face, noticing the way her eyes darted away from his. "You wanna go back with me, don't you?"

She nodded. "Armand called. You were right about Suzette. Anyway, I promised him I'd call my mom. I was going to do that this morning."

Rock's face hardened. He didn't like that she changed the fucking subject. *Doesn't she want to come back with me? What the fuck's going on with her?* "Isn't your mom going to be pissed at you?"

"Probably, but Armand acted like a big brother to me. *Finally*. It's taken what… twenty-nine years? Not too bad." She rolled her eyes and laughed.

"That's good. People can change as they get older. And sometimes life handing you a crock of shit can do it too. You and your family hit rock bottom after your dad died. That shit would have an impact on most people."

"True." She picked up his hand and kissed it. "I'm happy with you."

"Then why the fuck are we talkin' 'bout everything but *us*? You comin' back with me, or am I goin' alone? Don't fuckin' bullshit me,

Clotille."

She kissed his hand again. "I'm going back with you." She blinked several times.

She's fuckin' hedging. What the hell's the matter with her? He nodded. "Good. You call your mom, and I'm going to hang with my brothers. We got shit to discuss. I'll be back later."

Her face dropped but he didn't give a damn. The bitterness threatened to leak out of the compartment he'd locked it in for the last ten days. *I gotta get outta here before I say something I'm going to regret.* He rose from the table. "See you later." He strode toward the back door.

"Aren't you going to kiss me before you leave?" Her small voice held hurt, sadness, and regret.

He spun around, went up to her, and gave her a quick peck on her lips, moving away before her raised arms hooked around his neck. He slammed the screen door and sprinted to his Harley. Clenching the handlebars, he switched on his engine and broke the sound barrier with his cams. He sped away, forcing himself not to look back. If he did he would go to her, and he didn't want to. He had a funny feeling she was going to shatter his heart *again*. Hardness inched its way through him as he rode to the Devil's Legions' clubhouse to meet up with his Insurgents brothers.

★ ★ ★

SHE LEANED AGAINST the kitchen counter looking out the window, hoping he'd turn around and smile at her as he rode away, but he didn't. He hadn't even looked back before he roared away.

Why did he have to bring up the future today? I was hoping we could ride into Abbeville, have lunch, stroll around the town, and hold each other. I love him so much, but I'm scared he's going to run away from me when I tell him about all the lies and secrets I've kept in my heart. He deserves to know, but in telling him I'm pretty sure I'll lose him forever. I can't be selfish. If he walks away from me then he does. I love you so much, Roche.

She gripped the kitchen counter as she continued to stare out the window, hoping she'd see a flash of chrome come around the corner. He'd only been gone a few minutes and she was already missing him terribly. *I can't lose you, cher. I love you so much.* He was everything she'd wanted. She breathed in deeply and vowed to talk to him when he came home and tell him everything she had in her heart—the past, the present, and, hopefully, the future. And she'd make sure nothing interrupted their conversation. That night would either be a new beginning for them, or their final good-bye. Either way, she had to come clean.

She pushed away from the counter and picked up her phone, sitting back down as she plugged in her mother's phone number.

"Clotille? How wonderful to hear from you. How are you doing?"

"Okay. How are you, Mom?"

"Busy with all the different committees. I don't know why I take on so much. How's Frederick?"

She swallowed hard, then exhaled. "I've left him," she whispered, waiting for her mother's tirade of insults on what a fool she was.

"When? Why?"

"A few weeks ago. I couldn't live with him anymore. It wasn't working for me. I was dying inside." Silence. If she didn't hear her mother breathing, she'd have thought they'd been disconnected. "I know you're disappointed. I'm sorry."

"Where are you?"

"Lafayette. I needed time to think before I called you. I was so confused. I know I've made the right decision. I can help you financially. I just couldn't stay with him anymore," her voice cracked at the end.

"When your father died in the arms of that trashy woman, I was mortified. But when he left us destitute after spending all the money on *her* and the gambling tables, I was devastated. I didn't know how to be poor, and I was desperate to get my old life back. That's why I pushed you into being with Frederick. He could help us financially, and he was able to help you get your life on track. He took care of everything. Now things are different. I've made some sound investments. I don't need his money."

"I also agreed to be the woman he wanted me to be. I did it primarily for the family. To give you a good life. I'm happy I've done that, at least."

"If Frederick isn't for you anymore, then you did right in leaving him."

Clotille's heart soared. "Do you really mean that, Mom?"

"Of course. Where are you staying?"

"With friends."

"I insist that you come stay with me for as long as you like. I want to see you. It's been too long."

"I can come by to visit today if you're not busy."

"What time?"

"In an hour. Is that good?"

"Make it two hours. That'll work much better."

"See you soon."

Clotille leaped up in the air after she slipped her phone in her pocket. With her mother and Armand in her court, that part of her life was unfettered, and it would make things more bearable if Rock ended up throwing her aside after they had their talk. She'd been so worried her mother would've been furious at her for leaving Frederick—the goose with the golden egg, as her mother had called him—that she almost didn't call her. But she was so happy she had. She rushed to her room to fix up before she left.

Two hours later, Clotille paid the cab driver and walked up the stairs to her mother's home. She rang the doorbell, her stomach fluttering with thousands of butterflies. The door swung open and her mother greeted her with a wide smile. She looked older since Clotille had last seen her, but her forehead still had the perpetual crease that deepened when she was angry or upset. New frown lines had cropped up above her nose and the sides of her mouth. Her hair was still black and from the way her eyes stayed wide, Clotille guessed she'd had an eye lift fairly recently.

"Clotille, come in." Her mother hugged her stiffly, then moved aside so she could enter. "Let's go to the sun room. It's so bright and lovely in there. How do you like my house?"

"It's beautiful." *You've put Frederick's money to good use.* "Isn't the house too big for just you?"

"I love mansions. The bigger, the better." She laughed and led them to a sunny room filled with gorgeous plants and flowers. Overstuffed furniture gave the room a very homey feel. A pitcher of lemonade sat on the glass-topped coffee table, a plate of cookies beside it. "Help yourself."

Clotille poured a glass of lemonade for both of them and then chit-chatted with her mother. Every few minutes, her mother would look at her watch, and it was beginning to drive Clotille crazy. "Do you have to be somewhere?"

"No. Why?"

"You keep looking at your watch. I can leave if you need to go."

"I have a committee meeting. It's a charity that helps abused women and children. But the meeting's not for another hour. Let me get some more lemonade."

When her mother left, she picked up her phone and checked to see if Rock had called or texted. He hadn't. Disappointment ran through her veins. She then sent him a text.

Clotille: *Visiting @ my mom's. She seems cool. Sorry I didn't act 2 excited this morning about going back. I love u. I definitely want 2 go back with u 2 make a life with u. Before I can, we have 2 talk. When u get back 2nite, I have something VERY important 2 tell u. Then u decide if u still want me 2 come with u. Sorry for the long text. Let me know u got it. I ♥ u.*

She waited with bated breath for his response, but it never came. *He's so pissed at me.*

"Here you go. Freshly squeezed. By my maid, not me." Mrs. Boucher laughed.

Clotille heard footsteps behind her and she craned her neck over her shoulder to see Armand walking toward them. She stood up and went to him when he entered the room, giving him a hug. To her surprise, stiffness greeted her, and she pulled back. "You're looking good," she said.

"Thanks." He sneered at her, then went over and lightly kissed their mother on the cheek. "Have we come to any conclusion here?"

"What are you talking about?" she asked.

"About you getting your fucking ass back to Aspen where you belong."

Clotille's face turned white and her stomach knotted. "What? I told you I'm not going back to Frederick. You told me you were cool with my decision and that it's my life."

"You really are a stupid bitch, aren't you? Do you think for one minute that I'd let you ruin mine and *Maman's* life because you can't keep your legs closed? You love slumming it with white trash. You always have. So you spotted him at Frederick's and you left Frederick for *him*?"

A sudden coldness hit at her core and she jerked her head back. Looking at her mother, she saw the cruel eyes that were all too familiar. "You both lied to me. You pretended that you supported me just so you could gang up on me and convince me to go back to Frederick. Well, I'm not, and I don't have to stay here and listen to you." She whirled around and began to walk away, but Armand grabbed her wrist and yanked her back.

"There's no way you're ruining this for me," he hissed. "I'm sick of your fuckups and your spoiled brat ways. You're just like Dad. You've both brought shame to our family." His lips curled up. "I believe you have a visitor who wants to see you."

The room began to spin and she grabbed onto the arm of the love seat to steady herself. Heaviness weighed her down as she tried desperately to calm her racing heart.

"Hello, pet." His voice crawled all over her. "It's time for you to come home. You've been a very naughty girl, making me come all the way to Louisiana to fetch you." He paused and fear crept around her nerves as her knees buckled. She sat on the arm of the love seat, her heart sinking with every word he uttered. "And shacking up with that dirty biker. Tsk tsk. Yes, you've been very bad. You'll have to be punished."

Clotille pulled herself up and ran to her mother. "Get out of here or I'm going to call Rock." Frederick kept approaching. "I mean it." She fumbled in her pocket, trying to take out her phone, when her mother gripped her wrist like a vise. She stared at her mom.

"Frederick, come take this ungrateful little bitch and punish her good and hard." Her mother's words sucker punched her, the woman's face a mask of anger and cruelty. Her too-red lips looked like a gash across her face. "Since you're spreading your legs freely, it might as well be for a rich man rather than a dirty biker. You've always been a bad, spoiled girl."

Frederick grabbed her roughly and pulled her to him. He whispered in her ear, "You fucking cunt. Did you really think you could leave me?"

Scanning the faces of her brother and mother, she knew they wouldn't help her. They'd rather sell her to a life of hell than give up their lifestyle. *How can this be my family? I wish Dad were here.* She stifled a cry and willed herself to be calm, but as hard as she tried she couldn't stop trembling.

Her mother stood up. "Frederick, take your naughty girl out of my house. I have a committee meeting I have to go to." She passed by Clotille without looking at her.

"I'm not going with you!" Clotille made a dash for it, but Armand reached out and jerked her back. She screamed and struggled, but the more she screamed the brighter Frederick's eyes grew. Then Armand had her arms pinned behind her back, and she watched in horror as Frederick took out a syringe. She squirmed until he hit her hard across the face. The intensity of the blow stunned her, and he quickly injected her.

Soon everything faded away.

Chapter Twenty-Four

"PROBLEMS WITH YOUR woman? Not givin' you enough of that Southern charm the ladies around here are known for?" Bones nudged Rock with his elbow before he threw his third dart at the board. "Fuck yeah! Bullseye." He raised his arm in the air.

"Fuckin' luck, that's all." Rock picked up his three darts, each one landing further from the bullseye. He grumbled inaudibly and leaned against the wall. He took his phone out again and called Clotille. Again, no answer. He sent another text. "Want another drink?" he asked Bones.

"Is getting me drunk the only way you can beat me, bro?"

Rock scowled. "Do you want a fuckin' drink or not?"

"Fuck, will you chill? Yeah, get me a Jack and a beer." He picked up three more darts, then sat on one of the stools.

As Rock walked toward the bar, a pretty club girl came up to him and curled her hands around his arm. "Honey, you don't need to be getting your own drinks. Just tell me what you want and I'll bring it to you," she drawled.

"No worries. I can get my own." He shrugged her off and placed his order at the bar. *Why the hell isn't Clotille calling or texting me back? I know I acted like an asshole this morning, but this isn't her style. Anyway, she told me to text her back. Is she playing a fuckin' game with me? And what the fuck does she wanna talk to me about? I don't wanna hear why she married Luc. She's been tryin' to explain that shit since we've got here. I just wanna start new. Damn, Clotille. Answer or fuckin' text me!* A bad feeling circulated through him, his insides tensing the longer he didn't hear from her. He ambled back to Bones.

When he arrived, Chas, Axe, Wheelie, and Chicory were drinking at one of the tables and talking with Bones. "I'm just telling the guys how I'm beatin' your ass." Bones took the drinks Rock handed him. "I'm also sharing what a fuckin' pussy you are with your long goddamned face 'cause your woman's not putting out."

Before Bones finished his laugh, Rock had him by the throat, his back flat against the wall. "Don't fuckin' disrespect my woman. You don't know shit." He tightened his grip around Bones's neck until Chas and Wheelie pulled him off.

Bones gulped air and coughed as he threw daggered looks at Rock. "What the fuck is your problem?" He lunged for Rock and the two of them threw a few punches until the surrounding brothers pulled them apart.

"Will the two of you fucking calm down? What the hell?" Chas shoved Rock away from Bones.

"I don't like what he's saying about Clotille. And I'm fuckin' worried about her 'cause she's not answering my calls or texts. Shit!" He kicked over a couple stools, then tipped over the bar table. Several dudes from the Devil's Legions came over to see what all the ruckus was about.

"What the fuck's going on?" Catfish asked.

Axe and Wheelie went up to the host members. "It's cool. Our brother's just worried about his woman," Axe said.

"Need some help with it?" another member asked.

Rock shook his head and they sauntered away. "Something's not right," he said after the dudes were out of earshot. "My gut's telling me that."

Bones came over and gripped his shoulder. "Wouldn't have ribbed you if I knew your mood was because you were worried. Sorry, bro." Rock tilted his chin. "Why do you think something's up with her? Maybe she's just pissed or teaching you a lesson for something you did."

"Women love doing that," Chas said. "My wife's the queen of the cold shoulder, and it's fuckin' effective 'cause it drives me crazy and I always fuckin' give in. Am I right, Axe?"

Axe chuckled. "Yep. Baylee must've taken lessons from Addie 'cause she can go hours acting like I'm not in the same fuckin' room. Damn. How the hell do women do that?"

All the other brothers but Rock sniggered. "I don't think that's what's going on here. If she were doing that shit, she wouldn't have texted me that she was at her mother's and ask me to confirm the text. Fuck! I didn't really want her to go alone to visit her mom. I don't trust the fuckin' bitch."

"What's going on here?" Hawk asked as he walked up to the group.

"Rock thinks his woman's in trouble," Chas replied.

"Do you know what kind of trouble?" Hawk leaned against the table.

Rock nodded. "If something's wrong—and my gut's telling me it is—I know it involves that rich fuck we did the stint for in Aspen."

"Frederick Blair?" Hawk scrubbed his face. "He's the one you think killed your mother, and he's the one who wanted to sell the weapons to the Demon Riders. Why's his goddamned name all over the fuckin' place?"

"He wants Clotille back. I know he's been supporting her mother and she's a greedy bitch, so I wouldn't put anything past her. I'm going to go over there and see if my woman's still there. It's been a few hours since she texted me."

"You want me to go with you?" Bones said.

Rock shook his head. "No, I gotta do this on my own." He scanned his brothers' faces, a warm feeling spreading through him. They were ready to charge with him to the mean bitch's house and help him find his woman. He could *always* count on their loyalty and support no matter what. He pounded his fist against his chest a couple times, then headed out the door.

As he was about to switch on his Harley, Hawk came over to him. "You let us know what you find out about your woman. If this fucker is in town, I wanna know."

"Sure thing." They locked gazes for a few seconds and an understanding passed between them that the brothers were behind him and waiting to help in any way they could, even if it wasn't club business. Rock broke eye contact, switched on the ignition, and rode away.

After the second ring, he tried several bump keys that made getting into places a lot easier. The third one he used unlocked the door and he entered the house. Everything was quiet and he silently padded his way through the whole house looking for Clotille. No one was there. He went into one of the rooms that looked like an office and started rifling through the papers on top of the desk. Thumbing through a desk calendar, he noticed several notations that Mrs. Boucher had spoken to Frederick—one as recent as a couple of days before.

I fuckin' knew it! I wonder if he's taken Clotille back to Aspen. Fuck!

As he rummaged through the desk trying to find more information, he heard a door close. He froze as heels clacked on the floor. He hid behind the door and waited until the footsteps grew fainter, then quietly followed them to the other end of the house. He saw the woman he'd hated all through his growing years, the one who beat Clotille, underpaid his mother, and treated him like white trash.

Mrs. Boucher bent over and took off her high heels before massaging her foot. He waited until she straightened up and then came up behind her, grabbing her with one hand and covering her mouth with the other. She kicked and twisted, but he held her like a ragdoll. He let her carry on for a few minutes, and then he yanked her head back hard and snarled, "You're going to get one chance to tell me the truth. If you don't, I'll fuckin' peel your skin off before I rip out your intestines. Where the fuck is Clotille?" He put his hand over her throat and squeezed it hard before releasing.

"She's with Frederick," she said against his hand.

"Where the fuck is the sonofabitch?"

She shrugged. "I don't know. I just know she went with him."

He kneed her in the kidneys and Mrs. Boucher cried out as her legs buckled. He forced her to stand straight. "Wrong fuckin' answer, bitch. One last chance. Where the fuck is the asshole?"

Black streaks from her mascara ran down her tear-stained cheeks. "I have to look it up. Please. I don't remember. It's in my computer." She nodded toward the desk.

With an ironclad grip on her arms, he walked over with her to the desk and shoved her against the chair. "Please don't hurt me."

"Shut the fuck up and gimme the damn address." He watched her every move as she scrolled through her e-mails. She grabbed a pen and piece of paper, wrote down an address, and handed it to Rock. It was a local one in another parish about thirty minutes away. His heart leapt. *I gotta get to her before the motherfucker takes her away. I'm sure he's hurt her. I'm going to kill the bastard.* With Clotille's safety paramount, he was thinking with his heart when he ran out of the house, leaving a traumatized Mrs. Boucher collapsed in her chair. He jumped on his Harley and sped to rescue his woman.

★ ★ ★

FREDERICK HUNG UP the phone and smiled cruelly at Clotille. "That was your mother. We're going to have a visitor soon." He turned from her and dialed. "I need some reinforcements at the house. I'm expecting a jilted lover." He licked his lips as he stared at her. "You can't spare more than four? Well that'll have to work. I need them ASAP. Send over whoever is in the area."

Clotille's heart was in her throat. *Rock's going to step into an ambush and I can't do a goddamned thing about this.* She pulled at the cuffs around her wrists and ankles. He'd restrained her spread eagle on his favorite equipment—the St. Andrew's Cross. At first he'd attached her facing the cross when he exacted her punishment for being so disobedient. He'd started with his hands and then progressed to the flogger, the cat o' nine tails, and the cane. When he'd brought out the dreaded cane, she pleaded with him to stop, but he kept hitting her buttocks and thighs. She used her safe word, but he'd told her she had broken their contract by leaving him and they didn't have a new one in place yet, so there were no limits. The only thing that got her through the beating was thinking of Rock and their time together. Even though Frederick had made her count each blow aloud, her mind was on Rock.

"Getting tired, my pet? See what happens to naughty sluts who disobey?" He sat in a straight-backed chair, his leg folded over his pressed pants, and watched her. After he finished caning her, he turned her around so her back was against the cross and she faced him. Humiliation burned through her, and his eyes sparkled as he watched her shame.

"Please don't hurt Rock. I'll never leave you again. I'll do whatever you ask, but please don't hurt him."

"You've forgotten how to speak to me, pet. I'll have to retrain you when we get back to Aspen. But now, I must get you ready for your visitor." He laughed and unlatched the restraints. She fell onto the mat in front of the cross. Her arms ached from being held up so long, and her body hurt all over. After several minutes, he had her drink from a bowl of water, chuckling as she dipped her face in the bowl and lapped up the liquid.

"Ready?" He fastened her collar around her neck and attached her leash. As he walked up the stairs, she struggled to follow him on her hands and knees. When she slowed down, he'd jerk her hard, dragging her behind him.

Clotille assumed her slave position: naked on her knees, sitting upright on her heels, hands clasped behind her back, knees spread wide apart.

Frederick patted her head. "Good, pet."

Each minute that went by, each sound she heard, drove her further into a fit of frenzy. Frederick went to the door after reading a text, returning with four mean-looking bearded men. Their arms and necks were covered in tattoos, and one had skulls and demons tattooed on his shaved head. They were dressed in leather and denim and their black vests sported patches of numbers, guns, and wings. She trembled. *They must be the reinforcements. Rock, mon cher, stay away. Forget about me. I can't see you die. I love you so much.*

Frederick spoke in a low voice to the four men and they grunted and growled their replies. He looked at his watch again, then dropped to his knees next to her. "Soon it'll be show time," he cooed in her ear, "and I'm going to show you what happens to men who try and steal my pet." He pulled her head back and kissed her hard, then stood up and smoothed down his pants.

She swallowed down the bile rising in her throat as she fought against fainting. *Don't you dare pass out. Don't fucking do it! Breathe deeply. In and out. In and out. I'm with Rock and he's kissing me all over. His lips are so soft against my body. Don't fucking faint.* She steadied her nerves as she waited for Rock to walk into the web Frederick had spun.

Chapter Twenty-Five

On the way to Frederick's house, Rock called Bones and told him where he was headed. His friend had told him to wait until they came to join him, but he couldn't wait another minute. He had no idea what the sonofabitch was doing to his woman, but he'd guessed it was something awful. *She could be dead by the time my brothers get here.* He was almost there, driven by love, not logic, to get his woman out of the rich fucker's control.

He knew he'd fucked up when he left her mother unbound. All it would've taken was five minutes to tie the bitch up, but his head was on backwards with Clotille—always had been—and he made a stupid mistake. But it didn't matter because he was hell-bent on killing Frederick and taking his woman with him.

Figuring the bitch called the rich asshole, Rock decided he'd enter around the side of the house through a window. Again he cursed himself for leaving a loose thread, but he had to proceed regardless.

He parked his bike a few blocks away so as not to tip off Frederick that he'd arrived. He took alleys and cut through yards to get to the white plantation-style house. The lush foliage aided Rock in slinking to the back part of the house. He tried several windows but they were all secured. As he rounded the corner, he spotted a sliding glass door and pulled it. It opened and he went through. *That was too fuckin' easy.* His senses were on high alert as he took out his Glock and walked into the hallway. From the front of the house, a low murmur of deep voices floated down the hall.

His muscles tightened as he approached, dropping to his belly and slithering across the floor until he came upon a small room. He slid in and stood up, pressing himself against the wall. From what he could hear, it sounded like there may be three or four men in the larger room. He spotted a door and went to open it, hoping it wasn't a closet. The door opened into a large space that had a big fireplace and a lot of furniture. Next to the fireplace he saw her, naked and kneeling, a collar around her thin neck. He gritted his teeth when he saw the red slashes and angry welts across her soft body. *Steady, man. You've already made too many stupid mistakes.* Her eyes were downcast, but her swollen lids told him she'd been crying. *Don't worry,* chérie, *you'll be in my arms soon.*

Two burly men stood with their arms crossed, one by the door and the other across from Clotille. From their clothes, Rock knew they were bikers. He was positive they were from the Gypsy Fiends. He didn't feel any comfort in knowing that the Insurgents and the Fiends had just entered into a deal. He wouldn't put it past Copperhead to order the hit on him in order to remain on the good side of their rich pimp.

Frederick walked in looking cool and collected in his navy blue pants and pin-striped shirt. Rock wanted to rush out and beat the shit out of him, but he held steady watching the fucker run his fingers through Clotille's hair and glance at his watch several times. *He fuckin' knows I'm coming. Asshole.* The two bikers stood rigid, but their faces were slack from boredom. The one by the door yawned.

"Maybe I misjudged your biker, pet. He should've been here by now. Maybe he only saw you for what you are—a piece of slutty ass." He pulled her hair and she yelped, her cry lancing Rock's heart. Frederick took her nipple between his fingers and tweaked it hard, stretching it out while he began to unzip his pants.

Against his better judgment, Rock charged into the room, startling everyone. "Get the fuck away from her!" He rushed to Frederick and landed a solid punch in his stomach, causing him to bowl over. The two bikers recovered from their surprise and came after Rock, whose fist slammed into the jaw of one of them. He kicked backward, and from the low groan he knew he'd nailed the asshole in the balls.

The other biker came at Rock fast with a looping swing to his head, but he ducked it easily. He slammed the steel toe of his boot into the bearded man's knee and heard it pop as the man howled and went down. The biker behind him grasped Rock's shoulder and crashed his head into the back of his. Rock, dazed, stumbled forward and then whirled around, shooting his attacker in the leg. The biker crumpled to the floor.

Rock's gaze locked with Clotille's and the tears streaming down her face broke his heart. When he moved toward her, she screamed. "Rock! Behind you!" Before he could turn around, something hard hit him on the head. Warm, sticky liquid trailed down his face and he wiped it, his fingers coated in blood.

"You fucker!" A biker he hadn't seen before punched him in the face while another held him from behind.

Rock's head pounded like crazy and black spots danced in front of his eyes. *Where the fuck did these sonsofbitches come from? Where the hell is Bones?* Rock wasn't stupid; the odds were against him, especially since he was injured. He cursed himself for letting his heart rule his head.

Another biker entered the room. "You fuckin' shot my brother!" He came over and kicked Rock in the stomach. He groaned and they laughed. "You okay for a bit, Gater?" The man on the floor nodded. "We're gonna make this fucker pay for what he did to you."

Frederick, back on his feet, cleared his voice. "I'm calling the shots around here, not you. Stand this asshole up."

Three men dragged Rock to his feet. He noticed one of them had a Gypsy Fiends patch tattooed on his chest. Frederick looked hard at him. "You've caused all kinds of problems for me, you fucking lowlife. The first order of business is for you to understand that Clotille made the decision to come back freely to me. Isn't that true, pet?"

Clotille nodded. "I'm back with Frederick. We talked things over and we settled a lot of stuff. I'm sorry, Rock."

"Fuckin' bullshit! I want you to look me in the eyes, *chérie*, and tell me you don't love me. That it's over between us."

She kept her gaze downward.

"Go on, pet. Tell him you don't love him, that I'm the only one you love and want to be with." Frederick smirked at Rock.

With quivering lips, she looked up at Rock and her green gaze caught his. For a short moment they were connected, and then she broke away. "I can't," she whispered. "I love him with all my heart."

Rock smiled. "Oh, *chérie*."

"You fucking cunt! You will be punished long and hard for humiliating me. And your indiscretion will be felt beyond the whip on your flesh. I'm going to kill Andrew." Frederick's nostrils flared as spittle formed in the corners of his mouth.

"No. Frederick, no! I'll do anything but don't harm Andrew. You promised me." Clotille dropped her face in her hands.

"You promised me a lot of things too. It isn't fair that you can break your promises and I have to uphold mine. All bets are off, *pet*." He glanced at Rock. "Are you wondering who Andrew is?"

Rock stared expressionless at the man he wanted to tear apart. Clotille was extremely upset, and a tinge of curiosity weaved through him.

"Let me tell you." Frederick sneered.

"No, Frederick. Please. Not like this." Clotille glared at him "I'm the one who needs to tell him. I was going to do it tonight," she said softly.

"Shut the fuck up!" He turned to Rock. "He's your bastard son."

"What the fuck?" Rock stared at Clotille as tears streamed down her face. His heartbeat raced and the room spun. "I have a son?" Casting her gaze downward, she nodded. "How?"

"That night we were together in the park," she said softly.

"Clotille... what the fuck?" His head pounded as he tried to comprehend what she was saying.

"When I found out I was pregnant, you hadn't been sentenced yet. You dad was still I ICU barely alive." She locked onto his widening eyes. "I wanted to have our baby and wait to for you, even though I didn't know if you'd be in for life, but my mother and Armand threatened that they'd make me have an abortion. They didn't want me sullying our family reputation." She pushed her shoulders back. "You don't know how bad it was. I was desperate. I couldn't let them kill our baby, so I sought Luc out and pretended to want to reconcile. He fell for it, we had sex, and I told him a month later I was pregnant. I knew he'd do the honorable thing and marry me. I didn't have a choice, Roche. Not even my dad was on my side. I was seventeen and alone." She turned away, sobbing.

"I've been paying for your brat. That was the agreement." Frederick smiled broadly. "It doesn't feel good being betrayed by this whore, does it?"

Rock didn't answer, the reality that he had a son still ricocheting inside him.

She wiped the wetness off her cheeks. "It was either have an abortion or give our baby life and a chance of a good future. My whole family blamed you. After several years, Luc started fooling around on me, so I left him. I struggled to make it on my own, raising Andrew all by myself and juggling a couple jobs.

"My dad helped me a little without my mom knowing, but when he died, my world went from bad to hellish. After we lost all our money, Frederick spotted me at a charity function. My mom checked him out, and she and Armand concocted this plan where he would help our family financially if I'd be his partner." She crossed her arms over her chest. "The only reason I did it was because I wanted to give Andrew a chance at a good life. You were poor… you know how hard it could be. I wanted him to go to the best schools, travel the world, and not worry about money or anything, so I agreed to become Frederick's partner even though I knew the lifestyle he was into. I thought it would be okay, and it was until I saw you. Then I knew everything up to that point in my life had been a lie. You've always been the only one I've ever loved. I was going to tell you tonight when you got home. I swear it."

Rock shook his head. Adrenaline rushed through him as his muscles strained against his skin. He couldn't fathom that he had a child and she'd kept it from him. "How in the fuck could you not tell me I have a son?" he gritted. "We've been sharing the same fuckin' bed for the last few weeks and you never told me. Fuck, I knew you were hiding something, but I never imagined it was anything like this. You're cruel and cold-hearted. You always were." He darted his eyes between her and Frederick. "You and this fuckin' asshole deserve each other."

He tried to pull away from the three guys who held him, but they latched on tighter. "Get your fuckin' hands off me. I don't plan to fight for this woman." Out of the corner of his eye, he saw Clotille cover her face with her hands when she heard his words.

Frederick came in front of him and said, "It doesn't play out that easily. You soiled my pet, so now you have to pay."

Rock spat at Frederick, his spit trickling down the fucker's button-down shirt. "You asshole! You raped the bayou, my mother's land, so I call that even. Only an outsider could do what you did."

Frederick took out a handkerchief and wiped off the saliva. "Is that what you think? I don't think Armand or Henri are outsiders. Henri's your brother, isn't he? He was very anxious to kill your mother for the land. He'd been hoping you would've killed your dad and then that would've eliminated you from inheriting the land, but you couldn't even do that right, you fucking moron. Nevertheless, it all worked out." He straightened the cuff on his shirt. "By the way, condolences on the death of your father. You never know where they're buying the food in the prisons these days."

Rock felt like he'd been sucker punched and all the air had gone out of him. *Henri killed* Maman? *How could he have stabbed and strangled the life out of the woman who gave birth to him? Who cared for and held our misshapen family together?* A guttural roar came from his throat and, with a sudden burst of energy, he pulled away from the bikers and sprinted to the front door. The men were on him seconds later, fighting and punching him. In his weakened state, the three large men overpowered him.

Frederick came up to him. "I think since you're so careless about sticking your cock in women, it would be best if I got rid of it for you. Of course, pet would want to see this." He motioned for the men to take him in front of Clotille, who he forced to kneel on the floor while he held her leash tightly. The thugs laughed and dragged him over, pinning him to the floor. Rock kicked one of them hard in the crotch, but then someone hit him hard, again, over the head. Blood streamed down his face and his eyes went blurry. Frederick came over with a large pair of gardening shears and handed them to one of the bikers. "This should do the trick. After it's done, my pet can eat it. She loves cock, don't you?" He patted her hair before curling his hand around it and yanking hard. She yelped.

Rock kicked, pulled, punched, and cussed as they tried to pull his pants down. Just as they were ready to cut them off him, the front door flew open and gunshots rang out. The bikers trying to pin Rock down leapt to their feet, scrambling to take out their weapons. Rock grabbed one of their legs and pulled it back until he fell facedown onto the floor. He turned to the door and saw his Insurgent brothers streaming through it, rushing over to him.

Puck handed him a small throw from the back of the couch to put against the side of his head to stop the bleeding. As he stood there, he saw Frederick pull Clotille's leash, forcing her to come with him. Before Rock could react, she bit the asshole on the calf, and pulled back on her leash; it slipped from the fuckwad's hand. She unhooked it and then hit Frederick with it over and over, chasing him as he ran into another room.

Rock started to follow, but he saw Wheelie, Bones, Blade, and Tigger pushing the rich fuck back into the living room. Clotille was still striking him like a crazed woman, and she was still naked. Bones took the leash from her hand, took off his T-shirt, and handed it to her. She put it on, then sank down to the floor sobbing.

Bones walked over to Rock, who drew his brother into a bear hug. Pulling back, he said, "Fuck, am I glad to see your ugly face. I was too damn close to losing one of my best possessions." Bones winced and stared at the garden shears on the floor. Rock walked over to Frederick and glared at him. "You sonofabitch." He punched him hard, smirking when he heard the asshole's jaw shatter under his knuckles.

Bones went over and put his face a couple of inches in front of Frederick's. "You don't know shit about us. We got one law, asshole, and it's, 'You fuck with one, you fuck with all.'" Then he hauled off and slammed his fist into Frederick's nose, snapping it.

"Fuck, man. We didn't know you were an Insurgent. You shoulda told us. Copperhead didn't know Frederick wanted us to hurt an Insurgent," one of the Gypsy Fiends said. The one Rock shot had been taken by a couple of his brothers back to their clubhouse.

Hawk narrowed his eyes. "Yeah, right. Tell Copperhead he owes us big for this fuckin' mess. I'll be in touch with him. Now get the fuck outta here."

"You don't believe that bullshit, do you?" Rock said.

"Not for a fuckin' minute. I'll use it to get the price lowered and have them enter into an exclusive deal with us for future arms. I don't wanna have to haul my ass back to this humidity for a long time. I'm aching to get back to my woman." Hawk moved closer to Rock. "Speaking of women, yours is in a bad way."

"Yeah." Rock glanced over at Clotille, who sat on the floor, staring at it.

"You want me to go over to her?" Hawk pressed his lips together.

"Nah, I'll take care of it."

"Your head stop bleeding?"

"Yeah. It was just a gash, nothing major."

"You okay?"

"Not really. Some serious shit went down. I was right about Frederick being involved with my mom's death. Turns out Clotille's brother and mine did the murder-for-hire. Fuck, I can't believe it."

Hawk whistled under his breath. "Damn, dude… that's rough." He pulled Rock into a hug. "You know we're all here for you. We'll make sure the fucker gets his ass dumped at the badges' station. You go take care of your woman."

Rock tilted his chin and shuffled over to Clotille, who hadn't moved since Bones gave her his T-shirt. He knelt beside her. "Come on. Let's go."

She looked up at him, her eyes wildly scanning his face. "Do you hate me?"

He shrugged. "Right now I want you to stand up so I can take you back to Isa's."

"I couldn't stand it if you hated me. I did the best I could. Would I have done things differently if I could go back in time? Hell yes, I would. But I was a sheltered seventeen-year-old. I didn't know anything. I was scared shitless."

"You could have told me," he said in a low voice. "You chose not to, and you have to live with that choice because you can't go back and change it. I don't wanna talk about it anymore. I have some other things on my mind. Let's go." He held out his hand and she took it. He wrapped his arm around her as they walked out of the house.

And neither of them looked back.

Chapter Twenty-Six

Rock watched Henri cross the street in the middle and head for the park. He'd been waiting outside Suzette's apartment ever since Isa told him Henri spent all his evenings there, but never slept over. After two hours, his patience had paid off as he watched his brother disappear in the shadows of the cypress trees.

He quickened his step and soon he spotted Henri taking the path near the lake. He sped up and he could tell by the way Henri walked faster that he knew someone was behind him. Rock would bet the fucking wimp was second-guessing his decision to take the shortcut through the park. He was probably beginning to sweat, his blood pumping through his veins as he wondered if he should make a run for it. *I want you to feel fear the way* Maman *did, you motherfucker.* Rock clomped his boots loudly on the pavement just to make Henri shit his pants.

Henri whirled around, his eyes bulging and his chest heaving up and down. "What do you want—" He stopped short, then recognition spread over his face and he let out a long breath. "It's you. What a relief. I thought it was someone who wanted to mug me."

You're going to wish it were after I'm done with you. "Oh yeah? I was just in the area and thought I'd walk by the lake on the way to my bike. What're you doing in the park?"

"Suzette lives close to here, so I usually take a shortcut home. I live on the other side. Most of the time I drive, but she wanted to walk from my place to hers earlier today, so that's how I'm here."

Rock nodded. "Let's go by the lake. Remember how we used to throw stones at the lake near us? *Maman* would always collect just the right size of flat stones so we could skip them easier. Do you remember that?"

Henri shoved his hands in his pocket. "Yeah. I always wondered how we had so many rocks on our dresser. For the longest time I thought there was a rock fairy. I haven't thought about that in years."

I wonder if you thought about it as you and Armand plunged the knife in Maman's *neck over and over.* "She always thought about us. She was a great mom."

"She was." Henri stopped by the edge of the lake and bent over as if searching for something. "Let's skip a few rocks in memory of *Maman*."

Rock growled, hate riding up his spine. He stood behind Henri. "Why did you kill her?" he said in a low, hard voice.

Henri straightened up and spun around. "Kill who?"

Rock saw the fear and deceit in his brother's eyes, and he wanted to rip them out so they'd stop mocking him. "*Maman*." His voice was barely a whisper.

"Are you fucking drunk or stoned? I didn't kill *Maman*, Pa did. You know all this. I have to get home." He started to walk away but Rock blocked his path.

"You're not going anywhere until you tell me how you could kill our mother." A steel edge had crept into his voice.

"I can't believe you'd think I'd kill *Maman*! I was in St. Martin that night. Don't you remember? I was watching the traps Pa had set up. I'd thought it was unfair that I had to waste another weekend at the bayou while you had fun at your senior party, but I went. Don't you remember how fucking mad Pa was when I told him I didn't want to go? You have to remember that. I'd never do anything like that to *Maman*. How could you think such a thing? I was just as shocked as you were that Pa had killed her. You weren't the only one who loved her." Henri rambled on without taking a breath, and Rock just stood there holding back his urge to break his brother's neck. When he stopped to inhale, Rock said, "Are you finished?"

"You have to believe me, I—"

"That's where the problem is. I don't believe a fuckin' thing you're saying. I *know* you did it, so that's not what I'm asking you. What I've been asking is *why* you did it. That's what I wanna know. I'm real curious about that."

Henri slumped his shoulders. "Madame Vincennes told you, didn't she? I'd told Armand she'd be trouble, but he didn't listen to me. The asshole always thinks he knows everything."

"It wasn't Madame Vincennes. I guess you killed her for nothing."

"Armand offed her. I had nothing to do with that. If it wasn't her, then who told you?"

"It's none of your fuckin' business."

Henri nodded. "It doesn't matter anyway. Do Isa and Lille know?"

"Isa knows Pa was innocent. I haven't told her yet. I wanted to know why you did it. Frederick Blair has been arrested, as well as Armand. How in the fuck did you end up with Armand? He hated our family. He thought he was better than us."

"I know. Greed is an evil seducer. He was involved with Frederick, selling the land in the bayou for him. Frederick paid him well for each sale. Everyone was more than eager to sell their land for big bucks except for *Maman*. She held out. You know Pa wanted her to sell, that they fought about it all the time. I'd told Pa how much we could've made, and he tried to convince her, but she was a stubborn woman."

"Armand knew Frederick before his father died? Clotille said he didn't know them until after her father died and left them broke."

"Armand has known Blair for a long time, just acted like he didn't. He fixed it up so his sister would meet him. Blair had seen Clotille and wanted her. Armand basically gave her to him in exchange for a fat monthly stipend. Like I said, greed clouds all loyalties."

"You killed *Maman* for money?"

"Stop asking me these questions. Yes, I did, but it was her fault. If only she would've sold the land none of this would've happened. But she was selfish. Even if she didn't want money for herself, she should've thought about us. We deserved a better life. She wanted to be poor. I didn't."

Rock tackled Henri and pinned him down on his back. Straddling him, he pummeled his face over and over. "You fucking sonofabitch! You killed *Maman*! You took the one person away from me who loved me unconditionally. I wanted to give her a better life and you fuckin' took that away from me. You kept her from seeing Isa grow and have kids, from Lille becoming a young woman. You took her from us!" He panted heavily between his words as he continued to beat Henri senseless at the edge of the lake.

The scent of dirt wafted around him as he raised his arm to strike his brother yet another time. But he couldn't bring his arm down; it was like something was holding it back. Then the aroma of magnolias and passion flowers overwhelmed him, and he felt his mother's presence in the breeze, the rippling lake, the trees, the earth, and the flowers. He looked down and realized Henri was unconscious, his face bloodied and beginning to swell. Rock placed two fingers on the pulse in his neck and felt the strong beats.

He moved off Henri and sat on the ground, staring at the water as it reflected the moonlight. The lump in his throat grew larger until he rested his head on his bent knees and cried for the first time since he'd found his mother's butchered body. His whole body shook as the sobs ripped through his bones, muscles, and gut, the sound of them filling the spaces between the leaves on the trees, the soft moonlight caressing the ground as it shone above amid the shimmering stars.

★ ★ ★

POOR ISA HAD been in shock ever since Rock had told her what really happened to their mother. He'd called the badges after he'd reached his bike and told them where they could find Henri. After being released from the hospital, Henri was formally charged. Rock doubted if he'd stay loyal to Frederick and Armand. He gave him a week or less before he squealed.

"You'll be back for the trial?" Isa said.

She had dark circles under her eyes. It hurt him to see her suffering like she was. He leaned over and kissed her cheek. "Yeah. I'll be back if there's a trial." He squeezed her hand. "Now that I've seen Aline and Michael, I'll be coming back more often for a visit."

Her eyes shimmered. "I'd like that. What about your son?" He darted his eyes to hers. "Clotille told me everything. She's feeling awful about how everything turned out."

"She should be. Hawk's old lady is a lawyer. I'll talk to her when I get back home to see about visitation."

"Clotille won't keep you from seeing him. She wants to bring him to Lafayette so I can meet him. She's trying to make up for all the mistakes she's made over the years. Can't you give her a chance to do it? As a woman, I can understand to what lengths a mother will go to protect her child and give him a good life. You know, she loves you."

"She has a fuckin' funny way of showing it. Enough. I'll figure it out." He rose to his feet. "I'll be back." He left the room and ambled downstairs.

When he went into the bedroom, Clotille was sitting on the overstuffed chair. "Hi, Rock. I'm so glad to see you."

"Hey." He went to the closet, took out a small duffel bag, and began stuffing it with his clothes.

"What're you doing?"

"Packing."

"Are you going back to Colorado with the others?"

"Yeah."

"When are you going?" Her voice hitched.

"In a couple days. I'm going to stay at the Devil's Legions' clubhouse until we take off."

"I'll leave. I don't want to drive you away from here. I'm the intruder, not you. I'll go to a hotel."

"You can stay. Isa's cool with it. I wanna be with my brothers."

A tense silence engulfed them. He zipped up his bag and went to the bathroom to gather up his toiletries, coming out and putting his stuff in a black case.

"Are we okay?" she asked in a small voice.

He checked all the drawers in the dresser and nightstand, then turned to her. "No, we're not. You kept it secret all these years that we had a son? You had all those years to enjoy him, watch him grow, be his mother. How the fuck did you think it was okay to deny me the same things? I can't forgive you."

Her face fell. "I was seventeen years old and pregnant, and you were headed to prison for God knows how long. Would it have been better if I would've had an abortion? Would that make you feel better?"

"I'm not saying that."

"Then what are you saying? I had to give our baby a name, a chance at a life. You weren't around so I married Luc, and he played at being a mediocre daddy for seven years. You never once contacted me from prison. You ignored all my letters. When you got out, you never looked me up. You keep saying I deserted you, but you deserted me too. I didn't know where the hell you went. I'd heard at one of the high school reunions that you'd joined up with some biker gang."

"You could've called Isa to find out where I was."

"I guess I could've, but I barely knew Isa and I had no clue where she lived. I went to your house after I found out about the baby and it was boarded up. Your whole family scattered after you went to prison. I was trying to survive the best I knew how. When Luc and I divorced, I was a single mom working two jobs and trying to keep everything together. I'm sorry if you weren't on my mind daily. During that time, the only thing that was on my mind was how to give our son a better life. I love him so much." Her voice broke and she wiped her cheeks.

"Why didn't you tell me when I was in prison?"

"What could you have done about it? Could you have married me? Given Andrew a life? Damnit! I didn't even know if you were going down on an assault or murder charge. Your father was in ICU for a long time. I didn't know if you were going to spend the rest of your life in prison. My family would've disowned me. *Everything* I did, I did for

Andrew. I would've died for him if it meant giving him a better life. Do you seriously think I hooked up and stayed with Frederick for four years so my mother could have a big house and my insane brother could have Armani suits? I did it for our son. Every lash to my back, every humiliation Frederick threw my way, I did for Andrew. I knew if I told you, you would've charged in and rescued Andrew, but I also knew Frederick would've killed him before you got there. He held that over my head for all these years. Frederick threatened so many times, especially when I was with him in the beginning, that he'd make Andrew disappear. I couldn't bear it if I lost him too. Whenever I went to visit him at his boarding school, I'd think how wonderful it was to have a piece of you forever. He means everything to me and I couldn't lose him, even if it meant pretending you weren't his dad. I could never let Frederick know that Luc wasn't Andrew's father. And you can bet my mother and brother held that fact over my head." She took out a tissue and blew her nose. "Why didn't you bother to write me or try to look me up after you got out of prison?"

He shrugged. "Why would I? The way I saw it was that you left me. I wasn't a pussy. I wasn't going to beg after you."

"So it was your pride?"

"Fuck, woman. Don't be laying guilt and shit on me. You're the one to blame here, not me."

"I know," she said softly. "But your actions weren't exactly stellar either."

He stared at her. "Where's he now?"

"In Connecticut with a cousin of mine. When I left Frederick, I called her immediately and wired her some money to take him out of his boarding school. I knew Frederick would go after Andrew to hurt me, so I hid him with her. I've been planning to be with him before all this happened. That's why I was hesitant about going back to Pinewood Springs with you. It wasn't because I didn't love you; it was because I didn't want to be without Andrew anymore. I know you won't believe me, but I'd planned to tell you about Andrew the night everything got so crazy. I'd texted you telling you I wanted us to talk. Before we spent this time together in Lafayette, I wasn't sure. You'd told me back in Pinewood Springs that you weren't ready for a family. You said you liked your life easy and free, but after I fell in love with you all over again, I made up my mind to tell you about Andrew even if it meant I'd lose you. I didn't tell you right away because I didn't want to mess Andrew up. He's always thought Luc was his dad. How could I have told him that you were, only to have you walk away from him? Whether you believe me or not, I do love you and I'll never stop loving you."

"Too much too late, babe. I'm talking to a lawyer to find out what my rights are. You know, you're a real fuckin' piece of work. You crushed my heart years ago, and then you come back in my life and you fuckin' stomp on it. Now it's encased in steel, baby, and I don't need any woman taking a blowtorch to it."

"Please don't go, Roche. *Je t'aime.*"

"The name's Rock, babe. And I'm not too crazy about you anymore. Have a good life. Give your address to Isa. You'll hear from my lawyer."

He picked up his bag and walked past her, closing the door behind him. He told Isa he'd be back to say good-bye before he left for home. Placing his bag in his saddlebags, he hopped on his bike and rode away, his heart aching.

Love fuckin' sucks.

★ ★ ★

"WE'RE LEAVING IN one hour. I want everyone ready to go," Hawk said as he picked up his bag and headed out toward his Harley.

"You don't have to worry about us. We can't wait to get the fuck back home," Wheelie said.

"I miss our club girls. The ones here are good, but they can't give head like Lola or Wendy. And Rosie's ass… damn, I'm getting hard just thinkin' about it." Bones laughed as his fellow brothers voiced their agreement.

Rock went out and placed his case in his saddlebags. "I'll be back in an hour. There's something I gotta do before I leave." He swung a U-turn and sped off down the street.

When he arrived at the cemetery, he went straight to his parents' humble graves. There was no fancy headstone, just a simple placard with each of their names and their dates of birth and death. It was just the way his mother would have wanted it. He bent down and laid a bouquet of fresh magnolias on her grave. They were his mother's favorite flower in her favorite color—purple.

"I miss you a lot, *Maman*, but I'm okay." He looked at his dad's grave. "I hope you've found the peace you couldn't find in life. Rest easy, Pa."

On his way out, he looked around to find another grave he'd asked the caretaker about. He went over, slipped the mojo bag out of his pocket, and placed it on Madame Vincennes' grave. A sad smile whispered across his lips. "*Merci*," he said softly, then turned and walked toward his Harley, anxious to return to Pinewood Springs.

Chapter Twenty-Seven

One month later
Pinewood Springs

ROCK SAT IN the great room staring at the television as Dr. Phil tried to help another fucked-up family.

"Getting some pointers, dude?" Bones said as he sat next to Rock.

Rock laughed, shaking his head. "Why in the hell do the club girls like this shit so much?" He glanced at Lola, Rosie, Wendy, Kristy, Brandi, and Mary as they sat on the couch, transfixed by the program.

"'Cause it's always good to know there are people in the world more fucked up than you. Want one?" Bones handed Rock a joint. They both lit up and turned away from the television. "Did you hear that the Demons Riders—Dustin and Shack, in particular—went ballistic when the deal with the Gypsy Fiends fell through? Too fuckin' great."

Bones and Rock bumped their fists together. "Score one for the Insurgents. Anytime we fuck those assholes over is a great one." Rock inhaled deeply.

Buzz came over, placed two salami, cheese, and hot pepper sandwiches in front of them along with two bottles of Coors, and walked away.

Rock jerked his head toward Buzz. "He's shaping up to be a good prospect. Who sponsored him again?"

"Hawk. He's the nephew of one of his old Marine buddies. Seems like he's got the makings of a good Insurgent, but you never know. We'll have to see how he does when it gets real tough." Bones took a bite out of his sandwich. "How's that shit going with your brother and that rich fucker?"

Rock swallowed a gulp of beer. "Henri turned on both Armand and Frederick. I knew he would. He fuckin' gave them up the second day he was in the slammer. I always knew he was a sniveling piece of shit." Darkness passed through him. "He gave them up in exchange for life in the joint instead of lethal injection. I hope they beat and rape his ass in prison."

"Do you think the others will see it through?"

"Armand will probably cave. He's the one who killed the old lady and… my mother. The rich fucker will go to trial. People like him think they're above everything and everyone. He's going to be great feed for the inmates when his ass is sent away. No fuckin' way he's going to win this case."

"Unless he bribes the jury or judge, or both."

"If that happens, then I'll make sure he's dead." Rock crunched down on a potato chip.

"Count me in on that." Bones drained his beer and motioned the prospect for another one.

"Count me in too, even though I don't know what the fuck you're talking about," Wheelie said as he joined them.

"Killing the rich fuck if he gets off," Bones said.

Wheelie's eyes lit up. "Fuck yeah. I've been wanting to beat his ass since the first time we were at his house." The three of them chuckled, then glanced back at the television.

"Have you heard from Clotille?" Bones asked softly.

Rock tipped his head back and drank deeply before he nodded. "She keeps calling and texting, but I never respond. I'm done with her."

"It's too bad. It seemed like you had something going there."

"I thought we did too, but she wasn't the person I thought she was. That's the way women are."

Bones nodded. "Yep. They're nothing but ball busters. I keep sayin' it 'cause it's true. The club women are the way to go."

"Only thing is you ain't gettin' any from them. How the fuck can you go without pussy for so long?" Wheelie picked up the sandwich the prospect had just put in front of him.

"Why the hell you noticing that shit?" Rock smirked and Bones guffawed.

Wheelie jerked his head back. "Whoa, man. It's the club girls who've been complaining about it. I don't give a fuck if you get pussy or not."

"Wheelie's right. The girls are always asking me when you're gonna come out of celibacy. Dude, the best way to forget a chick is to fuck her out of your system. The girls want you back inside them."

Rock looked pointedly at Wheelie and Bones. "Stay the fuck outta my sex life. I'll get pussy when I want to. All this shit with my family in Louisiana is weighing on me. Isa's been bugging me 'bout coming back for Henri's sentencing. She wants me and Lille to make statements to the judge. Fuck all this shit."

Bones slapped his hand against Rock's shoulder. "We're there for you, bro, if you need us. Any fuckin' time." Rock nodded. "We should go to the rally in Lincoln. A ton of our charter brothers will be there. It'll be a good time. I think it'd be good if—" Bones put his beer on the table, his eyes fixed at the door. "Fuck," he muttered, "he looks just like you."

Rock turned around and saw Clotille, brown hair flowing around her. *Fuck, she's beautiful.* He sucked in his breath. She stood just inside the club by the door, holding the hand of a boy about twelve years old, who had a mop of dark hair and eyes black as coal. Rock's insides lurched when he saw the young boy. *That's my son.* He pushed back and went over to Clotille, her heady scent of vanilla, sandalwood, and juniper berries wrapping around him like a blanket.

"Hi, Rock." She smiled at him as she gently prodded the boy forward. "This is your son. Andrew, this is your father." The boy swallowed hard and cast his eyes downward.

Rock cleared his throat. "Hey there, buddy. It's good to meet you. We're going to have to spend some time getting to know each other."

The boy nodded. "My mom said you're a biker. Is one of those motorcycles outside yours?"

"Yeah. You wanna see?"

The boy craned his neck at Clotille. "Can I, Mom?"

She brushed his hair out of his eyes. "Yes. Go on. Maybe your dad can take you for a ride around the parking lot."

A big smile spread over Andrew's face before he looked shyly at Rock. "Would you take me for a ride?"

"You bet. Let's see if you can guess which bike is mine." Rock glanced at Clotille, and then he and his son walked out into the bright sunshine.

★ ★ ★

THE WEEK WENT by so fast, and it seemed to Clotille that Rock was trying to shove twelve years into those short seven days. At the end of each day, she and Andrew would fall down exhausted on their beds, but the way her son's eyes sparkled each time he saw or talked about Rock made every weary moment worth it.

For the past couple days, she'd left father and son alone while she'd taken long walks on the numerous hiking trails in the area. She loved the quaintness of the small town and the camaraderie of the club, and Andrew thrived in ways he'd never had before. When she went to Connecticut after Rock left, she'd told Andrew about Rock. At first the boy was angry, but the more she told him about what a wonderful person his father was and how he wanted to be a part of his life, the more he liked the idea.

Luc had never kept in contact with Andrew after they'd divorced. She'd always felt that Luc knew Andrew wasn't his son, thus he forgot about him. Frederick hadn't been a good father figure. He didn't like children and when Andrew had visited during the summer and school breaks, he was cold toward the boy and irritable to her during her son's stay. When Clotille visited her son at boarding school, Frederick never came.

The past week, Andrew had come alive, and he kept asking her if they could stay another week. And Rock had worn a perpetual smile, which was a nice change from his usual stony face. When he found out they were at the Palace Hotel, he'd promptly checked them out and given his room to them, taking an empty one in the basement. Andrew loved being around the club, and the guys tried to outdo each other on teaching him the right way to change a motorcycle tire and play darts, pool, and cards.

The only dark spot in the time she'd spent there was the way Rock interacted with her. He was polite and respectful, but he acted like they were social acquaintances and it broke her heart. *I still love him so much, but I think he's fallen out of love with me. It tears me up inside.*

Whenever the club had their parties, she'd take Andrew out for dinner and a movie or a game of miniature golf. Then they'd come in through the back and take the other set of stairs until they were safely in their room. After Andrew had fallen asleep, she'd sit in the room, staring out at the inky darkness, her heart lurching every time she heard a woman's voice or laughter. She'd drive herself crazy picturing Rosie or Lola kissing her Rock—she still considered him *hers*—and him hovering above the club girls, thrusting inside them. As hard as she tried, she couldn't stop the images.

One afternoon, she sat behind the club and watched the Colorado River gushing over the stones. Clotille turned around when she heard the pine needles crunch behind her. She shielded her eyes with her hand, smiling when she recognized Rock walking toward her.

He pulled over one of the lawn chairs and plopped down. "Where's Andrew?"

"Exhausted in the room. He's taking a nap. It's official—you've worn him out." She laughed when concern crossed his face. "The high altitude has a lot to do with it as well." She put her hand over his and he quickly moved it away. Her stomach twisted. "It's nice here," she said with a cheerfulness she wasn't feeling.

"Yeah. I like watching the river. Just thinking about where it goes is mind-blowing. It's fun to come here with a few brothers, smoke a few joints, and come up with ideas of where the water, rocks, and leaves end up. It can be fuckin' hilarious." He chuckled and then put his beer bottle to his lips.

"I'm sure what you guys come up with is pretty much out there." She laughed and turned back to gazing at the water. From the corner of her eye, she noticed him staring at her.

"You're a good mom. Andrew's a great kid."

She cocked her head and met his gaze. "That means a lot coming from you." *I miss you so much. I want to feel your lips on mine, your arms around my body. I want us to be back the way we were at Isa's. How can I melt your heart again?* "Addie told me the club's having a family barbecue in the yard this Sunday. She said her son, Jack, will be there, along with some other kids Andrew's age. He'll like that. Her daughter is so precious. She seems very happy." She sighed.

"I was going to mention it to you. It's a good time, and with the days growing shorter we don't have too much time left before it'll be too cold to do shit outside. Chas and Addie are solid. She's a good woman." He placed a joint in his mouth and cupped his hand around it as he lit it.

"All the old ladies I met seem real nice. Baylee said that if we wanted to stay in Pinewood Springs, she'd try and find us a place." She held her breath.

"You planning on staying? When did that come about?"

"I'm not sure. It's just that Andrew loves it here, and he's over the moon about spending time with you. I think Pinewood Springs would be a good place to raise a kid. I also want you to have the time with him. If we go back to Connecticut it'd be so far away. He needs you."

His smoke blew away from them, dissipating by the pine trees. "I'd love to be a full-time dad. We have a lot of catching up to do. What would you do?"

"Get a job. Cara said she could hook me up with something. She knows everyone." She smiled. "You could watch Andrew until I got home from work. I don't know… I'm just thinking about it."

"Sounds like you wanna do it. I'd love for Andrew to be here."

But not me. You deserve to have a chance with your son, but it rips me up inside that you've shut me out of your life. She glanced at her watch. "I better get going. There's some things I want to pick up at the grocery store before it gets too late. I was thinking I'd make a pot of gumbo. Do you think the guys will like that?"

"Fuck yeah. They're not too picky except when it comes to barbecue—then everyone is a critic. You need a lift into town? I could borrow Wheelie's SUV."

Her pulse quickened. "Let me see if Andrew's up. If he is, then we can all go together." She sprang up and dashed into the clubhouse.

Grocery shopping with Rock and Andrew was so enjoyable. It seemed like they were a happy family, and if she pretended hard enough, she believed it too. So many women blatantly flirted with Rock, acting like she was invisible. Even though she knew he enjoyed it, he didn't flirt back, but she did catch him take a few phone numbers when he thought she wasn't looking and it made her stomach plummet. *I'm being foolish. Why shouldn't he go out? We aren't together anymore. I should probably think about meeting someone. Maybe if I date a little I won't think of him as much.*

"Is that going to do it?" Rock asked as he and Andrew munched on some beef jerky.

"Done. How can you guys eat that?"

"It's super good, Mom. I never had it before until Dad gave me some a few days ago. Now I'm hooked." She and Rock laughed, and he ruffled his hand through Andrew's hair.

"Did your Dad tell you that the club's having a family barbecue this Sunday, and that there's a boy around your age who'll be there?"

Andrew bobbed his head up and down. "He said his name's Jack." He ripped off another hunk of jerky.

On the way back to the clubhouse, Andrew and Rock talked about everything and nothing, and their chatter was comforting to her. *I wish it could always be like this. It just feels so right.* When they arrived at the club, Rock and Andrew carried all the groceries in and placed them on the kitchen counter. Clotille busied herself in putting things away.

Bones walked in and high-fived Andrew. "You wanna find rocks for skipping? Your dad's taking you to Crystal Lake tomorrow, so you're gonna want the best rocks."

Andrew practically knocked Bones down in his haste to get to the door. "Can I, Mom?" he asked breathlessly as he leaned against the door frame. She nodded. "Yay! Let's go." Bones chuckled and followed the boy.

"He sure has taken to Bones," she said as she put the cans in the pantry.

Rock leaned against the counter, watching her. "And Bones to him. I know he always wanted kids with his ex from hell, but she wasn't into them. It's too bad he can't have one and skip the woman being around." He chuckled.

"Like you?" she said softly.

He stared hard at her, then pressed his lips together. "Yeah, like me." At that moment, Wendy came into the kitchen and grabbed an orange before she went up to Rock and ran her hand up and down his arm, her fingers lingering on his bulging bicep. "Hey, Wendy. What's shaking?"

"Bored out of my fuckin' mind." She licked her lips. "Wanna do something with me?"

Clotille buried her head in the refrigerator, pretending to clear off a shelf. *I want to grab the witch and shove her in here. I hate that he's letting her touch him when all he does is pull away from me like I'm a leper. I can't stay here anymore. I need to move us back to the hotel. I can't stand seeing him giving to other women what he should be giving to me.*

"You need me for anything else?" Rock said.

Clotille pulled herself out of the fridge. "No. You can go."

And much to her disappointment, he did—with Wendy hanging on his arm.

Chapter Twenty-Eight

Rock's gaze traveled up and down Clotille's body, lingering on the roundness of her ass as she bent over and pulled a big pot out of a cupboard. *I hate that I fuckin' want her so much. My goddamned cock has been constantly hard since she got here.* He'd done a pretty good job in avoiding being alone with her. Most of the time, it was the three of them, or if Andrew was doing something with one of the brothers, there'd be people around. It'd been safe, but the day before when he'd sat with her by the river, he'd wanted to pull her to him and kiss her. The truth was he'd sought her out and found her by the river. He acted nonchalant but a firestorm was raging inside him. When she'd placed her hand over his, he almost lost it and threw her on the ground, fucking her good and hard.

"I know it won't taste exactly like back home because I couldn't find some of the stuff I needed, but I'll make it work."

"They'll love it. You make a fuckin' awesome gumbo and jambalaya."

She smiled as she laid out her cooking utensils on the counter. "Remember how much you ate when I made jambalaya at Isa's house? Charlie wasn't too far behind you."

"It fuckin' kicked ass. It was better than my mother's, and that's sayin' a fuckin' lot." The time they spent in Lafayette was damn good, and the way she'd sway her hips to the music when she cooked turned him way the fuck on. *She still has a hold of your cock… and your heart.* He had to admit that the white-hot anger he felt toward her after she'd told him about Andrew had subsided a lot, especially since she'd brought his son to see him. *She's trying, and I can tell by the way she looks at me that she's still in love with me. Bringing Andrew without me asking was huge. Can I let her back into my life?* As much as he hated to admit it, he missed the hell out of her. He wanted to bury his dick inside her while she wrapped her long legs around his waist, moaning and writhing underneath him.

"Do you want something to drink? I can get you a beer." She poured a glass of white wine for herself.

"Nah. I gotta go." *I gotta go before I bend you over the counter and pound the fuck outta you.* "See you later." He strode out of the kitchen, went up to the bar, and hopped on a stool. A bottle of Coors and a shot of Jack were placed in front of him. He threw the shot back, the liquor going down smooth. "Fuck, that tastes good," he said to Rags and Bones, who were seated at the bar chomping on pretzels and drinking beer.

"Nothing like a good shot of Jack," Rags said.

"So, are you and Clotille together?" Bones asked.

Rock took a long pull on his beer. "Nah. We're just hanging out because of Andrew. Why?"

"Clark was asking."

A hot poker seared up his spine. "Who the fuck is Clark? And why the fuck is he asking?"

"You know him. He owns the gas station and convenience store right outside of town. We all go there. He's a damn nice guy. He noticed Clotille when she came in with you a few times. He thinks she's real pretty and asked if she was with you. I said I'd ask. I did, and so I'll let him know she's available." Bones grabbed a handful of nuts and popped a few in his mouth.

Rock glared at Bones, the veins on his neck straining against his skin. "You'll do no fuckin' thing. She's not available."

"She's got a dude? All the beautiful women are hooked up," Rags said, and Bones nodded.

"She's not fuckin' hooked up. I'm outta here." He jumped up so hard he knocked his stool over. He was so pissed off. *There's no fuckin' way Clotille's hooking up with any man. And this Clark fuck better back off. No one's taking her.* He stormed out of the great room, Rags and Bones's guffaws grating on his nerves.

He marched into the kitchen but it was empty, the large pot of gumbo simmering away on one of the burners. Sprinting up the stairs two at a time until he reached his room, he opened his door and Clotille yelped. She stood in the middle of the room in her bra and panties, trying to cover herself with her sweater.

His stare washed over her from head to toe. "Why're you hiding your body from me?"

Red stained her cheeks. "You startled me."

"You're not anymore. Let me see your body. It's not like I never have."

She shook her head. "We're not like that anymore. You can't just come in here and ask to see me, then walk out and take up with one of the club girls. That isn't the way it works with me."

"Who told you I was fucking the club women?"

"I can see what's going on. You left with Wendy yesterday. I don't have to have a high IQ to figure it out."

He walked to her and traced his finger down her jawline. "So you figured out I was screwing Wendy?" She nodded. "There's no way, *chérie*. The only one I've banged in the last four months is you."

She rolled her eyes. "You expect me to believe that?"

He shrugged. "You can believe it or not, but I know I haven't been with anyone since you and I were together in Lafayette. You fuckin' do something to me that makes me think and want only you. Did you get a mojo bag when we were back home?"

She laughed softly. "I've been wondering the same thing about you. You're all I ever think about. It's like you're pulling me to you all the time."

"Yeah, like a fuckin' magnet. I feel the same."

"You do? I thought you hated me," she whispered.

"Hate? I could never hate *mon petit chouchou*. Fuckin' pissed at you… yeah, I was."

"Was?"

"Not so much anymore. When I thought about it, I knew you did what you thought was best for our son. And you bringing him here just blew my mind." He stroked her cheek with his finger.

"I wanted you both to get to know each other, but I didn't realize how hard it would be to see you with other women."

"You're the only woman for me, always have been. Life just keeps kicking us in the ass, but I think it's time we kicked back." He took her face between his hands and kissed her gently on the lips. The contact with her skin was like touching a live wire, the spark going straight to his dick. He yanked away the sweater she held in front of her and she stood before him in a sheer bra and matching panties. He inhaled sharply, needing to lose himself in her lush body.

She trembled before him, tiny bumps peppering her skin as he glided his hands over her curves and softness. "Rock," she moaned, then grabbed a handful of his thick hair and pulled his face closer to hers.

He felt his pulse quicken when her lips parted and she closed her eyes, sighing as he whispered her name. He outlined her lips with the tip of his tongue while his hand grazed her neck. A soft moan escaped from her throat, and he felt his cock swell in his jeans. "It's been too long, *chérie*." His lips brushed against hers as he spoke before he sprinkled feathery kisses over her face, her eyelashes fluttering on his cheek. Then his lips caressed hers and she circled her arms around his neck, pulling him closer, returning his kiss with abandonment. Her tongue plunged into his mouth and he had to adjust his jeans to relieve the throbbing ache of his cock as it responded to her scent, her touch, her taste.

"I want you so bad," she whispered, her breath hot against his ear.

"I've been craving you since I saw you standing in the doorway holding Andrew's hand. Fuck, *chouchou*, you send all my goddamned senses reeling. I can never have enough of you."

He dipped his head and she cradled it against her soft breasts, his tongue lapping the thin fabric of her bra. With one fluid movement, he had her bra off and his mouth on her stiffening nipples. Each suck, bite, and pinch brought a melody of moans, whimpers, and cries of pleasure. He lowered her to the bed and hovered over her, his face only a few inches from hers. Tears prickled at the corners of her eyes, but he knew they were tears of desire, happiness, and love. Every time she kissed him, moaned his name, or held him, the steel around his heart melted. She was his and he was hers, and nothing could ever take that away from them.

"You make me so wet, *cher*. I love the way you feel inside me."

"I gotta have you now, *chérie*. We have time for slow lovemaking later, but now I gotta fuck you hard. I wanna hear you screaming as I slam into you. I'm not going to hold out much longer."

He quickly threw off his boots and clothes, then peeled off her bikini panties. His gaze devoured her ripe nakedness, his dick hard as granite. Her soft hands curled around his cock and he grunted from deep in his throat. "*Chérie*, I'm not gonna make it if you touch me. I'm so fuckin' turned on I'm going to blow." He spread her legs wide and smiled wickedly when he saw her glistening pussy. "I gotta have a taste." He went between her legs and swiped his tongue over her engorged clit, the tip of his tongue flicking her bud steadily. He pushed a couple fingers up her slit, and his pre-come smeared against her thigh. *She's so hot and sexy. Fuck, I love this woman.*

Kneeling, he leaned back and picked up her legs placing them over his shoulders. Grabbing a pillow, he put it under her sweet ass and then he pushed into her. Her cry almost made him lose it, but he pinched the base of his cock and pulled all the way out. He shoved in again, then out. Over and over he slammed in and out of her, the pillow making her ass higher so he could thrust more deeply into her heated wetness. His balls slapped against the underside of her butt and the room filled with the scent of their arousal. As he pounded in and out of her, he moved his finger over her clit until she thrashed her head about on the pillow, her moans filling his ears.

She went over the edge first and he watched as her whole body tightened and then shook, a feral look in her eyes. A sheen of sweat shone on her upper lip and forehead, and she scratched his chest with her nails. He pumped into her some more before his balls tightened and a rush of release shot through him as he pumped his hot streams inside her. Deep moans ripped from his throat as he thrust one last time, his spent cock warm in her tight pussy.

"Fuck, Clotille. That was fuckin' awesome." He kissed her lips, then rolled off her and lay by her side. He tucked her in close to him, her warm arm across his waist making him smile.

They lay sated, her fingertips drawing circles on his skin, his hand smoothing down her hair. "I want you and Andrew to stay. He needs me, and I need both of you."

"Are you sure about that?" she asked in a low voice. "It's not the incredible sex that's talking, is it?"

He squeezed her. "No. The fucking just makes it better. I love you. I always have, and there's no fuckin' way I'm letting you and Andrew walk out of my life. I want this to work between us. We gotta at least give it a shot."

"I'd like that. I love you too. Andrew adores you. We owe it to him to see if we can make it."

"I want it to work. You're the only woman for me."

"And never forget that."

He chuckled and held her close to him. "There's no fuckin' way I will."

He'd take her with him to look for a house. Andrew had to go to school, so he'd enroll him first thing on Monday. Rock's heart felt as though it would burst. Clotille had melted away the steel that had encased it, and she'd filled all the cracks in it. She was the reason he was whole again.

The storm had passed for them, and the two of them—once broken—had come out stronger. They were willing to fight for love.

And neither of them was ever going to quit.

Epilogue

Four months later

ANDREW AND JACK flew through the back door, their cheeks red from the cold. "Mom, you gotta come and see the baddest snowman *ever*!" Andrew stood next to his mother, his black eyes shining, as he gulped in air. "Come on."

Clotille laughed. "Okay. Can you give me a minute to put on my coat so I don't freeze to death?" She went to the mud room and put on her suede and shearling jacket. Opening the back door, she stood aside as the two boys ran out. As she approached one of the biggest snowmen she'd ever seen, Rock waved to her.

"Jack and I named our snowman Frostbite. Dad helped us with it."

"I figured as much," she said as she took in the leather jacket, skull bandana, and sunglasses. "All he needs is a motorcycle."

"That's for tomorrow." Rock smiled, his black eyes sparkling.

"That's gonna be so rad. My dad's coming over to help," Jack said as he jumped up and down in place.

"We've got all the brothers coming! I can't wait." Andrew picked up some snow and ate it.

"Is this an Insurgents' winter project?" she joked.

"A lot of the brothers are coming over to help make the Harley. I was going to tell you. They'd love a big pot of gumbo after all their hard work." Rock walked over to her and pulled her close to him, his cold, red nose nuzzling her ear.

"I'm glad you told me now instead of tomorrow morning." She kissed him on his cheek. "All of you are frozen. Inside for cookies and hot chocolate." The two boys dashed to the house, laughing and kicking up snow.

Rock turned her face and kissed her deeply. "Fuck the hot chocolate, kissing you is warming me up and then some." He winked at her, and she pressed closer against him—their breath was vapor.

They kissed until Andrew's voice broke them apart. "We better get inside. The boys want their cookies." Cold licked at her face as they walked to the house, the snow crunching beneath their feet.

After peeling off their coats, Clotille put the milk on the stove while Rock built a fire. It had always been her dream to have a large, cozy kitchen complete with fireplace. They'd searched for the perfect house, but never quite found the one that spoke to them. After much discussion, they'd agreed that the only way to get what they wanted was to build it themselves.

Baylee had been the architect on their home, and had understood their dream perfectly. Clotille loved her home; she loved her life with Rock and Andrew. When they'd reconciled that autumn day four months before, she wasn't sure if she could be part of the biker lifestyle. As time passed, she got to know the old ladies and see the workings of the club, and then she understood what the lure for Rock had been. Every brother was there for each other, the old ladies, the kids, and the club women. She'd been blown away by the loyalty and love the brotherhood shared.

She'd become fast friends with Cara, Addie, and Baylee, and they often got together for lunch. A couple of times a month the women and their men would go out for dinner and dancing. For Clotille, it was a fulfilling experience to go out with other couples. With Frederick she only had a couple of friends, and they were all in the lifestyle so their talk mostly revolved around their masters and the play parties.

She watched Rock as he stoked the fire. *He's just perfect, and he's all mine.* Every day that she spent with him, she loved him more and more. He was the missing piece in her life, and it'd taken her over a decade to figure it out.

"When the boys go upstairs to play video games, we should take advantage of the fire." He winked at her, melting her insides.

"They'll be playing for hours." She held his gaze, desire burning in it. "Are you up for good old-fashioned necking?"

With a seductive grin, he said, "I'm up for anything as long as it includes you and me together, *chérie*."

"Is the hot chocolate ready yet, Mom?" Andrew asked as he walked into the kitchen.

"It is. I'm just mixing in the cocoa." She took off the plastic covering a large plate of freshly baked cookies. "I want you and Jack to have your snack at the kitchen table. After that, you can go upstairs to your room."

Andrew nodded. "Jack! Cookies."

Jack's stockinged feet slid on the hardwood floors in the kitchen as he rushed in. When he saw the stack of chocolate chip cookies, his eyes grew big. He plopped down on the chair next to Andrew, both of them grabbing a cookie. She placed their steaming mugs in front of them, then set a place for her and Rock. As they ate, the boys recounted the building of the snowman. *This is just perfect. I couldn't be happier.* She reached out and squeezed Andrew's and Rock's hands.

It had been a series of upheavals for them to arrive at this point, but all of the evil things that surrounded them had gone away. Armand had admitted that he had participated in the murder of Rock's mother. He admitted it was solely for financial gain. He also admitted that he'd killed Madame Vincennes.

As Rock had predicted, both Henri and Armand turned against Frederick and testified at his trial. They had explained to the jury how Frederick had offered them a lot of money to kill Henri's mother. Henri had held his head down when he testified that in killing his mother, he profited by inheriting her land in addition to the large sum of money Frederick had paid him.

During Henri and Armand's testimony, Clotille held and stroked Rock's hand. His body had been so tense as he'd stared at his brother stone-faced. His expression had changed only when the pictures of his mother's battered, bloody body were shown to the jury; sadness and regret etched all over his face.

Frederick had kept turning around, staring at her and trying to hold her gaze, but she never looked at him directly. Her focus was on Rock—the love of her life. The jury had found Frederick guilty of conspiracy to commit murder on both counts. It had come out through Armand's testimony that Frederick had paid the cook a large sum of money to poison Rock's father; Henri didn't know about it. Frederick and Armand had tried to tie up all the loose ends, and when Rock had found out his father was innocent, the two culprits had planned on getting rid of him too. When the jury foreman had read the verdict, Frederick had seemed shocked. The court sentenced him to life without parole.

Henri and Armand had each received life sentences. At their sentencing, Rock, Isa, and Lille told the judge how empty their lives had been without their mother. Their statements were compelling, and Henri had cried like a baby. He asked his siblings for forgiveness, but Isa and Lille just shook their heads and Rock glared at him.

Clotille still couldn't believe she'd lived with the man who'd conspired to kill the love of her life's mother. And Armand… it was still unfathomable to her. She often wondered if her mother knew what Armand had done; she wouldn't put it past her. She had no idea what her mother was doing; Clotille didn't want anything to do with her anymore. When she'd turned Clotille over to Frederick, she'd known in that instant that her relationship with her mother was over forever. She hadn't even attempted to contact her when she and Rock were in Lafayette for Frederick's trial.

When their house was ready, Clotille promptly brought Stephan to live with her. At first he enjoyed being in her company, but then he began to feel sad about not having his roommate and friends around him. Rock had suggested she place him in a new home that had just been built in the valley. Each resident had a roommate and the facility looked like a large bed and breakfast.

She'd taken Stephan there, telling him that if he didn't like it he could come home with her, but his face lit up when he saw the cats and dogs the staff brought with them to work. After a couple of weeks he had settled in nicely. At least twice a week, Clotille went to see him and take him out for ice cream, a long walk, or whatever he wanted to do. Every Sunday he spent it over at Clotille and Rock's house. She was thrilled that Andrew was getting to know his uncle Stephan.

She placed the mugs and dishes in the dishwasher and turned to look at Rock, who was already on the small love seat next to the fireplace. She padded over to him. "You make a mean snowman," she said softly.

Gathering her in his arms, he held her snugly. "I'm a mean sonofabitch. That's the only kind of snowman I know how to make."

She giggled and looked up; his eyes brimmed with tenderness and passion, and his smile was as intimate as a kiss. Reaching out, she softly brushed her fingers against his cheek. "I'm so lucky to see the gentle, loving side of you."

"You're everything to me, *chouchou*." His last words were smothered on her lips, and his kiss sang through her veins.

As they sat by the fire, twisted together, they touched, kissed, and murmured loving words to each other. They had time to enjoy their time alone; Andrew and Jack would be engrossed in their video game until the gray skies turned inky.

And they'd planned to take full advantage of it.

★ ★ ★

A WEEK LATER, Rock and Clotille's house was bustling with people. It was the first formal party they'd thrown. Clotille wanted to make sure everything was perfect even though Rock kept telling her to "calm the fuck down."

"Clotille, your crab and shrimp étoufée was fantastic. You've got to give me the recipe," Cara said as she dried the pots and pans.

"I never cared much for Cajun food, but fuck, girl, you converted me." Cherri sat at the island folding the desert napkins.

Clotlille laughed. "That's a compliment, Cherri. When Rock and I left Lafayette after the trial, we went crazy and bought a bunch of spices, dried chiles, red beans, and other things. We had the back of the SUV filled. Andrew thought we were crazy as hell, but I still have some of the spices."

"You can order those things online, can't you?" Addie picked up a chocolate covered strawberry and popped it in her mouth.

"Yeah, but it's not the same as the local neighborhood markets."

"These are delicious." Addie took another strawberry. "You should have these at your wedding, Cara."

"I can't believe you're finally going to do it. I can't wait to see Hawk walk down the aisle in a tux." Belle laughed as she put the leftovers in tupperware that Clotille had given her.

"Hawk's wearin' a tux? No fuckin' way." Cherri clapped her hands while she laughed.

"Not so loud. If Hawk knows we're laughing about him wearing a tux, all my hard work in convincing him will be gone in a minute. In a few weeks, I'm dragging him to a cake tasting. He doesn't know it yet." Cara's bemused look made Clotille grin.

"I can't believe you talked Hawk into a country club wedding," Baylee said before taking a sip of her wine. "And he's been so involved in picking the furniture for your house. When I told Axe that, he didn't believe me. He thought I was exaggerating. These guys." Baylee rolled her eyes, but her smile was soft and tender.

"I can't picture Rock agreeing to a country club wedding." Clotille commented.

All the women stopped talking and stared at her. "Are you hiding something from us?" Addie asked. "Are you guys going to get married?"

"Axe will totally not believe *that*," Baylee said.

Clotille's face turned red and her fingers touched her lips. "No. Oh no. I didn't mean that. I just meant it's funny to think of one of these guys dressed up and in a country club. Rock and I are taking it slow."

"Taking it slow doesn't exist in these guys' vocabulary. When they want something they go for it no matter what." Cara shook her head. "Hawk was a persistent one, that's for sure." The group of women laughed.

"How did you get Hawk to agree not to have a biker wedding?" Belle asked. "Banger wouldn't even consider not having one."

"Chas and I had a beautiful one. I loved every minute of it." Addie leaned her chin on her hand.

"You had a fuckin' awesome wedding, Addie. If Jax and I decided to get married, I want you to help me plan it. I loved what you did." Cherri sat on one of the stools at the island.

"The compromise for Hawk indulging me and my parents was for me to agree to a biker wedding. So we're having two. I'll be dead before we go on our honeymoon." Cara folded the dish towel over the towel rack.

"Two weddings? That's insane." Baylee laughed.

"It's not as bad as it sounds. Hawk's planning the second one."

"What the fuck am I planning?" Hawk walked into the kitchen, and all the women stopped talking. "I knew you were talkin' about me. I could sense it in the other room. What shit you been telling the ladies about me, babe?" Hawk swung Cara into the circle of his arms and nuzzled her neck. She giggled. "You telling 'em about our love life? I fuckin' hope not 'cause the room's going to explode if you are." He kissed her, his hand running down her back.

"Aren't you inflating our love life just a bit?" Cara said, pressing closer to him.

"Am I, baby?"

"No. Not at all," she whispered, but Clotille overhead her and smiled. She really liked Cara, and she seemed to be able to handle Hawk, who usually had a scowl on his face except when Cara was around. Hawk sort of scared her, but Rock told her he wasn't as mean as he looked. Clotille wasn't too sure about that.

"What are you ladies up to?" Rock asked as he came over to Clotille and tugged her close to him.

"Just talking," she said.

"Talkin' or gossiping?" Banger's deep voice filled the room. His blue eyes twinkled as he went over to Belle.

"Talking. Don't you guys have some motorcycle stuff you need to discuss?" Addie placed her hands on her hips, smiling when Chas came into the room followed by Axe and Jax.

Soon the kitchen was filled with all the couples and Clotille and Cara laid out the pastries, cookies, and fruit on the island, creating a dessert bar. Rock poured shots of Jack, and opened up several more bottles of wine. They ate, talked, and laughed until late in the night.

After the last couple left in the frigid night air, Clotille closed the door. "I can't wait to take these damn heels off. My feet are killing me."

"I'll help you with those, *chérie*." Rock led her to the family room where they sat on the couch. She rested her back against the arm of the couch, and Rock, sitting next to her, took her feet and placed them in his lap. He took off her shoes and massaged her feet.

She groaned. "That feels so good, *cher*. You've got the right touch."

He chuckled and kept kneading her feet. "You did a good job with the dinner party. The food was excellent. Everyone had a real good time." He bent down and kissed her toes. She giggled. "I love you so much, *chouchou*."

She leaned forward and ran her fingers through his hair. "I love you, too. I'm so happy." She took a deep breath. "What would you say to us having another kid?"

Rock stopped massaging her feet. He looked at her. "Are you pregnant?"

A smile whispered across her lips. "No, but I'd like to be. I'm thinking of getting off the pill. I want another child. I'm hoping you do, too."

A wide grin spread over his face. "Fuck yeah. I wanna have more kids with you. What you told me has made me very happy, *chérie*." He held her hand and pulled her up with him. "Andrew's over at Jack's grandparents for the night. We've got all fuckin' night to love each other. Let's get started."

They climbed the stairs and when they went into their bedroom, he tenderly undressed her and kissed and caressed every inch of her body.

By the time they lay down on the bed, they were rabid for the feel of their skin against each other's. Flames of desire licked over them, and she spread herself wide, desperate to feel him inside of her. They had the whole night to savor, but for right then, she needed it fast and hard.

"You want it bad, *chouchou*." He chuckled, the vibration tickling her stomach as he slid his tongue further down her body. Then it landed on her aching, sweet spot, and she cried out, pulling at his hair. "I fuckin' can't wait anymore." And he pushed his hardness inside, and her walls clamped around him, and everything was a whirl of emotions, feelings, and ecstasy.

After their breathing returned to normal, he lightly fingered a loose tendril of hair on her cheek. "If we're going to start a family, we need to get hitched. I'm fuckin' old fashioned when it comes to that."

Her heart soared. "Me too."

He kissed her head. "I've loved you for years, *ma petite chérie. Je t'aime.* I'm never letting you go again."

She squeezed him tighter around his waist. "*Je t'aime, aussi.* Being with you is like a dream come true. For so long I was searching for something that was missing in my life, and now I've found it. I love you."

"We were both lost for a while, but we found our way back to each other. It's fuckin' awesome."

After a couple of minutes, she asked, "When we get married, will you wear a tux?"

"What the hell? Fuck no. It's leather and jeans all the way, *chérie.*" She laughed until her eyes watered. "What's so funny?" He stroked her cheek with his thumb.

"Nothing, *cher.* I love you so much."

He pulled her tight to him, and she relished the warmth of his body. As she looked out the window, watching the snowflakes dance in the sky, she realized that she and Rock were finally whole again.

And it was damned sweet.

The End

Make sure you sign up for my newsletter so you can keep up with my new releases, special sales, free short stories, and other treats only available to newsletter readers. When you sign up, you will receive a FREE hot and steamy novella. Sign up at:

http://eepurl.com/bACCL1

Visit me on Facebook

facebook.com/Chiah-Wilder-1625397261063989

Check out my other books at my Author Page

amazon.com/author/chiahwilder

Acknowledgments

I have so many people to thank who have made my writing endeavors a reality. It is the support, hard work, laughs, and love of reading that have made my dreams come true.

Thank you to my amazing Personal Assistant Amanda Faulkner who keeps me sane with all the social media, ideas, and know how in running the non-writing part smoothly. So happy YOU are on my team!

Thank you to my editor, Kristin, for all your insightful edits, excitement with the Insurgents MC series, and encouragement during the writing and editing process. I truly value your editorial eyes and suggestions as well as the time you've spent with the series. You're the best!

Thank you to my wonderful beta readers, Kolleen, Paula, Jessica, and Barb—my final-eyes reader. Your enthusiasm for the Insurgents Motorcycle Club series has pushed me to strive and set the bar higher with each book. Your dedication is amazing!

Thank you ARC readers you have helped make all my books so much stronger. I appreciate the effort and time you put in to reading and reviewing the books.

Thank you to my proofreader, Daryl, whose last set of eyes before the last once over I do, is invaluable. I appreciate the time and attention to detail you always give to each book.

Thank you to the bloggers for your support in reading my book, sharing it, reviewing it, and getting my name out there. I so appreciate all your efforts.

Thank you to Carrie from Cheeky Covers. You put up with numerous revisions, especially the color of Rock's tattoos until I said, "Yes, that's the cover!" Your patience is amazing. You totally rock. I love your artistic vision.

Thank you to Ena and Amanda with Enticing Journeys Promotions who have helped garner attention for and visibility to the Insurgents MC series. Couldn't do it without you!

Thank you to the readers who support the Insurgents MC series. You have made the hours of typing on the computer and the frustrations that come with the territory of writing books so worth it. You make it possible for writers to write because without you reading the books, we wouldn't exist. Thank you, thank you!

Rock's Redemption: Insurgents Motorcycle Club (Book 8)

Dear Readers,

Thank you for reading my book. I hope you enjoyed the eighth book in the Insurgents MC series as much as I enjoyed writing Clotille and Rock's story. This rough motorcycle club has a lot more to say, so I hope you will look for the upcoming books in the series. Romance makes life so much more colorful, and a rough, sexy bad boy makes life a whole lot more interesting.

    If you enjoyed the book, please consider leaving a review on Amazon. I read all of them and appreciate the time taken out of busy schedules to do that.

    I love hearing from my fans, so if you have any comments or questions, please email me at chiahwilder@gmail.com or visit my facebook page.

    To hear of **new releases**, **special sales**, **free short stories**, and **ARC opportunities**, please sign up for my **Newsletter** at http://eepurl.com/bACCL1.

    A big thank you to my readers whose love of stories and words enables authors to continue weaving stories. Without the love of words, books wouldn't exist.

Happy Reading,

Chiah

AN INSURGENT'S WEDDING

Book 9 in the Insurgents MC Series

Coming in December 2016

Note: This short excerpt is a ROUGH DRAFT. I am still writing the story about Hawk and Cara's wedding. It has only been self-edited in a rudimentary way. I share it with you to give you a bit of an insight into An Insurgent's Wedding.

PROLOGUE

Federal Correctional Institution
Florence, Colorado

HE WATCHED AS she shimmied down the hall, her big tits swaying, her keys clanging with each step. When she approached his cell, she threw him a quick, furtive glance then walked past, acting like he was just another inmate. His thin lips curled up, and he knew when she came back later with four other correctional officers to do a cell block inspection, he'd have her up against the wall and rubbing her breasts while she pressed into him, grinding her pussy against him like a slut. He counted on it; she was his ticket out of the hellhole he'd be sentenced to. Their time against the concrete wall would be fast, but it would be enough to wet her pussy and crave his tongue on it.

Viper sat on the edge of his hard bed. His cell was a cube of concrete with a small window placed in such a way that all he could see was the sky and the red tile of the adjacent buildings. Sounds echoed down the corridors, and the ever-present din of metal against metal filled his ears.

He'd been stuck in the high-security prison ever since he entered his plea of guilty more than two years before. Viper often entertained himself by recreating the events of that night in the way that they should have played out. He shook his head as the images of his downfall assaulted his mind. His unadulterated hatred for Hawk fueled him on; it kept him a model prisoner so he could lay low as he worked his magic on Officer Brenda Rourke.

A busty thirty-two year old, Brenda Rourke had worked as a correctional officer for the past ten years. She'd never been disciplined, and had a stellar employee record as she often told Viper. When he first spotted her six months before, she acted like he was just Inmate 10567, but the way she'd slide her eyes over him told him she was his ace in the hole in escaping. So he became the model prisoner. The fights between him and the Aryan gang members halted, he didn't cuss out the prison guards, and he did as he was told. It fucking tore him up inside each time he answered, "Yes sir," but the anticipation of sweet freedom made his words sound sincere.

He'd even gone so far as feigning remorse for all his bad actions that landed him in prison. And that gem earned him the privilege of working in the laundry room, and it was there that he kissed and touched Brenda, her small moans disgusting him. She'd been the one to tell him that the security camera did its sweep around the room at thirty second intervals. When it scanned past them, he had a half a minute to shove his hand down her pants and touch her damp pussy. And it was always wet for him. It amazed him how horny she was for him.

After six months, she'd proclaimed her love to him in simple notes she left under his pillow after she inspected his room. He read them with humor, pretending to be touched by her proclamations of love. Her note from the previous week had read "I love you. I can't live without you. I wish you were free." Those were the words he'd be waiting to hear. She'd be instrumental in getting him out of the razor-wired-fence compound that sat on a cleared patch of red-brown turf.

Viper leaned back against the cold wall, waiting for his favorite guard to come back for inspection when all of a sudden, loud shouts bounced off the walls. Pounding shoes on concrete filled the corridors as grunts and cries accompanied the thuds of bodies colliding. The stream of officers blurred past his cell as he fought to stay on his bed; he desperately wanted to be in the thick of the violence. He wanted to slam heads against the concrete, choke the life out of inmates and guards alike, and plunge his newly acquired shank deep into the belly of The Baron—the head of the Aryan gang who had a personal vendetta against all bikers.

Then suddenly, a deafening silence of voices.

Fuck! It's gonna be another goddamned lockdown. Lockdowns occurred almost weekly in the violent atmosphere of that prison. Race wars were brutal and constant, and the tension was so thick, it could be cut with a knife. Lockdowns meant no more laundry room duties, no mixing with the general population, staying twenty four seven in the cells, and no Brenda. *Fuckin' assholes!*

When she came to his cell with another colleague announcing that there was a lockdown, her blue eyes held sadness as they shined behind the taller guard. She mouthed, "I love you," to Viper and a faint smile twitched at his lips as she moved past his cell. He estimated that in less than two weeks, he'd be free. Dustin and Shack were already setting things up so he could lay low at the Demon Riders' clubhouse for a while. The fucking badges would never think to look there.

Dustin and Shack hated Hawk as much as he did. They also hated Banger, but even though he wasn't a fan of the Insurgents MC's president, Viper's focus stayed on Hawk, the club's vice president. He and his cunt were the reason he was locked up. And every time Brenda rubbed against his limp dick, his body burned with rage at what Hawk had done to him. He unclenched his fists and breathed in and out slowly. He'd have plenty of time to cool the rage that fired his soul, but for that moment, he had to remain calm and logical. In a short while, he'd be a free man.

★ ★ ★

"Do you love me?" Brenda gasped as his finger glided into her slippery hole.

"I fuckin' do, sweetheart," he whispered in her ear, his eyes fixed on the scanning camera. "I just wanna be with you all the time. We need more than snippets of thirty seconds, babe."

"I know," she breathed into his ear as she rode his fingers.

"I want us to live together. Get married. The whole fuckin' thing."

"I want that too." She jumped away from him and straightened her uniform. "We're on camera again." She moved away from him, and he hauled a pile of laundry into the dryer.

She stopped shy of the doorway. "I really can't stand not being able to love you the way I want to."

"I know. Me too. We're gonna have to do something about it, sweetie." She walked out of the room before the camera came back for another swipe. *I've just planted the seed in her empty head.* He shook his head, a faint smile on his lips. It didn't take much to make some women abandon everything for a man. He guessed Brenda hadn't been all that popular with men in her lifetime. She craved his attention to the point that she'd risk her job and her freedom for him. *What a pathetic whore.* He chuckled while he loaded the washing machine with more orange jumpsuits—courtesy of the prison.

In order to make his escape successful, Viper had to enlist the help of the maintenance worker, Buddy Riester. From the background checks Dustin performed, Riester was ripe for the picking. He was broke, a gambler, and in desperate need of cash to pay off the loan sharks who were breathing down his neck. When Viper offered him half a million dollars for his assistance, the pimply-faced Riester agreed.

Bed check was at eleven o'clock in the night, but Viper knew the officers on duty that night were the lazy ones who skipped opening up the cells and making sure the inmate was really the form in the bed. He counted on ineptness; it always made things easier.

Brenda had arranged for Buddy to place Viper in a laundry cart right after dinner. The maintenance workers usually took the laundry carts out to the back of the prison to change the canvas bag or repair the wheels and aluminum bars. Viper lay down in the bottom of the cart, old sheets piled on top of him. Buddy rolled through several doors and then out the back door. When he got there, Viper jumped out and then was transported in Reister's car trunk out of town.

Later that night, Brenda met him and Buddy in a small town a hundred miles from the prison. She threw her arms around him, but he pushed her away. "We have time for that later. We gotta keep moving." He handed the rest of the money to Reister, knowing that he'd be killed before he made his way back home. There was no way Viper was leaving a witness. Dustin had arranged for a couple of the brothers to intercept Buddy and put a permanent end to his gambling addiction.

Brenda chatted incessantly as they drove deep into the night on their way to Iowa. Viper had taken some plates off a junked car a hundred and fifty miles back, so he relaxed a bit as he tuned her off and took a deep drag on his joint. It was an eleven hour drive, and they'd already put a good seven hour distance between them and the prison. Viper knew they'd think he was either heading to the border or to stay with his brother or sister in nearby Kansas. They'd never think to look for him at the Demon Riders' clubhouse. He was a nomad biker so he didn't belong to any one club.

About a couple of hours from Johnston, Iowa, Viper leaned over and kissed Brenda on the cheek. "You ready to have a little fun before we get to the clubhouse?"

She smiled broadly, her blue eyes shining in her round, pasty face. "I've dying to be with you since we met up hours ago."

"Turn down this road and pull into the cornfield. We don't want anyone spotting us." He was grateful it was a dark moonless night.

She did as she was told, and then she turned off the engine and turned to him. "I love you so much. I can't believe we're together." She giggled.

"Yeah." He pulled her roughly to him and plunged his tongue down her mouth, chuckling as she gagged. He ripped open her blouse and stared at her white, full breasts. He grabbed and squeezed them, twisting her nipples until she cried out in pain. He laughed and brushed her hand away as she tried to stroke his cheek.

He pulled, pinched, and bit her as she squirmed under his touch. When her hand covered his crotch, a startled look crossed her face. "Aren't I exciting you? Don't you want me?"

A bitter smile settled on his lips as his forehead creased. "You excite me plenty. I haven't been with a woman since the night I was arrested. I got the desire, sweetheart. I'm just not able to get it up."

Her eyes were wide. "Really? What's the matter?"

"Hawk. The sonofabitch I'm gonna kill. I can still fuck you. It just won't be with my cock." Before she could answer, he was on top of her like a crazed animal, his hand over her mouth snuffing out her screams. He let his rage dictate his actions, and after some time, she quit trying to push him off, she quit crying against his palm… she just stopped. He released the hold he had on the belt he'd looped around her neck. He pushed her limp body aside and straightened up, and then lit a joint as he waited for the brothers to come and help him dispose of her body. He knew from the minute she checked him out that she had signed her death certificate. Outlaws never leave evidence. Her car would be sold to an unscrupulous dealer for scrap metal, and Brenda Rourke would become another disappearance.

His eyes narrowed. He'd strike Hawk where he was the most vulnerable—his old lady. He'd bide his time, striking when the sonofabitch least expected it.

I'm gonna have a good time with his slut, and then Hawk's a dead man.

Chapter One

Pinewood Springs, CO

"You didn't like the almond filling?" Cara asked as she moved the slice of cake away from her.

"Babe, they all taste the same to me. I can't believe we've been here for forty minutes and you still haven't picked a fuckin' cake for the wedding. What the hell?"

"If you were more helpful, it'd be easier." Cara tossed her hair over her shoulder. "The chef is bringing out a couple more pieces. We have to choose. I want your input."

He laughed. "I'm not a cake guy, you know that. Chocolate, vanilla, blue velvet, or whatever else is all the same to me." He scowled as she giggled. "What's so funny?"

"It's *red* velvet cake, not *blue*. You're sweet." She blew him a kiss.

He pressed his lips together. "Whatever. You're such a little smartass." He shook his head as he scooped up a glob of frosting on his finger. Leaning over, he smeared it lightly on her nose and lips. Instinctively, she pulled back and picked up a napkin. "No way, babe. I'll clean it up. Get over here."

"You're bad," she said as she licked some of the frosting off her lips.

"Thanks." He stood up and came over to her, bending down low, his hand tilting her head back. He licked off the icing from her nose and mouth, his tongue delving between her parted lips. She hooked her arms around his neck and his hand caressed her cheek as he kissed her deeper.

Someone behind them cleared his voice. Hawk kept kissing his woman, who brought her hands to his chest and pushed him back a little. Hawk straightened up and winked at her then sauntered back to his chair. Cara's face blushed red, and the chef, who held three more plates of cake samples, moved his eyes everywhere but on the two of them. Hawk threw his head back and laughed. The citizens' world never ceased to amuse him.

For the next twenty minutes, he passed the time by picturing Cara's body smeared in the white frosting she and the pastry chef were gushing about. He'd love to lick every bit of it off her luscious body. As he pictured her writhing underneath him, his jeans grew uncomfortable. *I'm gonna be pitchin' a tent if Cara doesn't hurry up and pick a damn cake.*

"Hawk. I'm asking you if the white cake with the white buttercream frosting is a good choice."

He nodded. *Just pick something, babe. All I wanna do is make love to you.* He didn't realize picking out wedding cake would be such a turn-on. He smiled as he watched the crease across her forehead deepen before she threw her shoulders back and said, "Let's go for it. I'm glad that's over with." She glanced at him, her eyes sparkling like a fresh glass of champagne.

"Let's get something to drink. I need a fuckin' beer after all this."

"Don't be so grumpy." She came over and draped her arms over his shoulder, dipping her head to kiss his jaw. "Thanks for pretending to help out." She slipped her fingers down the front of his T-shirt, her nail tugging at his nipple ring. A small grunt rose from his throat. "You like that, honey?" She ran her fingers over his every groove of his tight skin. "Love the way you feel," she whispered, her breath scorching on his neck.

He looped his arm around her waist and yanked her on his lap, his hard dick poking at her rounded ass. "Feel what you've done to me. How you gonna fix it?"

"When we get home, I'll treat you real good." She wiggled to get out of his grasp, but he held her firm.

"Fuck that. We're gonna take care of it now."

Wide-eyed, she put her hands on his chest. "Don't even think about doing it in the tasting room."

He lifted her off his lap and stood up. "Come on." He laced his fingers through hers and walked out of the dining room. Turning the corner, he stopped in front of the women's room.

Cara shook her head. "You've got to be joking."

"Didn't you tell me each stall is private? Come on." Before Cara could comment, he'd pushed open the bathroom door. The anteroom had a large couch, a couple of plush armchairs, a full length mirror, and a crystal chandelier. Their footsteps clacked on the marble floor.

Cara tried to pull out of his grip. "Hawk, this is insane. What if someone comes in here?"

He laughed. "That makes it more fun." He pulled her through the doorway into the bathroom where five sinks lined the wall, the white marble shone under the bright lighting. There were several wooden doors. Hawk opened one and closed it after Cara entered. The room was like a small bathroom: toilet, sink, and a small parlor chair upholstered in a fleur de lis design. The door was floor to ceiling. After turning the lock, he hoisted Cara up by the waist and plopped her down on the dusty rose granite counter. He shoved up her skirt and she moaned as she leaned back against the mirror. He bent his head and his mouth covered hers hungrily as his arm on the small of her back, drew her close to him, her breasts pressed against his chest.

"Oh, Hawk," she murmured.

"You're so hot," he whispered against her lips. He bit her bottom lip slowly and held it between his teeth for a few seconds before moving his mouth from hers to her cheeks then to her earlobes. She curled her arms around his neck. As he lavished kisses on her neck, his hand slowly inched toward her sex, tickling her inner thigh until she gasped loudly.

Chiah Wilder's Other Books

Hawk's Property: Insurgents Motorcycle Club Book 1
Jax's Dilemma: Insurgents Motorcycle Club Book 2
Chas's Fervor: Insurgents Motorcycle Club Book 3
Axe's Fall: Insurgents Motorcycle Club Book 4
Banger's Ride: Insurgents Motorcycle Club Book 5
Jerry's Passion: Insurgents Motorcycle Club Book 6
Throttle's Seduction: Insurgents Motorcycle Club Book 7

I love hearing from my readers. You can email me at: chiahwilder@gmail.com.

Sign up for my newsletter to receive updates on new books, special sales, free short stories, and ARC opportunities at: http://eepurl.com/bACCL1.

Visit me on facebook at:
www.facebook.com/Chiah-Wilder-1625397261063989

Made in the USA
San Bernardino, CA
04 November 2016